THE ULVERSCROFT FO
(registered UK charity nu
was established in 1972 to pr
research, diagnosis and treatment of eye diseases.
Examples of major projects funded by the
Ulverscroft Foundation are:

- The Children's Eye Unit at Moorfields Eye Hospital, London
- The Ulverscroft Children's Eye Unit at Great Ormond Street Hospital for Sick Children
- Funding research into eye diseases and treatment at the Department of Ophthalmology, University of Leicester
- The Ulverscroft Vision Research Group, Institute of Child Health
- Twin operating theatres at the Western Ophthalmic Hospital, London
- The Chair of Ophthalmology at the Royal Australian College of Ophthalmologists

You can help further the work of the Foundation by making a donation or leaving a legacy. Every contribution is gratefully received. If you would like to help support the Foundation or require further information, please contact:

THE ULVERSCROFT FOUNDATION
The Green, Bradgate Road, Anstey
Leicester LE7 7FU, England
Tel: (0116) 236 4325

website: w ... ndation.org.uk

A THIMBLE FOR CHRISTMAS

Living hand-to-mouth ever since her mother's tragic death, Amelia sells the last of her treasured possessions to avoid being cast out of her home onto London's streets.

Her estranged grandfather unexpectedly offers her a job as manager of a small, struggling factory making mourning dresses, and Amelia dares to dream . . . Drawing sketches by candlelight, she longs to sew elegant gowns from fine silks and beautiful ribbons for the rich.

As the cold winter wind begins to bite, Amelia's future hangs by a thread — can she keep her hopes alive?

DILLY COURT

A THIMBLE FOR CHRISTMAS

Complete and Unabridged

MAGNA
Leicester

First published in Great Britain in 2023 by
HarperCollins*Publishers*
London

First Ulverscroft Edition
published 2023
by arrangement with
HarperCollins*Publishers*
London

This novel is entirely a work of fiction. The names, characters and incidents portrayed in it are the work of the author's imagination. Any resemblance to actual persons, living or dead, events or localities is entirely coincidental.

A catalogue record for this book is available from the British Library.

ISBN 978–0–7505–5081–9

Published by
Ulverscroft Limited
Anstey, Leicestershire

Printed and bound in Great Britain by
TJ Books Ltd., Padstow, Cornwall

This book is printed on acid-free paper

For my new great-grandson, Riley Muggeridge

1

Long Acre, London, December 1875

It was snowing so hard that Amelia could barely see the houses on the other side of the narrow street. Large flakes swirled and whirled in an icy ballet, some of them sticking to the windowpanes like delicate feathers, only to curl up and vanish as if a conjuror had waved his magic wand. It would be dark soon and Amelia strained her eyes to peer at the street below. Her father, Dr Harold Sutton, had been called out on an emergency early that morning but he should have been home by now. Since her mother's death, ten years previously, when Amelia was just eleven, she had done her best to take care of her father, a selfless medical man, who put his patients first and his own wellbeing last.

Amelia shivered and wrapped her woollen shawl a little tighter around her slim shoulders. She had only just lit the fire, adding a miserly two lumps of coal to the burning kindling, but the feeble flames did little to warm the large room, with its high ceiling and badly fitting windows. The old brass coal scuttle was almost empty and if Pa did not get paid for his efforts today there would not be enough money to buy food, let alone fuel for the fire. Harold Sutton was no businessman, and he often refused to take payment from his poorer patients. It had been his late wife who brought money to the marriage, but her allowance had stopped abruptly on her death. It was only recently that Amelia realised they had been relying almost entirely on her mother's income. Her grandfather, Nathaniel Norris, a man who had accrued a fortune importing indigo and large amounts of guano, had never made them welcome at his grand house in Albemarle Street. Now his doors were firmly closed against both Amelia and her father.

Amelia sighed. There was no point dwelling on the past. She had never had anything like a close relationship with her maternal grandfather, and she would rather starve than go cap in hand to him and ask for help.

She moved away from the window and placed a soot-blackened saucepan on the trivet in front of the fire. She had made soup yesterday from a few vegetables she had bought in Covent Garden Market, together with a cabbage that had fallen off a barrow and been crushed underfoot. A few spoonfuls of pearl barley had thickened the rather tasteless concoction, which would have benefited greatly from the addition of meat or even some bones, but the butcher was no longer her friend. A large bill that she was unable to pay had soured their relationship to the extent that she was not a welcome customer. It was the same at the grocer's shop, although she had managed to keep the man in the dairy on her side by tending to a nasty cut he had suffered while slicing up a truckle of Cheddar cheese. In fact, people often came to their door asking for her help for minor injuries and ailments. Amelia was only too happy to share her practical medical knowledge for a small fee, although more often than not the remuneration was a poke of tea or sugar, a cup of milk or a couple of rashers of bacon.

It was getting darker by the minute and the lamplighter was on his rounds. The gaslights on the pavement below created a friendly glow in the room, but did not give enough light to see by. In the end Amelia took a spill from an old jam jar on the mantelshelf and lit the last candle. She added one more nugget of coal to the glowing embers and stirred the thick soup, although it remained stubbornly cold and unappetising. She picked up a pair of her father's socks that she had been attempting to darn, but it was a case of repairing what had already been mended several times, and in the poor light it was almost impossible to make out the tiny stitches. She had always loved sewing and, of necessity, had made her own clothes, but also because she enjoyed creating something out of next to nothing. She put the socks aside and rose to her feet. If Pa did not return within the next five or ten minutes, she would brave the snowstorm and go out to look for him. Perhaps there had been an accident in Oxford Street, which was not uncommon when the road was packed with all manner of horse-drawn vehicles, costermongers' barrows and careless pedestrians.

The small brass clock on the mantelshelf ticked on mercilessly. Only recently reclaimed from the pawnshop, it was Amelia's prized possession and had once belonged to her mother. At one time they had lived in a house filled with the pretty things her mother had loved, but the house and furniture had belonged to the Norris family. Pa had hoped they might be allowed to stay on, at least until Amelia was married and had a home of her own, but Nathaniel Norris was a hard man. He blamed his daughter's early demise on her husband, and nothing Harold said would change his mind. Amelia and her father had left their much-loved house, and gradually all the valuables had been pawned or had ended up in the auction rooms. Home now was a single living room and two small, cramped bedrooms on the third floor of the terraced townhouse in Long Acre, not far from Covent Garden Market.

Amelia was about to take her cape from the peg behind the door when she heard heavy footsteps on the bare floorboards outside. She rushed to open the door and saw her father looking like a snowman as he stomped wearily up the last few stairs. Lumps of ice fell from his top hat as he took it off and shook it.

'Are you all right, Pa?' Amelia asked anxiously. 'I was getting worried.'

'It was a very difficult birth. I thought I was going to lose both mother and child, but somehow they survived.'

'You saved them — that's wonderful. Well done, Pa. Come inside and get warm.'

Amelia held the door open for him to pass, closing it as soon as he was safely in the room. It was marginally warmer in here than on the narrow landing where draughts whistled eerily up and down the stairs, a sound that was particularly disturbing at night. Amelia helped him off with his greatcoat and hung it over the back of a chair by the fire, although with little hope of it drying out overnight.

'I'm glad it was a safe delivery, Pa.' She hesitated. Talking about money at such a time seemed harsh, and her father's face was grey with fatigue, but the rent was due and they were in desperate need of coal and candles. 'But did they pay you?' she added anxiously.

Harold reached for his coat and pulled a rather

squashed loaf of bread from the pocket. 'I couldn't demand money, my love. The poor woman has eight children already and all of them were clamouring for food. Their father works in the bakery and he promised us free bread for a month in payment.'

He looked so exhausted and disconsolate that Amelia had not the heart to scold him. She took the loaf from him and placed it on the table. 'Supper won't be long, Pa.'

'I'm sorry I've let you down again, Amelia.' Harold sank onto the chair by the fire. 'I should have insisted on payment, but the family are struggling as it is.'

'Don't worry, Pa. We'll manage somehow.' Amelia kneeled down and helped him off with his boots. She stifled a gasp of dismay. 'Your boots leak, Pa. Your socks are soaking.'

'Don't fuss, dear. I'm fine.'

'You won't be if you catch a cold or a chill, Pa.' Ignoring her father's protests, Amelia pulled off his socks and hung them from the mantelshelf. Despite the seriousness of their situation, she stifled a giggle. 'It looks as if we're waiting for Father Christmas to come down the chimney and fill your socks with nuts and oranges.'

Harold smiled tiredly. 'Trust you to find humour in a bleak situation, my love. I wish I had your spirit. You are so like your dear mama. You have her beautiful blue eyes and raven hair. She turned heads wherever we went.'

Amelia rose to her feet, gazing down at her father with a frown puckering her brow. She brushed back a lock of hair that had escaped from the chignon at the nape of her neck. 'You know, Pa, I don't like to keep on at you, but we are in desperate need of funds. I realise that you are the soul of generosity, but by giving your services virtually free, you are putting us in danger of being evicted if we can't pay next month's rent. We're living hand-to-mouth as it is.'

'I know, and I am thoroughly ashamed of bringing you to this sorry state of affairs. But the people around here are even poorer than we are. I haven't the money to set up in a wealthier area, and even if I had, I would still want to look after the sick and needy.'

Amelia sighed and reached out to take one of his cold hands in hers. 'I know, Pa. But we need to find money from somewhere. Perhaps I should go and see Grandpapa Norris and ask for his help?'

'No!' Harold snatched his hand free. 'I won't allow you to go cap in hand to that person, Amelia. I forbid it.'

'All right, Pa.' Amelia sighed. It was always like this: her father habitually shied away from the truth, and once again she had not the heart to press the point. 'Please don't distress yourself. I'll think of something, but now you need to eat.'

'I'm sorry, my dear, but I'm not hungry. I must get some sleep.' Harold raised himself from the chair with obvious difficulty. 'Wake me if I'm needed.' He walked slowly across the bare boards to the room where he slept on a narrow iron bed with a flock-filled mattress. A waft of cold air brought the temperature in the living room even lower as he closed the door.

Amelia placed her father's boots on the hearth in the vain hope that they too would be dry by morning. Her stomach rumbled, reminding her that she had eaten nothing since a slice of stale bread at breakfast. She gave the soup a stir and raised the spoon to her lips. It was lukewarm but reasonably palatable, and she was too hungry to wait for the feeble flames to heat it further. She filled a bowl with the soup and went to sit at the table. At least the bread was fresh, if rather doughy, and she cut a slice. At one time there would have been a golden pat of fresh butter set on the table in a pretty china dish, but that was long ago.

The food might not have tasted delicious, but it warmed her and was filling. She washed the dish and spoon in a bucket of water that she had carried up three flights of stairs earlier that afternoon. The pump and the privy were in the back yard. She would have to tramp through the snow to get to either of them, and that was not something that appealed to her, especially in the dark. There was little she could do now other than try to keep herself occupied until bedtime and she went to sit at the table with the only one of her father's medical books that remained in his possession.

She moved the candlestick nearer and opened the book at the place marked by a broken bootlace. A folded sheet of paper fell open to reveal some of her latest sketches. Designing beautiful gowns made her feel part of the world outside, but it was difficult to see in the flickering light of the candle, which had burned dangerously low. The fire had given way to ashes and it was so cold in the room that Amelia knew she had little alternative other than to go to bed in order to keep warm.

She was about to snuff out the candle when she heard footsteps on the stairs, although this in itself was not unusual. There was another floor above theirs and a further floor devoted to attics, which were occupied by a constantly changing flow of people, many of whom had fallen foul of the law. It was better not to ask questions.

However, the footsteps stopped outside her door and someone knocked.

'Doctor, are you there? We need you.'

Amelia hurried to open the door. It was dark on the windowless landing but she could see that the stranger was a child, although it was so muffled up against the cold she could not tell if it was a girl or a boy. 'What do you want?'

'Is the doctor there, miss?'

'He can't come at the moment. What is the problem?'

'It's little Percy, miss. He can't breathe. I think he's going to die.'

'Where do you live?' Amelia had often accompanied her father on his rounds. She had seen children suffering from a variety of ailments, including whooping cough and diphtheria, and she knew what Papa would do, given such circumstances.

'Not far from here, miss. I'll take the doctor.'

'I'm his assistant,' Amelia said firmly. 'I'll come and if I think it's very serious I'll fetch the doctor myself.' She snatched her thick cape from its peg and wrapped it around her shoulders. Having collected her father's medical bag, she followed the child downstairs to the ground-floor entrance. A gust of ice-cold air greeted them as Amelia opened the door, and a flurry of snow enveloped both her and the small girl as they stepped out onto the pavement.

'You'd better hold my hand. We don't want to get separated or I won't be able to help Percy. What's your name, anyway?'

The child's upturned face was pinched and pale in the fractured light from the gas lamp. 'I'm Betsy, miss. Betsy Simms. Please hurry.'

'Lead the way, Betsy.'

Amelia allowed Betsy to guide her along the slippery pavement in the direction of Bow Street. Walking against what was almost a blizzard, the journey took twice as long as normal, even though it was not very far to Betsy's home. Each step Amelia took, she felt as though she had slipped back at least two paces, but eventually they reached the tall, narrow dwelling not far from the courthouse. It was a much larger and better proportioned house than Amelia would have expected to be the home of a family who, judging by Betsy's appearance, were eking out an existence. However, this was not the time to ask questions. Betsy made her way to a side door, which she opened, and went inside, beckoning Amelia to follow her.

The passageway was dark and narrow but Betsy was on familiar territory and she hurried past several closed doors to open one at the back of the building. It seemed as though they were in the servants' quarters now, and that would explain how a poor child came to live in a relatively affluent area. Amelia followed her into the kitchen where a fire burned brightly in a black-leaded range. Rows of copper cooking pots and pans hung from the ceiling, together with bunches of dried herbs, their fragrance adding to the tempting aroma from a pan that was cooling on the side of the range.

'In here,' Betsy cried agitatedly as she ran to open a door on the far side of the room.

The sound of an infant coughing painfully reminded Amelia why they had come to this place and she followed Betsy into what appeared to be the family's bedroom. A thin woman was cradling a toddler in her arms. Tears ran down her cheeks as she looked up, but her lips trembled when she saw Amelia.

'I need the doctor, not you, miss.'

'Dr Sutton couldn't come, but I'm here to help you, Mrs Simms.'

'Percy is mortal sick. I'm afraid I'm going to lose him, like I lost his older brother to cholera last year.'

Amelia opened her father's medical bag. She had seen him treat such cases in the past and knew exactly what to do, or so she hoped and prayed. She took out a small bottle.

'This is oil of camphor. We'll rub a little of it on his chest and it will help him breathe. May I?' Amelia went to take the infant from his mother. 'I'll be very gentle.'

Reluctantly Mrs Simms allowed Amelia to hold the small boy, who was struggling to catch his breath. Amelia pulled back the flannel vest and very gently rubbed a little oil of camphor on his chest. Almost immediately his breathing eased a little and his mother snatched him from Amelia's arms.

'Ta, miss. That's the best he's been all day.'

Amelia delved into the bag again and produced two small bottles.

'What's that?' Mrs Simms demanded suspiciously. 'It's not a quack medicine, is it?'

'It's cochineal and salt of tartar.' Amelia turned to Betsy. 'I saw a steaming kettle on the range. Will you pour some hot water into a large cup for me?'

'Do it, Betsy,' Mrs Simms said urgently. 'I'll try anything to save Percy from this horrible illness.'

'And some sugar, if you have any,' Amelia added, raising her voice as Betsy rushed into the kitchen. She hurried back moments later.

'Here's the cup of water, miss.' Betsy placed the cup in Amelia's hands. 'And some sugar, although it belongs to the master and he keeps a count on how much is used.'

'Is that true, Mrs Simms?' Amelia asked incredulously. 'You are not allowed to take a little sugar in your tea?'

'No, miss. The master is very strict. Everything has to be accounted for.'

Amelia shook her head but she kept her thoughts to herself as she mixed the medicine. The result was a pretty pink colour, much admired by Betsy, although eyed a little suspiciously by her mother.

'I'm still not convinced, miss. What good will that do?'

'This has been proved to work, Mrs Simms. Allow the mixture to cool and give Percy a teaspoonful four times a day. That, together with the oil of camphor, should help greatly.'

'I don't know how to thank you, but I can't pay you until the end of the quarter, when I get my wages.' Mrs Simms's blue eyes filled with tears. 'Betsy shouldn't have asked you to help.'

Amelia glanced round the sparsely furnished parlour with just one bed set against the far wall. It was obvious that the small family were eating and sleeping in the same room, which was badly ventilated with a small window set high in the wall. All the fumes from the kitchen would circulate freely in this space and there were damp and mouldy patches on the walls and ceiling.

'It's all right, Mrs Simms,' Amelia said softly. 'Wait until Percy is well again. I think you'll need your money to buy nourishing food for him.' She found herself echoing the words that she had heard her father say to patients who could not afford to pay his fee, and she knew he would approve. But that was not going to help them pay the rent and buy necessities. 'I'll go now but I'll look in again tomorrow morning. If Percy should get worse, I can only suggest that you take him to the hospital.'

'Ta, miss,' Betsy said, grinning. 'You done good.'

'Thank you, Betsy. It's kind of you to say so. I hope Percy gets well soon.' Amelia placed the bottles on the dresser. 'You know how to use these, Mrs Simms. I'll leave them with you.'

'But I can't pay you for them, miss.'

Amelia glanced over her shoulder with a reassuring smile. 'It's more important to get your little boy better, Mrs Simms. No charge.' She crossed the flagstone floor and was about to leave the kitchen when the door opened and she found herself faced by a big man with a florid complexion and an uncompromising scowl.

'Who the hell are you?'

'I'm the doctor's daughter, sir. Are you the owner of the house?'

'I am Jasper Cook. Not that it's any of your business, miss. Why are you here, poking your nose into other people's business?'

'There is a very sick infant living in totally unsuitable conditions on your property, Mr Cook.'

'You should learn to mind your own business, miss. Get out, and don't come back.' Cook turned to Betsy, scowling. 'This is your doing, you miserable creature. If I have to reprimand you once more, I will turn you out on the street, together with your mother and the squalling brat.'

'It's not her fault,' Amelia said angrily. 'She came to me for help.'

'Who asked you for your opinion? Get out before I call for a constable and have you arrested for trespass.'

'All right,' Amelia said reluctantly. 'I'm going now.' She turned to give Betsy an encouraging smile. 'You know where I am should you need me.'

'Get out.' Cook took a step towards Amelia, shaking his fist.

She could see that he meant business and she ran.

However, when she reached the safety of home she suffered a pang of guilt. She had given help and advice for free and in doing so had depleted her father's meagre stock of medicines. She had criticised him on so many occasions for doing exactly the same thing and now they were even poorer than before. Not only that, but her clothes were soaked by melting snow and her boots leaked. She undressed and hung her damp garments over the back of the two chairs in the living room. Although it was still quite early Amelia knew she would be warmer in bed, but whether she would sleep was another matter. She could still hear baby Percy struggling to breathe, and the look of desperation on his mother's face would stay with her for a long time. She went to her small room, little bigger than a cupboard, and curled up on the truckle bed, pulling the worn coverlet up to her chin.

* * *

Next morning Amelia awakened early. It was still dark but the snow had settled, creating a pristine white blanket over the roofs, and the pavements where pedestrians had yet to trample it to slush. The outer garments she had worn the previous evening were still very wet, leaving her no alternative but to wear her Sunday-best black bombazine skirt. Fortunately her white blouse had dried overnight but her boots were still damp. Amelia put them on anyway, knowing that she would have to go out, no matter how deep the snow. There was no food in the cupboard, other than a crust of bread, and only one or two nuggets of coal left in the scuttle. She glanced at the brass clock on the mantelshelf and sighed. Mama had loved that pretty little clock with roses enamelled on its face, but it was the only thing left of any value to pawn, only this time she doubted if she would find enough money to redeem it in the allotted time. It would be heartbreaking to let it go, but it was a question of survival.

Amelia put on her best bonnet and wrapped a shawl around her shoulders before setting off for the pawnshop a couple of streets away.

The result was disappointing. Old Scoggins, the pawnbroker, was not in a good mood and the price he quoted for the clock was too low to keep them going for more than a few days. However, Amelia was forced to accept the ridiculously low price. She left the dingy shop, struggling to come to terms with the obvious answer to their problems. It was staring her in the face, even though she knew that it was the last thing her father wanted. But it was either take the matter in her own hands or end up in the workhouse. Pa might be a clever man and a dedicated physician, but he was not a businessman and he had left her with no alternative.

Amelia hailed a passing hansom cab.

'Albemarle Street, please, cabby.'

2

The cab was sheer extravagance but also a dire necessity. To walk all the way from Long Acre to Albemarle Street in such adverse weather conditions would be madness, even if it did take most of the money that Amelia had just received for her pledge. She sat back on the padded squabs, and gazed out at the familiar and not-so-familiar streets as they came into view. It was only when they drew nearer to her grandfather's imposing mansion that Amelia began to have second thoughts. Pa would be furious and also hurt by what he considered to be a betrayal of his principles, but having such uncompromising ethics did not put food on the table or pay the rent.

Amelia gazed at her hands, clenched tightly in her lap, and realised that her gloves had holes in them. She pulled them off and tucked them into her reticule, but in minutes her fingers had turned blue with cold. She was wondering what to do when the cab pulled up outside her grandfather's house and the cabby opened the flap in the roof.

'That'll be sixpence, miss.'

She paid him and the door flew open, allowing her to alight. She crossed the slippery pavement and raised the shiny brass lion's-head knocker, allowing it to fall with a loud clang. She waited, holding her breath as she gathered the last scrap of courage she possessed. Grandfather Norris was a forbidding sort of person at the best of times, and now she was about to put herself and her father at his mercy. It was Christmas Eve and the season of goodwill, but even so, she was tempted to turn and hurry away when the door opened and Hobbs, the butler, gazed at her with the stony expression he had practised for many years.

'Good morning, Hobbs,' Amelia said, forcing a smile. 'Is my grandfather at home?'

'Step inside, please, Miss Amelia. If you'll wait here, I'll go and see if he's receiving visitors.'

Hobbs's disapproving gaze took in the state of Amelia's clothes. He said nothing further, but it was obvious that he knew why she had come to the house uninvited, and so early in the morning. There was no going back now and she crossed the threshold. The wainscoted entrance hall was very familiar to her, due to the many visits she had made here with her mother, and nothing had changed. Of course, the flowers in the silver urns were fresh, and had no doubt been brought from the hothouse on the country estate her grandfather had bought after one particularly profitable voyage. The oil paintings on the walls had been purchased at auction sales, but to the uninitiated they could pass for depictions of illustrious ancestors of the Norris family. Amelia was well aware that her predecessors on the maternal side had been farm labourers and gardeners, but Grandpapa had risen above such humble beginnings. He was a successful businessman and he never allowed anyone to forget it.

Hobbs reappeared, walking with a measured tread. 'Mr Norris will see you now, Miss Amelia. You'll find him in his study.'

'Thank you, Hobbs. I know my way.'

Amelia crossed the black and white marble-tiled floor. In happier times, when she and her mother had been welcome visitors, Amelia had always trodden on the white squares, taking care to jump over the black tiles for fear that bears might leap out of the shadows and get her. Not that she had seen a bear anywhere outside the Zoological Gardens, but it was a game that Mama had often joined in, holding up her skirts and giggling like a child when she landed on the wrong square. Was it Amelia's imagination, or had the house seemed warmer and more welcoming in those far-off days? Today there was a feeling of foreboding in every shadowy corner, and it felt colder indoors than in the snow-covered world outside. Amelia shivered, but, ever practical, she blamed her parlous state on hunger.

She stopped outside the study door, took a deep breath and knocked.

'Enter.'

Amelia opened the door and stepped inside. The room had changed very little since she was a child. The oak panelling on the walls was partially concealed by paintings of Highland scenes with majestic stags at bay, or equally fashionable representations of game birds, hares and rabbits artistically arranged on a chopping block as if waiting for the cook to arrive and prepare them for the pot. Mama had tried to convince her that the birds and animals were merely sleeping, but even at a young age Amelia had suspected that this was said simply to comfort her. She dragged her gaze back from the offending work of art to give her grandfather a steady look.

'Good morning, Grandpapa.'

'How much do you want, Amelia? Let's not prevaricate. I know you would not be here unless you were in dire straits. Just looking at you is enough to convince me that things are not going well.'

'Yes, sir. You are right, of course. I have no excuse other than the fact that we are related, and for my poor dear mama's sake . . .'

Nathaniel held up his hand, his grey eyebrows knotting together over the bridge of his Roman nose. 'Don't bring your mother's name into this, Amelia. I warned her what would happen if she married a man who put charity above family and followed the Hippocratic Oath as if it were a religion.'

'My father is a good man, sir. And he is an excellent physician, but a poor businessman. You are quite correct. We are in desperate need of help and I didn't know where else to turn.'

'At least you are honest.' Nathaniel sat back in his chair, giving her a calculating look. 'This cannot go on, Amelia. You are a young woman now, not a child. Do you wish to live in the gutter for the rest of your life? I could see how it would be from the start.'

'Pa gives his help to those who need it most. Surely that is a good thing?'

'It is not good if it leaves his only child begging for sustenance. Take a look at yourself in a mirror, Amelia. You are unkempt and shabby. What man in his right mind would pick you for his wife? Or do you intend to dwindle into an old maid in the service of a very selfish man?'

Amelia shook her head. 'I knew it was a mistake coming here. I'm sorry I bothered you, Grandpapa. I'll go now and I won't return, ever.'

'No! Wait. I haven't finished, Amelia. Sit down, please.'

She had been feeling a little faint from lack of food and it was a relief to sink onto the padded leather seat of the chair facing her grandfather's desk. 'What else is there to say?'

'Maybe I'm getting soft in my old age, but I loved my daughter and, for her sake only, I am prepared to offer your father a chance to redeem himself.' Nathaniel held up his hand as Amelia was about to protest. 'Are you willing to hear me out?'

'Yes, sir.' Amelia shivered despite the warmth from the coals burning brightly in the grate. She forced herself to concentrate even though her stomach was rumbling painfully.

Nathaniel rose from his seat and went to stand with his back to the fire. 'I own a manufactory in East London.'

'Are you offering me a job, sir? I am very willing to earn my living.'

'But are you hardworking and trustworthy, Amelia? I know very little of you.'

'That is not my fault, sir. You wanted nothing to do with me and my papa after my mother's sad demise.'

'That is true, and for that reason I am willing to give you a chance to prove yourself and keep your sainted papa from bankruptcy.'

'What is it you require of me, Grandpapa?'

'As I said, I own a manufactory in Nightingale Lane, close to St Katharine Docks. I employ a dozen or so women, making mourning garments for the large department stores, which is the way forward as far as manufacturing clothes is concerned. There is a growing market for such items at a reasonable price.'

'I am willing to try anything, but I know nothing of manufacturing mourning gowns.'

'You will learn as you go. You are a bright young woman and I sense a determination to improve your lot in life, which will not happen if you continue to support your father.'

'It's quite a long way for me to travel every day, sir. Are there lodgings attached?'

'The manager's house is at present vacant. I had to sack the man who was supposed to be in charge of production when I discovered that he was lining his own pockets at my expense. The house is old, large and in need of improvement, but it goes with the job and will cost you nothing in rent. What do you say, Amelia? Is it yes or no?'

Amelia met his intense gaze with a determined lift of her chin. 'Even without seeing it I say yes. Our situation cannot be any worse than it is now. I accept your offer, Grandpapa.'

A flicker of admiration lit Nathaniel's pale blue eyes briefly before he turned back to his desk. He opened a drawer, took out a large bunch of keys and laid them on the desk.

'Very well. I appoint you manager for a trial period of three months, which I think is very generous, considering your lack of experience.'

'I accept,' Amelia said firmly. 'What exactly will I have to do?'

'My assistant will be here shortly. He will take you to the warehouse and show you round. He knows more about running the mourning warehouse than I do.'

'Thank you, sir.'

Nathaniel eyed her keenly. 'You look half-starved. Did you have breakfast?'

'No, sir.'

'And I would imagine that your supper was fairly meagre. Harold Sutton should be ashamed of himself.' Nathaniel held up his hand as Amelia was about to protest. 'Don't defend him. It's a pity he doesn't pay more attention to looking after his only child than wasting his time on trying to save the hopeless.' He reached out and rang a bell. 'You'll have something to eat before you go. Don't mistake me, Amelia. I am not being kind. I merely need to get the best use of any talents you might reveal.'

Hobbs answered the bell so promptly that Amelia suspected he had been waiting outside.

'You rang, sir?'

'Take Miss Sutton to the dining room, Hobbs. Make sure she has a decent breakfast, and send Mr Marsh to me as soon as he arrives.'

Hobbs inclined his head. 'Yes, sir. Please follow me, Miss Sutton.'

There was little that Amelia could do other than to obey her grandfather, and the thought of food was more than welcome. She hurried after Hobbs, who, despite his measured tread, seemed to cover the ground so quickly that she had almost to run in order to keep up with him.

Slightly out of breath, Amelia found herself in the dining room. It had been many years since she had been a guest at her grandparents' table, but here, too, little had changed. The sideboard still groaned beneath the weight of silver serving dishes and crystal decanters. The crimson velvet curtains were the same, although slightly faded from years of exposure to sunlight, and the Persian carpet closest to the window was similarly faded. Amelia was taking all this in when a housemaid appeared, bringing a plate of scrambled eggs and two rashers of crisp bacon. Another servant brought a rack of toast and a plate of butter, while Hobbs poured coffee from a silver pot.

Amelia forgot everything other than the pleasure of eating hot, savoury food and delicious coffee laced with cream and sugar. It was a long time since she had eaten so well, but a feeling of guilt assailed her when she finished the last crumb. She had left the remains of the stale loaf for her father's breakfast, while she had eaten like a princess.

Hobbs cleared his throat. 'Mr Marsh is waiting to take you to the warehouse, Miss Sutton. Unless you would like some more coffee or toast?'

'Thank you, Hobbs. That was excellent. Please thank Cook for me.' Amelia rose to her feet. 'I'm ready.'

'Mr Marsh is in the hall, miss.' Hobbs led the way although Amelia could have found it blindfold. The layout of the house was coming back to her in flashes of memory. She could almost hear the sound of her mother's laughter when they played hide-and-seek. There had been parties with music and dancing, and in those days Papa had been a handsome young doctor at the London Hospital. But all that was before a broken heart and overwork had aged him prematurely.

'Miss Sutton. How do you do?'

Startled out of her reverie, Amelia came to a sudden halt. 'Mr Marsh?' She looked up into the smiling face of a smartly dressed young man, perhaps twenty-five or twenty-six. His eyes were warm brown, fringed with thick lashes and his dark hair waved back from a high forehead. Amelia took to him immediately and she smiled in response.

'Yes, I'm Caleb Marsh. Your grandfather has asked me to take you to the warehouse. I believe you are taking the position as manager.'

Amelia was quick to hear the note of uncertainty in his voice. 'Do you disapprove, sir?'

'Of course not. I respect Mr Norris's judgement.'

'But you are not sure I can do it.'

'You haven't seen the warehouse yet. You might well decide that the position is not for you.'

'My mind is made up. I believe there is a manager's house.'

'There is accommodation,' Caleb said carefully. 'You will see it and judge for yourself, Miss Sutton. Shall we go now, before the weather closes in again? The sky looks quite threatening. We don't want to get caught in yet another snowstorm.'

'No, of course not. I'm ready and eager to see where I'll be living and working.'

* * *

The cab set them down in a gloomy street lined with warehouses on one side. They faced the red-brick walls, three times the height of an average man, which protected the docks from the outside world. A thick coating of snow softened the stark outlines of the commercial buildings, but it was obviously a rough area. Ragged individuals hung around braziers on street corners, huddling together to keep out the cold. Perhaps they were dockers waiting to be offered work that day. Whatever the reason for their presence, they had a look of desperation about them.

Amelia tried to ignore them, but she could not help wondering if her grandfather had chosen to offer her the job and accommodation as a way of testing her resolve to be independent. She glanced around and shivered, not entirely from the chill rising up through the thin soles of her boots. If this was a test, she would take it on and prove herself to be worthy of his trust.

'Which building is ours, Mr Marsh?'

'Caleb, please. We will be working together to bring the manufacturing business up to scratch. At least, I will be there to help you if needed. I believe you have the keys.' He held out his hand. 'I'll unlock the door to the private accommodation, which is probably what you need to see first.'

Amelia gave him the large bunch of keys and after a few tries he found the right one and opened the door to what appeared to be yet another warehouse. She followed him inside and he closed the door, leaving them in a narrow, dingy passageway with doors leading off on either side.

'The previous manager was a single man who spent most of his free time in the pub down the road, and he dipped into the petty cash to fund his drinking.' Caleb opened a door to the left. 'This is what you might call the front parlour.'

Amelia wrinkled her nose at the smell of stale alcohol and dead cockroaches, with a trace of mouse droppings thrown in. The floor was littered with old newspapers, and ashes spilled out of the fireplace onto the grate. Empty beer bottles were lined up on the floor, like soldiers on parade.

'It won't be too bad when it's been cleaned,' Amelia said hopefully. 'I'd like to see more.'

Caleb smiled. 'If this hasn't put you off I think you will be able to cope with the rest of the rooms.' He led the way to the large kitchen at the rear of the building. The range was old and in desperate need of cleaning. It was crying out for an application of black lead to keep rust at bay. The stone sink was chipped and the only good point that Amelia could see was the pump, which brought fresh water to the kitchen. The only furniture was a large pine table, which again was littered with empty beer bottles, scraps of mouldy bread and a heel of cheese that even the mice had ignored. There was a chair, but it leaned drunkenly against the wall, having lost one leg. Caleb picked it up, shaking his head.

'I'm afraid this will only be good for kindling, Miss Sutton.'

She laughed. 'If we are to be informal I suggest you call me Amelia. I would feel better if I knew I had at least one friend in this neighbourhood.'

'Of course, Amelia. Shall we go upstairs and take a look? Perhaps I'd better go first, just to make sure there is no broken glass or missing floorboards.'

'What's outside, Caleb?'

He unlocked the back door and opened it with difficulty, pushing aside a snowdrift. 'Not much out here, apart from the privy. The yard is very small and surrounded by the high walls of the other warehouses. I'll take you to see your business quarters after we've inspected the upper floors.'

Amelia tried to keep an open mind as they negotiated the steep and narrow staircase. Cobwebs hung from the ceiling and the banisters were thick with grease from years of unwashed hands trailing on the bare wood. There were three rooms on each of the upper three floors, the top floor being attics with sloping ceilings and dormer windows. The only room that the previous tenant inhabited was on the first floor, overlooking the street and the high wall surrounding St Katharine Docks. The state of it was predictable even before Caleb opened the door. The smell from the single mattress was nauseating and Amelia was tempted to fling open the windows, despite the cold outside. Caleb shut the door quickly. He led the way downstairs to the ground floor.

'We will get the old furniture removed, Amelia. You don't have to worry about that. Perhaps you know a couple of women who could clean this place for you. I wouldn't want you and your father to move in until the whole place has been scrubbed from top to bottom.'

'I'm sure that could be arranged,' Amelia said firmly, although, unless Grandpapa was feeling generous and offered to pay for cleaners, she knew that she would have to do most of the work herself. However, the prospect of rent-free accommodation was too tempting to throw away on a mere technicality, and she was not afraid of hard work.

'I'm sure the place could be made quite comfortable once you have your own furniture and things installed,' Caleb said hopefully. 'I realise it's a lot to take on.'

'As a matter of fact we have very few belongings. You can leave what's here and we'll throw out what we don't need.'

'In that case perhaps I can persuade Mr Norris to help financially. After all, the property still belongs to him. He would have to make it good if he employed someone who was not related to him.'

'Yes, I suppose so, but I'd rather not depend too much on my grandfather. I need to prove to him that I can manage on my own.'

'But what about your papa, Amelia? I don't wish to pry, but doesn't he have some say in all this?'

'My father is a dedicated medical man. Since my

mother died he has put all his strength and energy into trying to save his patients. He is completely selfless in his work and I try to help him.'

Caleb raised an eyebrow but merely nodded. 'I see. Well, you've been through the property and, if that hasn't put you off, perhaps you would like to come into the warehouse and meet the women who work there.'

'Yes, please. That's really why I am here.'

'Come along then. You don't have to go outside. There is a connecting door.' Caleb hesitated at the top of the stairs. 'They are working women and they don't mince words. You will need to keep them in order.'

'You need not worry about me, Caleb. I'm no shrinking violet.'

He smiled. 'I do hope not. Anyway, this is the door to the warehouse. You will see that it's fastened at the top and bottom as well as being locked. That is for security and you should keep it like this while you are in the accommodation.' He unbolted the door, turned the key in the lock and thrust it open.

Amelia's first impression of the workplace was the loud chatter of women and the clatter of the sewing machines.

'Ladies, may I have your attention.' Caleb had to raise his voice in order to be heard, and there was a sudden silence.

Amelia shifted nervously from one foot to the other as she found herself the object of overt curiosity.

'Who is she?' one woman demanded loudly. 'Have you come to join us, ducks? You don't look as though you know one end of a sewing machine from the other.'

This remark was met by a gale of laughter and a

few loud sniggers.

Caleb held up his hand for silence. 'We'll have less of that, please. This lady is Miss Sutton who is taking over from Mr Thomas, who has left the company.'

'Got the sack, did he? The old soak.'

'Thank you, Nellie,' Caleb said calmly. 'As a matter of fact you are right. Mr Thomas had problems and he is no longer working here. Miss Sutton is taking over. She will be living next door and I trust all of you to be your usual cooperative selves.'

A ripple of mirth greeted his last remark and Nellie, who was apparently the spokesperson for the whole group, stood up. She looked Amelia up and down. 'She don't look as if she's done a day's work in her whole life. Can you sew, love?'

'As a matter of fact I can,' Amelia said firmly. 'But I've never used a machine, so I will have to watch what all you experts do and learn. I hope we can all work together to make the business even more successful.'

'Well said.' Caleb glanced round at the sea of faces. 'Carry on with your work. However, you will all have tomorrow off, it being Christmas Day, and be back here on Monday as usual. I will be here every working day for the next week or two, until Miss Sutton has settled into her new home and into the position she now holds.'

'Yes, I hope to get to know you all individually,' Amelia added earnestly. 'In the meantime I am always ready to listen to any problems you might encounter and to help if and when needed. Thank you all for listening.'

'I hope you're not going to stop our money for the time we've been idling while you talked to us,' Nellie said suspiciously.

'Of course not.' Amelia looked to Caleb for confirmation. 'That doesn't happen, does it?'

'Don't ask him.' Nellie pushed her way to the front. 'That's what old Thomas done, time after time. He stopped our pay for going to the privy or if we broke a needle, or anything that held up production. He was a real b —'

'Thank you, Nellie,' Caleb said hastily. 'Mr Thomas has gone now and you'll find Miss Sutton much more sympathetic to your needs. We are turning over a new leaf and I'm sure that production will improve. That's all. You may get on with your work. And don't worry about your pay. Nothing will be deducted.'

Still muttering between themselves, the women returned to their machines and the clattering resumed. Amelia was impressed by the speed with which they worked, but their covert glances in her direction were unsettling. She realised that it would not be easy to win their trust and even more difficult to earn their loyalty. It was a challenge, but one that she was determined to accept. At least she would be in control of their finances.

A sudden thought struck her as she and Caleb retreated into the private accommodation.

'Mr Marsh — I mean Caleb — my grandfather didn't mention remuneration. I assume there is a salary to go with the position of manager.'

'Yes, of course there is, but I will check with Mr Norris before I commit myself.'

'What was Mr Thomas earning?'

Caleb hesitated. 'I can't say if you will warrant the same wage. I'm afraid it's a fact that women are paid at a lower rate. I know it doesn't sound fair, Amelia, but that's just the way things are done. I'll put your case to Mr Norris and see what he says. After all, you are his granddaughter. Maybe he will decide you are worth more.'

Amelia could see that he was embarrassed by the question she had raised. Even if she was paid less than the last manager, she would still be earning a wage, and living rent-free was a huge bonus, but she was not going to give in easily. She needed to press him on the subject.

'I would like to know how much I would be paid before I give you a definite answer.'

'I'll speak to Mr Norris, Amelia. However, he'll want to know your decision quite quickly as we have several applicants for the position waiting to be interviewed. What shall I tell him?'

3

Caleb managed to find a cab, which took them to Long Acre. He stepped down to proffer his hand to Amelia and, although she was perfectly capable of alighting on her own, she allowed him to help her. He had, after all, been quite charming and understanding during their tour of the house and workroom, and he had promised to speak to Grandpapa as soon as he returned to Albemarle Street.

'Will you be at home this afternoon?' Caleb released her hand somewhat reluctantly. 'You must understand that your grandfather will want an answer today.'

'Yes, of course. Just ask him that one thing and I'll say yes or no when you tell me his decision.'

'If he should offer less than Thomas was earning, would that affect your decision?'

'To be honest, I know I am inexperienced and have a lot to learn, and I don't expect to be paid as much as someone better qualified, but I think I can get on with those women, given time. I hope to establish a good relationship with them and that will make things better all round. I am serious about this, Caleb. I want to prove myself worthy of my hire. I would come with you now and put my case to Grandpapa, but as you advised against it, I will wait at home for his response.'

'I understand and I'll do my best. I'll be back as soon as I can.' Caleb climbed into the hansom cab. 'Albemarle Street, please, cabby.'

Amelia entered the building and climbed the stairs.

The smell of boiling boar's head and onions filtered up from the basement where Widow Chalker lived with her six adult sons, none of whom was currently employed. It was well-known locally that Widow Chalker did favours for the butcher on a fairly regular basis, and in return there was always a boar's head in the pot on a Friday. Amelia frowned thoughtfully as she let herself into the living room. Perhaps she should have accepted the position at the workroom without question. However, the sight of her father slumped in the armchair by the fireplace made her forget everything else.

'Papa, are you all right?' She rushed to his side and went down on her knees, taking his hand in hers. To her relief he opened his eyes.

'Amelia? Is anything wrong?'

She scrambled to her feet, laughing with relief. 'No, Pa. I'm sorry, I didn't mean to wake you.'

A slow smile creased Harold's face into even deeper lines. 'You thought I had slipped away in my sleep?'

'No, Pa. Of course not. You do look exhausted, though.'

'I was called out in the middle of the night again, my dear. I'm glad I didn't wake you.'

'Have you had anything to eat, Pa?'

'I don't remember. Probably not. It was a difficult case and I only got back about an hour ago.' Harold peered at the mantelshelf. 'Not again, Amelia. Have you popped the clock? You know it was your mother's favourite.'

'We needed the money for food, Pa. But I'll soon be able to redeem it.'

'Why? What have you done?'

She laid her hand on his arm. 'Don't get upset. I

went to see Grandpapa Norris. I didn't get enough for the clock to pay what we owe the landlord. It seemed the only way, Pa.'

'No! How could you, Amelia? You know he blames me for your mother's death. I want nothing from that man.'

'This isn't just about you, Pa. We are in desperate straits here. We need coal and candles, and the only food we have is the remains of that loaf you accepted in lieu of payment yesterday.'

'But we always manage, don't we? I will be paid for the care I gave my patient last night.'

'When, Pa? That's the trouble, isn't it? You believe these people when they promise to pay you, but they never do, or very rarely. You are wearing yourself out and we are living like paupers. It has to change, Pa. And that's why I am going to accept Grandpapa Norris's offer of a job.'

Harold stared at her open-mouthed. 'What? No! I won't allow it, Amelia.'

'I am over twenty-one, Pa. I can make my own decisions. Besides which, there is free accommodation for us both with the position. It's a fine house in Nightingale Lane, next door to the workroom. I am to supervise the women who make mourning garments for the department stores in the West End.'

'Nightingale Lane is opposite St Katharine Docks. It's a rough area, child. And my patients are in *this* vicinity.'

'You will have sick people to tend wherever you go. Maybe the dockers will pay you with real money for a change.'

Harold shook his head sadly. 'What has this life come to when my daughter has to work to support me? Your mama would be turning in her grave if she knew what was about to happen.'

'Mama was a practical woman, and it's time to forget past hurts and slights. Grandpapa Norris is a widower who has lost his only child. I think he wants to make amends, Pa. I really do.'

'Then you don't know him as I do. That man is hell-bent on humiliating me and he's using you to show me up. I am a physician. I took an oath to heal the sick. I don't exploit people like he does. I expect the women in the workroom are paid the bare minimum for long hours, working in unsanitary conditions. Don't fall for his clever talk, Amelia. Think for yourself.'

'That's exactly what I am doing, Pa. I am going to accept the position, no matter how much or how little the salary he offers me. You and I will have a roof over our heads and if I can improve the lot of the women I saw today, that's exactly what I will do.'

'What have we come to?' Harold said despondently.

'Times have changed. One day women might even be paid at the same rates as men, and we may even be able to vote, but that's in the future. For now, I will accept Grandpapa's offer and we will move to Nightingale Lane.'

'Never. I forbid you to talk about it, Amelia.'

'The rent collector will be round next week, Pa. We can't pay and we are two months in arrears. He only allowed us to stay because you treated his son when he had scarlet fever and the boy recovered. But he won't be so forgiving this time. There is free accommodation with the position I've been offered and I'm going to accept whether you agree or not.'

'Good heavens, Amelia. You are your mother's daughter. That's all I can say.'

'And I'm proud to be so, Pa. Now, I have a little money left from pawning the clock, and I'm going out to get some coal, kindling and something to eat. I won't be long.'

'Be careful, my love. The pavements are very slippery. I'd go for you, but I am a bit tired.'

'Don't worry about me, Pa. I'll be fine.' Amelia picked up a wicker basket on her way out. Downstairs in the entrance hall she almost bumped into Widow Chalker's youngest son, Ted, as he burst in through the front door.

'You look as if you've been in a snowball fight, Teddy.'

He gave her a gap-toothed grin. 'Don't tell Ma. She'll be furious. I tore my jacket.'

Amelia glanced at the sizeable rip in the cloth. 'I tell you what, Teddy. I'll mend that for you if you'll do me a favour.'

'Yes, Miss Amelia. Anything you like.'

She took her purse from her reticule and handed him some coins. 'I need a sack of coal from the coalmonger. Can you do that for me?'

'I certainly can and I will. But you look as if you're going out. You said you'd mend this tear.'

'I'm only going to the dairy. I expect I'll be back before you, or soon after. Just leave the coal inside the living-room door.'

'There's the coal cellar, miss.'

'And everyone in the building helps themselves whether or not they've bought any of the coal. Just leave it where I said, and I'll hurry back to mend your jacket.'

Ted saluted and raced off with total disregard to the adverse conditions outside. Amelia followed more slowly. She did not want to slip and break a bone, especially now, with the prospect of a home of their own so close at hand. She made her way carefully to Sainsbury's dairy in Drury Lane, where she purchased bread, milk, butter and cheese. The tempting aroma of baked ham was almost too much to resist, but she knew how much money she had left in her purse, and it would have to last for a while. Perhaps Grandpapa would give her an advance on her wages. She could only hope.

When she returned home, she found Teddy waiting at the door. 'I got some kindling as well, miss.'

'Thank you, Teddy. That's very thoughtful.' Amelia opened the door and went inside. Her father was nowhere to be seen but she could hear gentle snoring from his room. 'Come in, Teddy. I'll just get the fire going and then I'll mend your jacket.'

'I can light the fire, miss. Ma gives us all jobs to do and more often than not I have to light the fire in the range.' He hefted the sack of coal over to the fireplace and began to clean the grate in a methodical manner that gave Amelia confidence. She put the basket of provisions on the table and took off her cape and bonnet. Having found her sewing basket she sat down to mend the tear in Teddy's jacket while he worked hard to get the fire going, his breath forming clouds above his head in the cold air. Soon flames were licking round the coal and kindling, and he sat back on his heels, grinning.

'That's one thing I'm good at, miss. I can get a fire going better than all me brothers.'

'That is a skill worth having,' Amelia said, smiling. 'This won't take long. Luckily it's a clean tear so it shouldn't show.'

'It's been handed down to me. All me brothers wore it until they grew too tall. Now it's mine. I'm going to look for work, miss.'

Amelia snipped the cotton thread and examined the result. 'That's good, Teddy. It's a pity your brothers don't follow your example.' She handed him the jacket. 'There you are, not quite as good as new, but hopefully it will pass.'

'Ta, miss. Much obliged.' Teddy shrugged on the shabby jacket. 'I'd better go or Ma will be sending the boys out to find me. It's boiled boar's head for dinner today, and for the rest of the week, but the first day is the best.' He hurried from the room, closing the door behind him.

Amelia rose from the chair by the fire, which was beginning to throw out a decent amount of heat. She unpacked the basket and cut herself a generous slice of bread, which she spread sparingly with butter and thin slices of Cheddar cheese. She sat down to enjoy her meal while the kettle on the trivet began to boil the water for tea. The leaves had been dried several times after use and this would probably be the last cup they made before being consigned to the rubbish bin. She ate her meal slowly, savouring each mouthful. Today she had enjoyed a splendid breakfast and now she had the luxury of some bread, butter and cheese for a late luncheon. Perhaps it was a sign of better things to come.

She sat for a moment, gazing into the orange and scarlet flames, but her thoughts strayed back to the house in Bow Street and baby Percy. She could only hope that the medicine she had recommended had relieved the poor child's symptoms, but she could not forget young Betsy's pale face and skinny extremities.

Her condition was probably due to malnourishment, but with a master like Jasper Cook, there could be little hope for the small family. Mrs Simms herself had looked as though she was losing the will to survive and no wonder, living in such dire circumstances with a bully for an employer.

A loud rapping on the door brought Amelia back to the present and she jumped to her feet. Judging by the urgency of the summons it was almost certainly someone needing a doctor. She hurried to open the door.

'Is the doctor in, miss? We need him urgent, like.' A boy of ten or eleven stood on the threshold, shifting agitatedly from one foot to the other. 'Quick as you like.'

'Who is sick? Can you give me some details for the doctor?'

'It's me dad. The doctor saw him last night but he's got worse.'

'I'll fetch him. Wait there.' Amelia went to rap on her father's door. It was a routine they followed all too often. She managed to wake her father and he emerged from his room, running his hand through his tousled hair. She helped him on with his coat and top hat and handed him his medical bag.

'Shall I come with you, Pa?'

He shook his head. 'I doubt if there's anything anyone can do for the boy's father. He fell from some scaffolding yesterday and was seriously injured. The family can't afford hospital treatment and, to be honest, I doubt if anything can be done for him.'

'The boy seemed very agitated, Pa.'

'I'll do what I can.' Harold walked slowly from the room.

Amelia could hear her father's gentle tones as he comforted the boy before following him downstairs. She sighed. There was so much tragedy, especially amongst the poor. She took the kettle off the hob and placed it in the stone sink. She could not help her father today but she could visit the house in Bow Street and check on baby Percy. It would ease her mind if she knew he was getting better.

In a matter of minutes, she was hurrying towards Bow Street with her cape around her head and shoulders, paying little attention to the heavy dark clouds pregnant with yet another snowstorm.

She reached Jasper Cook's house to find Mrs Simms standing on the snowy pavement with baby Percy in her arms. Betsy was struggling with two hessian sacks, which she bumped down the front steps. Behind her, red-faced and angry, Jasper Cook stood, arms akimbo as he watched her struggles.

'I don't know why I kept you on for so long, Mariah Simms. You're a slut and a terrible cook. You and your brats can find some other gullible person to take you on.'

'It's Christmas Eve, Mr Cook,' Mariah said tearfully. 'Have a heart, sir.'

'Ma done nothing wrong, guv,' Betsy added angrily. 'You're a pig, that's what you are.'

Jasper swung his arm and caught her a blow around the head that sent her tumbling down the steps, landing at Amelia's feet. He threw the sacks after her and slammed the door.

Amelia bent down to lift Betsy to her feet. 'Are you all right?'

A livid mark on the side of Betsy's face was already turning into a purplish bruise. She shook herself, spitting a tooth onto a previously pristine patch of snow.

'I'm all right, ta. The tooth was loose anyway. But that man is a monster.'

'He most certainly is,' Amelia said with feeling. 'Are you sure you aren't hurt?'

Betsy nodded emphatically. 'It's not me you need to worry about, it's Ma and Percy.'

Amelia took a closer look at Percy. 'He seems a little better. What do you think, Mrs Simms?'

'The medicine you give him and the camphor oil both helped, but now we've got nowhere to go. It's the workhouse for us, I'm afraid. I never thought we'd come to this.' Tears poured down Mariah's thin cheeks. 'It's going to snow again. We'd best start walking, Betsy, love.'

Amelia was close to tears herself as she gazed at the small family. She had known hardships but this was above and beyond anything she had experienced. She thought quickly. 'I won't let you go into the workhouse. Come home with me and we'll sort something out. You can't go traipsing around the streets in this weather, especially with a sick child.' Amelia picked up one of the sacks. 'Is this all you have?'

Mariah nodded. 'That's all our possessions. At least it was all we could gather, given the short notice. He said it was because Percy was crying all night, but that ain't true. He's found someone else to slave away for him and he just wanted rid of us.'

'You're better off away from that house.' Amelia hefted the sack over her shoulder. 'Can you manage the other one, Betsy?'

'I can. I'm strong for me age.' As if to prove her point Betsy swung the sack over her shoulder, but she staggered beneath its weight and would have fallen if Amelia had not steadied her.

'Just drag it,' Amelia said, smiling. 'If it gets too heavy, I'll take it. Anyway, it's not far to my home.'

They made their way slowly to Long Acre, but when she reached the top of the stairs Amelia came to a sudden halt at the sight of Speke, the rent collector. He was standing outside the door to their rooms, talking to Caleb Marsh.

'I'm sorry,' Amelia said breathlessly as she dumped the sack on the bare floorboards. 'I didn't realise you were coming today, Mr Speke. Surely we have until nearer the end of the month?'

Speke shifted from one foot to the other. 'The landlord wants what you owe him, miss. It ain't up to me.'

'I arrived rather early,' Caleb said calmly. 'I was just having a friendly chat with Mr Speke. It seems you have had trouble finding the rent.'

'Yes, I did explain that this morning.'

Speke cleared his throat noisily. 'It's no use, Miss Sutton. I've got orders to evict you today unless you can pay up.'

Amelia opened her mouth to respond but Caleb held up his hand. 'I have authority to settle the debt, Mr Speke, although I believe Miss Sutton and the doctor will be moving out very soon.'

Speke turned to Amelia, eyebrows raised. 'Is that so, miss?'

'We ought to leave you to settle your affairs, miss. You have enough to do without worrying about us.' Mariah Simms beckoned to Betsy. 'Come on, love.'

'No, Ma. Miss Amelia promised to help us. Ain't that so, miss?'

Amelia unlocked the door and ushered the Simms

family into the room. She could feel the lodgers in the other rooms hanging on every word, even though she could not see them.

'Come in and get warm by the fire, Mrs Simms, and you, too, Betsy.' Amelia turned to Caleb, standing at the door. 'What did my grandfather say?'

'He said if you prove yourself better than Thomas you will get a similar wage. He is a fair man, Amelia. He gave me permission to settle what debts your father might have and to give you your wages in advance. He doesn't normally treat his employees so generously.'

'I am his only grandchild,' Amelia said stiffly. 'However, in the circumstances I accept my grandfather's offer, and I would be very grateful if you would pay Mr Speke up to the end of the month. It will give me time to make arrangements for moving to Nightingale Lane.'

'Of course.' Caleb took out a bulging purse. 'Right, Mr Speke. How much will it take to settle the debt . . . ?'

'Good luck, miss,' Speke called over his shoulder. 'I'm glad I didn't have to call in the bailiffs.'

'Goodbye, Mr Speke. Thank you for your patience in the past.' Amelia closed the door, leaving Caleb to settle the debt. 'I'll make us a cup of tea and then we can talk, Mariah.' She glanced at Betsy, who was eyeing the loaf on the table. 'Have you eaten today?'

Mariah shook her head. 'Old Jasper watched every morsel we ate, and I had to account for every penny I spent on housekeeping. He locked the larder at night so we couldn't help ourselves.'

'I'm glad we've left him,' Betsy said, sighing. 'I hate old Jasper.'

Amelia moved to the table and began slicing the

loaf. She set some bread and cheese aside for her father, but she divided the rest up between Betsy and her mother, with small fingers of bread and butter for Percy. They fell on the food, eating ravenously, and Amelia went to answer a knock on the door.

Caleb stood outside on the landing alone. 'Speke has gone,' he said, smiling. 'You were lucky: he seems to be a decent sort for a rent collector.'

'My father lanced his boils and didn't charge him. That's how we've been living since my mother passed away. Sometimes Pa gets paid, but mostly it's something in kind, like a few sausages or a poke of tea. Or, as you've just seen, a grateful rent collector.'

'But you've decided to accept your grandfather's offer of a job and a home next to the warehouse?'

'Yes. I don't think I have any real choice in the matter, besides which, I want to have some independence. Up to now I have had to rely entirely on my father. To have a secure home and a set income would seem like heaven to me.'

'I understand, and I admire your courage.' Caleb put his hand in his jacket pocket and took out a document, which he handed to Amelia. 'This is a contract between you and Mr Norris. I suggest you read it thoroughly before you sign it.'

'Do you know what's in it?'

'Yes, of course. I helped write it.'

'Is there anything against my taking other people to live with us at Nightingale Lane?'

'Are you thinking of giving Mrs Simms a position in your home?'

'I will need help to get that big house up to standard. I can't do it on my own as well as managing the workroom. The family are in even more dire straits than we were. I'd like to help them, if I can.'

'I see no reason why you should not take the family in. As far as I recall, there is nothing in the contract that would prevent you employing staff or even taking in lodgers. Mr Norris is a businessman first and foremost. If you manage to improve the rate of production, the quality and the eventual turnover, I'm sure he will be more than satisfied.'

'Thank you.' Amelia opened the document, which was thankfully short and business-like. She refolded it and placed it in her skirt pocket. 'I see nothing to change my mind. Please tell my grandfather that I accept his terms and conditions.'

Caleb smiled and produced a leather pouch from his inside pocket, which he placed on the table. 'An advance on your pay, Miss Sutton. I'm sure we will deal very well together in the future.'

4

'I'd be careful of that one if I was you, Miss Amelia,' Mariah said as the door closed on Caleb.

'I don't know what you mean.' Amelia smiled happily. The future had seemed so bleak first thing that morning and now it felt as if a Christmas miracle had happened. 'Caleb is a really nice man.'

'Handsome is as handsome does,' Mariah said grimly. 'But you've been good to us, miss. I think it's time we went on our way.'

'No, please stay, Mariah.' Amelia pushed all thoughts of Caleb to the back of her mind. Her immediate concern was for the two children. Percy was still unwell but sleeping relatively peacefully in his mother's arms. 'It's Christmas Eve, Mariah. I'm not going to turn you out into the cold snow.' She smiled ruefully. 'I know it's not much warmer in these draughty rooms, but it will do until we move into the new house.'

Mariah stared at her in astonishment. 'Are you offering to take us in?'

'Not exactly. I'm asking if you would come and live with us. I'll need help to run that big house and, to be honest, I'm not much of a cook.'

'Oh, please, Ma,' Betsy cried excitedly. 'Please say yes.'

'You don't know us, Miss Amelia. What would your father say?'

'He would agree with me, and you would be doing me a favour. I doubt if I could make the old place habitable on my own, and you seem like a very practical person. I think we need each other, Mariah.'

'I must say, it sounds too good to be true, but if you're sure . . .'

Amelia smiled mistily. 'I've never been more certain of anything in my life.'

* * *

It was crowded in the tiny apartment but Mariah slept on the sofa and the children shared a palliasse on the floor. First thing next morning Amelia was up early and, with money in her pocket and the shopping basket looped over her arm, she set off to find a shop that was open on Christmas morning. The dairy in Drury Lane, run by Mr and Mrs Sainsbury, was getting ready to do business and Amelia filled her basket with eggs, butter, cheese, tea and a large meat pie. The baker was also open and she collected the free loaf he had promised in lieu of payment, which she accepted gratefully. The greengrocer was also open and she bought two oranges for the children and a handful of walnuts. Walking home through a quiet Covent Garden, she found a broken branch that had come off a Christmas tree, which she tucked under her arm. Amelia was already laden and walking on the slippery pavement was hazardous, but she could not go back to their rooms without purchasing a couple of candy canes to hang on the branch.

She managed to get home without mishap and found everyone still asleep. Judging by the snores emanating from his room, her father must have returned after she had gone to bed. She would have a lot of explaining to do when he awakened.

It was a Christmas Day like no other that Amelia had experienced, and it was bittersweet with memories of her mother never far from her mind. However, Betsy was beside herself with excitement. She could not have been more overjoyed with her simple presents had they been the most expensive toys that money could buy. Percy was a lot better and Mariah was deeply touched by the trouble that Amelia had taken to make the day special.

Amelia took a cup of tea to her father and she explained her reasons for taking Mariah and the children into their home. Harold listened intently.

'You are so like your mother, Amelia. You have a good heart. I just hope you haven't taken on too much. I would just say one thing, though. Be careful about trusting Mr Marsh. I've met ambitious men before and I remember coming across him a few years ago when I had to visit your grandfather to ask for his help. Mind my words, that's all I'm saying.'

* * *

Next day Percy was left in Betsy's charge, while Amelia and Mariah trudged through the snow to work on the house in Nightingale Lane. They swept, scrubbed floors and generally spring-cleaned the house from top to bottom. Mariah took particular trouble with the kitchen range, scraping off the rust before cleaning it thoroughly, and finishing it off with a generous application of black lead. The privy in the back yard was in an appalling state and Amelia undertook this onerous task herself. She worked for an hour until she was satisfied that it was no longer a hazard to health, and she cleared a pathway to it, piling the snow against the high brick wall.

Having exhausted herself, she went into the kitchen and found Mariah gazing triumphantly at the now sparkling range in which she had lit a fire.

'Where did you get the coal?' Amelia gazed at the hod filled to the brim with shiny black nuggets.

'I found it in the cellar. I went down there hoping to find enough pieces of coal to get the fire going, and there was a sackful. The last tenant must have forgotten it.'

'That was a stroke of luck. We really need to warm the house. It smells of damp.' Amelia sank down on a rickety chair at the recently scrubbed pine table. 'I have enough money to buy necessities, Mariah. But we will have to be very careful until I get my next wage.'

'Yes, I understand. I'll work for you for just my board and keep, Miss Amelia. I'm more than grateful to you for taking us in.'

'I need your help as much as you need a home for yourself and your little ones. I can't do everything myself. We might even be able to make some extra money by taking in lodgers, but I'll see how things go before I do anything like that.'

'Your pa isn't too keen on moving to the docks area, miss.'

'Pa is very loyal to his patients, but we can't live on air. He heals the sick but they have to pay for his services. I know it seems cruel when so many people are poor, but we all have to live.'

'But will Dr Sutton want to live in a place like this?'

Amelia sighed. 'I'm afraid he has no choice. We have to move out of our rooms by the end of the month. Before then we must try to make this place habitable.'

'The bedsteads are all right, but the mattresses will have to be thrown out,' Mariah said, frowning. 'The nippers and I can manage with one bed, if necessary.'

'I don't think it will come to that,' Amelia said gravely. 'We'll go to the furniture warehouse tomorrow and get the cheapest mattresses we can find. There are plenty of second-hand salerooms where we can get oddments of furniture.'

'I'll make a pot of tea when the kettle boils. It's beginning to feel like home already.'

'With your help we'll make this into a comfortable place to live.' Amelia gazed down at her sore and reddened hands. 'I'm determined to do well with the business.'

* * *

Amelia was determined to be there to meet the women when they arrived for work on Monday morning. She left home very early to undertake the long walk. A thaw had set in overnight and the pavements were less dangerous, although wet and slushy. She let herself into the house and waited until she heard chatter and raucous laughter in the huge, high-ceilinged room that had once been a warehouse and was now the workroom. The women were so busy chatting about their Christmas break that nobody noticed when Amelia walked through the door. She stood for a moment, eyeing the idle sewing machines.

'Good morning,' Amelia said pleasantly.

There was a sudden hush and the women spun round to face her, their expressions ranging from mutinous to frankly scared.

'Nellie Dawson, you seem to be the spokeswoman

here. Step forward, please.' Amelia faced them with an air of assurance that she did not feel. Inside she was trembling but it was important to be in control. She could see that some of the workers were not going to make life easy for their new manager.

Nellie made her way to the front of the group. 'We was just having a chat before staring work, miss.'

'I'm not here to treat you like children,' Amelia said firmly. 'I expect a fair day's work for a fair day's pay. You are the overseer, so that is your job, and you report to me. If anyone is not up to scratch, I want to know.'

'We're keeping up with the orders, miss. Well, almost.'

'I'll speak to you in the office, Nellie.' Amelia walked purposefully to the small glass-fronted office at the back of the workroom. She ushered Nellie inside and closed the door. 'You know that I am new to the job, so I will need your help, Nellie. I am a fair-minded woman and I will see that good work is rewarded. I would like you to stay behind today, for which you will be paid, and you can show me the whole process from start to finish.'

Nellie eyed her warily. 'Mr Thomas used to punish us if we didn't make the targets he set for us. He used to patrol the shop floor with a cane in his hand. If he didn't think someone was working hard or fast enough he would swipe it across that person's back or hands.'

Amelia was horrified but she tried to keep her expression neutral. 'I see. Well, you won't find me a hard taskmaster, but I expect people to earn their wages. The better we do, the more we will all benefit. However, I will need your full cooperation, Nellie.'

'If you are fair with us we will do our bit, miss. I will stay on today.'

'Thank you. I need to know exactly how everything works. For a start, I'd like to meet each of the women in person. Who shall we begin with?'

At first the women workers were suspicious and some of them were reluctant to talk about themselves. It was obvious that they knew Amelia was the owner's granddaughter, and it seemed that many of them thought she had been planted amongst them as a spy. She realised that she would have to earn their respect, and the best way to do this was to learn as much as she possibly could about the work they did. She needed to understand the whole process from the beginning, when the bales of cloth were delivered from the warehouse, to the finished garments. It was a daunting prospect but interesting, and she decided to learn as much as possible about the way the women worked.

At midday Amelia joined Mariah in the kitchen for a meagre lunch of bread and a sliver of cheese, washed down with several cups of tea. The house now smelled of carbolic soap and furniture polish, which was a great improvement on the previous noxious odours. Mariah had cleared the outside drain of dead leaves, bits of string and scraps of newspaper, which allowed water to drain freely from the stone sink. There was still plenty of work to do in the rest of the house, but Amelia sent Mariah home in the middle of the afternoon. It was obvious that she was worrying about Percy, and as she had worked so hard it seemed unkind not to acknowledge her efforts. Mariah was unwilling at first, but after a little persuasion she left to walk home, despite the bad weather.

Amelia sat at the kitchen table, studying the list of

workers and notes she had made while she was interviewing them. She knew she must memorise their names and details if she was to make any impression on them. She did not intend to rule by fear, as Mr Thomas had done, but neither did she want to become too familiar with her staff. There was such a lot to learn. She was deep in thought when the sound of someone rapping on the door knocker made her jump to her feet. She went to open the door and was surprised to see Caleb Marsh standing outside on the pavement.

'Come in,' Amelia said, holding the door to allow him to enter. 'I wasn't expecting you.'

He stepped over the threshold, taking off his top hat. 'I know. I'm sorry if this is an inconvenient time, but I brought some paperwork you will need. I could see the way things were going under Thomas and I took the ledgers on the pretext of doing an audit for Mr Norris.'

'Did you suspect Mr Thomas of dishonesty?'

Caleb smiled. 'Yes, that's exactly what I thought and I was proved correct. Hence his speedy departure. Is this a convenient time for me to go over the books with you?'

'Yes, of course. I am just finding my feet, so to speak.'

He shrugged off his coat and hung it over a chair. 'How are you getting on with preparing the house for occupation? I must say, it smells a hundred times better than it did when I last visited.'

Amelia led the way to the kitchen, which was the only warm room in the house. 'I have Mariah to help me. She's worked so hard I sent her home early. Her little boy is just recovering from whooping cough, so naturally she doesn't like leaving him for too long.'

'It seems that you are both reaping the benefit of the arrangement.'

'Yes, I think so too. Would you like a cup of tea? There's some left in the pot, although it's only lukewarm.'

'A cup of tea would be most welcome. It's freezing hard out there.' Caleb picked up the notes she had written on the employees. 'You don't mind, do you?'

Amelia poured the tea. 'No, of course not. I am trying to get to know the women who work for us. I think some of them might be troublemakers.'

'I'm afraid you get that in any business. But it looks to me as if you know how to handle them. Thomas ruled by threats and fear. That's not the way to get the best out of people.'

'I do so agree.' Amelia set the cup and saucer down in front of him. 'Please take a seat and we'll go over the books. I'm beginning to feel more confident about taking over the business, despite my lack of experience.'

He sat down. 'You had doubts? You were very brave to take it on.'

'I had little choice. Anyway, I intend to make a success of it. I'm sure that Grandpapa thinks I will fail miserably, but I am determined to do well.'

Caleb studied her notes. 'This is an excellent start. They are good women who work for us, but they have had hard lives. They are used to fighting for what they have.'

'I gathered that from the little they told me. Nellie Dawson has agreed to stay on for a while today after the workroom closes. She's going to show me the whole process, from start to the finished garments.'

'Excellent. With Dawson on your side you should be able to control the others easily. She was always the ringleader when there were rumblings of trouble. Thomas was too stupid to see it and he met them head on, which solved nothing.'

Amelia eyed him curiously. 'Does my grandfather treat his employees like that?'

'No, certainly not. He's strict, but fair. There's no one I would rather work for than Mr Norris.'

'That's good to hear. I haven't seen much of my grandfather since my mother died. In fact, I wouldn't have approached him now if things had not been so desperate.'

Caleb drank the last of his tea. 'I can understand that, Amelia. We all have to do what is necessary to keep going.'

'Do you speak from experience?'

'I'm afraid I do. I was orphaned at an early age and raised by an elderly aunt, who did not like children.' Caleb pulled a face. 'But we aren't talking about me. I brought the ledgers for you to peruse at your leisure, but perhaps you would like me to go over them with you now.'

Amelia nodded. 'Yes, that would be a great help. I need to learn as much as I can about the business.'

Caleb took her through the accounts for the past year, and although Amelia had never been particularly good with figures, she could see that Thomas had quite literally been helping himself to the profits. He had taken small sums at first, getting larger as he had obviously gained confidence.

'He didn't think he would be found out,' Amelia said when they reached the last page.

'He was so sure of himself.' Caleb closed the ledger.

'I have a suggestion, Amelia. I don't want you to think that your grandfather has no faith in you, but I would be very happy to help you with the financial side of the business. At least until you are more experienced in running things. This is not a slur on your capabilities.'

'Was it my grandfather's idea in the first place?'

'Yes, it was. I'll always be perfectly honest with you, but I am more than willing to help. It is in all our interests to get the workroom running at a profit again.'

Amelia met his direct look and she could see that he meant what he said. She smiled. 'I think it would work well, but only if I am given free rein to run the workroom as I see fit.'

'There is no doubt about that. I am good with accounts but I know nothing about fashion. This was just a side-line, as far as your grandpapa is concerned. Maybe you can make it into a thriving business.' Caleb took out his pocket watch. 'I should be back in the office. You'll excuse me if I leave now?'

'Of course. Thank you for all your help.'

His dark brown eyes sparkled with topaz lights as he smiled. 'Not at all. It's a pleasure. I'll see you next week at the same time, if that's convenient with you. But you can contact me at the office if you need me before then.'

'Thank you, I will. And now I have to spend some time with Nellie Dawson.'

Caleb frowned. 'It's dark already. You do take a cab back to your lodgings, don't you?'

'No. It's not too far to walk.'

'You shouldn't go out on your own in this area.'

'Caleb, I'm used to the streets in deprived areas. I've been walking them sometimes with Pa but more often on my own when I see patients for him. I know how to look after myself.'

He did not look convinced. 'Your grandfather told me to give you money for expenses. He is not a mean man, whatever people say about him.' Caleb took a leather pouch from his inside pocket and laid it on the kitchen table. 'I suggest you get a cab tonight. I'm afraid the thaw was only temporary. It was freezing when I arrived and the temperature will have dropped again now.'

Amelia eyed the bulging pouch. 'Please thank him. I will take a cab tonight, but only because it's been a long day and I started early.'

'Of course. You've done wonders here. Good night, Amelia.'

He left the room and, as the front door closed behind him, the house felt suddenly very quiet and empty. Amelia quickly made the fire safe for the night before she went to find Dawson. She was almost too tired to take anything else in, but she was determined to prove herself. She was her father's daughter and she suspected that she had a streak of pragmatism and iron-clad determination to succeed that she had inherited from her grandfather. She hoped so, anyway.

* * *

One of the things that Amelia learned during the following few days was that her grandfather was not a mean man. The pouch that Caleb had passed on to her was heavy with golden guineas and small change. It enabled her to purchase mattresses for their beds in the new house and enough cheap second-hand furniture to make them comfortable on a day-to-day basis. She already had a small amount of crockery and some pots and pans, but a trip to the market was pleasurable and she succeeded in buying everything they needed without spending too much on any one thing.

Betsy came with her on most of her shopping trips and she was as excited as if the items were being bought for her alone. Amelia took Betsy to a dolly shop where she bought her warm winter clothes, including a serviceable woollen coat and matching beret, adding a blue woollen scarf and matching gloves for good measure. Betsy was thrilled, and when Amelia insisted on buying her a new pair of boots, Betsy burst into tears and flung her arms around Amelia. Baby Percy was not forgotten and he too was outfitted for the winter. Mariah refused to accept any money, but Amelia got round the problem by telling her it was an advance on her wages, which she invested wisely in warm clothing. The house in Nightingale Lane was still very chilly and although there were fireplaces in each of the rooms on the upper floors, coal was expensive and Amelia knew she must be careful with the remainder of the money her grandfather had given her.

The only person who was not excited by the move to the new property was Harold. He hated taking anything from Nathaniel Norris, and he was very unhappy at the thought of moving to a new area, particularly one close to the docks. But in the end he had no choice in the matter. Speke returned on Thursday morning, politely but firmly telling them to leave the premises or risk a visit from the bailiffs. Amelia and Mariah were ready with their few belongings packed.

Percy, who was almost fully recovered, was wrapped up against the cold and Betsy was jumping up and down with excitement. Harold, on the other hand, was determinedly gloomy. He made no secret of the fact that he expected Amelia to fail miserably. If she made one single error her ruthless grandfather would evict them all and they would end up living under the railway bridges, or worse. However, he climbed into the hackney carriage, grumbling beneath his breath and clutching his medical bag as if he was afraid that someone would snatch it from him.

Amelia breathed a sigh of relief. The worst was over, or so she hoped. Persuading Pa that the move was a good one had been the hardest part of leaving their old home. The icy weather did not help, and patients had been arriving day and night, complaining of sore throats, colds and high temperatures. Harold had barely slept and it had affected them all.

The cab made good speed despite the inclement weather. The brief thaw had cleared the roads of snow, but once again the heavy clouds were gathering over the rooftops and more snow was expected.

When they arrived in Nightingale Lane, Caleb was waiting for them. He was standing in the doorway of the house with his collar of his greatcoat pulled up to his chin. He stepped forward to open the cab door, but Harold rejected his proffered hand and alighted stiffly to the pavement.

'Have you come to gloat, young man?'

'No, sir. Of course not, sir.' Caleb stepped forward to assist Amelia and then Mariah, who was holding Percy in her arms. Betsy leaped to the ground, her thin cheeks glowing pink and her blue eyes sparkling with anticipation.

'Am I really to have my own room, Ma?'

'Let's get indoors out of the cold,' Mariah said hurriedly.

Amelia produced the bunch of keys from her pocket and unlocked the door. 'Step inside first, Pa. This is our new home.'

Harold stood back. 'No. You go first, Amelia. This is your house. I am merely the lodger.'

Amelia bit back a sharp retort. She loved her father dearly, but sometimes he was a very difficult man. She stepped over the threshold. 'Come in, Pa. I'm sure you'll change your mind when you see how nice we've made everything.' She opened the door to the parlour, where a fire burned brightly in the grate. 'This is our sitting room, and a little further along the passage there's another, slightly larger room where your patients can be seen, Pa. You don't have to visit them at home unless they are too sick to walk here.'

Harold glanced into the room. 'It's very bare.'

'We will get more furniture as we go on, Pa.'

Amelia followed Mariah and Betsy into the kitchen at the back of the building.

'Did you come here earlier just to light the fire?' Caleb gave her an encouraging smile. 'You are quite amazing.'

Amelia felt the blood rush to her cheeks. 'Not at all. I didn't want everyone to arrive in a cold house. I will have fires in all the rooms when I can afford to buy more coal.'

Caleb turned to Harold. 'If you could have seen this house before Amelia and Mariah started to work on it, you wouldn't believe your eyes, Dr Sutton.'

'If you are here to report back to Mr Norris, you can tell him that I accept his help for the sake of my daughter. In any event, we don't need your help, sir.'

'Pa, that's very uncivil. Caleb has been helping me with the accounts. I mean to do well on my own merit but I have to learn the business first.'

'My daughter in commerce. Your poor mama will be turning in her grave.'

'Mama grew up in the business world, Pa. She would be proud of me.' Amelia turned to Caleb with an attempt at a smile. 'I'm sorry. We don't mean to be rude. You've been most helpful.'

Caleb backed towards the doorway. 'I understand. I'll leave you to settle in, but I'll be back next week. Just send for me if you need help in any way.' He paused. 'I'll wish you good day, sir.'

'You're not needed here,' Harold said tiredly. 'Please leave.'

Caleb acknowledged him with a brief nod and left.

'Pa, how could you be so rude to Caleb? He's been nothing but helpful.' Amelia faced her father angrily. 'I know this is hard for you, and I'm sorry. But what alternative did I have?'

Mariah handed Percy to his sister. 'Take care of baby for a while, Betsy. I'll put the kettle on.'

'Can I see my room, Ma?'

'Yes, in a minute.'

'It's all right, Mariah,' Amelia said hastily. 'You take care of the children. I'll make the tea.' She turned to her father. 'Would you like me to show you your room, Pa?'

'I'm not in my dotage, Amelia. You told me it's situated on the first floor at the front of the building. I think I can manage to find it myself.'

Mariah hurried Betsy and Percy from the room, closing the door behind them.

'You might try to be more amenable, Pa,' Amelia said in desperation. 'I do understand how you feel.'

'No, you don't. I'm utterly humiliated, especially when that young man is here spying on us. Your grandfather will no doubt find my situation very amusing. He always said I would come to no good.'

'That is not true at all. Your patients love you, Pa. You've saved hundreds of lives during your career.'

'Your grandfather has made my life even more difficult by burying us in this rough neighbourhood, Amelia. Can't you see that? It's his final revenge on me for marrying his daughter.'

'You can set up again here, Pa. There are always sick people in need of a good doctor, and you *are* a good doctor.'

'I'm weary of this. I'm going to my room. You may bring me a cup of tea when it's ready, Amelia.' Harold went to the door and opened it. He glanced over his shoulder. 'It isn't your fault, my dear. You've done your best, I know. I blame Nathaniel Norris for my final humiliation.' He closed the door behind him.

Amelia shook her head. Tears stung her eyes but she wiped them away with the back of her hand. She respected her father, but at this moment she felt like telling him that he was behaving like a spoilt child. She had worked so hard to make a home for them all, and he had not a good word to say for anything she had done. She made the tea and sat down at the table to allow it to brew. She could hear the familiar whirring of the sewing machines coming from the workroom and it was oddly comforting. The little brass clock that she treasured so much had been redeemed from old Scoggins, and now sat in pride of place on a shelf above the range. She could see that it was almost time for her first visit to the workroom.

She would have to learn the business quickly. It was obvious that the women worked hard, turning out garments by the hundred over a week, and sales were regular, but the profits were small. When Amelia had gone over the figures in the ledgers she could see that they often made a loss. It was all very puzzling, but Caleb had told her it was usual in business. She need not worry about the actual figures.

She reached for the teapot and was filling her cup when Mariah walked into the kitchen.

'Percy is having a nap and Betsy is arranging her room. I haven't seen her this happy since before her dad died.'

Amelia passed the cup to Mariah. 'Sit down for a moment. We have all day to get everything straight.' Amelia filled another cup for herself. 'You've never spoken about your husband.'

'Ben was a wrong 'un from the start, but I loved him. He was a charmer and a rogue. I knew it would end badly, but we had ten years together and some of the time it was wonderful. Then he would slide back into his old ways and end up in prison for months on end, sometimes a year or two.'

'I'm so sorry. I had no idea. Betsy told me that her pa had died. That's all.'

'He caught typhoid in prison.' Mariah sipped her tea. 'He wasn't a bad man, miss. He was just weak and he was easily led. Betsy loved her pa. Thinks he was killed in an accident. She was only five years old when he died and I never told her the truth.'

'But you have Percy. He's a year old, so Betsy said.'

'Don't think too badly of me, miss. Sometimes we have to do things just to keep a roof over our heads. If you know what I mean.'

'Your employer, Mr Cook?'

Mariah nodded. 'He refused to believe that Percy was his, even though he knew it was true. If you hadn't come along when you did, me and the nippers would have ended up on the street. I think Mr Cook had his eye on another woman to keep house for him and warm his bed on a cold night, but I'm so glad to be away from there.'

'You've had a hard time, Mariah.' Amelia reached across the table to pat Mariah's hand. 'But things will be better from now on. You and the children are safe here.' Amelia rose to her feet. 'I have to take a cup of tea to my father and then I'll do my rounds in the workroom.'

'I'll make a stew for dinner. I really enjoy cooking.'

Amelia smiled. 'That's good because I am a terrible cook. The kitchen is all yours, Mariah. We'll do well together. This will be a happy home for you and your children. I promise you that.'

Amelia was halfway up the stairs, on her way to her father's room with a cup of rapidly cooling tea, when she heard urgent knocking on the front door. She retraced her steps and placed the cup on an old sea chest she had found in the pawnbroker's shop. She opened the door and found a man in dirty overalls about to raise the knocker yet again.

'Can I help you?'

'I heard there's a doctor moved in here. There's been an accident in the dockyard. It's urgent.'

5

It was almost like old times as Amelia carried her father's medical bag, following him across the slippery cobblestones to the docks entrance. The agitated dockworker hurried on ahead. Harold had answered the call without stopping to put on his greatcoat, but in passing the hallstand he had snatched his top hat and rammed it on his head. Amelia wrapped a woollen shawl around her head and shoulders, but the cold struck her like hundreds of icy needles pricking her skin. She followed her father, breaking into a run in an effort to keep up with him.

The injured man was lying on the cobbles, his legs twisted at impossible angles. He was unconscious and for a moment Amelia feared the worst, but her father was ahead of her and he went down on his knees. After a brief examination he stood up. 'This man is alive but he has multiple fractures. Fetch a stretcher of some sort. If you can't find one, then make one. He needs to be taken to hospital immediately.'

Nearby, a carter was unloading a dray with barrels of ale from one of the nearest breweries. Harold marched over to him. 'I'm commandeering your vehicle to take the injured man to hospital.'

'You can't do that, guv. It belongs to the brewery. I'll lose me job.'

'And this man will lose his legs and probably his life. Do as I say. I will square it with your employers.'

The startled drayman rolled the last barrel onto the ground, still muttering beneath his breath. Harold beckoned furiously to the men who had found a large pallet for use as a stretcher. 'Over here. I need three of you on either side. I'll support his head. Careful now or you'll do even more damage.'

Amelia could only watch as the men gently eased the prostrate dockworker onto the pallet, which they then lifted onto the dray. Harold leaped up to sit beside the driver.

'Give me my bag, Amelia. Go home now. I'll see this man to the London Hospital. I don't know when I'll be home.'

Amelia knew better than to argue. She made her way carefully across the frozen ground to the place they now called home. The sound of the sewing machines could be heard from outside. She opened the front door and went straight to the kitchen.

'What happened?' Mariah asked anxiously.

'There was an accident and a man was badly injured. Pa is taking him to the London Hospital. It's where Pa trained.'

'Let's hope they can help the poor man.'

Mariah put the last peeled potato into the saucepan. 'We need some more groceries. I don't like to ask you for more money but I haven't got a penny. Mr Cook didn't give me my wages and I daren't go back and ask for what he owes me.'

'You're right, Mariah. Keep well away from that man.' Amelia frowned thoughtfully. 'You're better off without him. I have got some money left, but not a lot. I really think we're going to need to take a couple of lodgers in. It's going to take some time for me to build up the business. It seems that Mr Thomas let everything slide even while he was helping himself to any profits he made.'

'There are two good rooms we could let, and there's even more space in the attics.'

'Unless Pa gets patients who can afford his fees, we won't have any choice other than to let rooms to paying guests.'

'This is a poor area, miss. The dockworkers don't get paid much and their families suffer. Your pa would need to set up in the West End if he wants to treat rich people.'

'Yes, I know that, Mariah. But I think my grandfather is testing me with this house and this job, and I intend to prove my worth.'

'You know that me and Betsy will help in any way we can.' Mariah hefted the pan onto the hob. 'There's not much meat in the stew but just enough to give it a bit of flavour. It's mainly potatoes, onions and carrots with a couple of spoonfuls of pearl barley.'

'It sounds delicious,' Amelia said earnestly. 'I'd better go and do my rounds in the workroom or the women will think I've lost interest.'

* * *

Nellie bustled forward to greet Amelia as she walked into the noisy workroom. 'We're up to date with all the funeral garments orders, miss.'

Amelia glanced at the pile of gowns in unrelieved black, which were laid out ready to be packed and sent to the mourning warehouses in Oxford Street and Regent Street.

'Do we ever get orders for any other type of clothing, Nellie?'

'Not that I knows of, miss. We just follow instructions.'

'But would it be nicer for everyone if we were to branch out into different fashions?'

There was a general nodding of heads and a hum of whispered agreement.

'I dare say it would make life more interesting, miss. Sometimes working on black material is hard on the eyes, particularly in winter, when the light is poor.'

'Maybe things will change,' Amelia said vaguely. 'But you certainly need better lighting. I might be able to do something about that.' She glanced at the flickering gaslights bracketed to the walls. 'Maybe I can persuade my grandfather to put in electric lights. Anyway, I would like to see the advance orders, Nellie.'

'Certainly, miss. The books are all in order.'

'Did Mr Thomas leave it to you to keep account of everything?'

Nellie puffed out her chest. 'Yes, miss. I am good with numbers and I won a prize for me handwriting at school.'

Amelia entered the small office, followed by Nellie, who closed the door.

'Do you get paid extra for bookkeeping, Nellie?'

'No, miss.'

'Then we must remedy that. I'll speak to Mr Marsh when I see him next.'

'That would be much appreciated, miss.' Nellie reached for a ledger and handed it to Amelia. 'This is the order book. I tick off everything as it's packaged and sent out.'

Amelia studied the neat rows of writing. 'This is very well kept. You deserve a raise in wages, and I'll see that you get it. However, if I were you I would not mention it outside this office.'

Nellie grinned, exposing a large gap between her front teeth. 'Don't want the rest of me teeth knocked out, miss.'

'You were in a fight?'

'Not at work, miss. It were all a mistake. I got in the way of a flying fist, so to speak.'

'That's too bad.' Amelia patted her on the shoulder. 'Expect to find a little extra in your wages every week, Nellie. I'll study the orders, but that will be all for now. Thank you.'

Amelia sat down to study the order book, although her thoughts were not of black crepe and bombazine, but of elegant fashions that would boost business to a different level. Caleb Marsh was a progressive thinker. She would suggest an additional line or two in gowns that the departmental stores could stock. Perhaps some that followed the current fashions from top designers, but at prices better-off middle-class women who aspired to dress well might purchase. It was an exciting thought. She had never had enough money to buy such gowns for herself, but that did not mean she was uninterested in beautiful clothes. Sometimes on long dark winter evenings in the past, she had filled a notebook with designs of her own with no thought to have the gowns made, although it had satisfied the artistic streak she had inherited from her mother. She made up her mind to speak to Caleb when he next called at the house. It was obvious that there was always a need for funeral wear, but she was certain the copies of high fashion would make much more money.

Amelia put the ledger away and let herself out

of the office. She walked slowly between the rows of seamstresses. Just looking at the dark depths of the material hurt her eyes. She wondered what effect it must have on those who had to spend ten hours a day staring at the cloth. With a few words of encouragement to the women, she left them to get on with their individual tasks. It had been something of a shock to discover how many hours they worked for very low wages. At one time she might not have understood the struggle that poor people had simply to survive. However, the experiences of the past years, living hand to mouth, had made her empathise with those who were less well off. Pa was devoted to helping the sick, but she now had the fate of these women in her hands. It was an onerous task, but one that Amelia hoped she might tackle successfully.

Already, she was beginning to think of ways in which to improve the lot of the workers as well as making the business more successful. The ideas that came to mind were exciting and challenging. She felt she owed it to her mother to make a success of her life, and to save Pa from his unswerving devotion to duty, which was threatening his health and his well-being.

* * *

Harold did not come home until suppertime that evening. He looked pale and worn, but there was a light in his eyes that surprised Amelia. She knew immediately that returning to his old teaching hospital had been a good thing, even though the circumstances were due to another's misfortune.

'How is the patient, Pa?' Amelia asked as she helped

her father off with his jacket. 'You're freezing. You should have stopped to get your overcoat.'

'There wasn't time, Amelia. The poor fellow would have died if we hadn't got him to hospital very quickly. As it is, he has only a fifty-fifty chance of survival. Luckily, I know the surgeon who operated on him. Delaney has had remarkable successes with patients who might otherwise have spent the rest of their lives as cripples.'

'Come and sit in the front parlour, Pa. I kept the fire going especially. I knew you would be dog-tired when you came home.'

'You're a thoughtful girl, my dear. I know I should have shown more gratitude to you for taking on this mammoth task. I am grateful, but I don't like to think you are supporting me.'

'Perhaps there is work at the hospital for you, Pa.'

A faint smile curved Harold's lips. 'As a matter of fact there is a vacancy for someone with my qualifications. Delaney is putting me forward as a candidate.'

'That's wonderful, Pa. Supper's ready when you are, but would you like a cup of tea first?'

'I'd appreciate a tot of brandy, if there's any left. It's been a long hard day.'

Amelia found just enough brandy left in the bottle to pour a small measure for her father. She sat watching the colour return to his thin cheeks as he drank.

'When will they let you know about the job, Pa? The money that Grandpapa Norris gave me has almost run out.'

'I thought it was a substantial amount, Amelia. Have you been extravagant?'

'No, Pa. It went on necessities.'

'But surely you are getting paid for running the workroom?'

'First, I have to make a profit, and that is going to take time. The business was almost run into the ground by the previous manager, who helped himself to the takings.'

'I thought Nathaniel was being suspiciously generous. That man never does anything unless it profits him. He is using you, Amelia.'

'Pa, we have a home. We would be living on the streets by now if we hadn't come here. I don't mind working — in fact I enjoy the challenge. All I want to know is when you are likely to be employed at the hospital so that I can work out our finances. We're running very low as it is.'

Harold drained the last drop of brandy from his glass. 'You're right, of course. I am supposed to be the breadwinner, my dear. I'm afraid I've let you down. I shouldn't blame you.'

'We just need to be practical, Pa.'

'Tomorrow, I promise I will go back to the hospital and speak to Delaney again; see if he can't hurry things along.'

'You will be better off working at the hospital. You might even enjoy being back in the world you knew so well.'

Harold smiled ruefully. 'Yes, you're right. Just the smell of carbolic reminded me of the time I worked at that hospital. Delaney and I were students in the same year, but now he is a well-paid orthopaedic surgeon and I am a penniless physician.'

'You won't be penniless if you accept the position at the hospital.' Amelia eyed him warily. 'In the meantime, I was wondering if we should take in a couple of lodgers. Just a temporary measure, of course.'

'No, Amelia. I won't have strangers living in my

home. I told you, I'll go to the hospital in the morning to see my patient, and I'll have another word with Delaney. *I* will put our finances straight, not your grandfather.'

'Yes, Pa. I'll go and help Mariah serve supper.'

Harold ate his food sitting by the fire in the front parlour, while Amelia, Mariah and Betsy ate in the kitchen. Percy had been fed earlier and was already asleep in a drawer pulled from the chest in Mariah's room. Amelia was determined to buy him a proper cot when funds allowed. She had seen an iron cot advertised in an old magazine but it cost one pound fifteen shillings, which was far too expensive to buy. Second-hand wooden cots were the answer, again when funds permitted.

After supper, Mariah and Betsy went upstairs to their rooms. Amelia took some paper from the office and a pencil. She sat at the kitchen table, sketching gowns that followed the latest fashions. When she was satisfied with the result she sat back and smiled. She would show them to Caleb at the first opportunity.

* * *

Next day Amelia saw her father off when he left for the hospital. She had half expected him to change his mind, but as there were no patients knocking at the door he was left with very little choice. She realised that it would hurt his pride to go looking for employment, even if his old friend had promised to put his name forward to fill the vacancy. However, having studied the accounts from the workroom, she was even more convinced that it would take time to build up enough profits to pay her a decent wage. It would be easy to blame her grandfather for placing her in such a position, but, on the other hand, he had provided them with a home, even if it was not in the most salubrious area. Last night she had been kept awake by the noise of drunks pouring out of the public houses that thrived in the docks area. There had been a fight too close to the house for comfort and she had feared someone might throw a brick through the window, but the piercing sound of a police whistle had dispersed the revellers. She had risen from her bed to look out of her window and had seen the men slipping and sliding on the packed snow, which at any other time might have been comical. Everything went quiet then, and she had slept undisturbed until morning.

Amelia decided to check on the workroom early. She liked to vary the time of her visits so that she could get an accurate picture of the daily routine. It also kept the workers on their toes, although she was satisfied that Nellie kept reasonable order. Amelia had no intention of being too strict, as she considered the workplace should be somewhere pleasant, as well as profitable for all concerned. Even at this early stage she had a good idea which of the women were doing the least work, and those who really earned their pay.

She was about to enter the workroom when someone knocked on the front door. She opened it and was surprised to see Caleb standing on the snow-covered pavement.

'I know it's early, but I've brought the pay packets. May I come in?'

'Yes, of course.' Amelia stood aside. 'I'd forgotten that it was Friday already. This week has flown by.'

'That sounds promising.' Caleb put down the

leather bag he had been carrying and took off his gloves. He hung his hat on a peg together with his greatcoat. 'Are you settling in comfortably?'

'Yes, thank you, Caleb. We're doing well.'

'And your papa?'

Amelia knew exactly what he meant and she did not prevaricate. 'He has been offered work at the London Hospital. He trained there years ago.' She hoped that this piece of news would go straight back to her grandfather.

'That's splendid. I was afraid this area might not provide patients who were able to pay for treatment and you would be no better off than you were before you moved.'

'But you encouraged me to take up Grandpapa's offer.'

'I believe he has your best interests at heart. It's not up to me to question his judgement.'

'Even so, the workroom doesn't really make a profit, does it?' Amelia gave him a questioning look. 'Tell me honestly.'

'It did in the beginning, so I've been told. But other manufacturers managed to make similar garments cheaper.'

'If Grandpapa is such a good businessman, why didn't he sell up?'

'You might find it hard to believe, but your grandfather started this business when he was a very young man. He only keeps it going to provide work for the women in this area. In the right hands it runs smoothly, and even if it doesn't make much money, at least it doesn't make a loss.'

'So I am never going to earn very much, no matter how hard I try?'

He avoided her direct gaze. 'I think it unlikely, but you have a rent-free home.'

'I don't wish to sound ungrateful, but, as you said, it is in a very rough area.'

'Yes, I know. I wish it weren't so.'

He looked so awkward that Amelia took pity on him. 'I have had an idea that might save the business, and even make it profitable.'

'I'd be very interested to hear it.'

'If you have the women's wages, you'd better give them out. I promised Nellie Dawson that she would have extra in her pay packet for acting as supervisor, which she does very well.'

'Yes, I had the message you sent to the office. That's taken care of. Will you come in with me?'

Amelia laughed. 'Are you afraid of them?'

'I would be if they were an angry mob. As it is, I am quite happy to do it alone. I just thought it would look better if we went in together.'

'Of course. Anyway, I locked my drawings in the office. I want you to see them and give me your opinion.'

Caleb smiled. 'I'm probably not the best person to ask about the latest fashions, but I'd be very interested to see them.'

* * *

There was an expectant hush when Amelia ushered Caleb into the workroom. He spoke to each of the women in turn as he handed out their wages. Nellie was the last to receive hers. She weighed it in her hand and grinned. 'Ta, guv.' She turned to Amelia and winked, as if to show she knew that the small packet contained extra money. 'Right, ladies. Back to work. Let's show Mr Marsh how we do it.'

'Good day, ladies,' Caleb said as he left the workroom.

'I'll be with you in a minute.' Amelia let herself into the office to retrieve the sketches she had made the previous evening, and she joined Caleb, who was waiting for her in the hallway. She locked the interconnecting door.

'Come into the front parlour, Caleb. It's lighter in there and you can take a look at my ideas. I'm afraid I haven't lit a fire. I only do that late in the afternoon so that Pa has somewhere cosy to sit when he comes home.' She took a seat at the small tea table in the window where she laid out the sketches. 'I think we should branch out, so to speak. The funeral business is all very well, but we would make more money selling copies of high fashion designs although at a much more affordable rate.'

Caleb examined the drawings carefully. 'I'm very impressed. These are excellent.'

'I have no training in design, but I used to watch the fashionable ladies when they attended the theatre in Drury Lane. One of the lodgers in Long Acre was a star at the opera house. She used to buy fashion magazines, and when she threw them out I would take them and study them. My drawings are based on them but are not exact copies. The materials and colours would be very important.'

'Your ideas are wonderful, but it would all come down to costing and, probably even more important, finding an outlet for them. Do you know any fashion buyers from the department stores?'

'I don't, Caleb, but I thought you might.'

'My experience has only been with the mourning departments of the stores in question, but I could make enquiries.'

'If you can do that, Caleb, I will work out how much material is needed for each gown. I could have one made as a sample, to demonstrate the quality and style, as well as the low price.'

'You have thought it all out, haven't you?'

'Yes, I have.' Amelia smiled proudly. 'What do you think?'

Caleb put his hand in his pocket and took out a purse. 'I think you might use this money to purchase the materials you need.' He handed it to her, smiling. 'Your grandfather insisted. He knows you've had a lot of expenses. I'd advise you to take the money and put it to good use. I think your idea is excellent and so are your sketches. However, I'm not going to mention any of this to Mr Norris because I know what his response will be.'

'He won't allow it?'

'Mr Norris is an importer. As I said, he only keeps this business on for sentimental reasons.'

'Yes, you did say that, but it doesn't make sense. Why would he care now, after all these years?'

'I believe he was working as a clerk in his father's shipping office on the docks when he met your grandmother. She was working here as a seamstress. Judging by the portrait of her that hangs in his study, she was quite a beauty.'

'I remember her fondly. She was lovely and very kind. But I had no idea that she came from the East End.'

'Everyone who knew her says she was a real lady, no matter where she was born and raised. I believe it is in memory of their meeting here that Mr Norris keeps the place going. Perhaps he sees a little of your grandmother in you, Amelia.'

'I can't think why my mother didn't tell me their story. It was very romantic.'

'I wouldn't know about that, but it's just possible Mr Norris *might* agree to your ideas, especially if he sees a good profit in them.'

Amelia clutched the money tightly in her hand. 'I'll put this to good use, as you say. I will show Grandpapa that he is not the only one in the family who has a talent for business. Pa and I have been too close to starvation and homelessness for me to treat this opportunity lightly.'

'I have to go now or Mr Norris will be getting impatient. We have an important appointment this morning and your grandfather demands punctuality, but I won't forget your proposition, Amelia. At the first opportunity I will speak to the buyers in the mourning departments, and see if they can give me the information we need.'

'And I will do my part. Who knows, this might be the start of a whole new trend in ladies' fashions, and more profit for the business. Thank you, Caleb.'

'Don't thank me yet. Wait until I have some good news for you.' Caleb took her hand and raised it to his lips. 'I'll see myself out.'

Amelia waited until she heard the front door close before hurrying to the kitchen. She could not wait to tell Mariah, and she found her in the kitchen mopping the floor.

'It's very quiet,' Amelia said, smiling. 'Where are the children?'

'Betsy's upstairs getting Percy ready to go out. I'm

going to enrol her in the Princes Street School. It's time Betsy started lessons again. I don't want her to grow up ignorant.'

'I agree,' Amelia said, nodding.

Mariah gave her a suspicious glance. 'What went on with you and Mr Marsh? Your cheeks are very flushed.'

Taking care not to step on the wet patches left on the flagstones, Amelia laid her sketches on the kitchen table. 'I showed these to Caleb. He's going to help and I think he's quite keen on my idea of making cheap copies of the gowns that wealthy women pay a fortune for. I'm going to get some material to make up one or two of these as samples so that I can demonstrate my ideas to the buyers at the departmental stores.'

'I might be able to help,' Mariah said casually.

'In what way?' Amelia looked up, eyeing her curiously. 'What could you do, Mariah?'

'I was trained as a dressmaker and pattern cutter in one of them high-class places, making gowns for rich women. I had to give it up when I was with my old man because we was always dodging the bailiffs or the police. But I haven't forgotten how to cut a pattern and sew a seam.'

'Can you work a sewing machine?'

'We was taught to do everything by hand, but I can always learn. It can't be too difficult. Maybe I could have a practice in the evenings, when the women have gone home?'

'That sounds like an excellent idea. There's a material warehouse not too far from here. We could go there after you've been to the school to enrol Betsy.'

'I've really missed making pretty things. I love the feel of silk and satins and the beautiful colours of the brocades. I lost all that, thanks to Simms, but I'm free now and I'll do anything I can to help you. If it weren't for you, we'd be existing in the workhouse.'

'We'll do this together, Mariah. We'll make a fortune.'

Mariah rolled her eyes. 'Until that happens, I still think we should take in a lodger or two, miss. We need money to buy some bread, butter and milk, and some meat or fish for supper.'

Amelia placed her sketches in a drawer of the oak dresser. 'You're right, but I've got enough cash for a day or two. First things first, however. We'll buy some cheap material to make an afternoon gown, and we'll make a start on it this evening. So you know how to make a pattern?'

'I do, and I've seen them pin the cloth on a model before cutting, but I never done it myself.'

'All right. I'll be your model, but I warn you, if you stick a pin in me I'll scream.' Amelia doubled up with laughter at the image this created in her mind's eye.

'Why are you both laughing?' Betsy appeared in the doorway with Percy clutched in her arms. 'What's funny?'

'Nothing, love,' Mariah said, smiling. 'We're just happy today.'

'And I'll treat you to some chocolate when we buy the groceries,' Amelia said, controlling her mild hysteria with an effort. 'You're such a good girl, Betsy. You deserve the best, and your ma is going to see that you get every chance in life. Starting right now.'

6

Betsy was successfully enrolled in the local school and she attended lessons every morning with a wide smile on her face. At nine years old she could read and write and do simple arithmetic, but she was eager to learn more and proved to be an apt pupil.

In the afternoons she looked after Percy while her mother and Amelia worked on their first creation — an evening gown in blue silk taffeta. The low-cut bodice was trimmed with glistening bugle beads and fitted tightly to the waist. The apron skirt was finished with a deep frill and drawn back into a low train that was also finished with deep frills. It was not an exact copy of a Paris fashion, but it followed the current trend and Amelia was excited by the way the sketch on paper was turning into something any woman would be happy to wear for a special occasion. It would have made their work easier if they had use of the machines in the workroom, but Amelia did not want to risk it in case they damaged them in some way. So every seam was sewn by hand, and she found hand sewing quite relaxing after a busy day.

It was now three weeks since his interview at the hospital and Harold waited anxiously to hear whether he had been selected for a position in the emergency department. His considerable experience in treating accident victims must have stood him in good stead as he returned home one day with a triumphant smile on his face.

'I couldn't wait any longer so I called in at the hospital, Amelia. I turns out that I was the successful applicant and I start tomorrow.'

'Oh, Pa! That's wonderful news.' Amelia gave him a hug and, even though he normally shied away from shows of emotion, Harold managed a wry smile.

'Despite what Delaney told me, I thought I might be too old to be considered seriously, but they chose me anyway.'

'I was sure they would, Pa. Did you find out how the poor fellow who had that dreadful accident on the docks is doing?'

'He's survived, but the doctors are doubtful whether he'll ever walk again. He might be able to get round with the aid of crutches, but he won't go back to his old job.'

'That's sad, Pa. How will his family survive if he can't work?'

'These things happen. We can only hope that he has friends and family who will help.' Harold glanced at the kitchen table, which was covered in scraps of material, cottons and Amelia's sketches. 'Are you making yourself a new gown, my dear?'

'No, Pa. It's not for me. I'm hoping to branch out from the plain black mourning gowns.'

'That certainly is a contrast.' Harold picked up a piece of silk taffeta. 'Very pretty, but what's for supper? I believe my appetite is returning.'

'It's oxtail stew,' Amelia said, smiling. 'There's a fire in the front parlour. I'll bring you a bowlful when I've tidied all this away.' She picked up the dress and handed it to Mariah. 'If we can finish the hemming tonight I'll show this to Caleb when he brings the wages tomorrow.'

Mariah nodded eagerly. 'It's beautiful, even if I say so myself, and it fits you perfectly.'

'It's a pity I'll never get the chance to wear it,' Amelia said wistfully. 'Some lucky lady will have it bought for her, if we can persuade one of the stores to take it, and any others we create.'

Harold shrugged. 'This is all beyond me. I'll be in the parlour when the food is ready, Amelia.' He headed towards the doorway, turning at the last minute to give Amelia a genuine smile. 'I believe you have your grandfather's head for business, my dear. I'm sure he thought you would fail when it came to running the workroom. I would dearly love to see his face when you turn around his failing business.'

Amelia cleared the scraps of cotton and material from the table. She could not help wondering if her father knew the real reason why Nathaniel Norris had kept the workroom going, even though it barely made a profit. It was such a romantic story. Just thinking about the love shared by her grandparents brought tears to her eyes. She wondered if she would ever meet someone who would care about her with such devotion. The young men she had met so far had shied away when they realised that she would never desert her father. Amelia knew that, but she loved Pa and had felt completely responsible for him since her mother died. She filled a bowl with stew and took it to the front parlour, together with cutlery and a starched white napkin.

Harold looked up and smiled. 'Thank you, Amelia. That smells really delicious. I didn't have time to eat at midday.'

'We're so lucky to have Mariah to cook for us. I wish I had half her skill in the kitchen.'

'You did well enough for me in the past, my dear. I have no complaints.' Harold unfolded the napkin and tucked it into his shirt collar.

Amelia was about to leave him to enjoy his supper when she hesitated. 'Pa, did you know that Grandmama used to work here when she was very young?'

Harold swallowed a mouthful of hot potato. 'Do you mean in the actual sewing room? Surely not.'

'Apparently this is where she and Grandpapa met. She was a seamstress and he was a clerk in his father's shipping office.'

'She was such a lady. I always imagined she came from a good family. Caroline was very kind to me when I was first introduced to the family, unlike your grandfather, who wanted to show me the door.'

'She was very beautiful when she was young, judging by the portrait in Grandpapa's study.'

'Your mama was exactly like that when I first knew her. In fact, you are the image of her, Amelia.'

Amelia smiled to herself as she left the room. It was kind of Pa to say so, but she knew she could never be as good-looking as her late mother or her grandmother. It made Pa happy to think so and it was wonderful to see him smile again. Returning to his old world at the hospital had been the best thing that could have happened to him. Now it was up to her to make sure that the workroom thrived under her management. She had just reached the kitchen when someone knocked on the front door. Thinking it must be a patient, she hurried to answer it. Snow had turned to steady drenching rain.

'Is this Dr Sutton's house?' The man had a wide-brimmed hat pulled down over his forehead, from which rain was dripping in cascades onto his tweed overcoat.

'Yes, it is. Who shall I say wishes to see him? Are you sick?'

'No, I'm not a patient. Dr Sutton asked me to come here this evening.'

Amelia opened the door wider. 'Come in out of the rain. Who shall I say wishes to see him?'

He took off his hat and shook it outside, sending a shower of raindrops to rejoin the downpour. 'My name is Todd Taylor. Dr Todd Taylor from the London Hospital.' He brushed his tousled fair hair back from his forehead.

Amelia was surprised to see that he was probably in his mid-twenties. Somehow she had assumed that anyone working at the hospital would be closer to middle age. He smiled, revealing a row of even white teeth, and his hazel eyes twinkled mischievously.

'I am a doctor, I promise you. I'm not here to sell him anything.'

'No, of course not,' Amelia said hastily. 'Please wait for a moment. I'll tell him you're here.'

She entered the parlour, closing the door behind her. 'Pa, there's a young man here to see you. He said you asked him to come.'

Harold laid his spoon and fork back on his empty plate. 'That was delicious stew. Congratulate Mariah for me.' He untucked the napkin and wiped his lips. 'That must be young Todd Taylor. I met him today at the hospital. Nice chap — you'll like him, Amelia.'

'I'm sure I will,' Amelia said cautiously. Pa was up to something. She was sure of it. 'Shall I send him in?'

'Yes, of course. Don't keep him waiting in the hall.'

Amelia opened the door. 'Dr Taylor, will you come

in, please?' She held out her hand. 'May I take your coat?'

He shrugged off the wet garment and hung it on the hallstand. 'One day I'll purchase another umbrella. The trouble is I'm always losing them. I leave them in cabs and omnibuses or they just seem to disappear.'

Amelia laughed. 'I'm sure someone profits from finding them.' She ushered him into the parlour and was about to leave them to talk when her father raised his hand.

'Don't go, Amelia. This concerns you so please stay.'

'Very well, Pa.' She closed the door and waited while her father and Todd exchanged pleasantries.

'Please sit down, Todd,' Harold said affably. 'It was good of you to turn out on a night like this.'

'It is to my advantage to come here, sir.' Todd pulled up a chair for Amelia and she sat down, waiting curiously to find out why this pleasant young doctor had trudged all the way from the hospital in the pouring rain. He took a seat opposite her.

'I expect you're wondering what this is all about, Amelia.' Harold met her enquiring gaze with a smile. 'Todd has only recently started work at the hospital. He came up from the country a few weeks ago and has been looking for decent lodgings ever since his arrival. I remembered what you said about renting out one of the rooms and I thought of him.'

'Please don't feel obliged to give me an answer immediately,' Todd said hastily. 'I realise that this has come as a surprise to you. I expect you would like to see some references before you make a decision.'

Amelia shook her head. 'My father is a very good judge of character, Dr Taylor. But we are new to taking in paying guests and the room is not yet ready. You might not think it suitable.'

'Miss Sutton, to be quite honest with you, anything would be better than the lodgings in which I find myself now. The only good thing about the damp, cold, rodent-infested house is that it's close to the hospital. I would be grateful for even a modicum of comfort.'

'You'd get more than that here, my boy.' Harold reached for his pipe and tobacco pouch. 'Amelia, I suggest you take Todd upstairs to see what is on offer. He can decide whether or not he wishes to join us here.'

'Yes, Pa. Of course.' Amelia rose to her feet. 'If I had known you were coming I would have made the room ready. But I'll show you the rest of the house and you can decide for yourself.'

Todd followed her from the room. 'I'm sorry if this is inconvenient. I thought that Dr Sutton would have told you about me.'

'It doesn't matter.' Amelia lit an oil lamp that was always kept at the foot of the stairs. 'There are two large rooms on the third floor, and a boxroom. There are more in the attic but we have yet to make them habitable.' She led the way, hoping that Mariah had found time to dust the rooms that day. It was bitterly cold and she wished she had thought to wrap her shawl around her shoulders. Todd Taylor seemed a nice enough person and the choice was his, but she found herself hoping that he would find one of the rooms to his liking. The sound of their footsteps on the bare boards echoed off the high ceilings. She turned to give him an encouraging smile.

'We haven't been in this house for long so there's

still a lot to do to make it more habitable.'

'I understand. It's good of you to take the trouble to show me round, especially at this time of night. I should have come in the day, but I am kept very busy at the hospital.'

'I'm sure you are.' Amelia reached the landing on the third floor. She held the lantern high as she entered the front room, which was the largest and benefited from two tall windows. The faint glow of the gaslight in the street below sent patterns from the windowpanes onto the bare walls. Mariah had obviously taken her household duties seriously and the scent of lavender polish filled the air. She had covered the mattress with a patchwork quilt and had added a couple of pillows. If a fire had been lit the room might even have appeared quite cosy.

'The room at the back is very similar.' Amelia put the lamp on a rather rickety table they had found in the pawnbroker's for next to nothing. 'You might prefer that as it's quieter away from the street.'

Todd shook his head. 'This is perfect. Would you mind if I added some furniture? I would need a desk so that I can continue my studies, and a bookcase or some shelves. I would pay for them myself, of course.'

'It would be your room,' Amelia said firmly. 'Would you expect to have meals here?'

'I do long hours, but yes, if it were possible I would appreciate at least one meal a day. The landlady where I lodge now serves cabbage soup with every meal, except breakfast, which is a cup of weak tea and a biscuit.'

'You would do much better here. Let's go downstairs and you can meet Mariah, who lives with us and does the cooking. She has two children and one of them is a baby. He cries at night sometimes. Would that disturb you?'

'Not at all. I am usually so tired by the time I get to bed that nothing on earth would wake me from my sleep.'

Amelia smiled. 'You haven't heard Percy when he's at his best.' She picked up the lamp and headed for the staircase. 'I know it's very chilly up here, but if you take the room I will see that a fire is lit every day in the cold weather.'

'I couldn't ask fairer than that.' Todd followed her downstairs.

* * *

In the kitchen Betsy was having her supper at the table and Percy was sitting on his mother's lap. Mariah half rose to her feet but Amelia signalled her to remain seated.

'Dr Taylor, may I introduce Mariah Simms and Percy, of course. And the young lady at the table is Betsy.'

Todd acknowledged each of them with a nod and a smile. 'It's a pleasure to meet you all.'

Betsy grinned. 'I like him, Ma. He's nice.'

'I think you are nice, too, Betsy,' Todd said seriously. 'I don't know what you're eating but it smells very tasty.'

'Is there any stew left, Mariah?' Amelia made a move towards the range, but Mariah was on her feet instantly. She handed Percy to Betsy. 'Yes, there is. Are you hungry, Dr Taylor?'

'It's Todd, and yes, please. I am starving and that smells wonderful.'

'Then you'd better sit down,' Amelia said, smiling. 'Mariah can't allow anyone to be hungry when she's in charge of the kitchen.' She took a bowl from the cupboard and passed it to Mariah who filled it to the brim with stew.

'It's still quite hot.' Mariah placed the food in front of Todd and handed him a spoon and fork. 'I'll cut some bread for you.'

'And I'll make a pot of tea. Pa always has a cup or two after dinner.' Amelia sidestepped Mariah to pick up the kettle and fill it at the sink. She glanced over her shoulder and was delighted to see Todd tucking into the food as if he had not eaten for days, let alone hours.

Mariah cut slices from the loaf and spread them generously with butter. Although Amelia approved, they were on a tight budget. She must remind Mariah of that when Todd had gone.

Todd looked up, smiling beatifically. 'I think I've died and gone to heaven. That is the best stew I've ever tasted. I can't thank you enough. When can I move in, Miss Sutton?'

Betsy eyed him curiously. 'You haven't died, guv. You're still breathing.'

'So I am, Betsy. Your diagnosis is quite correct. I think one day you will make a very good doctor.'

Amelia smiled as she made the tea. Betsy obviously had made a friend, and Todd certainly had a way with children.

'I'm making tea for my father, Dr Taylor. Would you like a cup?'

'Call me Todd, please. And yes, I would love a cup of tea.'

'I'm Amelia. Miss Sutton sounds so formal.'

‘Amelia,’ Todd said, smiling. ‘It’s such a pretty name.’

Amelia left Todd, Mariah and Betsy chatting amicably while she took the tea to her father. He was dozing with his pipe still clenched between his teeth, but he woke with a start as she placed the cup and saucer on the table beside him.

‘I was just resting my eyes, Amelia.’

‘Yes, Pa. I realised that.’

‘What did Todd think of the room? You told me you wanted to take in a lodger and when I met him at the hospital we started talking, and I thought he might be a suitable candidate.’

‘He seemed to like the room, Pa. What he liked even more is Mariah’s cooking. She took pity on him and gave him some of her delicious stew. He wants to take you up on your offer.’

‘Did he say how much rent he would pay?’

‘We didn’t talk about money, Pa. Didn’t you discuss it with him?’

‘Me? Heavens, no. I don’t deal in financial matters, you know that, Amelia.’

She sighed. ‘Yes, Pa. I know only too well.’

‘You’d better ask him then. I know nothing of these matters. I don’t suppose there’s any more brandy in the bottle, is there?’

‘No, Pa. You drank the last drop yourself.’

‘Oh well, if you take young Dr Taylor on, maybe we can afford a few luxuries for ourselves.’

‘Don’t forget you will be paid a salary, Pa. That, together with rent from Dr Taylor, should make life much easier for all of us.’

‘Yes, of course. I was forgetting that I can now rely on a wage from the hospital. Life is not so hard, after all, my dear.' Harold closed his eyes and smiled.

Amelia returned to the kitchen to find Todd on his own. He looked up and grinned. 'Thank you so much. I feel like a new man after that wonderful meal.'

'You have Mariah to thank for that. She's a truly amazing cook.' Amelia pulled up a chair and sat down. It was embarrassing to talk about money, especially to someone who was so overtly appreciative and grateful for everything, but it must be done. 'I wish we didn't have to talk about money, Todd, but how much rent do you pay at the moment?'

'Far too much for the discomfort I've suffered for the past six weeks. I would be more than willing to pay a guinea a week, especially if that were to include an evening meal. Although I should add that I am often on night duty.'

Amelia made an effort to appear nonchalant. 'A guinea a week is quite acceptable. I'm used to my father working very unsociable hours. I am sure we can accommodate you in that respect.'

'That is wonderful. I have to get back to the hospital for my night shift now, but I could move in tomorrow, if that is convenient?'

'I'll make sure your bed is aired and that the fire is lit in the morning. You'll have a nice warm room to come home to.'

'Thank you, Amelia. You don't know what that means to me.' Todd rose to his feet. 'I'd better leave now.'

'I'll see you out.' Amelia followed him into the hall where he put on his coat and hat.

'I can hardly believe my luck.'

'I think the arrangement will benefit all of us.' Amelia opened the front door and peered out into the rain.

'I hope you don't get too wet on the way back to the hospital.'

'I'd better find a cab or I'll be late for my shift and that will never do. Thank you again, Amelia. I'll see you tomorrow.' He stepped outside and walked briskly towards East Smithfield. He glanced over his shoulder and waved before disappearing into the rain and darkness.

Amelia closed the door with a feeling of sheer relief. She knew instinctively that Todd Taylor was a man to like and trust. She had no worries about taking him into their home, and the money would make the world of difference. She returned to the kitchen where Mariah was busy clearing the table.

'The children are in bed already?'

Mariah nodded. 'Betsy finds schoolwork very tiring and Percy was ready to go down half an hour ago. Did the young doctor agree to rent the room?'

'He did and he's going to pay a guinea a week for the privilege. He's on night duty so he might want to sleep when he gets here tomorrow. We'd better get the room ready first thing.'

'You like him, don't you?'

'Yes, I do. Who wouldn't find someone so obviously genuine a nice person to have around? Pa did well in choosing Todd. I can't wait for him to move in. I know I'll feel safer with another man in the house. It gets very rowdy round here in the early hours of the morning.'

'You're right. Dr Taylor looks as though he can handle himself in a difficult situation.'

'Let's hope we never have to put it to the test. Pass me a cloth, Mariah. I'll dry the dishes if you wash them.'

* * *

Next morning Amelia was up even earlier than usual. The prospect of earning a guinea a week for very little effort other than accepting a relative stranger into their home was enough to make the dull day seem brighter. She washed, dressed and went downstairs to find that Mariah was already in the kitchen, having stoked the fire in the range and was preparing the breakfast porridge.

'I've lit the fire in the guest room,' Mariah said with a satisfied smile. 'It will take a while to warm the room.'

'I'll make up the bed. It's fortunate we bought extra blankets in the market. We'll need more sheets and pillowcases but I'll get those when Todd pays his first week's rent.'

Mariah raised an eyebrow, a sure sign she had something important to say. 'Do you think using first names is a good idea? I mean, wouldn't it be better to be on formal terms at the start?'

'But he's Pa's colleague. Surely that makes a difference?'

'If you say so. I only speak from experience. I allowed Jasper Cook to be too friendly and look where it got me.'

'I understand, Mariah. But that won't happen here. I know how to keep my distance, but I don't imagine it will be necessary. Dr Taylor is a born gentleman. You can always tell.'

'I'd better get Betsy up or she'll be late for school.' Mariah placed the saucepan of porridge on the hob. 'I'm sure he's a very nice, upstanding man,' she added as she hurried from the kitchen.

'He is,' Amelia said, speaking to thin air. 'I'm sure of it.'

She tipped the tea leaves she had saved and left drying overnight into the warmed teapot and poured on the boiling water. It was part of the daily routine to take her father a cup of tea first thing in the morning, which was even more important now that he had a position at the hospital. When Todd paid his rent she would be able to buy tea on a regular basis and using the leaves again and again would be a thing of the past. She took a cup upstairs to her father's room. She could hear Betsy's loud protests that school was a waste of time and she did not like her teacher, with Mariah's voice growing louder until there was a sudden gloomy silence, broken only by Percy crying.

Amelia woke her father and left the tea on a table close to the bed. She was halfway down the staircase when someone knocked on the door. She hurried to answer its urgent summons and was surprised to see Caleb standing outside.

'It's very early.' Amelia gave him a searching look. 'Is anything wrong?'

'It's your grandfather. He's been taken ill and he's asking for you. You must come immediately.'

7

'Come inside for a moment, Caleb,' Amelia said urgently. 'I'll fetch Pa. He might be able to help.'

Caleb shook his head. 'No, please don't. Mr Norris was adamant that he wanted to see you on your own. It really is a matter of life and death. We should hurry.'

'All right, but I need to tell Mariah where I'm going. I can't just walk out and leave everything.'

'Of course. I understand, but we mustn't waste time.'

Amelia snatched her cape and bonnet from the hallstand. She put one foot on the bottom tread but at the sound of voices she hesitated. Mariah came down the stairs carrying Percy. Betsy followed them, protesting that she did not want to go to school.

'I heard the knock on the door,' Mariah said breathlessly. 'Is anything wrong?'

'Grandpapa has been taken ill. He wants to see me, not Pa. Will you tell my father when he comes down for breakfast? I really should go with Caleb.'

'Yes, of course. Don't worry, I can handle everything here.'

'Thank you, Mariah.' Amelia put on her bonnet and cape. 'I'm ready, Caleb.'

* * *

The cab ride through the busy London streets seemed to take far longer than usual and Amelia was increasingly nervous. She had no particular affection for Grandpapa Norris, who had always been remote, even when her mother was still alive, but he was someone she respected for his ability to create and control a thriving business. It was a shame that, even now, he seemed to be unable to accept his late daughter's husband into the family. Amelia still found that hard to forgive.

'Are you all right?' Caleb asked anxiously. 'I realise it must be an anxious time for you.'

She turned to meet his concerned look with an attempt at a smile. 'I've never been close to my grandpapa, but that doesn't mean I don't care about his suffering.'

'Of course not. He is very poorly, Amelia. I think you need to prepare yourself for the worst.'

'I'm a doctor's daughter. I've seen cases of terrible injury, pain and distress since Pa decided that I was old enough to accompany him on his rounds. I've also witnessed many deaths, which were sad but unrelated to me. This might be different but I don't understand why Grandpapa wants to see me. He's never shown much interest in my wellbeing until recently.'

'Perhaps he senses that his end is near. Who knows? Anyway, we'll be there soon. I just wanted you to be aware of the circumstances.'

They lapsed into silence during the last part of the journey and when they arrived outside the elegant townhouse, Caleb paid the cabby and alighted first, proffering his hand to Amelia. Albemarle Street was busy with carriages, cabs and gentlemen on horseback. Very few of the residents walked any great distance and, if they took exercise at all, they would ride in style to one of the great parks where, weather permitting, they would take a short stroll. Amelia remembered this with a wry smile as she crossed the pavement and was ushered inside by a liveried footman.

Hobbs, the butler and long-time servant to Nathaniel Norris, came hurrying towards them. Amelia was surprised to see that the old man's eyes were reddened as if he had been crying.

'How is my grandfather, Hobbs?' She remembered him in happier times when her mother was alive. Hobbs had always shown a marked fondness for Eleanor Sutton, having served the family since she was born. Amelia felt a wave of sympathy for Hobbs, who was about to lose yet another person whose life had been inextricably bound to his own.

'He's fighting to the last, miss,' Hobbs said with a break in his voice. 'He wishes to see you.'

'Would you like me to come with you?' Caleb asked gently.

Amelia shook her head. 'No, but thank you, anyway. I need to see my grandfather on my own.'

Hobbs nodded approvingly. 'Follow me, please, Miss Amelia.'

A cool winter light seemed to drain the colour from everything it touched in the grand entrance hall. The black and white marble squares were sharper than usual, and the chill of winter seemed to have found its way into the house. Even the plaster cherubs gambolling around the cornices, clutching lutes and garlands of roses, appeared to be frozen in time. The atmosphere in the building was tense, as if awaiting the master's demise. That feeling sent a shiver down Amelia's spine as she followed Hobbs up the wide staircase to her grandfather's enormous bedroom on the second floor.

It was almost too dark to make out the prone shape beneath the satin coverlet, but as she drew closer, she realised that Nathaniel was propped up on lace-trimmed pillows, his face as pale as the white silk.

'Miss Amelia has come to visit you, sir.' Hobbs backed respectfully towards the doorway.

'Come closer, Amelia.' Nathaniel's voice was weak but still commanding.

'I am here, Grandpapa.'

'Caleb has kept me informed of your progress at the workroom.'

'I am trying to make it more profitable, sir.'

Nathaniel paused, gasping for breath. He cleared his throat with an obvious effort. 'I wanted to tell you myself . . .'

'Yes, Grandpapa?'

'I have altered my will. I've left everything to my nephew Daniel Norris. Everything except the mourning clothes manufactory and the attached house. They now belong to you.'

'To me, sir?'

'Yes.' Nathaniel attempted to raise himself on one elbow, but failed. 'You have a chance to prove yourself, Amelia. Now go. Send Hobbs to me.'

Amelia backed away as Hobbs hurried to his master's bedside. There was nothing she could do other than to leave the room and make her way downstairs to the entrance hall. Stunned by what her grandfather had given her and hardly able to believe that it was true, she walked slowly as if in a dream. Perhaps that was what it was. She was asleep and would wake up in her comfortable bed at home. But the sight of Caleb pacing the marble tiles was enough to shake her out of her trance-like state.

'Are you all right, Amelia?' Caleb said for the second time that day. 'You are very pale.'

'He really is dying, isn't he?'

'I'm afraid so. The doctor doesn't think he has long to live.'

'Do you know what is in his will?'

Caleb shook his head. 'No. That is between Mr Norris and his solicitor, Edgar Musgrave.'

'Would you ask the footman to find me a cab, please, Caleb? I feel I ought to wait here in case Grandpapa wants to see me again, but I need to go home. They'll be worried about me and I have the business to consider.'

'Of course. I understand.' Caleb beckoned to the footman, who was staring into space although Amelia suspected that he was desperately trying to overhear their conversation. 'Hail a cab for Miss Sutton, if you please, James.'

'Sir.' James snapped to attention, opened the front door and stepped outside.

'May I ask what your grandfather said to you?' Caleb asked in a low voice.

'I wasn't expecting anything from him, but he's left me the manufactory and the house. They're both mine.'

'He didn't leave you this house or the rest of his business assets?'

'No. All of that goes to Daniel Norris, Grandpapa's nephew. I think I met him once, a long time ago.'

'That seems a little unfair, but it's not up to me to criticise my employer. Even so, I think he could have provided better for his only child's daughter.'

'The way things have been between Grandpapa and my father, I'm surprised to have anything, and grateful, too. Thank you for your concern but it really is more than I was expecting.'

'I should see you safely home,' Caleb said worriedly. 'But I have to remain here in case your grandfather needs me.'

'Of course you must.' Amelia laid her hand on Caleb's arm. 'Don't worry about me. I'm used to going everywhere on my own, and I don't always have the luxury of a hansom cab.'

'I have never met anyone like you,' Caleb said, smiling. 'Most young ladies would be having a fit of the vapours after what you've just been through.'

'I have seen much worse, but I am truly sorry to see my grandfather like this.'

James strode into the hall, attracting their attention with a polite cough. 'Your cab is waiting, miss.'

'Goodbye, Caleb. Please keep me informed as to my grandfather's condition. Who knows? He might rally.'

'I will, of course.' Caleb escorted her out of the house to the waiting cab. 'The Mourning Warehouse, Nightingale Lane, cabby.'

Amelia climbed into the cab and made herself comfortable. She was still in a daze as the driver urged his horse to a brisk walk, heading east. She genuinely hoped that her grandfather would recover his health and strength, but should he lose this battle, it was his wish that she should become a property owner. She leaned back in the seat and closed her eyes. Grandpapa had given her a chance to follow her dream, and her first task would be to change the manner of the business. Gradually, the mourning garments would be replaced by fashionable apparel in beautiful colours and lovely materials; just like Paris fashions, but at more affordable prices.

Still in a state of shock, Amelia went about her usual tasks for the rest of the day. She spent time with Nellie, going over the problems that arose in the workroom, but she decided not to mention her grandfather's failing health. As far as Amelia was concerned there was no question of the women losing their jobs, which would inevitably bring privations to them and their families. She had suffered enough herself to know the hardships of living hand to mouth. Nevertheless, she realised that the reality of being employed by a woman, and a very young one, would be hard for some to accept. When she officially inherited the business she would have to prove herself to her staff as well as the rest of the business world. It would not be easy.

Putting all such thoughts aside, Amelia congratulated Nellie on her efficient performance in the workplace and the calm atmosphere in which the women worked. Nellie was obviously unused to being thanked for anything to do with the garments they produced and she was smiling and crying at the same time. Amelia gave her a few moments to compose herself before sending her back to her machine. There was a rustle of whispers as Amelia left the workroom, having asked Nellie to pass on her appreciative comments.

* * *

During the next few hours Amelia tried hard to focus on the normal routine, although her grandfather's condition was uppermost in her mind.

She confided in Mariah, who was sympathetic but

practical, as always.

'He's an old man, miss. Maybe his time is up and he's ready to meet his Maker. But you have to concentrate on yourself and your papa now. If it was me, I'd take the gown we made to the big department stores up West and I'd convince them that my designs was just what they needed. Any seamstress can make a mourning gown, but it takes someone talented to create a beautiful ball gown at a reasonable cost.'

'You're right,' Amelia said slowly. 'Grandpapa is giving me a chance to make something of the business. I'll pick my best sketches and I'll take the gown with me. You should come too, Mariah. After all, you cut the pattern and did most of the sewing. We'll go together.'

The sound of someone knocking on the door made them both jump.

'I'll go. It might be Caleb again.' Amelia hurried from the kitchen, almost tripping over Percy who had made a dash for freedom in the hallway, but was scooped up by his mother.

Expecting the worst, Amelia opened the door, but it was Todd who stood outside on the pavement with furniture piled up on a handcart.

'I hope you don't mind, but I bought a desk and chair in old Scoggins's pawnshop.' He eyed her warily. 'Are you all right, Amelia? You look rather pale.'

'My grandfather is very ill and not expected to recover. I thought you were someone bringing me bad news.' Amelia held the door open wide. 'Please bring your things inside. It looks as if it's going to rain again.'

'Thank you.' Todd lifted the chair from the top of the pile and carried it into the hall. He put it down.

'I'm sorry to hear about your grandfather.'

'Let me help.' Amelia had spotted a couple of oil lamps balancing perilously on the cart and she stepped outside without waiting for Todd's response. She took a lamp in each hand and hurried inside as the first drops of rain fell from a threatening sky.

Todd and the ragged boy who had accompanied him brought the desk into the house and placed it at the foot of the stairs. Todd tipped the boy and patted him on the shoulder.

'Thanks, mate. Best hurry to get that cart back to the pawnshop or you'll get drenched.'

'Ta, mister. You're a toff.' The boy backed out of the door.

Todd turned to Amelia with a wry smile. 'To think I was like that at his age.'

Diverted, Amelia gazed at him in surprise. 'You were a street urchin?'

'Does that surprise you?'

'Yes, of course it does. You're an educated man.'

He laughed. 'It's a long story, but I was born in a workhouse, and I ended up living by my wits on the streets of London.' Todd closed the door and picked up the chair. 'I'll take this up first, if that's all right with you.'

'Yes, of course. But I really would love to hear more. I can't imagine how an orphan from the mean streets of London became a respected doctor at the London Hospital.'

'I'd be happy to tell you when you have time to spare.'

'I'll bring your oil lamps upstairs, so you can tell me at least part of your story. It will take my mind off things.' Amelia followed him upstairs to his room on the third floor.

She was pleased to see that Mariah had made up the bed and a fire burned brightly in the grate. The room was still quite bare, but it felt warm and even welcoming. She set the lamps down on the mantelshelf and sat in the chair, waiting while Todd went downstairs to fetch the desk.

He manoeuvred it through the doorway and set it down in front of the window. 'Perfect,' he said, smiling. 'Now I will be able to write notes and study in my spare time.'

Amelia eyed him curiously. 'I thought you were a qualified doctor.'

'I am, but I hope to specialise in paediatrics. My experiences as a child made a great impression on me. The number of children who die before their fifth birthday is shocking.'

'How did you overcome such a difficult start in life, Todd?'

'I ran wild when I left the workhouse. I was the leader of a gang of street urchins when I was thirteen. I did many things of which I am not proud.'

'I find that hard to believe.' Amelia eyed him curiously. 'Go on, please.'

Todd perched on the edge of the desk. 'There were twelve of us, counting myself. We lived in a cellar and survived by picking pockets and petty theft. Then one day we were desperate for food and we kidnapped a young woman, who chanced to wander into our territory.'

'That's really shocking.' Amelia stared at him in disbelief.

'We didn't hurt her, and it turned out that our bad deed saved us all from a life of crime and degradation.'

'How did that happen?'

'Nancy is the kindest, most caring person I've ever met. She saw something in us that was worth saving, and she realised that we were driven by hunger and desperation. She took us back to her home in Devonshire. You won't believe this, but she lived in a castle.'

'It sounds like a fairy tale.'

'I suppose it was, in a way. Nancy herself was a foundling and had been taken in by the Carey family who lived at Rockwood Castle. They raised her as one of their own and her story is even more remarkable than mine.'

'I would love to hear the rest of it, Todd.'

'It would take too long to go into detail now, but Nancy made it possible for us boys to receive a good education, and I was apprenticed to the local doctor. Eventually I attained the necessary qualifications at the London Hospital, and I took over the practice when the doctor retired, but I still had a burning ambition to give young children a better start in life — hence my return to London.'

'But you never married?'

'I did love a beautiful, well-born girl, but my best friend won her heart, and that's another story. I am now a confirmed bachelor.'

Amelia put her head on one side, regarding him seriously. 'That would be a shame, Todd. Perhaps you haven't met the right woman.'

He smiled ruefully. 'Who knows?'

Amelia rose to her feet. 'Thank you for confiding in me. I can't wait to hear the rest of your life story, but I have work to do and I'm sure you have, too. If there's anything you need, just let me know.'

'I will, thank you.' Todd put his hand in his pocket

and took out a small leather pouch. 'Just a moment. I expect you want an advance on the rent.'

Amelia hesitated in the doorway. 'That would be helpful. I hope we aren't overcharging you, Todd. I have no experience of letting rooms.'

'It's only a little more than I was paying for really dreadful lodgings and even worse food. I can assure you that it's the going rate here in London.'

'We'll try to make you comfortable.' Amelia made an effort to sound casual. Perhaps she would get used to taking money merely for offering hospitality to a guest in her home, but it felt wrong somehow. She supposed it would be easier next time, and at least Todd had paid up without her having to badger him for the rent. She went downstairs to join Mariah in the kitchen.

They were having a quick luncheon of bread and cheese when Todd put his head round the door to say he was due back at the hospital, and would not finish until late that evening.

'Don't worry, sir,' Mariah said quickly. 'I'll leave something out for your supper. It will be kept warm on top of the range.'

'You are very kind, Mariah. Thank you.' Todd gave her a smile that brought the roses to Mariah's pale cheeks. 'I'll leave you in peace now. Thank you both for making me so welcome.'

Amelia opened her mouth to tell him it was no trouble, and the extra money would be a great help, but he had gone before she could say anything. His footsteps on the bare boards echoed throughout the house, followed by the sound of the front door closing with a thud.

'He's a lovely gentleman,' Mariah said enthusiastically. 'Your pa picked a good 'un there, miss.'

'Yes, he certainly did.' Amelia pushed her plate away. 'I really like Todd. He's paid the rent in advance, so you and I can go up West when we have time. If we can interest a buyer to take our creations it would be wonderful.'

Mariah nodded in agreement. 'I'm sure that Nellie and the other women would be glad to work on something other than such dark material. She told me it hurts their eyes, particularly in winter when the days are so short and it gets dark early.'

'I really want to cut down on the mourning garments. I'm sure they will love making beautiful gowns in fine materials. I know I would if I were them.'

Mariah stood up and scooped Percy into her arms as he began to cry. 'I've made you some bread and milk, poppet. You're getting to be such a big boy now.'

Percy gurgled in response and Mariah resumed her seat so that she could spoon the mixture into his eager mouth.

'We should go up West as soon as possible,' Amelia said firmly. 'Maybe one of the women in the workroom would look after Percy for a couple of hours tomorrow morning, which would leave you and I free to get the bus to Oxford Street. What do you think, Mariah?'

'I'd trust Nellie. I don't know about the others.'

'They'll love having a baby to coo over, especially if it's only for a short while. I'll give Nellie a little extra in her pay packet for taking care of Percy.'

'I don't know about that. He's doing his best to walk. Heaven help us when he's fully mobile.' Mariah sighed. 'I haven't left him before, at least not with a stranger. Betsy looks after him sometimes, but he knows her.'

'We won't be away for long, but if you don't want to leave him I suppose I could take Nellie with me. After all, she would be in charge of the workroom when they make the gowns.'

'No. Don't do that. I am the pattern maker and I helped make the gown. I'll come with you.'

'Excellent. We'll start at Peter Robinson and go on from there. If Grandpapa rallies, I'll go and see him again, and I'll be able to tell him about my plans. I think he'll be proud of me.'

'I'm sure he is already proud of you. After all, why would he leave you the business and a big house if he didn't think a lot of you? You're a young lady of property now. You can hold your head up high wherever you go.'

Amelia smiled ruefully. 'I've never thought of myself like that.'

'You, miss, are an heiress.'

'Perhaps it would be better to keep quiet about that when we visit the buyers. I want to appear business-like and knowledgeable. I need to convince them that I can produce the items quickly and relatively cheaply. We will start a new line in fashion, Mariah. Starting tomorrow.'

8

The first buyer they met next day was in charge of purchasing for a newly opened store at the end of Oxford Street. Amelia decided she would start there in order to gain some experience, but unfortunately she and Mariah must have caught the man on a bad day. He was both supercilious and patronising, and he dismissed them with barely a second glance at the sketches or the gown. Mariah was very downhearted, but Amelia refused to take it personally. They received a better reception from the person in charge of buying at the next store, but he was hesitant about taking on a new supplier who had virtually no experience in the trade.

After an unsuccessful morning, Amelia's feet were aching and she was beginning to feel dispirited. There was only one store left to try and it was the largest and most prestigious, which was why she had left it until last. There seemed little hope of even seeing the head buyer. However, Amelia put on a brave front and requested an interview with as much confidence as she could muster.

The fashion department in Harrison's department store was so luxurious that Amelia was even more conscious of her well-worn boots and outdated garments. Mariah seemed to have shrunk into herself as she gazed around at the sumptuous red velvet curtains and gilded fittings. The rich chestnut of the highly polished floorboards was partially covered by thick-piled carpet runners in red and gold. The female shop assistants looked as if they had been invited to an elegant house party rather than were being paid to sell clothes.

'I think we should leave now before we're thrown out,' Mariah said in a low voice. 'I don't like the way those hoity-toity girls are staring at us.'

'We are as good as them, if not better. I won't be put off so easily. We're waiting to speak to Mr Barnet, the chief buyer. I'm not leaving until I've seen him.'

'I can't expect Nellie to look after Percy all day. I should be going home.'

'Percy has a roomful of doting women to take care of him. If he holds up production for a few hours that is my worry, not yours, Mariah.'

In her head Amelia knew that Mariah was right. The senior assistant who had agreed to tell Mr Barnet that they were waiting to see him did not seem to be carrying out her promise. Instead, she was giving her full attention to an overdressed dowager and her pale companion. When a man wearing a frock coat and pin-striped trousers entered the department with a train of followers, it was obvious that he was a person of some standing in the store. He strolled past Amelia and Mariah without a second glance, but Amelia was tired and desperate. She jumped to her feet and followed him, edging her way between the young men in tailcoats and the black-clad women shop assistants until she reached his side.

'Mr Barnet?'

He shot her a sideways glance. 'Do I know you?'

'No, you don't.' Amelia came to a halt in front of him, causing him to stop, which created a ripple effect as his entourage almost cannoned into each other.

'But if you don't spare me a few minutes of your time you will find yourself regretting it.' For a moment she thought she had gone too far. She sensed the tension in the room and fully expected to be escorted out of the building.

The woman assistant who had abandoned Amelia and Mariah came hurrying forward, frowning ominously. 'Mr Barnet, I am so sorry, sir. This person came here demanding to see you. I told her that you are a very busy man.'

Barnet held up his hand. 'It's all right, Miss Perkins. Leave this to me.'

'Certainly, sir. Shall I call the doorman to show these people out?'

'That won't be necessary.' Barnet turned to Amelia and his lips twitched. 'You have five minutes to convince me why I should not have you removed from the building. Come into my office.' He turned to his followers. 'That will be all for today. You may return to your posts.'

Amelia followed him through the rest of the department, aware that all eyes were upon her and Mariah, but she did not care. She had made this haughty man take notice of her and that was a small triumph even if nothing came of it. Barnet let himself into his glass-fronted office and ushered Amelia and Mariah inside before closing the door.

'Please take a seat, and tell me exactly why you have caused this diversion in my department.' He went to sit behind an ornate French desk with ormolu mounts, which Amelia secretly thought was rather vulgar.

She remained standing. 'I am sorry to disturb your routine, sir. But I have something to offer your department, which I think will not only bring in more customers, but will give you a wider range of clientele.'

'And how will I do that, Miss, er — I don't know your name.'

'I am Amelia Sutton and this is my assistant, Mrs Mariah Simms. I am the owner of the Mourning Warehouse in Nightingale Lane,' Amelia said, embroidering the truth slightly. 'However, I intend to branch out.' She turned to Mariah. 'Will you kindly show Mr Barnet the gown?'

Mariah obliged instantly, producing the shimmering silk taffeta creation. She held it up, shaking out the folds.

'This is my design,' Amelia said proudly. 'It was made in my workshop. My intention is to produce elegant creations based on the latest Paris fashions, but at a fraction of the cost.'

Barnet rose from his seat and walked round the desk to take the gown from Mariah. He examined the garment closely. 'I need to see it on a model. It looks to be about your size, Miss Sutton. Put it on, if you please.'

'Of course, sir.' Amelia took it from him. 'I need somewhere to undress.'

He walked to the door and opened it. 'Your five minutes is almost up. I suggest you hurry.' He stepped outside, closing the door behind him.

'Everyone can see you,' Mariah said anxiously.

'You heard what Barnet said. Stand in front of me, Mariah. This is not the time to be prudish. I refuse to be beaten.' Amelia undressed more quickly than she would have thought possible and Mariah helped her to put on the gown. Almost before the last button had been secured Barnet entered without knocking. He held the door open.

'Now walk the length of the department and return slowly, so that I can see how the material moves with your body.'

Amelia ignored the muffled tut-tutting from Mariah and paraded the gown through the department and back again, walking slowly and gracefully so that the bugle beads caught the light and the folds of silk taffeta emphasised her slender figure. She came to a halt in front of Barnet.

'Well?' Amelia said eagerly. 'What do you think?'

A faint smile softened his granite-grey eyes. 'I think you make an excellent model. I might offer you that position if I decide to use live models.'

'I am a manufacturer, Mr Barnet, not a model.'

'Is this your only sample?'

Amelia had hoped he would not ask that question, but it was important to be frank with him. 'Yes, sir. But I have sketches of my other designs.' She turned to Mariah, who handed her a sheaf of papers, which Amelia passed on to Barnet.

He flicked through them. 'These are interesting. However, I cannot consider what you have to offer until I have visited your premises. I need to see your workroom. Harrison's is a reputable store, as you must know. I can't afford to deal with companies who are unreliable.'

'You will be most welcome, sir. If you will give me pen and paper I will write down our address. It's in Nightingale Lane, close to St Katharine Docks.'

'I know where Nightingale Lane is.' Barnet took paper from a desk drawer and laid it in front of Amelia, together with the silver inkstand. 'I have to get back to my rounds. Leave the address on my desk.

Good day, ladies.' He let himself out into the department.

Amelia turned to Mariah. 'Get me out of this dress, please. I don't want to risk spilling ink on it.'

'He'll probably tear up the paper or simply forget all about it.' Mariah applied herself to undoing the tiny pearl buttons.

'I don't think so,' Amelia said thoughtfully. 'I have a feeling that he's really interested in our plans, Mariah. This is the best reaction we've had so far. I think he was impressed. What we need to do now is to go home and make up one or even more garments from my sketches.'

'We certainly need to get home as soon as possible.' Mariah allowed the gown to fall to the floor so that Amelia could step out of it. 'Put your clothes on quickly, miss. Those blooming shop assistants are gawping at us.'

'I don't care. I've done what I came to do,' Amelia said happily. 'I am sure that Mr Barnet will visit us in Nightingale Lane.'

Mariah folded the sample dress and stowed it carefully in its bag. 'You can't trust men to keep their word.'

'They aren't all like that, Mariah. My pa is the most honourable man I've ever met.'

'Let's hope your grandpa keeps his promise then, deathbed or no deathbed. If he doesn't leave the premises in Nightingale Lane to you, we'll all be out on the street.'

Amelia shook her head. 'I think you're hungry, Mariah. You and I both need sustenance. We'll hurry home and I'll collect Percy while you get luncheon. Who knows? We might be celebrating later in the week if Mr Barnet likes what he sees.'

* * *

The next few days were nerve-racking for Amelia. She waited anxiously for news from Caleb as to her grandfather's condition. Her father refused to visit the house in Albemarle Street, using his work at the hospital as an excuse, but Amelia knew that he could have found time had he really wanted to see his ailing father-in-law. The rift between them was too deep and too bitter to be healed, even on Nathaniel's deathbed.

It was beginning to feel as if Mariah's gloomy prognosis was correct when she said that men never kept their promises as there was no word from Barnet. Todd was the only cheerful and optimistic person in the house, but like her father, he was spending long hours on duty at the hospital. The harsh winter weather always claimed many victims with lung complaints and diseases associated with overcrowded accommodation and unsanitary conditions. Then there were the injuries caused by falls on icy surfaces, although March winds had brought slightly warmer weather, with the hope of spring arriving a little early.

Despite everything, Amelia kept working on her designs. With Mariah's help she made two more gowns: one a simple afternoon gown in lavender linen and the other a dinner gown in emerald-green velvet. Mariah was pessimistic, but nonetheless she put all her enthusiasm and skill into her work. They used the machines in the workroom in the evenings after Percy was in bed and supper had been cooked and eaten. Food was always set aside for Harold and Todd when they were working late at the hospital.

One evening, after a long session working on the velvet evening gown, which was almost finished,

Amelia realised that Mariah was exhausted and she sent her to bed. Amelia was tidying up the workroom so that it was ready for the women when they arrived next morning, when she heard someone hammering on the front door. She picked up the oil lamp and made her way as quickly as possible between the work benches to the interconnecting door. 'I'm coming.' She hurried to open the door and Caleb stepped inside without waiting to be asked.

'I'm sorry to come so late, but it's your grandfather, Amelia. He's sinking fast and he's asking for you.'

She stared at him in surprise. 'He wants to see me? Surely not. He said everything he had to say when I visited last time.'

'That's as maybe, but he hasn't long and he was most insistent. The carriage is outside.'

Amelia plucked her cape and bonnet from the hall-stand. 'Of course I'll come.'

They had just stepped outside into the cold night air when Amelia spotted Todd hurrying towards them. 'Just a moment, Caleb. I need to tell Todd what's happened and he can pass the message on to my papa when he comes home from the hospital.'

Caleb held the carriage door open. 'We mustn't waste time.'

'I'll be very quick.' Amelia ran to meet Todd. 'It's my grandfather, Todd. He's been asking for me.'

Todd eyed Caleb suspiciously. 'It's very late. Would you like me to come with you?'

'Thank you, but Caleb will see me home. I don't know how long I'll be there and you need your sleep. Will you tell Pa for me, if you're still up when he returns?'

'Of course.'

'Your supper is on the top of the range.'

Todd smiled. 'You are very kind. I wouldn't get this consideration anywhere else.'

'We need to hurry, Amelia,' Caleb said urgently.

'I'm coming.' Amelia walked briskly back to the carriage, where she allowed Caleb to help her climb into the luxurious vehicle. She had never travelled in anything quite so grand. The scent of leather, polish and simple cleanliness was so different from the stale tobacco smoke, residual alcohol fumes and unwashed body odours that lingered in hackney carriages.

'He seems to have insinuated himself into the family,' Caleb said sourly.

'Todd is an ideal tenant. He's always pleasant and polite. He doesn't cause any trouble and he keeps his room clean.'

Amelia leaned back and closed her eyes. She did not want to discuss Todd with Caleb, who, if anything, sounded jealous, which was ridiculous. Todd had rapidly become a friend and it was good to have someone with whom she could talk freely. Besides which, he was a good listener and was never judgemental. She could tell him anything and he would always have a positive response. She loved his quiet sense of humour and innate kindness, but she sensed a sadness deep within him, which he kept locked away.

'I didn't mean to offend you.' Caleb laid a tentative hand on her sleeve. 'I'm sorry.'

'I'm a little tired. It's been a long day.' Amelia stifled a yawn.

'You were working late when I arrived. I saw the light in the workroom.'

'I'm expecting a visit from the head buyer from

Harrison's very soon. I showed him my designs and a sample gown that Mariah and I made, and he is quite interested. At least I hope he is.'

'You met Oscar Barnet?' Caleb peered at her in the darkness. 'How did you manage to get an interview with him? He's the most difficult to reach of all the buyers in the new department stores.'

'I went to the store and was waiting to see him when he marched past me, followed by all his menials. He didn't give me a second glance, so I followed him into his office. I think I took him by surprise and he gave me five minutes of his time. I did my best to convince him that I was capable of providing Harrison's with elegant designs based on Paris originals.'

'I am impressed. I don't know him personally, of course, but he is notorious for being difficult to deal with. But then there are very few, if any, lady commercial travellers. I doubt if a man would have been so lucky.'

'You don't think much of my chances, do you, Caleb? Please be honest with me.'

'I know it is almost impossible for a woman to enter the world of commerce, let alone to succeed.'

'Times are changing very slowly, but there are women entering some of the professions that up until now have been a male domain.'

'I hadn't noticed it myself.' Caleb peered out of the window. 'The streets are fairly clear at this time of night. We'll be there soon. I hope we're in time.'

* * *

Hobbs opened the door to admit them to the house in Albemarle Street and Amelia could see that he was deeply distressed, despite his brave attempt at concealing his feelings.

'Are we in time, Hobbs?' Caleb asked anxiously.

'The master passed away some ten minutes ago, sir. My condolences, Miss Sutton.'

'I'm so sorry I wasn't here when Grandpapa needed me.' Amelia's voice broke on a suppressed sob. 'We were never close, but that wasn't my fault. I wanted him to know that I cared.'

'I'd better take you home,' Caleb said gently. 'There's nothing you can do here, Amelia.'

Hobbs cleared his throat. 'If you'll pardon the intrusion, sir, Miss Amelia might wish to speak to Mr Daniel Norris. He arrived shortly after you left, Mr Marsh.'

Amelia frowned. 'I haven't seen him since Mama died. I only vaguely remember him.'

'Mr Norris is in the morning parlour with Mr Musgrave,' Hobbs said stiffly.

'He's probably going over the will as we speak.' Caleb spoke lightly but Amelia was quick to note the sarcasm in his voice.

'I will see him, Hobbs. Will you announce me?'

Hobbs snapped to attention. 'Of course, Miss Amelia.' He marched off in the direction of the morning parlour.

Amelia turned to Caleb. 'I think it best if I see him alone. If I remember rightly, my mother and her cousin Daniel were not on the best of terms. Perhaps even now, I can heal the rift in the family.'

Caleb inclined his head. 'If that's what you want. I'll wait here and I'll take you home when you're ready.'

Amelia crossed the marble-tiled floor, following Hobbs to the morning parlour. Every step brought back memories of the time when the house was filled with guests. Many of them were her mother's admirers — she had realised that, even at such a young age. Mama seemed to attract both men and women, who clustered round, eager to be noticed by her. There had been parties, although of course Amelia had only seen the wonderful gowns, jewels and dashing men from the top floor where the nursery suite was situated. She had crept out of bed to peer through the banisters, breathing in the heady perfumes and scent of Macassar oil, melting candlewax and cigar smoke. The strains of an orchestra playing in the ballroom had made her small feet tap on the thick pile of the carpet. Sometimes she had fallen asleep where she sat, curled up like a kitten, until Nanny came looking for her and carried her back to her bed. But all that was long ago; things were different now.

Hobbs held the morning-parlour door open for her. 'Miss Amelia Sutton.' He closed the door after her as she stepped into the familiar room.

Daniel Norris was a year or two younger than Amelia's father, but he looked older. His once luxuriant dark hair was receding from his forehead and was streaked with grey. His slender figure had become corpulent and his complexion was a little too ruddy.

'Amelia. You are no longer the little girl I knew.'

'No, sir. I think we have both changed over the passing years. I am sorry to hear that Grandpapa has passed away. I regret that I was not in time to say a final farewell.'

'I doubt if he would have recognised you, Amelia. The end was quite sudden.' Daniel turned to the gentleman who was standing quietly behind him. 'This gentleman is handling the legal side of things.'

Amelia managed a faint smile. 'I understand you were my grandfather's solicitor, Mr Musgrave.'

'I was indeed, Miss Sutton. It's a pleasure to make your acquaintance, even in such sad circumstances.'

Daniel cleared his throat. 'Musgrave and I have been going over my uncle Nathaniel's will, which is why I wanted to speak to you, Amelia.'

'Surely he has left everything to you, Cousin Daniel. That is what he told me.'

'That is correct, except for a significant property in Nightingale Lane, which I believe is a manufactory of mourning clothes.'

'Yes, that's correct. Grandpapa gave it to me.'

'Together with a large house,' Daniel added sharply.

'It is written in the will, Mr Norris,' Musgrave said quickly. 'Once probate is granted it will be a legal bequest.'

'Nevertheless I disagree with those particular terms of my uncle's will. You are too young and inexperienced to acquire such valuable property, Amelia. I suggest you start looking for somewhere else to live because I will challenge the will in court, if necessary.'

'Really, sir. Is this the time or place to discuss such matters?' Musgrave glanced anxiously at Amelia. 'Miss Sutton must be allowed time to grieve for her late grandpapa.'

'Nonsense, Musgrave. You know as well as I do that the rift between my uncle and his late daughter's family was irreconcilable. My uncle was not in his right mind when he left such an important property to a young inexperienced woman.'

'But Grandpapa was in his right mind when he left everything to you. Is that so?' Amelia stood her ground, glaring at Daniel.

Musgrave cleared his throat nervously. 'Let us not argue. Mr Norris would not approve of this behaviour.'

'Quite right,' Amelia said firmly. 'I am clear in my mind that Grandpapa meant me to have the workroom and the accommodation. You are being mean, Cousin Daniel. Haven't you got enough with the other businesses? Do you really want to see me and my papa evicted and living on the street?'

'You are a very pretty young woman, Amelia. I am sure that there is a clerk or a shop keeper somewhere in London who would marry you and give you and your papa a home. Now, much as I am enjoying your company, I would ask you to leave my house. You will be hearing from Musgrave when the will is returned from probate. If you don't agree with my decision I suggest you employ a solicitor. Musgrave will represent me.'

Musgrave folded the document and placed it back in his briefcase. 'I was your uncle's solicitor, Mr Norris. I do not work for you, so I suggest you look for someone who will.' He marched to the door, but paused and glanced over his shoulder. 'Miss Sutton, I will be pleased to take your case on, should you need my services.' He took a card from his breast pocket and handed it to her. 'Please don't hesitate to contact me.'

'Wait a minute, Musgrave. You can't just walk out.' Daniel's complexion darkened to a deeper shade of red. 'I refuse to settle your bill if you leave now.'

'Then I'll see you in court, Mr Norris, but I will be the complainant and you will be in the dock for debt. Good evening, sir.' Musgrave opened the door and ushered Amelia out into the hall. 'I want nothing to do with that gentleman, Miss Sutton. Please believe me, I had no notion of his intentions. They are beyond despicable.'

'Thank you, Mr Musgrave. If I need a solicitor, please be sure I will think of you.' Amelia could see Caleb waiting for her by the door. 'Good night, and thank you for putting Mr Norris in his place.'

Musgrave nodded and beckoned to a maidservant. 'My coat and hat, if you please.' He turned to give Amelia a wry smile. 'Mr Norris needs to know that I meant what I said. It saddens me to have to behave like this, but I owe it to my late client. Whatever people might think of him, Nathaniel Norris was a fair man. He would not be pleased with his nephew.'

Amelia shuddered. She felt a cold wind ruffle her skirts and the candles in the sconces and candelabra flickered as if they were in danger of being extinguished by a strong wind. It was eerie, but she realised it was not the ghostly presence of her grandfather. Hobbs had opened the front door and Caleb was waiting to escort her home. Anger directed towards her mother's cousin had dried any tears she might have shed for her late grandfather. He had relented and tried to make amends for the way he had treated her and her father, but now it seemed that Daniel Norris had inherited the disastrous trait of alienating family members. It was almost impossible to believe that they were related. There was certainly no sentiment in Cousin Daniel's decision to try to cut her out of the will. If he succeeded it would be just her and her father, on their own again, with their bright future hanging in the balance.

9

'What did Mr Norris say?' Caleb asked as he handed her into the waiting carriage. 'I can see that you're upset.'

'My cousin is going to challenge Grandpapa's will. He doesn't want me to have the business or the house.'

Caleb climbed in and sat beside her. 'That's ridiculous. I know that Mr Norris fully intended you to have the mourning warehouse and the accommodation. I'll testify that in court, if necessary.'

Amelia sighed. 'I think it might come to that. I'd rather not talk about it now, if you don't mind. I need time to think things over.'

'I understand, but if there's anything I can do to help, please let me know.'

'You might find that your position in the household is in jeopardy, Caleb. Mr Norris might decide he doesn't need any of the people closest to Grandpapa.'

'You're right, of course. I expect I'll find out very soon. My new employer doesn't seem to be a person who is prepared to take things slowly.'

They lapsed into silence until they reached Nightingale Lane. The carriage drew to a halt and Caleb alighted first, proffering a hand to Amelia.

'Good night, Caleb,' she said tiredly as she opened the front door. 'I hope things go well for you.'

'If I hear anything that concerns you I will be sure to let you know. I don't hold out much hope of keeping my position, but I don't wish to work for someone who treats his family as Mr Norris is treating you. Good night, Amelia.' Caleb turned on his heel and walked back to the carriage.

Amelia let herself into the house and saw a glow of light from the kitchen. She went to make sure that a candle had not been left burning and found her father seated at the table, finishing the plate of mutton stew that Mariah had left for him.

'Amelia, I didn't know you were out. Where have you been at this time of night?'

She sank down on a chair opposite him. 'Sad news, Pa. Grandpapa Norris passed away earlier this evening. Caleb took me to Albemarle Street, but I was too late to say goodbye.'

Harold sighed. 'I suppose he tried to make amends by giving you the business and this house, but I think it was more a matter of conscience. Perhaps he knew he had not much longer on this earth.'

'That's a little harsh, Pa.'

'I see people dying every day at the hospital, Amelia. Most of them are far too young to lose their lives, and I see the awful suffering of their loved ones, some of whom are left destitute as well as heartbroken.'

'I know, Pa. But I like to think that Grandpapa really did have a change of heart. He's gone now so we'll never know.'

Harold wiped his lips on a table napkin. 'Is there something else bothering you, dear? I know when you are keeping something from me.'

'Mama's cousin, Daniel, was at the house and he asked to see me.'

'Daniel was there? That man is like a vulture. He must have been there simply waiting for the old man to die.'

'You're probably right, but the worst part is that he is going to contest the will. He doesn't want us to have the house or the business.'

'Damn it.' Harold jumped to his feet. 'I apologise for my bad language, my dear. But that Daniel Norris is a mean-spirited fellow, and that's being kind. He always went out of his way to cause trouble for your poor dear mama and me. I will see him through every court in the land if he tries to make trouble for my only child.'

Amelia cast off her cape and stood up. She caught her father's hand and raised it to her cheek. 'Please don't upset yourself, Pa. You will make yourself ill.'

'I am just furious, Amelia.' Harold clutched her hand and brushed it with a kiss. 'I'm exhausted after everything that's happened at the hospital today. I'll think more clearly when I've had some sleep. However, rest assured I won't allow Daniel Norris to take this away from us. We will need a good solicitor.'

'Mr Musgrave was there also, Pa. He refused to work for Cousin Daniel and he offered us his services, should we need them.'

'Then we'll take him up on that. I know Musgrave. He's a reliable chap and I trust him.'

'Let's hope it doesn't come to a court case. Anyway, I'm worn out. I'm going to bed now. What about you, Pa?'

'Yes, me too. There's little point discussing this now, my love. We'll wait and see if Daniel carries out his threat. In the meantime, I'll say good night. Sweet dreams, my dear.'

'You go up first, Pa. I need to make sure I've locked the workroom as well as the front door. I'll follow on.'

'I hate to see you working so hard.' Harold made

his way from the kitchen, taking a lighted candle with him so that Amelia had the benefit of the oil lamp.

She checked the locks and was on her way to her room when she heard footsteps on the stairs to the second floor. She looked up and saw Todd.

'It's very late,' he said anxiously. 'Is everything all right?'

'Grandpapa Norris died this evening. He had passed away before I got there.'

'Would you like to talk about it?'

Suddenly the need to speak to someone who was not connected to the family business was overwhelming. 'Yes, I would. If you're not too tired.'

'Never too tired to listen to a friend's problems.' Todd retraced his steps to his room and Amelia negotiated the stairs, taking care not to make a noise.

'Make yourself comfortable,' Todd said as Amelia closed the door behind her. 'I've made some cocoa. Would you like some?' He took a pan of hot milk off the trivet in front of the fire. 'I learned to do this in my student days. I used to make porridge for myself in a Dutch oven left all night in front of the embers. It's surprising what you can do when needs be.'

Amelia sat on the edge of the bed. 'I shouldn't be here, Todd. And I'm keeping you up. You'll have another busy day in front of you tomorrow.'

He glanced at a small brass travelling clock on the mantelshelf. 'It is tomorrow already. Another half an hour won't make much difference, and it might help you to talk to me.'

Amelia smiled. 'Is that your professional opinion, Doctor?'

'I suppose it might be, but I'm speaking as a friend. I consider myself very fortunate to be here, Amelia.

You've taken me into your home, and Mariah is the best cook in London. What more could I ask for?'

Amelia laughed and held out her hand for the cocoa. 'You seem easily satisfied, Todd.' She clasped the warm mug in both hands, staring into the milky drink. 'I didn't have a chance to say goodbye.'

'I'm sorry. That must have been hard for you.'

'I really didn't know him too well. He wanted nothing to do with us after Mama died, but just recently he relented and gave me the business and this house. Now it looks as if I might lose both.'

'How could that be?'

'My mother's cousin, Daniel Norris, has inherited the estate. He was there this evening, waiting for Grandpapa to pass away, or that's how it seemed. Anyway, he told me he would contest the will and take all this from me.'

'That's awful. What sort of man would do that?'

'Someone like Daniel Norris. I don't know if he would be successful in court, but it's very worrying.'

'Have you told your father?'

'Yes, just now. He was still up when I arrived home. He was too tired for much discussion, but he did say he would fight the case in court, if necessary. There's no love lost between Pa and the Norris family.'

'It does sound as if Mr Norris is acting out of spite. No doubt his inheritance is considerable.'

Amelia nodded. 'It's pure vindictiveness. But what he doesn't know is that I've got the head buyer from Harrison's store interested in my own creations. Mr Barnet said he would visit the workroom, although on second thoughts maybe he was simply trying to get rid of me.'

'And perhaps he saw the talent you have for

designing beautiful clothes,' Todd said, smiling. 'You are too modest.'

'You don't know that, Todd. I haven't shown you the gowns that Mariah and I have made.'

'I admit I know nothing about fashion, but I would like to see them. I'm sure they are as fine as any I've seen on guests to Rockwood Castle.'

'Was it very fine? Did they have wonderful parties and grand balls?'

Todd smiled. 'It certainly wasn't a fairy-tale palace. It is very large, impressive and parts of it are always in need of repair. The Careys and the Blanchards are just normal people who happen to have inherited a great deal of history.' Todd leaned forward, lowering his voice. 'There is an ancient suit of armour in the vast, cold and draughty entrance hall. They say it's haunted by a knight called Sir Denys, an ancestor who died in battle hundreds of years ago.'

'You don't believe that, do you?' Amelia asked incredulously.

Todd pulled a face. 'All I can say is that the family think the legend is true. They greet Sir Denys as if he were an old friend every time they enter the castle, and the visor does seem to open of its own accord. I've seen it myself.'

'How odd, but fascinating. I like the sound of your castle. Is there a beautiful princess who lives there?'

'Maybe, but that's a story for another time.' Todd took the empty mug from her hand. 'You're half asleep already. I think we both need to get some rest.'

Amelia rose to her feet. 'You're right, of course. I would love to hear more about your life in Rockwood, Todd. But I don't think I can stay awake for much longer.'

He stood up and went to open the door. 'Good night, Amelia. Get some sleep and try not to worry. I'll do anything I can to help you.'

'I can't make any promises.' She managed a weary smile. 'Thank you for the cocoa, Todd. Good night.'

Amelia went to her room, and undressed slowly. She reached for her flannel nightgown and slipped it on, hugging the soft folds around her slender body in an effort to keep warm. The worst of the winter weather might be over but it was still cold, particularly at night, and she climbed into bed, pulling the coverlet up to her chin. She was comforted by her talk with Todd, and fascinated by his story, but she had a feeling that this was only the beginning of her problems with Daniel Norris.

* * *

Despite her worries, Amelia had little option other than to carry on with work as usual. The following week went by with no word from Daniel or his solicitor. Mr Barnet had not contacted her either, and Amelia was beginning to think that he had forgotten about her visit to his department. However, business in the mourning clothes warehouse was booming. According to reports in the newspapers, the necropolis railway carrying coffins and mourners from Waterloo station to the cemetery at Brookwood was busier than usual, and the sale of mourning gowns and crepe veils had doubled. Amelia put the time to good use. She studied fashion plates and worked on her designs, which Mariah interpreted by cutting paper patterns. They cut, tacked and finished the garments on the machines in the workroom after the women had gone home for the night.

A month later, almost to the day after Nathaniel Norris's death, Amelia was in the workroom going over the books with Nellie when they were interrupted by Maisie Lugg, the senior seamstress.

'Mr Marsh is here, miss. He's asking for you.'

Amelia closed the ledger. 'I'll take him through to the house. I don't want to cause a distraction when we're working on such a large order.'

'Of course, miss.' Nellie opened the door and Amelia stepped into the workroom.

'Good morning, Mr Marsh,' she said politely. 'Come this way, if you please.'

'Good morning, Miss Sutton.' Caleb acknowledged the curious glances of the women with a nod and a smile.

Amelia went on ahead. 'How are you?' She eyed him warily as she closed the door to the workroom. 'You don't look as if you've brought good news.'

He shook his head. 'I'm sorry, but you are right.'

'Come into the front parlour. It's a bit chilly but we won't be disturbed.' Amelia went in first. 'Do sit down and tell me what's happened.'

'Mr Norris dispensed with my services last evening.'

Amelia sank down on the sofa. 'I'm sorry, Caleb.'

He stood with his back to the empty grate. 'He's instructed his new solicitor to contest the will. It seems that he's determined to have you and your father evicted from this house, and it looks as if he wants the business for himself.'

'I think he's doing it out of spite. He hasn't even seen the books, but for the first time we are running at a decent profit.'

'Is that from the mourning garments?'

'Yes, it is. Although Mariah and I have made several gowns from my designs, Mr Barnet seems to have forgotten us. I will just have to start again and visit some of the smaller and less exclusive shops.'

'As I'm no longer employed by the Norris Company I am free to help you, Amelia. I don't know Barnet personally, although I am familiar with Mr Sydney Harrison, who has shares in the Norris Company. I hesitated to mention this before because I could hardly approach Mr Harrison while I was employed by Mr Norris. Anyway, I thought that Barnet would have kept his word.'

'Evidently he didn't think enough of my creations to bother. I suppose he's a busy man.'

'Will you give me permission to approach Mr Sydney Harrison? I can't promise anything, but I can at least try. I am a good salesman, as your grandfather discovered.'

'I can't afford to pay you for your services, Caleb. Perhaps you should concentrate on finding another employer.'

'Maybe, but I want to help you, and to be honest I have nowhere to go. I need somewhere to stay and I know you have taken in one paying guest. I thought perhaps we could have an arrangement, until such time as I find paid employment.'

'You want to lodge here with us?'

'To put it candidly, yes, that would suit me very well.'

'There is a room on the second floor. It's at the back of the house, but it is nice and quiet away from the street noises. You are welcome to move in there for as long as you want.'

Caleb sighed with relief. 'Thank you, Amelia.

That's what I was hoping you would say. If Mr Harrison won't help then I will make it my business to find someone who will.'

Amelia picked up a sheaf of papers and handed them to him. 'You ought to look at my sketches before you make up your mind.'

Caleb took them and sat down. He studied each one before looking up and smiling. 'These are really wonderful. The little I know of fashion is what I've observed when your grandfather entertained his wealthy friends and clients, and these compare most favourably. You say you can make them relatively cheaply?'

Amelia nodded. 'Much cheaper than the gowns from the Parisian couturiers or even the designers in London. I can purchase bales of material from the warehouses around the docks, and there are places I know of where I can buy the trimmings.'

'I see you have it all worked out. I think it's an excellent idea.'

'If you can get me my first order, I'm sure that others will follow.'

Caleb laid the sketches on the small side table. 'May I take these with me? I'd like to start as soon as possible. And please don't worry about the financial side. I've saved money from my salary and there'll be no difficulty in paying my rent.'

'I have no doubts about that, Caleb. You are a man of business, which is what I need.'

'I just hope my presence won't put too much of a burden on you and Mariah.'

Amelia smiled. 'Mariah might grumble, but that's her way. I think secretly she'll be delighted to have another gentleman to cook for. You'll have to get used to homely meals, though. I'm sure that you and Grandpa lived like lords.'

'Not to speak ill of the dead, but in truth your grandfather was a bit of a miser where food was concerned. I think the servants ate better than we did.'

'Then you will be in for a pleasant surprise, and with your rent money added to what Todd pays, I expect we can have a few luxuries every now and then.' Amelia rose to her feet. 'Perhaps you would like to see your room before you go collect your things.'

'Yes, please. I'm sure it will be far better than my present accommodation in the attics at Albemarle Street. Mr Norris classified me as an underling and I slept in the servants' quarters.'

'Why did you put up with such treatment, Caleb? You could have worked for anyone in London — why did you stay with my grandfather?'

'It was an interesting job and I enjoyed working for him. He took me in when I was little more than a boy. He could be difficult but that was because he wanted everything to be done properly. He rewarded hard work with extra pay, although praise was thin on the ground.'

'That I can believe, but it's not difficult to imagine that he was very exacting.'

Caleb smiled ruefully. 'I was used to living with harsh criticism.'

'In what way?'

'I think I told you that I was brought up by my aunt Mildred, who took me on when my parents were lost at sea. Apparently, they had been travelling back from the Continent when their ship went down in a storm. There were no survivors.'

'How awful.' Amelia sank back onto the sofa. 'How

old were you?'

'I was just two. I don't remember my parents. Aunt Mildred took me in out of duty and never allowed me to forget it. We lived in a large house on the edge of Hackney Marshes, and I was cared for by a nanny and then a governess. I was fond of Nanny, but Miss Grice used the cane to beat knowledge into my head.'

'Poor boy.' Amelia swallowed hard to prevent herself from shedding tears at the thought of a lost and lonely child being so abused. 'How unkind of your aunt to allow such a vicious person to be in charge of a child.'

'Aunt Mildred applauded the woman's methods. I used to escape from the house whenever I had the opportunity. There was a dead tree in the grounds. The gardener told me it had been struck by lightning, killing the person who sheltered beneath its branches. I don't know if it was true, but that tree saved me from many a hiding. I used to climb into its bare branches and stay there until it was too dark for anyone to see me creep back into the house.'

'What can I say? I can't imagine how anyone could be so cruel to a child. Did you spend all night out in the cold?'

'I was locked out but I knew there was a broken catch on the window in the flower room. If Cook realised I had not been in for supper she would leave me something to eat. On other occasions I used to steal food from the larder and creep upstairs to my room.'

'Was it all forgotten next morning?'

Caleb laughed. 'The beatings were memorable.'

'You must have grown up hating women.'

'I had no love for my aunt, and I did envisage Miss

Grice suffering all manner of tortures, but I loved Nanny, and Cook was kind to me. She used to make my favourite cakes and jam tarts. She gave me salve for the weals left by the canings, and she told me stories about my mother, who had been born and raised in that house.'

'I've never met your aunt but I hate her.' Amelia searched for her hanky and blew her nose. 'Thank goodness you had at least one person in the house who cared for you. What happened to your aunt?'

'She is now a recluse, living in the house with just a couple of servants to look after her.'

'Do you ever visit her?'

'I have on several occasions, but she doesn't want anything to do with me. She considers that I am a failure because I am not a professional man like my father.'

'What did your father do?'

'He was a barrister of some note. Aunt Mildred looks down on me because she says I am little more than a clerk.'

'I'm sure that's not true. From what I observed, my grandfather relied on you for almost everything.' Taking a deep breath Amelia stood up. She was still upset by Caleb's revelations about his childhood, but she sensed that the subject was closed — for now. 'I'll show you your room, and then you can decide if you wish to stay with us, Caleb.'

'There is no doubt about that. I feel at home already. I believe we can help each other. First thing tomorrow morning I am going to take the omnibus to Oxford Street and I'll make an appointment to see Mr Sydney Harrison himself. With his backing you can't go wrong.'

* * *

When Caleb had returned to Albemarle Street to collect his possessions, Amelia went straight to the kitchen to tell Mariah that they had a second paying guest. As she expected, Mariah was busy preparing the meal for that evening with Percy having a nap in a cot they had recently purchased.

'He looks like a little angel when he's asleep,' Amelia said fondly.

'It's a pity he's not always so well behaved.' Mariah added the last of the sliced carrots to the pot and carried it over to the range. 'I hope Dr Taylor doesn't mind having stew again tonight. I managed to get some beef bones with a little meat left on them.'

'What would you say if I took on another lodger, Mariah?' Amelia waited anxiously for an answer.

'Is it Mr Marsh from your grandfather's office?'

'How did you know?'

Mariah grinned. 'It's funny how the single young men suddenly show an interest in renting rooms in this house.'

'They need somewhere to stay,' Amelia said firmly.

'And the landlady happens to be young and beautiful, with a business of her own. I'd say that has something to do with it.'

'Not to mention the fact that I have a friend who is the best cook in London,' Amelia countered, laughing. 'I don't think either of them is interested in me in that way. They are genuinely looking for somewhere comfortable and affordable, and that is what we can offer.'

'I hope Mr Marsh realises that there's a toddler living in the same house, and he often cries at night when the gentleman would want peace and quiet. Not to mention my Betsy, who is a lively little soul, even after being in school all day.'

'I'm sure Mr Marsh will enjoy feeling part of a family. I just don't want to put too much work on your shoulders, Mariah.'

'One more mouth to feed don't make much difference. Anyway, it's Betsy's tenth birthday in a week's time. She can leave school at the end of the Easter term and she'll help in the house.'

'Just so long as you won't find it all too much, and we do need the money.'

'I agree. You won't get any arguments from me.'

'Maybe one day we'll earn enough to share some of the profits,' Amelia said, sighing.

'I'm happy to work for me keep. I can't see anyone else taking me in with my nippers as well.'

'We're a family now, Mariah. I couldn't manage without you. We met by chance and we're not blood related, but that doesn't matter. We look after each other and we share the good times as well as the bad.'

Mariah pulled a cotton handkerchief from her pocket and mopped her eyes. 'Blooming onions. They always make me eyes water something horrible.'

Amelia found that her own eyes were moist and she turned away, sniffing. 'I'd better get back to the office. I hadn't finished going over the accounts with Nellie when Caleb arrived.'

'The women in the workroom will be agog with curiosity.' Mariah gave her a watery smile. 'I expect they've already got you engaged to Mr Marsh.'

'Then they'll be disappointed,' Amelia said firmly. 'I am going to concentrate on building my fashion business. I haven't time for flirtation.'

10

Caleb was true to his word and a day or two after he moved into his room in Nightingale Lane he managed to arrange an appointment with Mr Sydney Harrison himself.

Dressed in one of her own creations, a smart grey woollen travelling costume with a matching cape and bonnet, Amelia waited in Mr Harrison's outer office with Caleb. She had been excited but calm when she awakened that morning, although now she was nervous. So much depended upon her making a good impression on one of the most influential men in London, and possibly the wealthiest. Sydney Harrison had many business interests, the store in Oxford Street being just one of them. She clutched the portfolio containing her sketches as she perched on the edge of her chair with a portmanteau at her feet. It was too valuable to be allowed out of her sight, as it contained a selection of her creations that she and Mariah had wrapped in muslin to minimise creasing.

'There's no need to worry, Amelia,' Caleb said gently. 'Mr Harrison is very approachable.'

'I hope you're right. So much depends upon this.'

'There are other places we can try. Don't be disheartened if we don't succeed this time.'

'Now I am worried,' Amelia said, smiling. 'You are not doing a very good job of calming me down.'

The inner door opened before Caleb had a chance to respond and a young man entered the waiting room.

He was wearing an immaculate swallow-tail jacket and black trousers with a crease that was so sharp it looked almost dangerous. Amelia was quick to notice such details and she was impressed. She rose to her feet, as did Caleb, who picked up the portmanteau.

'Good morning, Miss Sutton, Mr Marsh. My name is Frank Chance and I am Mr Harrison's personal assistant.'

'Good morning, Mr Chance,' Amelia said shyly.

'Come this way, please. Mr Harrison will see you now.' Chance hesitated in the doorway, lowering his voice. 'Just remember that he is a very busy man. Please be brief.' He did not wait for a reply as he turned away and entered the large office. 'Miss Sutton and Mr Marsh, sir.' He backed out of the room, closing the door behind him.

Amelia tried hard not to appear impressed by the size and the luxurious furnishings in the room. She reminded herself that she had spent the first six years of her life living in Grandpapa's mansion, which by any standards was a fine house, filled with precious artefacts. She held her head high as her feet sank into the deep pile of the carpet, but her knees were shaking as she approached the antique Louis Quinze desk. Mr Harrison sat in an equally elegant chair, but he rose gallantly to his feet as she approached.

'Miss Sutton, it's a pleasure to meet you. I knew your grandfather well. He was an excellent businessman and a good friend.'

'How do you do, sir?' Amelia could have cried with relief. Sydney Harrison was human after all. Moreover, he had a charming smile and she decided that he had excellent manners when he walked swiftly round his desk to pull up a chair for her. 'Thank you, Mr

Harrison.' She laid her portfolio on the desk before taking her seat.

'It's good to see you again, Marsh.' Sydney shook Caleb's hand. 'You must miss your former employer. How long were you with him?'

'Ten years, sir. I was a boy of sixteen when Mr Norris took me on to run errands for him.'

'Yes, he told me the story.' Sydney motioned Caleb to sit down before resuming his position behind his desk. 'Well now, Miss Sutton. I've heard all about your success in the mourning warehouse, but I understand from Marsh that you intend to branch out into ladies' fashions.'

'Yes, sir. I've brought some of my designs.'

Sydney opened the portfolio and took out the sketches. Amelia exchanged glances with Caleb, who gave her an encouraging smile. Sydney took his time, examining each drawing carefully before placing them back in the folder.

'Excellent. Now I believe from the size of that portmanteau you have either come to stay or these are examples of your work.'

This made Amelia laugh and she relaxed completely. She stood up and did a twirl. 'This is my first example, sir. As you can see, it is a travelling costume in fine merino wool, with a matching cape. The bonnet was purchased from a milliner, but I intend to take on and train extra staff to work in millinery, should it become necessary.'

Caleb undid the leather straps on the case and handed the first gown to Amelia. Soon the chairs and sofa in the office were draped in colourful silks, satins and velvets. Sydney Harrison rose from his chair and walked round slowly, picking up random garments.

He turned them inside out, examining the stitching in nerve-racking silence. Amelia could not tell if he approved or not, and she crossed her fingers nervously. Caleb laid his hand on her arm, but she could feel the tension radiating from him and she knew that he, too, was anxious.

At last, having examined every single article, Sydney returned to his chair and sat down. 'I have to admit that I was not holding out much hope for someone as young and inexperienced as you, Miss Sutton. But I have been agreeably surprised. You might not have been trained in a fashion house, but your sketches are very well executed and original. You say you have based them on the latest Paris fashion, and I can see that, but somehow you have made them your own. That takes talent.'

'Thank you, sir.' Amelia's knees really did give way beneath the weight of her relief, and she sat down rather more quickly than she intended. Caleb sighed audibly.

'I was not wrong, was I, Mr Harrison?'

'You showed excellent judgement, Marsh. No wonder Mr Norris put so much faith in you.' Sydney leaned his elbows on his desk and steepled his fingers. 'Now we need to talk business.'

An hour later Amelia and Caleb left the department store and stepped out into a blustery April wind. Fragments of straw, dead leaves and odd pieces of detritus that the street sweeper had missed whirled round in a bizarre aerial ballet.

'I can't believe it,' Amelia said dazedly. 'He not only bought the samples but he's going to give us a big order, depending upon the success of the garments we left with him.'

'I was certain he would appreciate them, otherwise I wouldn't have gone to the trouble of arranging a meeting. Luckily I've had dealings with Frank Chance in the past, and Mr Harrison values his opinion. Frank is keen to promote the fashion department at Harrison's.'

Amelia smiled. 'I noticed that Mr Chance is a very smartly dressed man. Anyway, it's a bit chilly. Hail a cab, please, Caleb. This is not the day to wait around for an omnibus. I want to get home quickly so that I can give Mariah the good news.'

* * *

Mariah was ecstatic and full of plans for making paper patterns that could be reused, but already Amelia was developing other ideas. She sat at the kitchen table sipping a cup of tea that Mariah had just poured from the Brown Betty teapot.

'I want our creations to be designed specifically for each individual, so that the customer can be assured that they will not meet anyone else wearing something similar.'

'We can vary the gowns with different materials and trimmings,' Mariah said thoughtfully. 'You could design garments to suit each customer's particular preferences.'

'I could. You're right. I just hope that Mr Harrison orders more gowns.' Amelia turned to Caleb, who had been sitting quietly drinking his tea. 'Could you keep in touch with Mr Chance? You said you have had dealings with him in the past?'

'Of course. I was going to suggest that anyway. He's a decent enough chap when you get to know him. I could approach other stores, too. That's if you would allow me to do so, Amelia. Now we've actually sold some to Harrison's I think the others will follow. They won't want to be left out now you've started a new trend.'

'A new trend!' Amelia sighed. 'I have to keep pinching myself or I think I am dreaming.'

Mariah cocked her head on one side at the sound of a baby crying. 'That's Percy. He's woken from his nap. I put him in the front parlour, I hope you don't mind, Amelia. Only it is too hot and steamy in the kitchen.'

'Of course not,' Amelia said quickly.

'I'll never forget how you took us in,' Mariah said emotionally. 'Not many people would have done so in the circumstances.' She hurried from the kitchen.

'She's a good woman.' Caleb pushed his empty cup away, frowning. 'But you've taken on a lot with her and her children. There might come a day when you would rather that they were not living here.'

Amelia shook her head emphatically. 'The idea never occurred to me, Caleb. Mariah has been a great help to me, and I love her children.'

'I think they are very fortunate. I'm just saying that things might change.'

'It's better not to look too far ahead at the moment. I don't know if my cousin Daniel is going to carry out his threat to challenge Grandpapa's will. We could all find ourselves homeless.'

'We can only hope it was an idle threat, but even if he did go that far, I can't see a magistrate ruling in his favour, especially when he's inherited a fortune and huge business assets.'

'I really hope it doesn't go to court, but if it does, I

will fight him every inch of the way. Grandpapa never gave me anything until now, and I don't intend to give it up without a struggle.' Amelia met his gaze with a straight look. 'But what about you, Caleb, now you have lost your position in my grandfather's company?'

'I will find a new position eventually, but in the meantime I'll do anything I can to assist you.'

'Thank you, Caleb. I really could do with some help.'

'I have faith in you. I know you can do whatever you set out to do. I just wish I had had someone to say that to me when I was starting out.'

Amelia eyed him curiously. 'You told Mr Harrison that my grandpapa took you on when you were sixteen. How did that happen?'

'My aunt decided that I was not clever enough to go to university,' Caleb sighed, shaking his head. 'She simply wanted me out of the house and so she apprenticed me to a bookbinder in Shoe Lane.'

'That seems a strange choice. Was it what you wanted to do?'

'No, not at all. The worst part of it was that I had no aptitude for such work. I was all fingers and thumbs, as they say. Poor old Tomkins, the printer, was very patient with me but I must have driven him to distraction.'

'How did you meet my grandpapa? It seems such an unlikely occurrence, given the circumstances.'

'It was fate, I suppose. Your grandfather had sent a very old and valuable book to Tomkins to have the binding replaced. Needless to say, I wasn't allowed to touch it, but when the work was completed I was given the task of delivering it to the house in Albemarle Street.' Caleb paused, as if reliving the moment.

'Go on, please. I'm really interested.'

'I walked all the way from Shoe Lane and had reached the front entrance in Albemarle Street when a rough-looking individual tried to snatch the parcel from my hand. He couldn't have known what it was, but I suppose he was desperate. Anyway, I brought him to the ground just as your grandfather's carriage drew up. I managed to wrest the book from my assailant, who scrambled to his feet and ran off.'

'Were you hurt?'

'I was cut and bruised, but as luck would have it your grandfather had seen the whole thing. He insisted on taking me into the house and instructed his housekeeper to clean me up. She fussed around me and brought me tea and a sweet cake.'

'And did you see Grandpapa again that day?'

'No. I walked back to Shoe Lane and forgot all about it until a couple of days later when Mr Norris arrived at the workshop. He told Tomkins what I'd done and he said he needed a bright lad to work for him. Tomkins said that I was legally apprenticed to him, but your grandfather wasn't going to be gainsaid. He literally bought my freedom and gave me a job.'

'And you worked your way up from being an errand boy?'

'Yes, that's how it was.'

'Amazing. Especially as Grandpapa was not the most generous or kindly person I've ever met. Even when I was only a small child I realised that he disliked my pa. I don't think he had wanted Mama to marry a doctor who was struggling to make a living. We lived with Grandpapa until Pa could afford to rent somewhere for us. When Mama died of a fever her allowance from Grandpapa stopped and we had to move into cheaper accommodation. I think Grandpapa wanted me to stay with him, but Papa was not going to allow that. He did his best to look after me, and we learned how to take care of each other.'

'It's strange how things work out,' Caleb said slowly. 'And now here we are, helping each other out in a difficult situation.'

'I would love to see Grandpapa's face if he knew that he'd literally thrown us together. Although perhaps he would approve. He obviously thought a lot of you, and I think, in his own way, he was fond of me too.'

'I am very sure of that, Amelia. He would not have remembered you in his will if he did not care about you. He was a strange man in many ways, but an honest one. Unlike Mr Daniel Norris, who is the very opposite. I cannot abide that person.'

'He can't be all bad,' Amelia said thoughtfully. 'Most people have a decent side to their nature, if you can find it.'

Caleb rose to his feet. 'I suppose that's true in most cases, but I think Daniel Norris is rotten to the core and that wife of his is no better. Anyway, I should make a start on looking for employment. Your late grandfather gave me a good reference.'

'I wish I could help you.'

'One day, maybe, but for now you should concentrate on making more of those lovely gowns. I have great faith in you, Amelia.' Caleb strolled out of the kitchen.

Amelia finished her tea and sat back in her chair. Mr Harrison might have bought the garments she had taken to his store, but that did not necessarily mean there would be future orders. However, she must be positive — it was a good start. If she failed it would not be for the want of trying, and there was always the mourning warehouse to provide a steady income. Papa had established himself at the hospital, and she had two paying guests. They would manage, but only if Cousin Daniel could be persuaded that contesting the will was not the right course for him to take.

She was deep in thought but the sudden urgent knocking on the front door made her jump to her feet. Caleb had gone to his room and Mariah was busy with Percy.

Amelia opened the door and found Nellie standing on the step outside. 'What is it, Nellie? Is something wrong?'

'I dunno, miss.' Nellie wrapped her shawl more tightly around her as a chill wind from the east caused her teeth to chatter audibly.

'Come inside. Why didn't you knock on the inner door?'

'I did, miss. But I couldn't make you hear me.' Nellie stepped into the hall with a sigh of relief. 'That wind cuts right through you.'

'Come into the kitchen. It's much warmer in there.' Amelia did not wait for an answer and she led the way to the kitchen. 'What's wrong, Nellie? You look troubled?'

'A man come to the workroom. I never seen him before and I wouldn't let him in.'

'What did he want? Perhaps he was selling something.'

'He was peering over me shoulder, squinting his eyes as he peered through the window. I dunno what he was looking for, but he was very insistent. He said he wanted to inspect the premises, but I wouldn't let him in, and he went away muttering beneath his breath. I'm glad I couldn't hear what he was saying.'

'Did he give a name, or any hint as to why he wanted to look at the workroom?'

'I think he said something about Mr Norris sending him, but we all know that Mr Norris has passed away. In fact, it's been a bit of a joke amongst the girls. I mean we're making mourning garments and now his family will be wanting them.' Nellie clapped her hand over her mouth and her eyes widened in horror. 'I'm ever so sorry, miss. I clean forgot that Mr Norris was your granddad. No offence meant, I'm sure.'

Amelia laid her hand on Nellie's shoulder. 'It's quite all right. I can see the irony of the situation. No offence taken.'

'Thank you, miss. I'm sorry, me tongue runs away with me sometimes. But he weren't a nice person. He looked like he wanted to come in and smash up all our machines.'

'That's very unfortunate, but I think I know who sent him. My cousin has inherited my grandfather's estate, but Grandpapa left the workroom and the house to me.'

'Then your cousin has got designs on the place, by the looks of things.'

'I think you could be right, Nellie. But please don't mention any of this to the other women. I'm going to call on my cousin and I'll make it very plain that such visits are unwelcome and intrusive.'

'What shall I tell the others, miss?'

Amelia thought for a moment. 'Tell them that he was sent by a competitor to spy on our work here. That's not too far from the truth. And if he or anyone like him should try to gain entry to the premises, do exactly what you just did. Slam the door in his face and let me know. I'll get someone to fix a bell on the connecting door, should you need me urgently at any time.'

'Yes, miss. Thank you. I won't tell the girls anything until you say I can.'

Amelia saw Nellie safely back in the workroom and closed the door.

'What was that all about?' Mariah emerged from the front parlour, clutching Percy in her arms.

'I think my cousin sent someone to spy on the workroom. Nellie didn't let him in.'

'You didn't tell her that he wants to throw us all out, did you?'

'No, of course not. But I know now what I have to do. It's too late to do it now, but first thing in the morning I'm going to take a cab to Albemarle Street and I'll have words with Cousin Daniel.'

* * *

Amelia had not told anyone other than Mariah about her plan to visit her cousin next day. She managed to leave the house without either her father or Caleb seeing her, although she almost bumped into Todd as he was about to set off for the hospital.

'You're in a hurry. Is the house on fire and no one thought to warn me?' Todd said, smiling.

Amelia laid her finger on her lips. 'I don't want anyone to know I'm going out, Todd.'

His hazel eyes twinkled with amber lights. 'Please don't tell me you have a romantic assignation?'

'Nothing so exciting,' Amelia said, giggling. Todd

always managed to cheer her up, even when she was really downcast. 'If you promise not to say anything I'll tell you. I'm going to Albemarle Street to face my cousin. I think he sent someone to spy on the business. He's trying to take it away from me.'

Todd's smile faded and his brow creased in a frown. 'Surely he can't do that. It was left to you. It has nothing to do with him now.'

'That's what I'm going to tell him. I refuse to be bullied into giving up the opportunity that my grandfather gave me in his will.'

'I'd come with you, but I'm already late for work.'

Amelia laid her hand on his sleeve. 'Thank you, Todd. I know I can rely on you, but this is something I must do alone anyway.'

'Be careful. I don't know your cousin, but he's not behaving like a gentleman. I think your grandfather would be furious if he could see what was going on.' Todd opened the front door and Amelia stepped outside onto the pavement. 'Let me know if he oversteps the mark. I'd be more than happy to take him on.'

'I know you would and that gives me comfort, but I'll do this my way.' Amelia hailed a cab. 'Wish me luck, Todd.'

He handed her into the hansom cab. 'You don't need luck. I can tell by the militant sparkle in your eyes that you mean business.'

'Albemarle Street, please, cabby.' Amelia blew a kiss to Todd as the cab drew away from the kerb. She sat back, planning what she would say to Daniel Norris.

When the cabby reined in his horse outside the house in Albemarle Street, Amelia was surprised to see Hobbs standing on the pavement, with a heavy valise in either hand. She paid the cabby and alighted.

'Hobbs?' Amelia hurried to his side. 'Where are you going?' Once again she could see from his red-rimmed eyes that he had been crying and even now his lips trembled.

'Thirty years I served the master, and now it's come to this.'

'What do you mean?'

'I've been sacked, to put it bluntly, miss. I know that Mr Daniel is related to you but he had no reason to treat a loyal servant like this.'

'He's thrown you out, Hobbs? Why?'

'Not for anything other than the fact I'm not as young as I was. He said I was too old to be of any use to him and he told me to leave immediately.'

'Have you anywhere to go? Any family who would take you in?'

'None that has room for me, Miss Amelia. I will have to seek another position, but I'm afraid my age will go against me.'

'I have business with Mr Norris, but it won't take very long. There's a coffee shop in Piccadilly. Go there and wait for me. You're coming home with me, Hobbs. I won't take no for an answer.'

'Thank you, miss. Just for a day or so until I can find work elsewhere.'

Amelia crossed the pavement and rapped on the door knocker. 'Please wait for me in the coffee shop, Hobbs.'

'Very well, miss. If you say so.'

Amelia was in no mood to be put off by the new footman who opened the door and looked down his nose at her. But a few sharp words from her and he ushered her inside, bidding her to wait while he checked to see if the master was at home. He returned moments later to say that Mr Norris was not available at the moment. Amelia had spotted her cousin heading towards the dining room. He did not know it, but he was about to have his breakfast interrupted. She pushed past the footman and ignored all his efforts to prevent her from reaching the dining room. He strode on ahead and placed himself in front of the door.

'You cannot go in there, miss. The master is not available.'

'We'll see about that.' Amelia made as if to pass him on one side but dodged him nimbly and opened the door. She burst into the room to find her cousin at the sideboard, helping himself from an array of her late grandfather's silver dishes.

'What's going on?' Daniel Norris demanded. 'I thought I gave instructions that I was not to be disturbed.'

Amelia crossed the floor and took a seat at the table. 'Don't blame him. It was not his fault.' She beckoned to onc of the startled parlourmaids. 'Coffee, please.'

The girl paled visibly and looked to her new employer for affirmation.

'Do not give her anything. Miss Sutton is not stopping.' Daniel carried a plate heaped with bacon, sausages, devilled kidneys and buttered eggs to his place at the head of the table. 'You are not welcome here, Amelia. I'm asking you to leave, or shall I have you thrown out?'

'You will probably do that anyway; it seems to be the way you go about things. However, you will hear me out first.' Amelia reached for the silver coffee pot and filled a cup without waiting for the maid to do it for her. She added a dash of cream and raised it to her lips. 'I am here to discuss business with you.'

'I do not speak about such matters at breakfast. You must leave or I shall send for a constable.'

'You would look very foolish if you did. Can you imagine the headline in the newspapers? Wealthy businessman, Daniel Norris, has his young cousin arrested for paying a visit to his house and interrupting his breakfast? You would be the laughing stock of the city.'

Daniel jerked his head in the direction of the footman, who was hovering nervously at his side. 'Get out. I'll ring for you if necessary.' Daniel leaned forward, narrowing his eyes. 'Say what you came to say and then leave.'

'Very well. I'll be blunt. I know you sent one of your minions to spy on my workroom yesterday. I warn you that if you do so again *I* will send for a constable and have him arrested. Not only that, but I will give my side of the story to the newspapers. I will tell them that my cousin is threatening to have me evicted from a humble workshop in the docks area, where poor women work hard to support their families by making cheap garments for the bereaved.'

'I heard that you want to launch out into the world of fashion. That doesn't make such a sympathetic story, does it? You shouldn't be living in that house or managing the workroom. I'm going to win this contest of wills, Amelia Sutton.'

Amelia pushed back her chair and stood up. 'We'll see about that. I came here with the best of intentions to speak nicely, but I can see that you don't understand such polite treatment. If you want to challenge Grandpapa's will in court I warn you that I will fight it with everything I have. Don't underestimate me. I am not a silly little girl who doesn't know her own mind. I have been trained in a hard school and you are not going to ruin my life, no matter how hard you try. Enjoy your breakfast, cousin.'

11

Hobbs was hovering in the doorway of the coffee shop, clutching his battered leather case and a neatly furled black umbrella. He shifted anxiously from one foot to the other as Amelia hurried up to him.

'I'm sorry if I kept you waiting. I had words to say to Mr Norris.'

'He's not like the master, Miss Amelia. Mr Daniel terminated my employment without giving me a character. After all these years of service.'

'I know. It's so unfair. But it's settled: you're coming home with me, Hobbs.'

'I can't impose on you, Miss Amelia.'

'It's not an imposition. I can't leave you here.' Amelia moved to the kerb and hailed a hansom cab. 'Come along, Hobbs. At least we can have a talk in private. I know Papa would want to see you.'

The cab drew to a halt and somewhat reluctantly Hobbs accepted Amelia's invitation to accompany her. It was a largely silent carriage ride through the busy streets. Amelia was wrapped in her own thoughts and Hobbs seemed to have lost the power of speech.

* * *

When they reached Nightingale Lane Amelia was surprised to see her father's overcoat hanging on the hallstand. She opened the parlour door and saw him seated by a newly lit fire, reading a copy of the *Daily Telegraph*.

'Pa, I've just been to see Cousin Daniel.' Amelia ushered Hobbs into the parlour. 'Hobbs has been sacked without a reference for no reason.'

'I apologise for the intrusion, Dr Sutton,' Hobbs said nervously.

Harold set the newspaper to one side. 'Come in, Hobbs, and take a seat.'

'I really shouldn't impose, sir.' Hobbs stared down at his shiny black shoes and tears trickled down his cheeks.

Amelia guided him to a chair by the fire. 'Please sit down. I'll bring you a nice hot cup of tea.' She turned to her father. 'I wasn't expecting you to be home so early, Pa.'

'I am going back to the hospital after luncheon and I'll probably be on duty all night. I'll have a cup of tea, too. And a biscuit, if we have any.'

Amelia smiled. 'I'll see what I can do. Anyway, I think Hobbs should stay here with us until he's decided what he wants to do next.' She did not wait for either of them to respond and she repeated her suggestion when she told Mariah that she had invited him to stay.

'Are you sure the old gent wants to live here, miss? I mean, it's a bit of a come-down from living in a mansion in Mayfair, ain't it?'

'Hobbs was a servant in that house. I believe that my grandpapa treated him well enough, but Cousin Daniel has cast the poor old man aside as if he was worth less than nothing.'

'Mr Hobbs ain't your responsibility, miss. We can manage as we are, but another mouth to feed is not going to be easy.'

'Nevertheless, I can't just abandon the poor man. He might think of a distant relative who will take him in, if we take care of him now. I think he's in a state of shock after being treated so badly.'

Mariah filled two cups with tea and added milk. 'The tea is ready. I suppose the old man will want something to eat at midday, as well as Dr Sutton.'

'Hobbs can have my portion if there's not enough to go round.'

Mariah sniffed. 'I'll add more water to the soup. We'll manage.'

'Thank you, Mariah. I knew you would. You're an angel.'

'A fallen one, more like.'

Amelia chose to ignore that remark and she picked up the tea tray. 'I don't suppose we have any biscuits? Pa asked for one to go with his tea.'

'Someone keeps sneaking them out of the tin. I don't know if it's that young doctor or if it's Mr Marsh, but we have a thief amongst us.'

'I don't think taking a biscuit or two is a capital offence. It could be Pa who takes them. He loves anything sweet and your biscuits melt in the mouth.' Amelia had the satisfaction of seeing Mariah's frown wiped away by a smile. She returned to the parlour with a determined set to her shoulders. One thing was for certain: Hobbs would not be cast out onto the street again. He was an elderly man who had served her grandfather well. Hobbs deserved to be treated with kindness and respect.

Whether it was the warmth of the fire or the sweetness and strength of the tea, Hobbs began to relax visibly and Amelia chose her moment in which to press her point.

'Mr Hobbs, you will stay with us, won't you? Just for a while, until you decide what it is you want to do next.'

'Amelia is right,' Harold added firmly. 'You cannot wander round London looking for cheap accommodation. You are more than welcome to reside here for as long as you like. I am at the hospital, working long hours, and it would give me peace of mind to know that there was a man here to protect the women and children during the day.'

Hobbs replaced his cup and saucer on the tray. 'You are both too kind. How could I refuse such a generous offer, but I will pay my way. I have some savings.'

'We'll talk about that later.' Amelia tried to keep a note of triumph from her voice. She could see that Hobbs was a proud man and used to controlling a large staff, which gave her an idea. 'You know, Mr Hobbs, I have been looking for someone with authority to oversee the women who work for me. Sometimes they get a little out of hand, but you are used to that, I'm sure.'

'I will do anything you ask, Miss Amelia. I cannot tell you how grateful I am.'

'Perhaps you would like to see your room.'

Hobbs rose to his feet and reached for his case. 'Of course, thank you.'

Amelia led the way to the second floor where Todd and Caleb had the largest of the three rooms. She opened the door to the smallest room, which contained a single bed, a chest and a washstand, as well as a comfortable but shabby armchair.

'If this is too small there are rooms on the top floor, but we haven't furnished them yet.'

Hobbs laid his case on the patchwork quilt. 'This is most acceptable, Miss Amelia. I have everything I could wish for here.'

'I'll get Mariah to light a fire for you, but you must feel free to use our parlour, too. You won't be alone on this floor. You know Mr Marsh well — he has the room next to yours — and Dr Taylor has the front room.'

'I can't thank you enough,' Hobbs said, smiling for the first time that day.

'There's no need. You were kind to me when I was a small girl. I remember that very well. Now it's my turn to help you.' Amelia stepped out onto the landing. 'I'll leave you to settle in. Luncheon is at midday.'

* * *

After everyone had eaten their meal and Harold had returned to the hospital, Amelia took Hobbs into the workroom and then ushered him into the office, where she introduced him to Nellie.

'Mr Hobbs has many years' experience in handling staff, Nellie,' Amelia said firmly. 'I think you might find his expertise useful, and he will deter any unwanted visitors.'

Nellie glanced at him suspiciously. 'He ain't after my job, is he, miss?'

'No, of course not. Mr Hobbs doesn't know anything about making mourning gowns. He is here to assist where needed. I know there are occasional arguments that can get out of hand, and someone like Mr Hobbs could calm the situation with a few words. He has also been accustomed to handling household accounts.'

'That is my job,' Nellie protested.

'You will do what you always do, of course. Mr Hobbs will go over the books with you as I have done in the past, which gives me more time for other important tasks. As I told you in confidence, Nellie, I am hoping to branch out into manufacturing fashionable garments. I am just waiting to see if the ones I took to the big department store in Oxford Street have sold quickly.'

'I ain't said nothing to the others,' Nellie said stiffly. 'I can keep me trap shut when I has to.'

'Yes, and I appreciate your discretion. Mr Hobbs is here to help, and your job remains the same as it has always been. It's just that you don't have to send for me if there is a problem. I'd like you to explain that to the other women.'

'They ain't keen on change,' Nellie said gloomily. 'They won't like a man telling them what to do.'

'I can assure you that I am tact itself.' Hobbs drew himself up to his full height. 'I know how to handle people, Mrs Dawson. But I will defer to you in difficult cases.'

'I'm glad that's understood.' Nellie puffed out her chest. 'I've been in charge here for many years, Mr Hobbs.'

'I respect that, Mrs Dawson.'

'It's important that you two work together,' Amelia said, smiling. 'Mr Hobbs will start his duties tomorrow morning.' She opened the office door. 'Ladies, I would like to introduce Mr Hobbs, who will be working with us. Nellie will explain everything to you.' Amelia left the workroom with Hobbs close on her heels.

'Are you sure about this, Miss Amelia?' Hobbs

asked as she locked the connecting door.

'It is a position made for you, Mr Hobbs. You have thirty years of experience handling female servants. This is no different. If you find the position isn't to your liking you can look for something better, but you will still be welcome to stay with us for as long as it suits you.'

'I am overwhelmed by your kindness, Miss Amelia. When Mr Norris sacked me this morning I felt as if it was the end of the world. You have given me hope and I won't let you down.'

'I am certain of that. I just need to have good news from Mr Harrison and then I know everything will fall into place.'

* * *

Todd arrived home that evening looking pale and exhausted after a long shift at the hospital. Amelia served the meal in the dining room, and Hobbs retired to his room as soon as he finished eating. Mariah, however, insisted on eating in the kitchen with the children, despite Amelia's pleas for her to bring them to dine with the rest of the family. Caleb had been out all day and had not yet returned. Amelia put food aside for him, but she was curious as to what could have been so important that he had missed luncheon as well as dinner. If she were to be honest she was a little put out by his casual attitude, and she had to remind herself that he was simply a lodger in her home. He was under no obligation to share personal details with them. She waited until Todd had eaten before taking a tray of coffee to the dining room. She filled two cups and passed one to Todd.

'A penny for them,' Todd said, smiling tiredly.

'I was just thinking about everything that's happened recently, Todd. So much has changed since Grandpapa died.'

'How did it go with your cousin this morning? Did you win?'

'Hardly that, Todd. If my cousin succeeds in his threat to challenge the will, everything will change again. We will all be looking for somewhere to live.'

'Did you try appealing to his better nature?'

'You don't know my cousin. He wouldn't take any notice if I went down on bended knee and begged him to relent.'

'What does your father say to all this?'

Amelia pulled a face. 'I think you know Pa well enough by now, Todd. He lives for his profession. It's always been the same.'

'He is a very good physician and well thought of at the hospital.'

'He's in his element there.' Amelia refilled Todd's coffee cup. 'But what about you? Are you happy or do you miss your patients in the village — what was it called?'

'Rockwood. Yes, I suppose I do. I was fourteen when I went to live in the country and at first I hated it. I missed London, although I was grateful to Miss Nancy for saving me from a miserable life on the streets. Then I began to settle down and when I was finishing my training in London I really missed everyone at home.'

'I've always lived in London. I know nothing about the countryside, but if you loved Rockwood so much, why did you come back to town, Todd? What made you give up your practice? You mentioned that you had feelings for a lady. Was she the reason you decided to return to London?'

'Dolly and I more or less grew up together, thanks to Nancy, or rather Lady Carey, as she is now. Nancy saw to it that all of us boys had what education we needed and I had an aptitude for medicine.'

'Did Dolly live in the castle?'

'She is Sir Thomas's niece and she was brought up to be a lady.' Todd smiled and shook his head. 'But Dolly was a rebel and she wanted a different life.'

'She fell in love with someone else?'

'With my best friend, Gus. It's a long story, and it's all in the past now. I was happy in the country, but I think this is where I really belong.'

Amelia was about to question him more about his lost love, but the door opened and Caleb breezed into the room.

'I apologise for missing dinner.' Caleb paused, his eyes sparkling with suppressed excitement. 'Something extraordinary happened to me today.'

Amelia picked up the coffee pot. 'There's some left. Would you like a cup?'

'I would, yes, please.' Caleb pulled up a chair and sat down. 'I went to Harrison's this morning. I wanted to question Frank Chance. I thought he might be able to tell me if your designs are attracting any interest.'

'It's early days yet, surely?' Amelia filled a cup with coffee and passed it to him.

'True, but I wanted to make sure that Frank was on our side, which he is, by the way.'

'This took all day?' Todd raised an eyebrow.

'Frank and I were simply chatting when Sydney himself walked into the office. He started asking questions about your late grandfather's businesses.

Apparently, Sydney Harrison is very interested in some of them. His financial dealings are legendary in the City.'

'But what has it got to do with you, Caleb?' Amelia gave him a steady look.

'Sydney suggested that I try to get my job back. It could be very useful to him to have someone close to Mr Norris, and I would be handsomely rewarded for information he requires.'

'You mean he wants you to spy on Amelia's uncle?' Todd shook his head. 'Not a nice business to be in.'

'But I would earn more in a month than you do in a year, Doctor.' Caleb turned to Amelia. 'I wouldn't even think about it, but for the fact that if I were close to your cousin I might be able to dissuade him from challenging the will.'

Amelia pushed back her chair and stood up. 'I don't like it, Caleb. The whole business sounds suspicious, and spying for Mr Harrison is just nasty. I can look after myself and I don't need you to break the law to help me.'

Caleb shook his head. 'I wouldn't be doing anything illegal. You ought to know me better than that.'

'No, Caleb.' Amelia met his smiling gaze with a frown. 'I don't think I do, and I don't want any part of it.'

'But I will be doing it for you,' Caleb protested.

'You're not listening to me, Caleb. I don't want any part in your nefarious dealings with Mr Harrison.'

'She's right,' Todd said firmly. 'It's not how things are done. You should know better, Marsh.'

Caleb rounded on him. 'What would you know about it, Doctor? You're a simpleton up from the country. You know nothing of business matters.'

'Don't speak to Todd like that.' Amelia faced Caleb angrily. 'I agree with Todd. You might think it's the way to do things, but I disagree.'

'You are never going to get anywhere if you don't take a few short cuts,' Caleb said tersely. 'I know what I'm doing.'

Amelia stared at him in disbelief. This was not the sort of help she wanted or expected from Caleb. 'What you do for yourself is your business, but please leave me well and truly out of any plans you might make.' She stormed out of the dining room and went straight to the kitchen.

Betsy was just about to carry her sleeping brother from the room and Amelia held the door for her. She managed a smile. 'Good night, Percy,' she said, dropping a kiss on his curly head.

'He can't hear you, he's asleep.' Betsy giggled as she headed for the staircase.

'What's wrong?' Mariah demanded. 'You don't look happy.'

Amelia closed the door. 'I need to speak to you, Mariah. Maybe I'm wrong but I've just listened to Caleb talking and I really don't think I know him. He's not the person I thought he was.'

'You're just getting to know him,' Mariah said evenly. 'What has he done to upset you?'

'I'm too angry to talk about it now.' Amelia frowned. 'I'd better fetch the coffee tray so that we can get everything cleared away.' She returned to the dining room but as she opened the door she was aware of raised voices.

Todd and Caleb were standing on opposite sides of the table, facing each other angrily. There was a heavy silence as she entered the room.

'What's the matter now?' Amelia demanded crossly.

'We were just having a discussion,' Caleb said glibly. 'But it got rather heated.'

'You and I will never agree, Marsh.' Todd made a move towards the door. 'Please don't worry about it, Amelia.' He left the room, allowing the door to swing shut of its own accord.

Amelia faced Caleb with a defiant stare. 'I suppose you'll be moving back to the house in Albemarle Street.'

'I wasn't intending to. Are you throwing me out, Amelia?'

'No, but I don't see how you can live here and yet work for my cousin, who is threatening to take everything away from me.'

'That is the whole point of my actions. I can keep you informed of his intentions as well as helping Mr Harrison to get what he wants.'

'But you were dismissed. How do you propose to gain his favour?'

'I can be very persuasive when necessary,' Caleb said with a disarming smile. 'I am on your side, I promise you.'

'You seem very sure that you can persuade him to take you back.'

'As a matter of fact it is done. I went to see him this afternoon and pleaded my case. To be honest, I think he regretted sacking me. He's taking over a business about which he knows next to nothing. I, on the other hand, have learned it by starting from the bottom.'

'You must do what you wish, but how do I know that you are not spying on us and reporting to my cousin?'

Caleb reached out to take her hand in his. 'You will

just have to trust me, Amelia. I promise that I will do nothing to jeopardise your business.'

Amelia snatched her hand free from his grasp. 'I would rather you left me out of this. I have no love for my cousin, but I don't agree with playing one person off against another.'

She hurried from the room and made her way to the parlour where she was surprised to find Todd, seated by the fire. He jumped to his feet.

'I hope you don't mind me being here. I've used up my ration of coal for the week.'

'Your ration?' Amelia stared at him blankly.

'Mariah tells us how much we can take. I thought you knew.'

'I didn't, although I expect she is trying to save money, but you pay a good rent, Todd. You can take as much coal as you need.'

'Thank you. I hope I haven't caused trouble between you and Mariah.'

'Of course not. I know she would be acting with my best interests at heart. I'll have a word with her in the morning.'

'There's another thing,' Todd said awkwardly.

'If you're going to say something about Caleb and his decision to return to working for my cousin — I've already spoken to him about that. I don't like it and I've made that very plain.'

'Is he going to take any notice of what you said?'

'I don't know. I think Caleb does as he pleases, but I want nothing to do with his scheme.'

Todd smiled as he resumed his seat. 'Well said. Do you mind if I sit here for a while?'

'Of course not. This is your home.' Amelia picked up her portfolio and took her drawing to the table in the window. She moved the lamp a little closer in order to see the sketches more clearly. Just looking at them calmed her down and she put Caleb and his schemes to the back of her mind.

'I have so many ideas for lovely garments,' she said with a sigh. 'I just wish I knew if the gowns we left at the store have been sold.'

'Didn't Harrison's purchase them from you?'

'They wanted to see if there was any interest first. I'm so new to the fashion business.'

'I saw some of the gowns that you and Mariah made. They were very fine. I could just see Lady Carey wearing them at one of the Rockwood balls.'

Amelia eyed him curiously. 'You are very fond of her, aren't you?'

'I owe everything to Nancy. If you could have seen how we boys were living in a damp, dirty cellar, you would understand. It seemed like a miracle to be rescued from a life of crime and treated like decent human beings.'

'But your friend Gus stole the young lady you loved?'

'They were better suited to each other.'

'Where are they now?'

'I believe Gus's regiment was sent to India, but I haven't heard from him for some time. I think Dolly will make a wonderful army wife. She'll enjoy every challenge that presents itself.'

Amelia smiled sympathetically. 'I think you are still a little in love with her.'

'I'll always be fond of Dolly, but that life is behind me now. I know I am doing what I was meant to do. Maybe one day I can help children from any background to a better and healthier life. Then I'll know

I've repaid my debt to society for the wrongs I did as a child.'

'But that's just it, Todd. You were a child when you were forced to live on the streets.' Amelia met his gaze with an encouraging smile. 'You've turned out well in spite of your early days.'

Todd laughed. 'You always know what to say to make me feel better about myself.' He rose to his feet. 'May I see your sketches? Not that I'm an expert in such things.'

'Of course.' Amelia patted the seat of the chair beside her. 'Come and sit down. I'll explain them all to you. I have so many ideas in my head — I need to get them down on paper.'

Todd studied the drawings intently. 'I think these are marvellous. I know little or nothing about fashion but I've seen the ladies at the castle in their fine clothes and I'm sure they would be happy to wear gowns like these.'

'I do hope so. I'm trying to be patient but it's not easy. Maybe I should just go on as I am and make even more mourning apparel. What do you think, Todd?'

'I think you should follow your heart. Those designs are lovely. I think you should continue to make beautiful gowns. If Harrison's don't take advantage of your offer, then try elsewhere, or even sell them yourself.'

Amelia met his earnest gaze with a smile. 'You're right, Todd. You've given me a wonderful idea.' She rose swiftly to her feet and kissed him on the cheek. Realising what she had done she sat down hastily. 'I'm sorry. I didn't mean to embarrass you. I was just so excited by the idea you've given me.'

'Don't apologise. I haven't been kissed by a beautiful woman for so long I'd almost forgotten how delightful it is.'

The irresistible twinkle in Todd's eyes made Amelia laugh. 'I'm not usually so forward, but thank you for giving me such a good idea.'

'Would you like to share it with me?'

'I will, when I've thought it through properly. In the meantime, it's a secret, but I promise you that you will be the first to know if I decide to go ahead.'

12

Amelia worked on her designs until the small hours of the morning and even when she went to bed she found it hard to get to sleep. Her mind was filled with plans for developing her own business, completely separate from the mourning warehouse. She wanted something that no one could take away from her. The only problem was how to do it with little or no finance behind her. She fell asleep finally and awakened later than usual. After a lick and a promise at the wash-stand she dressed hastily, brushed her hair and tied it back with a ribbon, before hurrying downstairs to the kitchen.

Mariah was giving Percy his breakfast porridge, which was going everywhere apart from Percy's eager little mouth.

'I'm sorry I'm too late to help with the breakfasts,' Amelia said hastily. 'I overslept.'

Mariah smiled. 'No matter. Caleb was up and out before I came down to get the fire going in the range. Your pa and Todd have had their breakfasts and they left for the hospital a good half an hour since. Betsy's gone to school all excited because this is her last day as she'll be ten on Sunday.'

Amelia helped herself to a bowl of porridge from the pan on the hob before taking a seat at the table. 'Caleb will be returning to Albemarle Street, Mariah. He has his job back with Cousin Daniel, but he intends to spy on him and report to Mr Harrison, who has similar business interests. Caleb said that would benefit us as well and I strongly disagreed. I want nothing to do with such dirty dealing.'

'No wonder you were upset last night.'

'I don't want any part of it, even if Daniel is trying to take this house and the business away from me.'

Mariah picked up a cloth and wiped Percy's face. 'Caleb is an ambitious man. I think he'll do anything to make his mark on the world.'

Amelia tasted the porridge but it was very hot and she rested her spoon on a side plate. 'I had a wonderful idea last evening, Mariah. Actually, it was Todd who put the thought in my mind.'

'What is the brilliant notion?' Mariah lifted Percy from his seat and set him down on the floor. She pulled up a chair and sat opposite Amelia. 'Go on, tell me.'

'I think our designs and clothes are worthy of being sold by us as a company in our own right. I think we could be a leader of fashion like the House of Worth.'

'I like the idea, but isn't that a bit ambitious, considering we are totally unknown?'

'Everyone has to start somewhere, Mariah. Even Charles Frederick Worth was a humble sales assistant to begin with.'

Mariah sipped her tea and pulled a face. 'It's cold. I'll make another pot.'

'Don't you like my idea?' Amelia asked, frowning. 'It wouldn't happen overnight. I realise that.'

Mariah bustled about making a fresh pot of tea. 'It's good to have a plan, but we need money to live on in the meantime. If you've sent Caleb packing that means one less person paying rent.'

'We'll manage somehow. I just want to be independent of my cousin. I don't know if he can take all this from us, but the thought of that is enough to make me anxious. Anyway, there isn't much joy in creating mourning garments in black bombazine and crepe. I want to make people look beautiful and feel happy.' Amelia swallowed a mouthful of porridge. 'By the way, where is Hobbs? Is he still in bed?'

'No, indeed. Mr Hobbs was up before me. He ate a quick breakfast and then he went into the workshop. He's determined to prove that your faith in him is not misplaced.'

'Of course not. He's a good man and he deserves better than being treated so badly by my cousin. I'll finish my food and then I'll go to market. We'll need extra supplies, but at least Hobbs can pay his way.'

'You might like to visit one of the textile warehouses,' Mariah said calmly. 'Maybe we can get what we need at a much lower price by purchasing fabric bales. Then we can work out the cost of each garment more exactly.'

'Of course. You're right. I am getting carried away with the designs and how to sell them, but we need to make a profit, too. I'll do just that, Mariah. What would I do without you?'

Amelia finished her breakfast and left Mariah preparing vegetables for soup, which they would have at midday. She went into the workshop first, and found everything running smoothly. Hobbs was in the office, checking through the ledgers. Nellie looked anxious but Amelia reassured her once again that Hobbs was there simply to help and her job was not in jeopardy.

The clatter of the sewing machines was almost deafening and Amelia was glad to escape to the street with her shopping basket over her arm. Not that it was particularly quiet in the docks area, but it was a different sort of noise. The hoots from the boats on the river and the distant thunder of barrels being rolled over the cobblestones mingled with the pounding of horses' hoofs and the rumble of the drays, delivering and collecting heavy goods. The shouts of the warehousemen and the dockers combined in a chorus of male voices that echoed off the high walls surrounding the docks. Dizzy with the sights, sounds and the smell of the river, she walked briskly to the market a few streets away, where she purchased the food on the list that Mariah had given her.

With her shopping accomplished, Amelia visited a couple of the large warehouses that sold textiles of all kinds, from heavy satins and rich velvets, to delicate silks and fresh cottons. She enquired as to the cost of each bale and committed them to memory. Even so, it was obvious that buying material in large quantities would be cheaper in the long run, and the same went for the purchase of trimmings. She could have spent a fortune in each place, but lack of funds prevented her from acting rashly. However, in her mind she knew exactly what she would do when the time came.

She made her way home with a feeling of excitement and anticipation. However, when she opened the front door, the sound of Mariah's raised voice and Percy's screams made her abandon her basket and run to the kitchen. The sight that met her eyes made her cry out in alarm.

Jasper Cook, the man who had beaten and bullied Mariah when she was his housekeeper, had Percy tucked under one arm while he held Mariah off with his free hand.

'Let him go,' Mariah screamed. 'Put my baby down.'

Percy's frightened cries made Amelia shiver with

rage. She ran at Cook and grabbed his sleeve.

'Put that child down, sir.'

Cook turned on her, his face purple with rage. 'Keep out of this. I've come to claim my son from his whore of a mother.'

'No,' Mariah cried in desperation. 'Please, give him back to me. He's my little boy.'

'He's my flesh and blood,' Cook countered, snarling. 'I'm taking him with me. You'll never see him again.'

Amelia clutched Cook's free arm. 'Please, put Percy down. You don't want the child. Give him back to his mother.'

Cook flung her away with a strong thrust that sent her toppling onto the floor.

Mariah's screams brought Hobbs hurrying into the kitchen. 'What's going on? Who is this person?'

'Get out of my way, old man.' Cook glared at Hobbs. 'I'm taking my son home where he belongs.'

'You can't take Mrs Simms's child from her,' Hobbs said calmly. 'Can't you see that the boy is terrified?'

'He'll learn to obey his father.' Cook lashed out at Mariah, catching her on the side of her face and toppling her to the ground. 'She's a whore and she isn't fit to raise a child.'

Amelia scrambled to her feet. 'You are a brute and a rapist. Mariah didn't stand a chance when you attacked her. Percy is the only good thing that came out of a terrible situation and you shan't take him from his mother.'

Cook headed towards the door, carrying a struggling, screaming Percy, but was stopped in the doorway by Todd, who barred his way.

'Stop him, please,' Mariah sobbed as Amelia helped

her to stand.

'That brute is stealing Mariah's baby,' Amelia added angrily. 'Don't let him take Percy.'

Todd caught Cook a blow on the chin that sent him staggering into the hall. Losing his balance, he dropped Percy, but Amelia caught the child before he fell to the ground.

Mariah rushed forward to take Percy in her arms.

Bruised and furious, Amelia faced up to Cook. 'Get out of my house and don't ever show your face here again or I'll have you arrested.'

Cook wiped a trickle of blood from his chin. 'That child belongs to me. I'll have him one way or the other.' He stomped out of the house, Hobbs holding the door open for him.

'Your forehead is bleeding.' Todd produced a handkerchief and stanched the blood from a cut just above Amelia's right eye.

'Are you all right, miss?' Hobbs asked anxiously.

'Yes, I'm fine, thanks to you and Todd.' Amelia clutched Todd's hanky to her head. 'Are you all right, Mariah? Cook lashed out at you.'

'I don't care. He didn't get Percy.' Mariah subsided onto a chair cuddling him to her bosom. 'Thank you, Todd, and you, too, Mr Hobbs. Jasper Cook would have taken my boy, although I can't think why. He never wanted him when I was forced to live in that man's house.'

'He's gone now, Mariah,' Amelia said gently. 'If he comes here again we'll be prepared. He'll never take Percy from you.'

'Let me look at your cheek, Mariah.' Todd went over to her. 'It needs a dressing, but I don't think you require stitches.'

'I keep Pa's medical bag for such emergencies,' Amelia said hastily. 'I'll fetch it for you.' She hurried to the dining room, where she kept the well-worn leather bag in a cupboard. She was about to take it to the kitchen when Caleb appeared in the doorway.

'I don't know what's been going on here, but I need to speak to you urgently,' he said in a low voice.

'Todd needs this. Can't it wait until later, Caleb?'

'I've just come from Albemarle Street. I came to warn you, Amelia. Mr Norris intends to challenge your grandfather's will on the grounds that he was of unsound mind when the will was altered in your favour.'

'Cousin Daniel told you all this?'

'Yes, he did.'

'Are you telling me that you broached the subject of Grandpapa's will in the short time you've been back in his favour?'

'No, as a matter of fact it was your cousin who brought it up. He seems to hate your father, although he didn't say as much. It is his premise that Mr Norris altered his will while under the influence of laudanum, administered by your papa.'

'That's a lie,' Amelia said angrily. 'Pa would never do such a thing. Neither of us even knew about the mourning warehouse.'

'Then the onus is on you to prove it,' Caleb said seriously. 'I can do no more, Amelia. I would just say that fighting the challenge to Mr Norris's will would be very costly, and under the circumstances I fear the court might come down on your cousin's side.'

Amelia pushed past him. 'I can't think about that now. I must take this to Todd.' She took the medical bag to the kitchen where Todd had just bathed the cut on Mariah's cheek. Percy had quietened down but Mariah was trembling visibly.

'I'll go back to the workroom. They'll be wondering what has happened.' Hobbs nodded to Amelia as he walked past her. 'Don't worry, Miss Amelia. I'll make sure that fellow doesn't gain entrance to this premises again.'

'Thank you, Hobbs.' Amelia passed the bag to Todd. 'Is the cut deep?'

Todd shook his head. 'No. Luckily for Mariah he only caught her a glancing blow. The bleeding made it look worse.' He opened the bag and took out a piece of lint and a roll of bandages. 'I'm afraid you'll have a black eye, Mariah. But you shouldn't have a scar.'

Mariah pulled a face and winced. 'He used to beat me regularly, so this is nothing. I don't care about anything just so long as he doesn't get his hands on Percy.'

Amelia filled the kettle. 'I'll make us all a nice hot cup of tea. We won't let Cook near Percy again, so don't worry, Mariah.'

'That man couldn't wait to get rid of us. I don't understand why he's suddenly changed his mind.'

Todd rose to his feet. 'Try not to dwell on it, Mariah. Percy is safe now and we'll keep it that way.'

'I should get back to Albemarle Street.' Caleb stood in the doorway, frowning. 'It seems odd that this happened on the same day that Mr Norris announced his intention to challenge the will.'

Amelia turned her head to give him a searching look. 'What do you mean by that?'

'Nothing. I was just surmising. I must go now or I will lose my position with Mr Norris before I've even begun.'

Amelia followed him to the front door. 'Just a moment, Caleb. Were you hinting that my cousin might have some connection to Jasper Cook?'

'It doesn't seem possible and perhaps it's a coincidence, but Frank Chance might have the answer. He and I started working for Nathaniel Norris at about the same time. That's how I came to know him.'

'Do you mean Frank Chance who works for Mr Harrison?'

'Yes, I only know one fellow by that name.' Caleb gave her a wry smile. 'I'm not laughing at you, Amelia. I know how much all this means to you, including the garments you left in Mr Harrison's personal care.'

'And Mr Harrison is paying you to spy on my cousin. Is Frank Chance spying on me?'

'I wouldn't put it quite like that, but there is an obvious connection. I dare say he has made some enquiries as to your probity and that of the people who work with you.'

'Are you telling me that Frank Chance might have contacted Mariah's former employer to find out if she is honest and trustworthy?'

'It's possible, that's all I'm saying. I am on your side, believe me, Amelia.'

Amelia frowned. 'I don't know who to trust, and I certainly didn't expect Mr Harrison to go into my background and Mariah's, too. Jasper Cook obviously thinks there is money to be made out of all this.'

'It's just a conjecture on my part, so please don't worry. I'll speak to Frank at the first possible opportunity. I'd better go now but I'll let you know if I find out anything definite. In the meantime, keep that man Cook out of your house.'

'He'll never be allowed near Mariah or her children.

But I'm confused — are you definitely moving back to Albemarle Street?'

'I think it's the right thing to do.'

'So you don't need your room. I could rent it out to someone else.'

'Keep it for me for now. I know you don't approve of my methods, but I am on your side. I want you to believe that.'

'We hardly know each other. Why would you risk everything to help people who are not related to you in any way?'

'I respected your grandfather. I intend to make sure his wishes were carried out and I think you and your father deserve better. Mr Daniel Norris is not a man I could ever like and respect in the same way, but he pays well.' Caleb opened the front door and stepped out onto the pavement. 'Don't forget to keep this door locked at all times.'

Amelia closed the door and automatically turned the key in the lock. Somehow she believed Caleb, or perhaps she simply needed to trust someone. She was shocked to think that Frank Chance might have been making enquiries about them, and what was even more worrying was the fact that it had brought Jasper Cook into their lives once again.

Amelia returned to the kitchen where Mariah was cuddling Percy, who had fallen asleep in her arms, and Todd was in the process of making the tea.

'Sit down, Amelia,' Todd said firmly. 'I'm making tea for you for a change. You've had quite a morning.'

'That's putting it mildly.' Amelia shot a worried glance in Mariah's direction. 'Are you all right?'

Mariah nodded with an attempt at a smile, but the bandage only allowed her a lop-sided grin. 'I've suffered worse, as I said. But it scares me to think that Jasper wants to take Percy from me. He refused to believe that Percy was his, so why has he suddenly changed his mind?'

'The main thing is to keep him away from you.' Todd filled three cups with tea and placed one within Mariah's reach, passing another to Amelia. 'It was pure luck that I happened to arrive here at the right moment. I don't think Mr Hobbs could have handled Cook on his own.'

Amelia sipped her tea. 'I think Nellie and the other women might have come to his aid. They wouldn't have shown any mercy to a man like Cook. But there's even worse news.'

Mariah stood up and placed Percy in his cot, although he would soon be too big for it. 'What could be worse?'

'Caleb has already discovered that my cousin is going to challenge the will. He's planning to say that my father drugged Grandpapa with laudanum and forced him to leave the business and this house to us. It's totally untrue, of course, but Caleb said the legal costs of fighting the case would be enormous.'

'Oh, my goodness!' Mariah clapped her hand to her mouth. 'What will we do? We have nowhere else to go.'

'I don't know, but I'll think of something.' Amelia turned to Todd with a sympathetic smile. 'I'm sorry, Todd. Just as you were settling in here, too. We might all be looking for alternative accommodation.'

'And another way to support ourselves,' Mariah added glumly. 'If we lose the mourning warehouse we will end up in the workhouse.'

'That will never happen,' Amelia said firmly. 'We

will stand up to them all, Mariah, and we will triumph. I promise you that.'

* * *

Despite her brave words Amelia was not entirely convinced that she could win against rich and powerful men like her cousin. Even Sydney Harrison, who had seemed such a benign person, willing to take a chance on an unknown designer and manufacturer of high fashion, now seemed a lesser man. If it were true that Frank Chance, acting on his behalf, had stirred up trouble for Mariah, it might be time to think again. Perhaps Harrison's was not the best place to sell the garments that they had made with such hope and enthusiasm. She needed to claim them back without delay.

Amelia left Mariah soothing her nerves by making a cake for Betsy's birthday, with Percy having apparently forgotten his fright as he played happily on the floor with a pile of bricks that Todd had bought for him. Amelia put on her mantle, bonnet and gloves and was about to leave when she almost bumped into Todd in the entrance hall.

'Where are you off to?' Todd asked casually. 'Would you like some company? I've got the rest of the day free.'

'As a matter of fact I'm going to Oxford Street. I intend to take my creations away from Harrison's.'

'Why would you do that? I thought they were going to promote them for you.'

'Because of something Caleb told me. He thinks that Mr Harrison told Frank Chance, his assistant, to check up on me and Mariah, too. It seems the only possible explanation for Jasper Cook coming here looking for Percy. He thinks there is money to be made out of us, but he couldn't be more mistaken.'

'It doesn't seem unreasonable to check on the people they are dealing with,' Todd said evenly. 'You would probably do the same in similar circumstances.'

'I agree with you, but it's the way it was done, Todd. Mr Harrison could have asked me to give him references, but instead he sent his assistant to make enquiries about Mariah and myself. I find that unforgivable, especially as Frank Chance worked for my grandfather when he was younger. That's how Caleb came to know him.'

'If it's true then I agree, it's unforgivable.'

'You mean that Caleb could be lying?'

'He hasn't exactly been straight with you, has he?'

'No, but I don't want to risk it, Todd. Mr Harrison hasn't paid me for the gowns. For all I know, they've been sold and he doesn't intend to give me what I'm owed.'

Todd frowned. 'Caleb has put these ideas into your head.'

'Yes, he has, but now I don't want Harrison's to have my gowns. I've lost faith in them and I intend to set up on my own. It won't be easy and it will probably take longer, but I know that Mariah and I can do it on our own.'

'I believe you.' Todd took his overcoat from the hall-stand and shrugged it on, adding his hat and gloves. 'I'm coming with you.'

* * *

An hour later, Amelia and Todd were sitting in the outer office, waiting to speak to Frank Chance. The officious and somewhat forbidding secretary had told them that they needed to make an appointment, but Amelia was not in the mood to be put off and, backed by Todd, she had insisted on seeing Mr Chance even if she had to sit in the office for the rest of the day.

Eventually the door opened and Frank Chance entered, smiling blandly and extending his hand to Amelia. He eyed Todd curiously.

'I haven't had the pleasure, sir.'

Amelia stepped in between them. 'This is my good friend, Dr Todd Taylor. He has come to assist me.'

Frank raised an eyebrow. 'I'm sorry. I don't understand.'

'I've decided to take back the garments I left here, Mr Chance. They have not been sold.'

'It's early days, Miss Sutton. Surely you don't want to lose the opportunity of dealing with a prestigious store like Harrison's?'

'My decision is final, Mr Chance. Would you be kind enough to have my creations brought to me?'

Frank's smile faded. 'I think you are making a grave mistake.'

'Maybe, but we'll see.'

'Are you absolutely certain you wish to do this?'

Todd cleared his throat. 'That is what Miss Sutton said, sir. Perhaps you would be kind enough to oblige?'

Frank glanced anxiously at the formidable secretary. 'Send someone to collect the gowns that Miss Sutton left with us, if you please, Miss Dodgson.'

'Yes, Mr Chance.' With a scornful curl of her lip, Miss Dodgson rose from her desk and let herself out of the office.

'I hope you won't regret this, Miss Sutton,' Frank

said icily.

Amelia faced him with a stony stare. 'Tell me, Mr Chance, did you make enquiries about Mrs Simms to her former employer?'

Frank looked from one to the other, his lips moving silently. 'Er, yes. Well, it's purely routine these days, Miss Sutton. Especially where trust between associates is paramount.'

'I don't think that going behind an associate's back is synonymous with trust,' Todd said coldly. 'You created a situation that could have had disastrous effects on an innocent woman and her child.'

'For that I apologise. I was only carrying out Mr Harrison's instructions.'

'But you worked for my grandfather, Nathaniel Norris,' Amelia said slowly. 'You know my family well enough, Mr Chance. And I would never employ anybody I suspected of being dishonest.'

Frank glanced anxiously over his shoulder. 'I see your garments are here. I suggest you take them and leave, Miss Sutton. It seems that our association is at an end.' He backed towards the door, eyeing Todd nervously before letting himself into the fashion department.

Amelia laid her hand on Todd's arm. 'Thank you for coming with me. I could have handled Frank Chance, but I think your presence made him much more amenable.'

Todd grinned. 'I learned how to handle myself on the streets of London. It's all about having confidence in oneself and making the other fellow think they don't stand a chance if it came to fisticuffs. No pun intended,' he added, smiling.

Amelia giggled. 'Could you teach me self-defence?'

'You could disarm anyone with your smile, Amelia. Chance would have given up in the end, even if I hadn't been here.'

The door opened before Amelia had time to reply and a young shop assistant staggered in, half-concealed by an armful of silks and satins. Amelia sighed with relief. She would take the garments home and she and Mariah would start again from the beginning.

The gowns were stored in Caleb's room as a temporary measure, but as days turned into weeks it seemed that he was a permanent fixture in Albemarle Street.

Having left much of the day-to-day running of the workroom in Hobbs's capable hands, Amelia concentrated on her designs, but money was always a problem and she could not afford to purchase materials she needed in order to turn her sketches into garments. It was frustrating but there seemed to be no answer to the problem. Betsy, at ten years old, considered herself to be a grown-up. She was keen to learn how to use a sewing machine but Amelia thought she was too young to be exposed to the colourful language and chit-chat in the workroom. Mariah disagreed and, somewhat reluctantly, Amelia asked Nellie to take Betsy under her wing. Surprisingly, Nellie was eager to train the child. Having daughters of her own, and grandchildren, Nellie was in favour of teaching girls how to support themselves. Betsy started in the sewing room, picking up stray threads and doing odd jobs. She was a willing worker and a great favourite with the women.

There had been no sign of Jasper Cook returning and no word from Caleb concerning the challenge to Nathaniel Norris's will. The showers of April gave way to the promise of summer in May. Everything was running smoothly, but Amelia was restless. They were managing well enough with the money that her father was earning, combined with Todd's rent and the small profit from the mourning warehouse. However, the threat of losing everything to Daniel Norris was ever present in Amelia's mind, and she knew that Mariah was constantly on the alert for another visit from Percy's father. A loud knock on the front door or the sound of male voices, other than those of Harold or Todd, caused Mariah to tremble uncontrollably. She hardly allowed Percy out of her sight and her nervousness was being transmitted to him. He was now fully mobile and into everything, making it difficult to keep an eye on him. He was adventurous and apparently fearless. If a door was left ajar Percy would find a way to get to the other side and it seemed that his main ambition was either to get out onto the street, or to climb the stairs to the top floor.

One morning at the beginning of June, Amelia had just managed to catch Percy before he was more than halfway up the first flight of stairs, when someone knocked on the front door. With a protesting Percy tucked under her arm, she hurried to open the door, and was surprised to see a liveried footman standing on the step.

'Is this the domicile of Miss Amelia Sutton?'

Amelia glanced over his shoulder to see a well-dressed lady, seated in an open landau. The matched pair of bays were snorting and restless.

'Yes, I am she.'

'Lady Galton wishes to speak to you.'

'Will she come inside? As you can see, I have my hands full at the moment.'

'Please approach the carriage. Leave the child inside.'

Amelia was about to refuse but Mariah appeared at her side, slightly breathless. 'I'll take him.' She took Percy in her arms and backed away.

Amelia stepped outside and crossed the pavement to stand beside the elegant carriage. 'You wanted to speak to me, my lady?'

'I saw some of your creations at Harrison's department store. However, I understand you no longer supply your work to them.'

'That's correct.'

'Has someone purchased the garments?'

Amelia was suddenly suspicious. Although the lady in question was undoubtedly wealthy and lovely to look at, she could not help wondering if this was a trap set up either by Frank Chance or Daniel Norris.

'Might I ask what is your interest in my creations, ma'am?'

'You have a very strange attitude for someone wishing to sell their work.'

'I have experienced some antagonism towards me because I am a woman attempting to enter a man's world.'

A slow smile lit Lady Galton's grey eyes and she beckoned to her footman, who hurried forward to open the carriage door and let down the steps. He proffered his gloved hand to help her alight.

'I will come inside.' Lady Galton glided past Amelia, holding her skirt just high enough to keep it from sweeping the pavement.

Amelia followed her into the house. 'Perhaps you would like to wait in the parlour, Lady Galton?'

'I will, and you will kindly fetch the garments you

wish to sell.'

Amelia held the door open and waited until Lady Galton had settled herself before going upstairs. She returned to the parlour and laid her creations on a chair. 'Which one was it that interested you, ma'am?'

'Hold them up against you. I can't remember exactly.'

Amelia did as she asked and paraded the gowns round the small parlour, one at a time. The last garment was a burgundy velvet dinner gown with a décolleté neckline and the overskirt drawn back into a low bustle. It had taken all Mariah's skill as a pattern maker to cut the cloth and Amelia had stitched some of it by hand, although she used one of the machines in the workroom for the long seams. It was the piece of which she was most proud.

'I will take this one with me,' Lady Galton said firmly.

'Don't you want to try it on, my lady?'

'I will do that in the privacy of my own dressing room with my maid to assist me. If it doesn't suit I will have it returned to you. However, if I like it I will invite you to design more gowns, on the understanding that they are for me only, and I will never see anyone in something similar.'

'It would be my pleasure, ma'am.'

'I will take it with me now. Please wrap it in something so that the city dust and dirt won't ruin it.' Lady Galton rose from her seat.

'I'll bring it out to your carriage, my lady.'

Amelia saw Lady Galton out of the house before rushing to the kitchen to find Mariah. 'A wealthy titled lady is going to buy this gown, if it fits to her satisfaction.'

'How much is she prepared to pay?'

Amelia came to a sudden halt. 'She asked me to wrap it for her. We didn't discuss the price.'

'I don't know if that's a good thing or a terrible mistake.' Mariah took a roll of butter muslin from the cupboard. 'You wrap and I'll find the scissors. Let's hope she really loves the gown. It was the last one we made, but the best, in my opinion.'

Amelia took the wrapped gown out to the carriage and handed it to the footman.

'Should I decide to keep the gown, my amanuensis will settle with you, Miss Sutton. She will contact you.' Lady Galton signalled to the coachman. 'Drive on.'

Amelia watched the smart equipage until it was out of sight, but a hansom cab drew up just as she was about to enter the house. Caleb leaped to the ground.

'Wait here for me, cabby.' He crossed the pavement in two strides. 'I'm afraid I have bad news for you, Amelia. Mr Norris's solicitor has lodged a caveat on the probate. He is contesting your late grandfather's will, and I believe he has every chance of succeeding.'

13

Caleb followed Amelia into the kitchen where she sank down onto the nearest chair.

'What's the matter?' Mariah demanded. 'Has he said something to upset you?'

'I have,' Caleb said evenly. 'But I was only passing on the news that Mr Norris is definitely contesting his uncle's will.'

'You said that he is sure to win.' Amelia eyed him suspiciously. 'What aren't you telling us, Caleb?'

He pulled up a chair and sat next to her. 'I'm afraid Frank Chance has been making mischief again. He told your cousin about Mariah's involvement with Jasper Cook, and Mr Norris paid a visit to Cook at his home in Bow Street.'

Mariah stared at him in horror. 'I've never met this fellow. Why would he make trouble for me?'

'I heard that Mr Harrison reprimanded Frank for letting Cook know your whereabouts, Mariah. It seems that Frank Chance decided to take his spite out on you by going straight to Mr Norris, who has been searching for evidence to discredit both Amelia and yourself.'

'What lies did Cook tell him about me?' Mariah picked up Percy and thrust him into Betsy's arms. 'Take your brother into the parlour, there's a good girl.'

'I always get sent out when something interesting is happening,' Betsy said crossly.

'Less of your cheek, my girl.' Mariah stood, arms akimbo, and one look at her mother's angry expression convinced Betsy to do as she was told. She ran from the room carrying a protesting Percy.

'That was a bit harsh,' Amelia said wearily. 'She'll have to know what's happening sooner or later.'

'I don't want her to hear all the sordid details again. Jasper Cook is determined to ruin my life, but he won't take my child away from me.'

Amelia reached out to clutch Mariah's hand. 'Don't fret, Mariah. I won't allow him to do any such thing.'

Caleb shook his head. 'Cook would probably win if it came to court, Mariah. He's well situated, with a house of his own. If he put his mind to it, he could convince a magistrate that he was more suitable to raise the boy than you are.'

'He's only well off because he deals in stolen goods. He's just lucky he's never been caught.'

'Can you prove it?' Amelia asked eagerly. 'If you can, he might be sent to prison.'

'It would be my word against his,' Mariah said sadly. 'He's managed to evade the law for years. I don't think we've seen the last of Cook.'

'Hobbs is keeping an eye open,' Amelia said firmly. 'He won't let him into the workroom or the house.'

Caleb shook his head. 'Hobbs is an old man. He couldn't stand up to someone like Cook.'

'This is all very well, Caleb.' Amelia eyed him suspiciously. 'But how do we know that you are telling the truth? You are working for my cousin. You could be trying to scare me into giving way to his demands without the necessity of going to court.'

'Yes, I could, but you'll just have to trust me. I'm not a bad person, Amelia. After all, I worked for your grandfather for ten years. Doesn't that tell you something?'

'I suppose so,' Amelia said warily. She was still not sure whether Caleb was being entirely honest, and now she had more to lose. If her cousin decided to take over the mourning warehouse or, even worse, to sell it on to a competitor, she would lose her home as well as her business. She met Caleb's bland gaze with a questioning look. 'What do you suggest we do?'

'I think you should find somewhere else to live, in the first place.'

Mariah sniffed and rolled her eyes. 'That would not be easy, as you well know, sir.'

'Of course,' Caleb said smoothly. 'But what alternative have you got? Anyway, Dr Sutton is employed at the hospital and so is Todd Taylor. They should support you ladies, not the other way around.'

'My pa does his best and Todd pays his rent regularly. We all do what we can.' Amelia rose to her feet. 'I don't think there's much point in continuing this conversation, Caleb. Go back to Albemarle Street and do whatever it is you are doing for my cousin. If the court decides in his favour, I am sure he will contact me himself.'

'You really don't believe me, do you?' Caleb stood up, facing her with a straight look. 'Why don't you trust me?'

'For one thing, you change sides too easily. And for another, I hardly know you.' Amelia went to open the kitchen door. 'For all I know it could have been you who told Frank Chance about Jasper Cook.'

'I'm not going to let that person harm me further.' Mariah thumped her fist on the pine table top. 'Jasper is never going to take my son from me.'

Caleb shook his head. 'I'm sorry you don't take what I've said seriously. I really am on your side.' He left the room and Amelia closed the door with unnecessary force.

'I wish I knew whether he was lying or not,' she said, sighing.

'It's just possible that what he said was true. What will we do now?'

'We'll be extra careful.' Amelia leaned against the closed door. 'We must not panic, Mariah.'

'Perhaps Lady Galton will order more gowns. That would be the making of us.'

Amelia nodded. 'I hope so. If she will just purchase the gown she took home with her, and if she were to wear it to one of her social functions, we might get orders from her friends and acquaintances. We mustn't give up hope, Mariah. It's all we have at the moment.'

* * *

That evening after supper, Mariah took the children to her room and Amelia sat alone in the parlour, her sketchbook on the table in front of her, but somehow the ideas would not come. She had been anxious all day and she could not help wondering whether she had judged Caleb too hastily. He had accepted his old position with a view to keeping an eye on Daniel Norris's actions, but he seemed to be a little too comfortable with the arrangement. She could not help wondering if it was all part of a plan to scare her into giving up the mourning warehouse, which he had worked out with her cousin.

Amelia looked up as the door opened and Todd

strolled into the room.

'Am I disturbing you, Emmie?'

'Ma used to call me that,' Amelia said, smiling.

'I'm sorry. It slipped out. I didn't mean to offend you.'

'I'm not offended.' Amelia smiled at the sound of her baby name being used by someone she had grown to like very much. 'I like being called Emmie. It reminds me of Ma, and I have many happy memories of her. Come and sit with me, Todd.'

'I thought you looked a little down at supper.'

'It was something Caleb told us. I didn't want to talk about it in front of Mariah. She was very upset after it happened.'

'What was it that disturbed her so much?'

'We knew that Frank Chance had been spying on us, which is how Jasper Cook found out where Mariah and the children were living. Anyway, Chance was in trouble with Mr Harrison and he went straight to Cousin Daniel, who visited Cook to find out anything he could to discredit Mariah and me.'

'I thought that Mariah was his cook and he sacked her. Why would he come looking for her?'

'Cook forced himself on Mariah when she was living in his house and Percy is his son, which he denied when he threw her out. However, he seems to have changed his mind. Perhaps he sees money in the relationship now, due to our connection with my cousin.'

Todd frowned as he took a seat opposite her. 'No wonder Mariah is shut in her room with Betsy and the young one. I could tell that something was wrong the moment I walked into the house.'

'Caleb also confirmed that Cousin Daniel is definitely contesting the will, so we might all have to find somewhere else to live.'

'I don't know how that man sleeps at night.' Todd leaned forward to take her hand in his. 'What can I do to help?'

'There's nothing anyone can do for us. I'm not even sure about Caleb,' Amelia said wearily. 'I don't know if I can trust him now he's changed sides.'

'Have you talked this over with your father?'

'I've hardly seen Pa since he started back at the hospital. His duties seem to take up so much of his time, and when he comes home he just eats his supper and goes straight to bed. I don't like to worry him.'

'It's not for me to say, but it doesn't seem as though your father takes his family responsibilities very seriously. I know you love him dearly,' Todd added hastily, 'but I think he leaves too much to you.'

'It's the way it's always been, Todd. Pa is dedicated to his work and I respect that.'

'Maybe things aren't as bad as they seem. You need to enjoy yourself occasionally, Emmie.' Todd glanced at the small brass clock on the mantelshelf that Amelia had rescued once again from Old Scoggins, the pawnbroker. 'It's still early enough to catch a show. Would you like to go to Wilton's Music Hall?'

Amelia stared at him in astonishment. 'I've never been to a music hall. I'm not sure that Pa approves of such entertainments. Anyway, I need to think things through. This is serious, Todd.'

'All the more reason for you to do something to take your mind off things. We have an excellent theatre in Rockwood. I used to go there whenever my finances allowed, and it really helped to cheer me up if I felt low.'

Amelia smiled. 'I hadn't put you down as such a

romantic, Todd.'

'I have hidden depths. But seriously, I think you should judge the entertainment for yourself. Come on, it's a fine evening and it's not very far to walk from here. What do you say?'

Amelia hesitated. She had grown so used to staying at home in the evenings in order to take messages from desperate patients when her father was out on a call. Even to consider going out to something as indecorous as a place where ribald songs were sung and scantily clad women danced, was quite shocking and yet exciting.

Todd stood up and pulled her to her feet. 'Come with me, please.'

'I think it would be all right,' Amelia said doubtfully.

'I wouldn't take you anywhere you might come to harm. I think you'll enjoy yourself. I'll eat my hat if you don't.'

Amelia laughed. There was something irresistible in Todd's smile. 'Now that I would like to see.'

'Come on then. We'd best hurry or we'll miss the first half of the show.'

* * *

Wearing her best bonnet trimmed with cream roses, and a lace shawl, Amelia set off with Todd, feeling like a child going to her first party. It was a fine evening, balmy but cool enough for the stench of the river mud and the exotic smells from the warehouses and manufactories to be wafted away on a gentle breeze. Todd took her hand and tucked it into the crook of his arm. They walked briskly to the theatre in Graces

Alley where Todd bought tickets and they were shown into the auditorium. The audience was rowdy and noisy, but appreciative of each act and Amelia found herself joining in the clapping and stamping shows of enjoyment. She leaned against Todd, listening emotionally to heart-rending ballads sung by a beautiful young woman wearing a garland of silk roses. There were more songs from a powerful baritone and a tenor who sang 'Champagne Charlie', which brought roars of applause and cries of 'Encore'. Amelia could hardly believe it was all over when the entertainers took their bows before leaving the stage.

'Well, did you enjoy your first visit to the music hall?' Todd asked as they emerged into Graces Alley.

'I loved it,' Amelia said breathlessly. 'It was so entertaining.'

Todd placed a protective arm around her shoulders as they were jostled by the crowd emerging from the theatre, and she did not protest. She felt safe with Todd and was happy to walk home arm in arm, despite the fact that her father would have considered it totally inappropriate behaviour. However, Pa was still at the hospital and the early summer evening had darkened into night with stars sparkling in the sky above them. They strolled home at a leisurely pace.

Amelia came back to earth with a sudden jolt when they walked into the kitchen to find Mariah seated at the table with a look of disapproval on her face.

'Do you know what time this is?' she demanded angrily. 'Where have you been and why didn't you tell me you were going out? I've been worried sick.'

Amelia exchanged rueful glances with Todd, but she did not let go of his hand. She felt a warm pressure as he squeezed her fingers.

'I'm sorry, Mariah,' Todd said earnestly. 'It was my fault entirely. I took Emmie to Wilton's Music Hall. It was a sudden decision and we had to hurry or we would have missed the start of the show.'

'You could have left a note,' Mariah said grudgingly. 'I had no idea where Amelia was. I most certainly don't worry about you, Todd Taylor.'

Amelia stepped forward, releasing Todd's hand as she did so. 'I am truly sorry I didn't tell you, Mariah. As Todd said, it was a spur-of-the-moment decision. I'd never been to a music hall and it was such a wonderful show. I've never enjoyed anything as much.'

Mariah's angry expression softened and she rose to her feet. 'Sit down, both of you. I'll make some cocoa.'

'Thank you,' Todd said hastily. 'That's very kind of you. I am so sorry you were anxious. It won't happen again, I promise you.'

'Yes, I'm sorry, too,' Amelia added. 'It was thoughtless, but I did have a wonderful evening, Mariah. After such a difficult day it was so good to be able to forget everything and simply enjoy myself.'

'Let's forget about it now.' Mariah poured milk from an earthenware jug into a saucepan and placed it on the hob. She busied herself making the cocoa while Amelia and Todd sat at the table as obediently as two children who had been thoroughly scolded for misbehaviour.

'You know if we go to Wilton's again it would be good if you could come with us, Mariah,' Todd said seriously. 'You've gone through a terrible time yourself.'

'That's such a nice thought,' Amelia said eagerly. 'We could go on a night when Pa is here to make sure the children are safe. Not that anything untoward is likely to happen to them.'

'We don't know if we'll be living here for much longer.' Mariah poured hot milk into the jug in which she had mixed cocoa and sugar with a little cold water. She stirred it vigorously. 'We can't take anything for granted now that Jasper is involved. He's a mean man and he won't rest until he gets what he wants. I should know.'

'We have to keep our spirits up. We can't allow anyone to beat us down.' Amelia looked to Todd for support and he nodded.

'Of course, and I'll do anything I can to help.'

Mariah poured the cocoa into cups and passed them round. 'I know you will, Todd. I didn't mean to snap at you both, but I can't help worrying.'

Amelia jumped to her feet and gave her a hug. 'We are in this together, Mariah. Whatever happens we won't let Cook take Percy, even if we have to run away and live in a field.'

This brought a reluctant smile from Mariah as she held the brimming cup of cocoa away from her. 'Be careful, Amelia. You'll spill cocoa all over me.'

'I'm sorry.' Amelia resumed her seat and picked up her cup. She sipped and smiled. 'You make the best cocoa in the world, Mariah.'

'I second that,' Todd added, grinning. 'And you're the best cook in London.'

'Flattery will get you nowhere.' Despite her words, Mariah was smiling, but as she was about to sit down she seemed to change her mind and she walked over to the dresser. She picked up a folded sheet of expensive-looking notepaper sealed with red wax. 'I almost forgot. This was delivered earlier. It must have come soon after you left.' She laid the document on the table in front of Amelia, who picked it up nervously.

'Oh dear. It looks official. Surely it's too soon for a court to have made a decision. I don't think I can open it.' She handed it back to Mariah. 'You do it, please. Break the seal and tell me the worst.'

Todd slipped his arm around her waist, taking care to keep the action away from Mariah's eagle eye, but she was staring at the letter, her expression unreadable.

'What does it say?' Amelia demanded. 'Don't keep us in suspense.'

Mariah passed the letter to her with a wide smile. 'It's not a demand to vacate this property. It's addressed to you.'

Amelia's hand shook as she took the piece of paper and spread it out on the table in front of her. 'Oh my goodness! It's from Lady Galton. She wants to purchase the evening gown that she took home with her, and she wants to order more garments. I'm to go to her house tomorrow at midday and take my portfolio of sketches with me.'

'Good news at last.' Todd raised his cup. 'Here's a toast to your new business. Congratulations.'

* * *

Lady Galton's residence in Dover Street boasted an impressive Georgian façade, as did the other equally fashionable houses in the terrace. Amelia had been brimming with confidence in the hackney carriage, but she was suddenly stricken with nerves. It was one thing to make a few gowns with the hope of selling them in a department store, but quite another to make garments for someone who possessed such obvious wealth and standing. Betsy accompanied her as Mariah refused to leave Percy, even though Harold had risen early and intended to spend the whole day at home. Mariah's fears that Jasper would descend upon them unexpectedly and snatch her precious little boy were based on her years of working for the bully.

Betsy was only too pleased to stand in for her mother. She was dressed in her best clothes and bursting with importance as they alighted from the cab with a selection of Amelia's creations carefully wrapped in butter muslin.

Amelia paid the cabby and crossed the pavement, but she stopped on the bottom step, wondering whether she ought to use the tradesmen's entrance. She took a deep breath and climbed the steps to knock on the front door. Confidence was the answer, she told herself firmly, but for a moment her self-control faltered when the butler opened the door and looked at her down his nose.

'I have an appointment with Lady Galton,' Amelia said firmly. 'Please inform her that Miss Sutton has arrived.'

There was a slight pause and Amelia held her breath. She was neither a servant nor an invited guest, and she was half expecting to be sent round to the tradesmen's entrance. However, her confident attitude seemed to have the desired effect as the butler stood aside to usher her and Betsy into the elegant entrance hall. After a brief wait, they were shown into a parlour decorated in Chinoiserie style with hand-painted wallpaper depicting colourful exotic birds and flowers. Betsy gazed round open-mouthed, which made Amelia smile.

'It's so beautiful,' Betsy said in awe. 'Lady Galton must be very rich.'

'It certainly seems so.' Amelia smiled at Betsy's reaction. 'This is all very fine.'

'I am glad you think so,' Lady Galton's crisp tone made both Amelia and Betsy turn with a start.

'Good morning, my lady.' Amelia curtseyed and Betsy was quick to copy her.

'Never mind the formalities, Miss Sutton. I have another appointment shortly so perhaps we can get down to business. Have you brought your portfolio?'

'Yes, my lady.'

'Then we will go through the sketches together.' Lady Galton turned her attention to Betsy. 'You may unwrap the samples you have brought to show me. Hold them up so that I can see them.'

Betsy shot an anxious glance at Amelia, who nodded in assent. Lady Galton took a seat on a small sofa, and sat there without inviting Amelia to join her as she went through the portfolio of designs without comment. Amelia shifted from one foot to the other as she waited for some reaction, whether good or bad. Lady Galton's expression was unreadable.

'Interesting,' she said as she closed the portfolio. 'Now let me see the actual garments.'

Betsy passed the gowns to Amelia one at a time and she held them up against her. Lady Galton examined each one, fingering the material and checking the seams. By the time she had looked at the last creation Amelia was beginning to think their journey had been a waste of time. She fully expected her wealthy client to send them away without any further ado.

Lady Galton rose to her feet. 'You may leave the gowns here. I will try them on to see if they fit and if

I think they suit me.'

Amelia stared at her in disbelief. 'You want them all?'

'Did I not just say that? Yes, I quite like them, but I want you to design my autumn and winter outfits. If I think they are good enough I will ask you to make them for me. Do you think you can do that?'

'Of course, my lady. I would be delighted to design garments especially for you.'

'I would want your guarantee that the garments would be exclusive. I don't want to see anyone else wearing anything similar.'

'There is no way I can prevent my designs being copied by others, but I can guarantee that I will never replicate anything I make for you.'

'I suppose that is all anyone can do. Leave those garments.'

Amelia cleared her throat nervously. 'There is the question of remuneration, my lady.'

'I never discuss financial matters. Send a note of your charges to my husband, Sir Oswald.' Lady Galton gave a gentle tug at an embroidered bell pull and within seconds a servant appeared.

'Miss Sutton is just leaving, Flanders.' Lady Galton swept out of the room.

* * *

Amelia could hardly wait to give Mariah the good news, but Betsy was equally excited and she reached the kitchen first.

'Ma, Ma, you'll never guess what happened at Lady Galton's big house. It was so grand and there were such beautiful things everywhere. I can't imagine ever being so rich.'

Mariah stopped kneading bread dough and wiped her hands on her apron. 'That does sound wonderful, love. What did her ladyship say?' Mariah looked to Amelia for an answer.

'She's taken all the garments,' Amelia said happily. 'She's going to try them on and she's asked me to design new outfits for the changing seasons.'

Mariah's expectant smile faded. 'But did she pay you for the gown she took last time?'

'Well, no. Not exactly. I mean I did ask her about payment, although it seemed a little impertinent. She said we were to send the bill to her husband, Sir Oswald.'

'You know what that means.' Mariah punched the dough as if to emphasise her point.

'I suppose he will send us a bank draft or a cheque.'

'People like that pay up when they feel like it. They live on credit and the tradesmen suffer for it. I've worked in big houses since I was Betsy's age and I know how they work.'

'But they are so wealthy, Mariah. You should see the mansion in Dover Street and the beautiful things they have. We only saw the magnificent entrance hall and one room, but it was all so fine, wasn't it, Betsy?'

'I'll say it was.' Betsy sighed. 'You never saw the like, Ma.'

'Probably not,' Mariah said, laughing. 'I spent all my time below stairs and it was hard work, which is what made me leave, when I was old enough, and I trained to become a pattern cutter.'

Amelia took off her bonnet and shawl. 'Let's hope that Sir Oswald pays up promptly. I need money to purchase material and trimmings for the garments I intend to design and make, with your help, of course, Mariah.'

'Could you add them on to the order for black bombazine and crepe for the mourning warehouse?'

'I suppose so. It is my business, isn't it? I can do as I please.' Amelia turned her head as the door opened and Caleb strode into the kitchen. 'How did you get into the house? I made sure I locked the front door.'

'I still have my key.' Caleb eyed Amelia warily. 'I think you should sit down. I'm afraid what I have to say is not good.'

Amelia clasped her hands tightly in front of her. 'Has my cousin succeeded in contesting the will?'

'The magistrate decided that your grandfather, Nathaniel Norris, was not of sound mind when he altered his will. It's his original testament that has been sent for probate, Amelia. I am so sorry, it's not the message I wanted to bring, but I'm afraid you've been given seven days' notice to leave the premises and hand over the keys to the workroom and the house.'

14

'He can't do that, can he?' Mariah gasped, clutching her hands to her bosom. 'Surely not.'

'I'm afraid he can,' Caleb said calmly. 'The law is on his side.'

Amelia faced him angrily. 'I think you'd better leave, Caleb. You're working for my cousin now, so don't pretend that you're trying to help me.'

'I'm just the messenger. I don't agree with what Mr Norris is doing,' Caleb protested.

Mariah fisted her hands and advanced on him purposefully. 'You heard what she said. Get out before I pitch into you. I've floored bigger men than you, Caleb Marsh.'

'You've had a shock.' Caleb held up his hands. 'I'm leaving, but I will be back, if only to collect the things I left here. I really didn't mean it to happen this way.'

'Get out.' Mariah took a swing at him but Caleb backed away.

'I am truly sorry, Amelia. But you're wrong about me. I spoke up for you.'

'You can't be on both sides at the same time,' Amelia said stiffly. 'I think you'd better go, Caleb.'

Mariah took a step towards him and Caleb made a hasty retreat, all the time protesting his innocence.

'What will we do now?' Betsy wailed. 'Not the workhouse, Ma?'

'No, little one. I'd as soon live under the railway arches as take you and Percy to the workhouse.'

Mariah wrapped her arms around Betsy, their tears mingling.

Amelia took a deep breath. 'My cousin is not going to beat us, Mariah,' she said firmly. 'We are just starting out in our own business. The main thing is to find alternative accommodation.'

'Where will we go?' Mariah's voice broke on a sob. 'It's been good here, or it was until Jasper found out where we were.'

'Then we'll live somewhere he cannot trace us. London is a huge city. There must be an empty house we can rent for an affordable sum. We're not going to give up, Mariah. You and I have been through worse. We must stick together.' Amelia picked up her bonnet and shawl and put them on. 'I'm going to the hospital to tell Todd and my father. They will have to help us find somewhere to live. We can't do it on our own.'

Mariah released Betsy with a heartfelt sigh. 'I don't see how either of them can make this situation better.'

'Pa knows the other doctors at the hospital. The more people who are aware of our situation, the more likely it is that someone will come up with suitable premises for us to rent. We need a good address, Mariah, if we're going to get on with our business.'

'How can we afford to rent in a nice area? We haven't received a penny from Lady Galton.'

'I don't know, but I'm not giving in. Daniel Norris is not going to ruin me out of spite. Besides which, Pa needs to know we have to leave, and so does Todd. After all, they will be homeless as well if we are forced from this house.'

'We only have a week. That's what Caleb said.'

'So I must act quickly.' Amelia laid her hand on Betsy's shoulder. 'Don't cry, dear. I won't let anyone put you and your ma and Percy in the workhouse. We'll be all right, I promise.'

* * *

It was a long walk to the London Hospital in Whitechapel Road, but Amelia was so determined to get the better of the situation that she hardly noticed her sore feet and aching legs. She knew that Todd was on duty in the emergency department and she marched into the hospital, catching her breath on the strong smell of carbolic that assailed her nostrils. She was met by a nurse in a starched white cap and apron, who thought she was yet another patient. Amelia claimed to be Todd's sister, in urgent need of speaking to him on a family matter and, to her relief, she was shown into a cubicle and told to wait.

After an agonising ten or fifteen minutes that felt more like hours, Todd pulled back the curtains. 'Emmie! What's wrong? You're very pale — are you ill?'

She shook her head. 'No, I'm sorry to come when you're on duty, but Caleb has just told me that my cousin has successfully contested the will. The magistrate, who I suspect must be a friend of his, has declared the alterations Grandpapa made to his will as being unenforceable due to his state of mind at the time. The previous will is the one being sent for probate. Pa and I are not mentioned in that one.'

'So you are to lose the house and the business?'

'We have seven days to find somewhere else. I'm sorry, Todd. I had to come and tell you. I can't really talk about it to Mariah because she's too upset on her own account.'

Todd slipped his arm around her shoulders. 'This affects me too. We'll find somewhere to live. I'll ask my colleagues and friends here if they know of any large premises to rent. You mustn't worry.'

'I knew you would want to help. Now I'd better tell Pa.'

'He's on a ward round with a consultant. You won't be able to reach him. You can tell him tonight when he comes home. We're both on the same hours this week.' Todd gave her a searching look. 'There's something else. What is it?'

'Lady Galton has asked me to design and make garments for her, but Mariah says people like her are very bad at paying. I desperately need the money so that I can purchase the materials I need to make the outfits for her ladyship.'

'I would help you if I could, but a doctor's salary is just enough to live on.'

'I wouldn't take your money even if you had any to spare. I have to become independent, Todd.' Amelia glanced over his shoulder as a nurse pulled back the curtains. 'I think you're needed.'

'There's an urgent case just come in, Doctor,' the nurse said crisply.

'I'm coming right away.' Todd gave Amelia an apologetic smile. 'I'm sorry. I'll try to think of something. I'll see you when I get off duty.'

Amelia left the hospital and walked home. She felt oddly relieved at having shared the bad news with Todd, but she dreaded having to pass the information on to her father when he came home. She had yet to break the news to Nellie and the women who worked in the sewing room, and no doubt they would be anxious as to their futures, should Mr Norris decide to sell the business. Amelia had learned a little of the problems that beset many of them, and she knew that their families depended on the money the seamstresses earned. Without it many of them would become destitute. She could only hope that her cousin had a shred of common decency in his soul when it came to his employees, but the way he had treated his own flesh and blood made that doubtful.

Amelia arrived home to find Caleb hammering on the front door. She could see the frightened faces of the women in the workroom as they peered out of the window.

'Caleb! What are you doing here? Haven't you brought enough evil tidings today?'

'I know I upset you earlier. It really was none of my doing.'

'So you keep saying, but you chose to take up your old position with my cousin. How do I know that you aren't his man still?'

'I never was Mr Daniel's man, as you call it. I worked for Mr Nathaniel and, despite his idiosyncrasies, he was a good person. May I come in? I don't want your workers to send for a constable. They look terrified.'

'Can you blame them? You were making such a din, no wonder they are frightened. We've had Jasper Cook threatening to kidnap Percy and now you are behaving like a lunatic.' Amelia took the key from her reticule and opened the door. She stepped inside and he followed her.

'Well, what have you got to say?'

'This concerns Mariah as well as yourself. Perhaps I should tell you together.'

Amelia eyed him suspiciously. 'Tell me and I'll be the judge of that. Mariah and Betsy are upset enough as it is.'

Caleb took a document from his inside pocket and handed it to her. 'Read it for yourself and you'll see that I am telling the truth.'

'Come into the parlour. The wall separating the house and the workroom is so thin you can hear everything.' Amelia ushered him into the room. She sat down, unfolding the sheet of parchment carefully. 'It's a will.'

'It's a copy I made. The original has gone for probate.' Caleb looked over her shoulder as she read the transcript. 'The aunt who raised me died recently. I was notified, but I couldn't mourn a woman who made my life miserable throughout my childhood. This was waiting for me when I returned to Albemarle Street — it would have been the last address she had for me.'

'You hated her but you kept in touch?'

'She was a lonely old woman with just an aged servant to tend to her needs. I gave her money occasionally but I suppose I could have done more.'

Amelia read the legal jargon carefully, although the will was short and to the point. 'She's left you the house and contents.'

Caleb pulled a face. 'The furniture is old and shabby. It would probably make a good bonfire, but yes, as her only living relative I have inherited the house and grounds.'

'What has this got to do with me, Caleb?'

'I want you to have the house. I hate the place and I'll never live there myself. I want you to believe that I'm not a bad fellow, Amelia. I have done things in the past of which I am not proud, but this is my chance to make amends in a small way.'

Amelia stared at him in astonishment. 'But you could sell it and purchase somewhere else.'

'You haven't seen the place. I'm not doing you any favours, Amelia. The house is in need of complete renovation, and if I tried to sell it I would get next to nothing for it. No one wants to live on the edge of the marsh.'

'You could rent it out to someone who would do what is required to make it habitable.'

'I'm offering it to you for a minimal rent. I'll keep the title deeds until I decide to sell it or until such time as you want to buy it off me. I know you don't approve, but I've decided to stay with your cousin. He's paying me an excellent salary and I have a suite of rooms in Albemarle Street. To be honest, I'm living like a lord, but I don't want to see you thrown out on the street. Please believe me.'

Amelia met his direct gaze with a sigh. 'I do believe you, Caleb. Strange as it seems, I think you are being straight with me, probably for the first time.'

'Then you accept my offer with no strings attached?'

'It's a very generous offer but I need time to think. It's rather a long way from the centre of town. Then there's Mariah to consider as well. We should talk it over together.'

'Of course. I understand.' Caleb turned to leave, but hesitated. 'Perhaps it would help if I took you all there to see the place. You might decide it's all right for you.'

'I think that's a good idea. Thank you.'

'Talk things over with Mariah and your father. I'll come for you tomorrow morning.'

'Wait. You'll want this.' Amelia rose to her feet and handed him the will. 'It's a very generous offer, Caleb.'

He grinned. 'Wait until you've seen the house. You might not think so then.'

* * *

Marsh House lived up to its name. Situated on the edge of Hackney Marshes, it was surrounded by a high brick wall, covered in moss and ivy-leaved toad-flax. Rusty iron gates hung despondently from broken hinges and the gravelled carriage sweep was pock-marked with weeds. The grounds had long ago been reclaimed from the boggy marsh but the once neatly clipped lawns had been invaded by twitch grass and ground elder. Even though the sun was shining from a cloudless sky, there was still an air of melancholy looming over the flat landscape. A solitary dead tree shed strips of bark onto the ground below as if tearing itself apart. Amelia suppressed a shiver.

'Is that the tree where you used to hide, Caleb?'

He glanced out of the carriage window. 'Yes, that's the one. It should have been chopped down years ago.'

Mariah craned her neck to look. 'I see a good supply of firewood. We'll be warm in the winter.'

'You are so practical,' Amelia said, laughing. 'It's certainly isolated here.' She caught her breath as the house came into view. 'It's enormous. You didn't tell me it was a mansion, Caleb.'

'It was once the home of a sea captain, who I suspect was a free trader, judging by the former grandeur of the house he had built for himself.'

'A smuggler?' Mariah pursed her lips.

'It's just a story,' Caleb said, smiling. 'The house has stood here for two or three hundred years and it's feeling its age. I did warn you both. When you see inside you might not think I am doing you any favours by suggesting you live here.'

Betsy kneeled on the seat in order to get a better look. 'I think it looks as if it's haunted. Is it, Caleb?'

'If there are ghosts they never bothered me, but then I was so miserable during my time here I wouldn't have noticed any unquiet spirits.'

'I don't believe in that silly nonsense,' Mariah said firmly. She shifted a sleeping Percy onto her other shoulder, just as the coachman reined in and the carriage slowed down, coming to a halt outside the front entrance.

Caleb alighted first and held out his hand to assist Amelia. Betsy jumped to the ground and raced to the front door. She reached up and tugged at a metal pull and the sound of the bell pealing inside the house echoed eerily.

'Don't do that, love,' Mariah said as she stepped down from the carriage. 'You'll wake up the evil spirits in an empty house.'

'I thought you didn't believe in that sort of thing,' Caleb said, smiling.

'I don't, but there's no need to take chances.' Mariah walked past him with her head held high.

Amelia suppressed a giggle. 'Well, if it is true, they'll all be wide awake by now.' She stood aside as Caleb produced a large iron key and inserted it into the lock. It made a grinding sound and the door opened with a protest from rusty hinges. Amelia entered first and was struck by the smell of must, cockroaches and rodent droppings. The sudden gust of fresh air disturbed clouds of dust and the cobwebs, which hung from the banisters like net curtains.

'When did your aunt pass away?' Amelia asked in

amazement. 'It doesn't look as if anyone has lived here for years.'

'I'm not sure exactly. It took several months for the will to go to probate and for the lawyers to track me down. She lived like this in her latter years anyway, having become rather eccentric. She didn't want cleaning women to disturb her peace.'

Mariah sniffed. 'It will take an army of charwomen to deal with this mess.'

'I think this house is splendid,' Betsy said, dancing across the hall. She flung open a door and entered the room, popping out again with a big grin on her face. 'The rooms are enormous, Ma. There's a piano in there, and bird feathers all over the floor.'

Amelia took a look for herself. It was obvious that a large bird had fallen down the chimney and been trapped in the room.

'I was forced to have lessons on that piano,' Caleb said, glancing over her shoulder. 'I am not in the least musical, as my teacher discovered. My knuckles were sore for days after a session as he took pleasure in slapping them with a cane every time I hit a wrong note.'

Betsy perched on the stool and lifted the piano lid. She began tinkling on the keys and the discordant, but joyous sound filled the room.

Mariah put Percy down and he toddled over to try to get up beside his sister, which of course was impossible. Amelia laughed at his antics.

'Let's explore the rest of the house, Mariah. I think the piano will keep the children amused for a while.'

Mariah shook her finger at Betsy. 'Keep an eye on your brother. Don't let him leave the room unless you go with him.'

'All right, Ma.' Betsy executed a crescendo on the

keys and Mariah closed the door on them.

'You'd better lead the way, Caleb,' Amelia said hastily. 'You obvious know all the nooks and crannies in the house.'

'I do indeed. Follow me.' Caleb led the way down a long passage, opening doors on either side. There was an oak-panelled dining room, several parlours and a large drawing room. Then there was the servants' domain, all of which was above stairs.

'The cellars were only used for storage, which was probably my ancestor's illegal cargo originally,' Caleb said as he showed them the kitchen, scullery and pantries. 'The kitchens were often built on at the back of older houses,' he added knowledgeably. 'So many fires were accidentally started there that some were even constructed away from the main dwelling.' He showed them the dingy utility rooms, still stocked with mops and brooms, and the butler's pantry together with the housekeeper's office. The kitchen was huge and the range was enormous, but very dilapidated.

'I could have fun with that,' Mariah said excitedly. 'It would take days to get it clean and in good working order, but I would really enjoy doing it.'

Amelia raised her eyebrows but said nothing to dull Mariah's enthusiasm. She could not imagine anything less enjoyable than scraping rust and dirt off an old range, but Mariah seemed to relish the thought. However, there were more pressing matters of concern, especially the cockroaches that scattered and hid at the sound of their footsteps, and the large holes in cupboard doors, gnawed by rats and mice.

'This place is of little interest to me,' Caleb said, shifting from foot to foot. 'There wasn't much cooking going on when I was a boy.' He waited until Amelia and Mariah had finished opening cupboard doors and inspecting the drawers in the dresser. 'Shall we go upstairs now?'

'Yes, of course.' Amelia closed the larder door. She had not inspected the detritus too closely. That would be another task for Mariah, who seemed to revel in cleaning up other people's mess.

On the first floor there were seven bedchambers, all of them a good size and furnished after a fashion, although, as Caleb pointed out, there was woodworm in most of the chests and the mattresses were so old they practically disintegrated at a touch. There was a long gallery on the second floor, and above that the attic rooms, which had once been home to the servants, were sadly neglected. It was obvious that the roof leaked in places.

Having inspected everything, they returned to the large reception room, following the sound of the piano being played with enthusiasm but no recognisable melody.

'I think we've seen enough, Caleb,' Amelia said as they reached the entrance hall. 'What do you think, Mariah?'

'It does need a lot of work, but I've been in worse places.'

Caleb laughed. 'My aunt will be turning in her grave. She loved this old house and it's true that the family lived here for so many generations I wouldn't like to count them, but not me. I would be more than happy to hand it over to you, Amelia.'

'We're a long way from the West End,' Amelia said thoughtfully. 'That would be my only criticism. If we're to run our business from here it's too far for wealthy ladies to come for fittings.'

'But being realistic, we have only a few days before we're turned out of the house in Nightingale Lane. We need somewhere to live, Amelia. As to the business,' Mariah added, frowning. 'We've only Lady Galton's word that she will order a whole new outfit. She hasn't settled up for the one gown she has definitely taken.'

'Shall we head back now?' Caleb glanced round the entrance hall and shuddered. 'This house gives me the shakes. To me it will always be haunted by that sad, lonely little boy. You can let me know your decision at any time.'

Amelia suppressed a surge of sympathy for him. She knew that he could be cold and calculating when it suited him, but she could see that he was telling the truth now.

'I think we'll take you up on your offer, Caleb. After all, we are in desperate need of somewhere safe to live, and the old house needs someone to bring it back to life. What do you say, Mariah? You'll have to live here, too.'

'Yes, but I think I would feel safer here than in Nightingale Lane. I doubt if Jasper would find us so easily.'

'We'd be taking on all sorts of problems with the house, and little or no money to spend on fixing them.'

Mariah smiled. 'I love a challenge and this is a very big one.'

'Me, too,' Amelia said simply.

'Does that mean you'll accept my offer?' Caleb looked from one to the other.

Amelia frowned. 'I should really speak to Pa before I make such a decision. It's a long way from the hospital, and then there's Todd.'

'He can find lodgings elsewhere,' Caleb said sharply. 'You don't owe him anything.'

'If I didn't know better I'd say you was jealous.' Mariah beckoned to Betsy. 'Come along, love. Bring Percy with you. I think it's time we went home.'

'Are we going to live in this funny old house?' Betsy asked eagerly.

'Would you like to live here?' Amelia eyed her curiously. It seemed strange for a child to want to live in such a neglected and isolated property.

'Yes, I would.' Betsy jumped up and down. 'I want to learn to play the piano.'

Caleb laughed. 'There you have a young lady with ambition, Mariah. I suggest you both listen to her.'

'First things first,' Amelia said firmly. 'It's only right I discuss this with Pa, but for my part I think it would be wonderful to have somewhere to live where we would all feel safe. I'll be sorry to leave Nellie and the other women, who've all worked so hard for next to nothing, but I haven't got much choice.'

'I'll take you home.' Caleb strode to the front door and opened it. 'I should warn you that this place seems pleasant enough in summer, but come winter it's another matter. Cold thick fog creeps over the marshes and envelops the house and grounds in a blanket so thick you feel you could cut it with a knife. Then in midwinter it freezes, and howling east winds rattle the old building to the foundations.'

'You're not a very good salesman, are you, Caleb?' Mariah picked up Percy and walked out into the summer sunshine.

* * *

When they arrived back in Nightingale Lane Caleb assisted Amelia and Mariah from the carriage. 'I'll leave you to think it over and talk to your father,' he said in a low voice. 'I have business to do in the docks tomorrow so I'll call in then and you can give me your decision.'

'I am truly grateful for the offer, Caleb,' Amelia said earnestly. 'You didn't have to do this, you know.'

He nodded. 'Yes, I did. If only to salve my own conscience. I haven't always been the most honourable man, but you have suffered a cruel injustice. This is my way of making amends.'

'It wasn't your fault. It was my cousin who did this to us.'

'I know what sort of man he is and yet I work for him. I take his money and I live in his house — that makes me an accomplice in all the shady deals he is prepared to mount in order to boost his wealth. Your late grandfather was a hard man, but honest and trustworthy. Daniel Norris is neither.' Caleb climbed into the carriage and slammed the door as if to underline his words.

* * *

That evening Harold and Todd arrived home at the same time. Amelia greeted them eagerly and shooed them into the parlour.

Harold sank down in the armchair he had appropriated for his own. 'What is all this, my love? I've had a hard day and all I want is my supper and then a pipe of tobacco before I go to bed.'

Todd gave her a searching glance. 'Have you found somewhere to rent? You seem excited.'

‘Yes, I have and I am delighted, but it affects both of you, and I don’t know if I will be able to accept unless you agree.’

‘We can neither agree nor disagree until you tell us where this place is, Amelia.’

‘Well, Pa. It’s like this.’ Amelia launched into an explanation of how Caleb came up with the offer, followed by a lengthy description of the house, sparing no ugly detail.

‘It sounds fascinating.’ Todd sat down, frowning. ‘But I doubt if I could lodge so far from the hospital.’

‘That goes for me, too, my dear,’ Harold said slowly. ‘But as it happens, I’ve been offered accommodation in a very respectable household. I might consider taking it up if you insist on moving so far from town.’

‘It’s not a matter of insisting, Pa. It’s pure necessity. Where are you thinking of lodging?’

‘My old friend Delaney’s sister-in-law is recently widowed — a charming woman. I met her a few days ago. She has been left in straitened circumstances and needs to let rooms to professional gentlemen in order to make ends meet. I wasn’t tempted to accept until now.’

Amelia and Todd exchanged amused glances.

‘Is she a nice lady, Pa?’

‘Yes, indeed, she’s very presentable, but of course you are my first consideration, Amelia. I won’t leave you in difficulties without my share of the rent.’

‘We have only a small amount of rent to pay at the new property. Caleb is giving it to us for as long as we want it.’

‘That sounds very odd. Why would he do something like that?’ Todd demanded suspiciously.

‘I’ve explained all that, Todd. What about you?

Could you make the journey into town every day?'

He shook his head. 'I don't know. If it were possible I most certainly would. I don't like the idea of you and Mariah living in a place that sounds so isolated. I'm not sure I trust Caleb either.'

'I will think it over tonight and let Caleb know tomorrow,' Amelia said slowly. 'But to put it bluntly, what choice do we have?'

15

It was decided and done so quickly that Amelia barely had time to draw breath. Next day when Caleb called for her answer Amelia thanked him and accepted his offer. During the next couple of days she had helped her father to pack and take his few belongings to the house in Charlotte Street, which was close enough to the hospital for Harold to walk there each morning.

Ruby Delaney was a plump, handsome woman in her late forties with a suspiciously glowing complexion and red lips, which Mariah dismissed as 'rouged'. Amelia gave Mrs Delaney the benefit of the doubt, and was relieved to witness the warm welcome that her father received. Harold responded with a beaming smile, and whatever his landlady's motives, Amelia decided that her beloved pa would be well looked after in Charlotte Street. That was one worry less. Todd decided to take a room there also, although with obvious reluctance, but he promised to take time off to help Amelia and Mariah to move to Marsh House.

Nellie and Maisie expressed deep sorrow and consternation when they were told that Amelia would be leaving. They were afraid for their jobs and Amelia did not have any words of comfort for them. As far as she knew, her cousin had decided to sell the property, and the future of the mourning warehouse looked very uncertain.

As they parted on the pavement outside the building, Amelia gave Nellie a hug. 'If ever I need a competent seamstress to manage my business I will call on you, and of course Maisie, too. In fact I would be happy to employ any of your girls should the opportunity arise.'

Nellie sniffed and wiped her nose on her sleeve. 'Ta, miss. I never thought I'd see the day when Mr Norris let us down. He was proud of the garments we made, God rest his soul.'

'Mr Daniel is a mean man,' Maisie added tearfully. 'I dunno how I'm going to feed my family if I get the sack.'

'If there was anything I could do for you I would do it right away,' Amelia said with feeling. 'I will come back and see you, and if I can get Mr Marsh to put in a good word for you all, that's what I'll do.'

Amelia went round the other women who had lined up outside the workroom and she shook hands with some and was hugged by others. Hobbs was last in line.

'Mr Hobbs, I am so sorry. I don't know if my cousin will keep you in his employ.' Amelia grasped his hand. 'I wish there was something I could do.'

'You mustn't worry about me, miss. I have a sister who lives across the river in Walworth. She's recently widowed and she's asked me if I would go and live with her. I was thinking about it, but now I'm certain. I want to thank you for helping me when I needed it most.'

Amelia leaned forward and kissed him on the cheek. 'I wish you well, Mr Hobbs.'

There were tears in her eyes when she climbed into the waiting hackney carriage. Todd took his seat next to her, Mariah and the children having gone on ahead.

'Mr Hobbs will be all right, but I wonder what

will happen to those poor women,' Amelia said sadly. 'Cousin Daniel is quite ruthless.'

'I know little of running a business.' Todd took her hand and gave it a comforting squeeze. 'But I agree it's very hard on those women.'

'I wish I could take them on, but I don't even know how I'm going to manage.'

'You know that I would lodge with you if it were possible,' Todd said anxiously. 'But I couldn't get to the hospital on time. The only consolation is that you and Mariah and the children should be safe from Jasper Cook. I'll visit you whenever I can.'

Amelia was about to tell the cabby to drive on when she spotted a liveried footman knocking on the door of the home she had just left. 'Wait! That looks like Lady Galton's servant. Maybe he's come to pay me for the gown she purchased. I'd almost given up hope.'

Todd flung the door open and leaped out. He crossed the pavement and exchanged words with the footman, turning to point to Amelia as she leaned out of the cab. The footman walked past him and stepped up to the kerb.

'Are you Miss Amelia Sutton?'

'Yes, I am.'

He handed her a folded document and a small leather pouch, which jingled encouragingly as he placed it in her hand. 'From Lady Galton. Is there any reply, miss?'

Amelia opened the letter with trembling fingers. She read the brief note, suppressing the desire to crow with delight.

'Yes, please tell Lady Galton that I will be delighted to call upon her tomorrow at the time stated. Thank you.'

The man nodded and stepped away. Todd climbed back into the cab.

'Tell the cabby to drive on, Todd,' Amelia said excitedly. 'Lady Galton has paid me and given me an order for several new outfits. I can't believe it.'

Todd tapped on the roof of the cab and it lurched into motion. 'I believe it, Emmie. You deserve to succeed. With a wealthy patron you could go far.'

'I know it won't be easy, but the trouble with Marsh House is that it's so far from the centre of London.'

Todd leaned back against the squabs. 'You will probably get most of your work visiting clients' houses, but you could always hire a room in a more central area of town in order to show your creations.'

'It's looking ahead, but I think that's a wonderful idea. You are clever, Todd.'

He laughed. 'I'm used to being practical. Never having had much money, I have had to be inventive, particularly when I was the village doctor in Rockwood. People often paid me in kind. I'd get a dozen eggs or a pound of butter and cheese.'

'It was the same for my pa when we lived in Long Acre.' Amelia weighed the pouch in her hand. 'I will probably have enough to purchase the materials I need to make the gowns for her ladyship. If not, by using her name I can prove that I'm good for credit.'

'Let's get you settled into that mournful mansion first and then you can start working out how to manage your fashion empire.'

'Fashion empire!' Amelia smiled. 'I rather like the sound of that, Todd. I think you should give up medicine and become my business manager.'

'And then you'd be paid in butter and cheese. Maybe I'm better at being a medical man.'

Amelia relaxed as she sat beside him, clutching the bag of coins in her hand with the letter from Lady Galton safely tucked away in her reticule.

* * *

The sun was shining on Marsh House when the cabby dropped them off outside the main entrance.

Betsy rushed out of the house giggling with barely suppressed excitement. 'It's so big. I've got my own room, if you agree, miss.'

Amelia stepped down from the cab, leaving Todd to help the cabby with the baggage. She followed Betsy into the house. 'Of course you may have your own room. There are plenty to go round.'

Mariah appeared from the depths of the house. Her sleeves were rolled up and she wore a once clean apron that was now covered in rust from the range.

'You're looking very chirpy, miss.'

'I've had wonderful news, Mariah. The money from Lady Galton was delivered just as Todd and I were about to leave Nightingale Lane, and she's ordered several outfits. I'm to go there tomorrow morning to discuss the details.'

Mariah stood with arms akimbo. 'That's all very fine, but I've got to get back to that dratted range. It's nearly dead, but it's fighting back.'

'Perhaps I can help?' Amelia suggested faintly.

'No, this is my job. I won't be beaten.' Mariah glanced over Amelia's shoulder as Todd staggered in with two heavy valises. 'Leave those at the foot of the stairs. We'll worry about taking them up to the bedrooms later.'

'It's all right,' Todd said calmly. 'I'm going to stay

tonight. I want to make sure you are settled in before I go back to the hospital. It's my day off anyway.'

Amelia had a sudden thought. 'Has the cabby driven off?'

'Yes. Why?' Todd eyed her curiously. 'You're not leaving already, are you, Emmie?'

'No, of course not, but I wanted to ask him to pick me up tomorrow so that I can get to Lady Galton's house on time.'

Todd frowned. 'That's a good point. We are very out of the way here. What you need is a pony and trap or something similar.'

'I saw a gig of some sort in the stables,' Betsy said excitedly. 'Shall I show you, Todd?'

'Dr Taylor, you cheeky girl,' Mariah admonished sternly.

'No, it's all right,' Todd said smiling. 'She can call me Todd.'

'I think we should all be on first-name terms,' Amelia added seriously. 'We really are all in this together. I'll come with you, Todd. But even if there's a vehicle, we still need a horse to pull it.'

'One thing at a time. Let's take a look round the outbuildings. You can lead the way, Betsy.'

'I know where to go. Come with me.' She skipped on ahead, her flaxen hair shining in the golden sunshine.

Amelia smiled at Betsy's innocent enthusiasm as they followed her more slowly. When they reached the stables it was in a similar state of dilapidation to the house. Betsy ran inside and attempted to drag a tarpaulin off a wooden vehicle covered in cobwebs.

'You were right, Betsy.' Todd lifted the covering and laid it in an empty stall. He walked round the vehicle, examining it carefully. 'There's no rot or woodworm that I can see. It looks to be reasonably roadworthy.'

'Except for the animal to pull it,' Amelia reminded him.

'Well, I have to get to the hospital in the morning and you have an appointment with Lady Galton, so we are in dire need of some sort of transport.' Todd frowned thoughtfully. 'I think you and I should go for a walk, Betsy. We'll see if we can find a friendly farmer who has a horse for hire.'

'Maybe I could learn to ride,' Betsy said excitedly. 'This is such a lovely place to live.'

Amelia glanced at the surrounding marsh, which did look quite pretty in the bright sunshine, but she could imagine it in winter and that was not so appealing. She smiled up at Todd. 'How will you pay the farmer? Or is that a mere detail?'

'Free medical treatment for six months or more. I might have been born in the city but I've become used to country ways. Leave it to us, Emmie. We'll find a healthy animal to take us into town, even if it's a donkey.'

'And I'd better get back to the house to help Mariah,' Amelia said hastily. 'She's trying desperately to get the range going.'

'You'll need coal as well as logs. If I meet a friendly farmer I'll ask him where to find the nearest coal merchant.'

'You're always so practical, Todd. I hadn't thought of that.'

He grinned. 'I might not be as good-looking and dashing as Caleb Marsh, but I have my uses.'

'You're too modest, Todd,' Amelia said earnestly. 'You certainly were not behind the door when looks were handed out.'

Todd laughed. 'Thank you for the compliment. Come on, Betsy. We've got work to do.' Todd walked off with Betsy skipping along at his side.

Amelia returned to the house. She had never thought of Caleb as being debonair. In fact, she had spent most of their short acquaintance suspecting him of ulterior motives and placing him in the same category as her cousin Daniel. However, by providing them with a safe place to live he had proved himself to be a good friend and she was deeply in his debt. The house might be isolated and in a poor state, but it was a roof over their heads and, she hoped, would prove too far from the city for Jasper to bother them.

She returned to the kitchen to find Mariah even more exasperated with the stubborn rust on the ancient range, even though she had scrubbed most of it away.

'It looks wonderful,' Amelia said encouragingly. 'It will probably be easier to clean when you have hot water. If we can get the fire going, some of the remaining rust will probably drop off anyway.'

Mariah shook her head. 'This thing and I are going to fall out, but you're probably right. I found a scuttle filled with coal in the shed across the back yard, and there are some logs as well.'

'Why don't you have a rest for a few minutes and I'll try to light the fire?' Amelia suggested tentatively.

'No, but thank you for the offer. Range and I have a score to settle. This is where I have the upper hand.'

Amelia sighed. 'All right. I'll take a broom and make a start on the front parlour, where we found the piano. I suggest we make one room habitable at a time. When the carter arrives with our furniture and mattresses we'll be ready.'

'Where's Betsy? I want her to look after Percy.' Mariah glanced at him as he played happily with his wooden bricks.

'She went on an errand with Todd. They should be back soon.' Amelia did not go into details. She knew Mariah well enough not to aggravate her further when she was in this mood, and she made her escape, taking with her a broom, dustpan and brush. She had to dispose of the dead bird and its feathers as well as dried leaves and soot from the chimneypiece. There was a chill in the front parlour, despite the fact that it was hot and sunny out of doors. Amelia's attempts to light a fire came to nothing and she had to seek Mariah's help. However, by now Mariah was in jubilant mood. The range had reluctantly allowed her to get a blaze going and the kettle was bubbling away on the hob.

'That showed the brute who's who,' Mariah said proudly. 'We can have a cup of tea, but unfortunately the milk I brought with me has curdled, so I'll have to make it into cream cheese.'

'Well done.' Amelia breathed a sigh of relief. 'I could do with a cup of tea, milk or no milk, and I need your expert touch to get a fire going in the front parlour. It's chilly in there, and it feels damp.'

'You make the tea and keep an eye on Percy. I'll deal with the fire.' Mariah bustled out of the kitchen, leaving Amelia to placate Percy, who began to snivel.

Moments later the back door opened and Betsy rushed in through the scullery. 'Guess what, Emmie?' She came to a halt, clapping her hand over her mouth. 'I may call you, Emmie, mayn't I?'

Amelia smiled. 'Yes, of course.'

'Well, we found a small farm about a mile away, on

the other side of the river, and Todd bargained with the farmer. We've got a pony to go with the trap.'

'That's marvellous,' Amelia said smiling. 'Where is Todd now?'

'He's settling the little horse in the stable. Not only that, but we bought butter, milk and eggs from the man. He was so pleased to have a sale. He gave me an egg all to myself for free.' Betsy stepped back into the scullery and returned with a wicker basket, which she placed on the table. 'There, see for yourself. Todd paid the man in money, but he's buying the pony with free doctoring for the farmer and his family for a whole year. Isn't Todd clever?'

'Todd is very clever, and the farmer sounds like a very kind man.' Amelia examined the contents of the basket. 'Your ma will be very proud of you, Betsy. I'm sure you had a hand in this.'

Betsy puffed out her chest. 'I did tell the man how hungry me and Percy get at times, and how good you've been to us.'

'I don't know about that, but you did well. Why don't you go and tell your ma all about it?'

'I will. It's so good here. Much better than Nightingale Lane.' Betsy picked up her brother as she hurried from the room.

Amelia left the things in the basket for Mariah to crow over and she made her way to the stables where Todd was filling the manger with hay for the grey Welsh cob. Amelia went to the pony and stroked his neck.

'He's wonderful, Todd. How did you do it?'

'I offered the farmer free treatment for him and his family for a year. He was only too pleased to accept as he has five children, the youngest of them being rather sickly.'

'It's a very good bargain, but how will you cope? What happens if you're on duty at the hospital when they need you?'

'I have some savings. I thought I'd purchase a horse and leave it at livery when I'm on duty. Then I can lodge here instead of with Mrs Delaney. If that's all right with you, of course?'

'Yes, that would be really good, but you're giving yourself a heavy burden for our sake, Todd. I don't feel right in allowing you to make such a sacrifice.'

'Being a country doctor is much more my style. If there was a living round here, I would far rather do that than work in the hospital, and it would give me more free time to study for the qualifications I need to become a paediatrician.'

Amelia met his intense gaze but looked away quickly. She was very fond of Todd, but she was not ready for a deeper relationship. At least not yet, which was what she kept telling herself. Tomorrow would be the beginning of a business career that she could never have imagined. In her mind she could see herself reaching a level close to that of the House of Worth. Love and marriage might come later. Todd had already told her about his unrequited love for the beautiful young woman who had married his best friend. She did not want to give him false hope, and yet somehow she could not imagine life without him.

She turned back to the pony and stroked his muzzle. 'What shall we call him? Or does he already have a name?'

Todd laughed. 'Betsy has already named him 'Grey', which is fitting, if not very original.'

'It's easy to remember. If Betsy wants to call him

Grey, I think it's a good choice. But do we have enough food for him? And the outer door is hanging off its hinges. He'll be cold at night.'

'I can mend that this afternoon, and I bought a sack of hay from Farmer Allen. Later on I'll harness Grey to the trap and I'll go and collect it. Also, I found out where to get coal, so I can do that, too.'

Amelia sighed. 'What would we have done without you, Todd?'

'I'm just glad I can help. You deserve someone to take the burden from you, Emmie.'

She cocked her head on one side. 'That sounds like the carter with our furniture and bedding. I'd better go and make sure everything is put in the right place.' She hurried from the stable without giving him a chance to respond.

* * *

That evening, when the children were in bed asleep, exhausted after a long and exciting day, Amelia, Mariah and Todd sat round the fire in the front parlour, or piano room, as Betsy had named it. Their furniture from Nightingale Lane looked rather lost in the large room, but at least they had the sofa and two armchairs, a tea table and a couple of small side tables.

Amelia poured tea from the Brown Betty pot and handed a cup to Mariah and one to Todd. 'This place feels like home already.'

'There's still a lot to do,' Mariah said gloomily. 'I know we're lucky to have somewhere to live, but it's going to take a month of Sundays to clean and furnish every room.'

'As I said before, we'll take it one room at a time,' Amelia said, smiling. 'I feel safe here, and even safer knowing that you are going to live with us, Todd.'

Todd raised his cup to them. 'You've both done wonders. Anyway, I'm not on duty until tomorrow afternoon, so if it's all right with you, Emmie, I'll drive you to Lady Galton's house and after you've finished your business I'll go on to Tattersall's to buy a horse so that I can get about easily.'

'That means I'll have to handle the reins on the way home,' Amelia said doubtfully.

'It's easy. I'll show you how to do it on the way into town. You'll need to be able to drive yourself. That is, until you're rich enough to employ a coachman of your own.'

Amelia laughed. 'That will be the day.'

* * *

The meeting with Lady Galton next day went well. She had obviously been studying Amelia's sketches and she had a clear idea of the wardrobe she wanted. Money seemed to be no object and she brushed aside any doubts Amelia had on that score. Above all, Lady Galton wanted to outshine all the other wealthy women of her acquaintance.

'This is your chance to make a name for yourself, Miss Sutton,' Lady Galton said as she rang the bell to summon a servant at the end of the session. 'If I create the sensation I expect to make while wearing your designs, your reputation will be made. You will have wealthy clients queuing up to order whole wardrobes from you.'

'I won't let you down, Lady Galton,' Amelia said

simply. 'I will set to work immediately.'

Lady Galton acknowledged this with a slight nod of her head. She turned to the maid who had appeared as if from nowhere. 'Show Miss Sutton out.'

Todd was waiting outside with the trap and he leaned over to hold out his hand. Amelia grasped it as she climbed up onto the seat beside him.

'She loves the designs, Todd. I have an order for an entire autumn wardrobe, and she's considering another for winter clothes, providing my garments live up to her expectations.'

'That's wonderful.' Todd flicked the reins. 'Walk on, Grey.'

'But now I have to purchase the materials I'll need, and the thread and trimmings. I'll have to work really hard to get everything ready for her first fitting.'

'You'll do it. You have Mariah to help you.'

'I really need a sewing machine. When I first thought of making garments to order I was certain of using one or two of the machines in the workroom.'

'Are they all being used?'

Amelia frowned thoughtfully. 'I'm not sure. I suppose I could ask Nellie. I could do that after I've visited the material warehouses.'

'I'd like to come with you, but it depends upon the horse sale. I have to purchase a mount today or else it's a room at Mother Delaney's for me.'

His comical expression made Amelia laugh and she relaxed against him as he expertly handled the reins. She could only hope that she would manage as well on the return journey.

They reached Tattersall's in Knightsbridge just before the sale started. Todd left Grey and the gig in the care of a young boy, giving him tuppence with the promise of more when they returned. Satisfied that their modest mode of transport would be safe, Amelia and Todd walked arm in arm to the area where the sale was about to begin, but Todd came to a sudden halt as they came face to face with an army officer with a beautiful lady on his arm.

'No!' Todd said in amazement. 'Gus! I can't believe it. And Dolly, too.'

Gus threw his arms around Todd and gave him a brotherly hug, while Dolly clapped her hands in delight. Amelia stared at them both, realising instantly that this handsome chestnut-haired man in the red jacket uniform of the Devonshire Regiment was none other than Todd's childhood friend, Gus Baker. That meant that the beautiful, golden-haired lady who was clinging to both of them with tears of delight running down her cheeks must be Dolly, the love of Todd's life. Amelia eyed her warily. She could see why Todd had been attracted to the lovely, vivacious young woman, but somehow the idea did not please her.

Todd broke free from his friends, turning to Amelia with an apologetic smile. 'I'm sorry, Emmie. I want you to meet my old friend Gus and his wife, Adela.'

Dolly broke away from her husband to clasp Amelia's hands. 'It's Dolly. No one calls me Adela except my grandmother.'

'I'm Amelia Sutton. How do you do?'

Gus gave her a hug. 'It's wonderful to see my old pal has made friends. I never thought he'd leave Rockwood, but I can see why he wants to stay in London.'

Dolly slapped him on the arm. 'You don't say things like that, Gus.' She turned back to Amelia with a charming smile. 'It's really lovely to meet you. I want to hear all about you and how you came to meet our dear Todd. You and I can have a chat, Amelia, while the gentlemen talk horses.' She propelled Amelia away from the men who crowded the area, bidding for the animals. 'It seems like ages since I last saw Todd. They told me at home that he had come to London to work in a hospital. That really surprised me.'

Amelia edged away from Dolly's affectionate grasp. 'Why would it? He's a very good doctor.'

'Of course, but he seemed so settled in Rockwood. We've just returned from South Africa and expect to be posted to India next.'

'Do you enjoy being an army wife?' Amelia asked for want of anything better to say. She was unsure how to treat the young woman who had captured Todd's heart and probably still held it in her small hands.

'I love being married to Gus. We are a perfect couple, but it isn't an easy life. I have to admit that. However, it's the one I've chosen and I am not complaining.' Dolly eyed Amelia curiously. 'But what about you? Tell me all about yourself, Amelia. How did you meet Todd?'

Amelia found herself talking to Dolly as if they had known each other for years instead of minutes, but the sound of raised men's voices as they bid for the animals and the general hubbub was quite deafening. It was a relief when Todd and Gus strolled over to them, smiling broadly.

'I own a bay mare,' Todd said happily. 'She's just what I want and need.'

'You had a good deal there.' Gus slapped him on the back. 'But you're not going to hurry off now, are you? We've much to catch up on, Todd, old chap.'

'We could go to luncheon somewhere,' Dolly

suggested airily. 'I'm starving, I don't know about you, Emmie?'

'I suppose I am. I hadn't given it much thought.'

'I don't know why, but I'm always hungry recently,' Dolly said, sighing. 'At this rate I will have to order a whole new wardrobe from you, Emmie, in a size larger than I'm wearing now.'

'You always used to eat like a sparrow.' Gus smiled affectionately. 'It's married bliss that has given you an appetite, my darling.'

'You flatter yourself,' Dolly said, laughing. 'We'll find a nice restaurant and we can all chat over a good meal.' Even as she spoke, the colour drained from her cheeks and she crumpled to the ground in a dead faint.

Gus rushed forward but was too late to catch her. He lifted her in his arms. 'Todd. For God's sake, help her.'

'Let's get her to somewhere quieter,' Todd said firmly. 'It could be simply that she needs food, but I'll examine her.'

Amelia caught him by the sleeve as he was about to follow them into the office building. 'I think it might be something even more obvious, Todd,' she said in a low voice.

He nodded. 'I agree, but I'll take a look at her anyway. Who knows? I might have some good news for the happy couple.'

16

As the four sat around a table in the busy restaurant, the conversation was all about the wonderful news that Dolly and Gus were expecting an addition to their family. Dolly was clearly overjoyed and so was Gus, although Amelia could see that he was concerned for his wife's health and wellbeing.

'We will probably sail for India in late October or early November, Todd,' Gus said, frowning. 'I'm not sure if Dolly should accompany me this time.'

'It's not your decision, Gus,' Dolly said firmly. 'I am the one who is in the family way and I will decide what is best for all of us, the infant included. I am coming with you and that's that.'

Todd laughed. 'It seems you have little choice, Gus. Your wife has spoken.'

'I don't want to put her and the child in harm's way.' Gus stared down at his plate, frowning. 'Being a father is a big responsibility.'

'Neither of us had parents to bring us up,' Todd said equably. 'But if you are half as good as Dolly's papa, you won't go wrong.'

'I think you will make amazing parents.' Amelia squeezed Dolly's hand. 'It's wonderful news and we should be celebrating. I'm sure everything will work out perfectly for you.'

'We have everyone to tell at home,' Dolly said dreamily. 'My sisters will be so happy for us, as will Mama and Aunt Nancy.' She turned to Amelia with a smile. 'I'm sure Todd must have told you about Nancy. Her story is so remarkable and so is she.'

Gus slipped his arm around Dolly's shoulders. 'We'll travel down to Devonshire when Todd thinks you're well enough, my love. We're taking no chances.'

'I think Dolly is in excellent health,' Todd said, smiling. 'But it would be good if we could have at least a couple of days together, Gus. You and I haven't seen each other since you were stationed abroad so we have a lot to catch up on.'

'Maybe you could come to Marsh House and see what we've taken on,' Amelia suggested shyly. 'Of course, it's nothing like you're used to. I mean, you were brought up in a castle, so Todd told me, Dolly. We've only just moved into a very old and dilapidated house on the other side of town. You might describe it as a challenge.'

'It sounds very exciting,' Dolly said eagerly. 'We're staying in Chelsea Barracks while Gus awaits orders so we are free to visit you.'

'Are you sure the coach journey across town won't be too much for you, sweetheart?' Gus asked tenderly.

'Of course not.' Dolly tossed her head. 'I am not made of glass, Gus Baker, and I don't expect to be treated as if I am fragile. Women have babies all the time and I am fit and well. Todd will agree with me, I'm sure.' She gave Todd a winning smile.

'You're fighting a losing battle, Gus,' Todd said, laughing. 'I'd pit Dolly against the enemy any day, and I know who'd win.'

Amelia smiled, but the idea that Todd was still a little in love with Dolly persisted and would not go away. She managed to put such thoughts to the back of her mind as she listened to Todd and Gus reminiscing about their boyhood in the Devonshire village, but there was still the worrying matter of driving the pony and cart through town to the warehouses close to the docks before she could think of making her way back to Marsh House.

Amelia cleared her throat as she rose to her feet. 'I'm truly sorry to leave you, but I have business in town before I go home.'

Gus half rose to his feet. 'Then you must go with her, Todd. I wouldn't want Dolly to drive through the East End on her own.'

'Unfortunately I am on duty at the hospital at two o'clock.' Todd examined his pocket watch, frowning. 'I really should be on my way. I have to collect my horse and find a livery stable near the hospital, so I'm afraid I will have to leave now.'

Dolly smiled, holding out her hand. 'Never mind. We'll have a lovely day together tomorrow. I can't wait to see this old haunted house on the eerie marsh.'

* * *

It was getting late but Amelia had successfully driven the cart laden with bolts of silk, taffeta, cotton and fine woollen material. There was also a linen bag filled with beads, reels of cotton, needles and lengths of satin ribbon. The order that Lady Galton had placed was substantial and she wanted the garments quickly. Amelia knew that she needed at least one sewing machine, preferably two, and she stopped off outside the workroom in Nightingale Lane. The women were just leaving, but through the glass window she could see Nellie in the office. Amelia greeted her former employees with a wide smile.

'Can't keep away, can yer?' Maisie Lugg said, grinning and exposing a wide gap where she had lost two front teeth.

'It's good to see you all.' Amelia returned a hug from Sadie, the youngest person in the sewing room. 'I just want a word with Nellie.'

'Well, don't forget us when you have a clothes factory on the marsh,' Maisie said cheerfully. 'I reckon we'll all be trooping out there to work for you.'

'I'll let you know if and when I'm in a position to employ you, but I must catch Nellie before she leaves for home.' Amelia broke away from them, shaking the outstretched hands as she made her way to the main entrance.

Nellie emerged from the office. 'What have you forgotten —' she broke off, smiling. 'Miss Sutton. I thought one of the girls had left her purse behind.'

'I came to beg a favour, Nellie.'

'Anything I can do, I will.'

'I need a sewing machine, preferably two. I know there are spares and I just wanted to borrow them until I can afford to buy machines of my own.'

'Mr Marsh knows how many we have, but I doubt if we will see much of him now. We don't know if the place has been sold, or even if it's going to continue as a mourning warehouse.'

'I can't help you there with any certainty, but I will make enquiries when I see Mr Marsh again.'

Nellie bustled over to the machine that was kept as a spare and picked it up. 'I'll take this outside. Have you hired a cab?'

'No, Nellie. I am the proud owner of a pony and trap. If you take that machine, I'll bring the other one. Mariah and I can work twice as hard with two, and I'll bring them back as soon as I have no need for them.'

Nellie put the machine down just long enough to allow her to open the door. 'You go first, miss. I'll follow.'

With the two machines tucked under the bolts of material, Amelia gave Nellie a warm hug. 'I'll always remember this. Thank you.'

'That's all right, miss. Just send for me as soon as you can afford to pay me wages. I'll gladly traipse out to the marsh, if only to get away from here. That's if I have a job in a week's time anyway.'

'I'll certainly remember you, Nellie. Goodbye and thank you again.' Amelia climbed onto the driver's seat and picked up the reins. She gave them a flick. 'Walk on, Grey.'

* * *

It was late evening by the time Amelia drove the cart through the open gates of Marsh House. It had been a hot day and now, in the cool of evening, a white mist had curled up from the boggy ground and shrouded the house from view. The damp cloud captured the smoke from the range and it mingled with the smell of wet mud and rotting vegetation. A shiver ran down Amelia's spine as she drew Grey to a halt outside the front door. For a moment it seemed the house was empty again but then the door flew open and Mariah rushed out to meet her, followed by Betsy. There were cries of excitement when they unloaded the valuable contents of the cart and carried them into the front parlour. Mariah picked up one of the sewing machines as if it weighed less than nothing.

'How did you manage to get these?' she said delightedly. 'We can both work at the same time. I gather her ladyship gave you a big order.'

'I'll tell you all about it over supper. Can I smell something cooking? I didn't realise how hungry I am until now.'

'It's only stew,' Mariah said apologetically. 'That farmer who let you have Grey brought a couple of rabbits he'd caught. I guessed you'd be starving by the time you got home, although I was expecting you a lot earlier.'

'Yes,' Betsy added, nodding seriously. 'We thought you'd had a mishap.'

'As you can see, I've been very busy. Moreover, Todd has bought a fine horse, and the strange thing is that he met up with two of his old friends from Devonshire.'

Mariah hefted several bolts of material from the cart. 'You don't sound very pleased.'

'I am, of course.' Amelia waited until Betsy had run indoors with the bag of trimmings. 'Except that one of them is the young woman he fell in love with years ago. She married his best friend.'

'I see. Well, if she's safely married you don't have to worry.'

Amelia shrugged. 'It's none of my business, anyway. I hope that stew is ready, Mariah. I am very hungry.'

'Betsy will serve it up for you. I'll unharness Grey and settle him for the night.'

'I didn't know you were good with horses, Mariah?'

'There ain't much I haven't done in my life. I had to learn to be useful when I was a girl in Hoxton, and after I got married I had to support my old man most of the time.' Mariah took the reins and led Grey towards the stables.

It was only then that Amelia realised how little she

knew about Mariah's past.

She was very grateful for the opportunity to go indoors and sit down to a tasty meal. As she entered the house she had a sudden eerie feeling that someone was watching her. The light was fading fast and some of the mist had trickled into the hall through broken windowpanes. She felt compelled to glance up the stairs but the top was in deep shadow, and all was quiet. She told herself it was fatigue and hunger that were making her nervous and she hurried through to the kitchen where Betsy was buttering a thick slice of bread.

'Sit down, Emmie,' Betsy said cheerfully. 'Ma said I could serve the soup.'

Amelia pulled up a chair and sank onto it. The kitchen was warm and the delicious aroma of rabbit stew made her stomach rumble with anticipation.

'The soup smells so good,' Amelia said appreciatively. 'Thank you, Betsy,' she added, as Betsy filled a bowl to the brim and set it in front of her.

'Thank Ma. She made it, but she's teaching me to cook. I don't think I'll ever be as good as her, but I want to learn.'

Amelia ate hungrily, allowing Betsy to chatter on about her day and the things she had done during Amelia's absence. She had almost finished the stew when Mariah strolled into the room and sat down by the range.

'It's a bit chilly out there with that thick mist coming from the marsh. Anyway, I've made Grey comfortable for the night and locked up.'

'We have visitors coming tomorrow,' Amelia said, sighing. 'It's Todd's friends, the lady I told you about, Mariah. She grew up in a castle and I'm afraid she will look down on this place. I wish we'd had time to make it look better.'

'If she's so inclined she's no friend. That's all I can say.' Mariah pulled Betsy onto her knee and cuddled her, despite loud protests.

'Ma, I'm not a baby like Percy.' Betsy wriggled free and stood up, brushing down imagined creases in her skirt.

'You are still my baby, Betsy, and always will be.' Mariah laughed. 'Make your poor old ma a pot of tea, will you, please? I'm sure Emmie would like some, too.'

'Yes, indeed I would,' Amelia said, smiling. 'I haven't had a drink since lunchtime so I am very thirsty. We ate in a very nice restaurant, which I'm sure was very expensive. I think Todd was showing off a bit in front of Dolly.'

Betsy picked up the teapot and warmed it with a little water from the bubbling kettle. 'I don't think I'm going to like that person. Todd belongs to us, don't he, Ma?'

'Not exactly, darling,' Mariah said hastily. 'We all love Todd, but you can't own a person.'

'That's very true.' Amelia laid her spoon back in the empty plate. 'That was delicious, Mariah. I really enjoyed it. Thank you.'

'It's me job, ain't it? Cooking, I mean, and cleaning, too.'

Amelia shook her head. 'You mustn't think like that. We are all equal here. You don't work for me, or I for you. We look after each other in this house.' She shivered, glancing over her shoulder as a cold draught blew in from the hallway.

'What's wrong?' Mariah asking, frowning. 'You

look like someone walked over your grave.'

Amelia managed a smile. 'It's my imagination playing tricks on me, but I can't help wishing Todd was sleeping here tonight. I feel safe when he's here and the rest of the world doesn't seem so far away.'

'What nonsense you talk, Amelia Sutton,' Mariah said severely. 'Betsy, hurry up with that tea. I think it's time Emmie was in her bed. In fact, we all need to get some sleep. We should rise early in the morning and make the parts of the house where the rich lady will go as neat and clean as possible.'

Betsy placed the teapot on the table. 'Yes, Ma. Of course.'

* * *

Despite her misgivings, Amelia slept well and rose early. She could hear Mariah and Betsy moving around in the front parlour, with Percy's baby chatter in the background, as she descended the stairs.

'Good morning,' Mariah said cheerfully when Amelia walked into the parlour. 'We're just about finished in here. There's tea and fresh bread on the table in the kitchen. We've had our breakfasts so it's just you, and there's enough for Todd if he gets home early.'

'Mariah, you and Betsy are marvels.' Amelia turned on her heel and made her way to the kitchen to snatch a quick breakfast. However, when she went to help Mariah and Betsy, she realised that they had scrubbed and polished everything they could find, and there was little they could do with the empty rooms other than close the doors on them. Having done that and assured herself that they had done what they could, Amelia decided to take the bolts of material and all her sewing equipment upstairs to the long gallery on the second floor. With Mariah and Betsy's help, she had everything laid out on a trestle table they had brought down from the attic. Sunlight poured through the lattice windows, and Amelia's fears from last evening seemed far off and frankly ridiculous. The old house creaked and groaned even in daylight, but it was simply the aged timbers contracting and expanding and nothing more sinister.

'I can't wait to start,' Amelia said eagerly as she fingered a fine ring velvet in a deep shade of crimson, which would make a wonderful evening gown. 'As soon as our guests have gone we can make a start, Mariah. With your pattern-cutting skills and with two sewing machines to work on, we will be able to work really quickly.'

'That's if Caleb doesn't turn up demanding the return of the machines,' Mariah said gloomily. 'I don't trust that man, Emmie. I never did.'

'Nor I, but we have to hope that my cousin will keep him too busy to bother about the mourning warehouse. It never made a huge profit anyway.'

Betsy had gone downstairs but the sound of her feet pounding on the wooden stair treads echoed throughout the house as she returned. She burst into the long gallery.

'Ma, Emmie. They're here. Todd has brought his friends with him.'

'I'm coming.' Amelia picked up her skirts and ran, but she slowed down as she reached the landing on the first floor, and she walked sedately downstairs, trailing her fingers on the banister rail in an attempt to appear nonchalant. Even so, her emotions were in turmoil. She had seen the way Todd looked at the beautiful Dolly, and heard the tender note in his voice when he spoke to her. Adela Baker might be a married woman and unattainable, but Amelia was convinced more than ever that Todd was still in love with her. She painted a smile on her face.

'Dolly, Gus. Welcome to our home.'

Todd shot her a grateful smile. 'You and Mariah have worked wonders, Emmie. The old place might be tumbling down but it's looking so much better than it did.'

'I think it's charming,' Dolly said enthusiastically. 'It looks like an old haunted house when viewed from the lane, but it feels very warm and welcoming now we're actually here.'

Gus took Amelia's hand and raised it to his lips. 'I'd say you've done a cracking job, Emmie. Todd warned us that the old place needed a lot of work doing to make it habitable. I'd say you were more than halfway there.'

'Do show us the rest of the house.' Dolly bent down and scooped Percy up in her arms. 'Who is this young man? I don't think we've been introduced.'

Betsy hurried up to her, holding out her hands. 'I'm sorry, my lady. I'm supposed to be looking after him.'

'No need to apologise,' Dolly said, laughing. 'You must be Betsy. I've heard all about you, and so this little fellow is your brother, Percy.'

Percy responded by tugging at Dolly's bonnet strings and gurgling.

'You have another admirer there, darling,' Gus said fondly. He took Percy from Dolly's arms. 'You are a fine chap, Percy, but you'd better go back to your sister. We have a lot of house to see.' He handed Percy to Betsy, who took him into the front parlour. Moments later the sound of discordant notes on the piano was followed by shrieks of laughter.

'Two budding musicians,' Dolly said, smiling. 'I love children and I can't wait to hold my baby in my arms. I'd love half a dozen, at least.'

Gus pulled a face. 'We'll see how we get on with this one, Dolly.'

'Why don't we start in the kitchen?' Amelia suggested hastily. 'I'm sure you would like some refreshment after travelling all the way across London to get here. Although I should add that we live very simply. I hope perhaps to get the garden tidied up at some point so I can grow fruit and vegetables.'

'You could keep chickens,' Dolly said enthusiastically. 'And you have room for a cow or two, or perhaps a goat. I suppose I am a countrywoman at heart.'

'But we knew you hadn't had time to settle in,' Gus added. 'So we took the liberty of bringing a picnic hamper. I hope you don't mind.'

Todd slapped him on the back. 'Mind? That's the best news I've had today.'

'I'll fetch it from the chaise.' Gus headed for the front entrance.

'I'll help,' Todd said eagerly. 'What a kind thought, Gus, old man. I can guess whose idea it was.' He followed Gus outside.

Dolly blushed rosily. 'I'd really love a cup of tea, Amelia. If it's not too much trouble.'

'Of course not. Come with me.' Amelia led the way to the kitchen, where she pulled up a chair for Dolly before filling the kettle at the sink. She placed it on the hob and took a seat at the table opposite her. 'Do you feel all right after the journey across town? Would you like to lie down, perhaps?'

'No, really. I am perfectly well. Apart from that swoon yesterday and some mornings when I feel very sick, there's nothing wrong with me.' Dolly leaned her elbows on the table. 'Tell me all about yourself, Amelia. I can see that Todd is very fond of you.'

'I don't know about that. We're just friends.'

'Well, he's a very lucky fellow to have someone like you on his side. Todd had a difficult childhood, as did Gus and the other boys that Aunt Nancy saved. They've all turned out to be fine men, although living very different lives. One day Todd must bring you to Rockwood and you will meet them all.' Dolly looked up as Gus breezed into the kitchen carrying a wicker hamper, followed by Todd with a basket crammed with bottles of beer and cider.

Mariah was close on their heels, but she stopped in the doorway, arms akimbo.

'I don't think this is a suitable place to entertain your guests, Todd. Her ladyship ought to be seated in a comfortable chair in the morning parlour.'

Dolly shook her head. 'I am really fine, thank you, Mariah.' She rose to her feet and walked towards Mariah, holding out her hand. 'We haven't been properly introduced, but I know you are the person who holds everything together in this household. You must call me Dolly. I am not a titled lady.'

Mariah shook hands tentatively, as if afraid that Dolly might shatter into shards at any moment. 'How do you do, ma'am?'

'It's Dolly.'

'Well, Dolly. You have to take care of yourself and the baby, so I suggest you sit back down and I'll make a pot of tea.' Mariah glanced disapprovingly at the bottles. 'You gentlemen might want to imbibe but it's not for ladies in the family way.'

Gus moved to Mariah's side and slipped his arm around her shoulders. 'You are very kind, but you do not have to wait upon us. My wife and I are hardened troopers, used to army life. I will wait upon you for a change, Mariah, my dear lady. What do you say to that?'

Mariah fluttered her eyelashes and her colour deepened. 'I don't know what to say, sir.'

Gus guided her to the table and pulled up a chair. 'Take a seat, Mariah. I suggest we sample the delights of Mr Fortnum's provisions here at the kitchen table. Todd, be a good chap and fetch the youngsters. We'll all eat together, unless anyone objects?'

'I must confess to being hungry,' Dolly added, hastily. 'What about you, Amelia?'

'I think it's a very good idea,' Amelia said, smiling. 'You sit there, Mariah. I'll fetch the plates and cutlery. It will be like having Christmas in midsummer.' She rose from her seat just as the door flew open and Betsy rushed into the room with Percy in her arms. Her eyes widened when she spotted the open hamper.

'Oh! Just look at that. I've never seen the like.'

'You and Percy can sit on the window seat,' Mariah said in a voice that meant business. 'There aren't enough chairs for everyone. I'll pass you your share so don't worry, Betsy, love.'

Amelia laid the table and stood back, enjoying the scene. It was obvious that Dolly and Gus were very much in love, and Todd was their very good friend. She chided herself for being jealous. After all, she and Todd were just friends, too. There had never been any hint of romance between them, and that was the best way to keep things. She took her seat at the table and helped Mariah to take the delicacies from the hamper, and pass them around. It was a merry meal with good-natured banter between Todd and Gus, which made everyone laugh. The food was delicious and Amelia enjoyed a glass of cider, leaving the others to drink the beer while Dolly stuck to tea. Betsy took a crafty sip or two of the cider, which brought the colour to her cheeks and a mischievous sparkle to her eyes. However, Mariah snatched the bottle from her daughter and placed it out of reach on a shelf above the sink.

When all the food had been eaten and everyone was replete it was Mariah's turn to take command. She shooed them from the kitchen, insisting that she had been waited upon for long enough and now she was going to wash the dishes and put them away. No one was to help, not even Amelia, and they were sent like schoolchildren to sit in the front parlour while digesting their meal. Dolly rose to the occasion and, to Betsy's delight, she sat at the piano and played so expertly that it brought tears to Amelia's eyes.

'I once thought I was going to be a great actress or a singer,' Dolly said, running her fingers over the keys in an arpeggio. 'But instead I married my Gus, and now I am going to be a mother, although I am happier now than I have ever been.' She blew a kiss to her husband.

Gus strolled over to the piano and dropped a kiss on her flaxen curls. 'You inherited your grandmother's talent, my love. Do play again.'

Amelia had been so intent on watching the tender scene between husband and wife that she was startled when the door opened and Caleb strode into the parlour. He stood in the doorway, peeling off his peccary-leather gloves as he glanced at each person in turn.

'Well, this is a pleasant party,' he said, curling his lip. 'Why wasn't I invited, Amelia? After all, this is my house.'

Amelia stood up quickly and went over to him. 'What are you doing here, Caleb?'

'I came to collect the rent you agreed to pay, but I didn't expect to find you entertaining all and sundry. I allowed you to stay here as a favour.'

'I don't know what you're talking about,' Amelia said, frowning. 'You didn't put any restrictions on how we would use the property, Caleb. Why have you changed your mind?'

Todd stood up, placing himself between Amelia and Caleb. 'I thought it was too good to be true. I should have guessed that you had an ulterior motive, when you made such a generous offer.'

'Mind your own business, Taylor. My agreement was made for Amelia's benefit and it has nothing to do with you.'

Gus moved swiftly to Todd's side. 'Who is this ill-mannered fellow, Todd? Would you like me to throw him out?'

'Move aside, soldier,' Caleb said angrily. 'This is still my house and I didn't invite you to visit. I suggest you leave and take your woman with you. Or do I have to throw you out?'

17

'Stop this at once, Caleb,' Amelia said angrily. 'These are my guests and this is my home. At least you said it was mine to do as I wished. Are you telling me now that this isn't the case?'

'Shame on you, sir,' Mariah said fiercely as she scooped a sobbing Percy into her arms. 'How dare you come here creating a scene? You're frightening my children.'

'Step outside, Caleb.' Todd grabbed him by the arm. 'We'll sort this out once and for all.'

'This has nothing to do with you, Todd. Let go of me or I'll forget I'm a gentleman and I'll floor you in front of the ladies.'

Gus seized Caleb by the scruff of the neck and propelled him from the room. Caleb's angry protests grew fainter as Gus and Todd ejected him from the premises.

'Really, that wasn't necessary,' Amelia said wearily. 'I'll go and talk to him,' she added as Todd returned, followed by Gus.

'Is it true that he owns this property?' Gus asked, frowning. 'It seems an odd arrangement.'

'It really is none of our business, darling.' Dolly rose from the piano stool. 'Perhaps we had better leave now. It was lovely to see you again, Amelia. And to meet you, Mariah, and your delightful children.'

Betsy clutched Dolly's hand. 'Don't go, miss. You play the piano so beautifully. Do you think you could teach me?'

'I'm afraid I play very badly. My aunt Nancy is the one with real talent at the pianoforte in my family. My husband and I have to travel to Devonshire tomorrow, but maybe when we return I can come here to see you and I'll give you a lesson on the piano.'

'Do you have to leave right away?' Amelia asked anxiously. 'We're only just getting to know each other.'

Dolly smiled. 'There will be other times, Amelia. I have very few female friends but I would love to count you as one of them.'

'I would like that,' Amelia said simply.

'We will come again,' Gus promised. 'But I don't like leaving you with that fellow still around.'

Todd shook his head. 'Don't worry about Caleb. I can handle him. I haven't forgotten how to deal with a bully. I'll go outside and make sure he's on his way before you leave.'

Amelia held up her hand. 'No, Todd. I'll deal with Caleb. Please wait here and let me have my say.'

'I'm coming with you.' Mariah took a step towards Amelia. 'He won't get the better of me.'

'I know that,' Amelia said gently. 'But this is my problem. Please stay here with the children, Mariah. I'll sort this out once and for all.' She hurried from the room, closing the door firmly behind her.

The front door was wide open and she could see Caleb pacing up and down on the gravel carriage sweep. She walked purposefully towards him.

'What was that all about, Caleb? Why did you come here today, anyway?'

He came to a halt, glaring at her. 'You have abused my hospitality.'

'Nonsense. You allowed me to have this house for

a low rent, providing I brought it back to life and undertook the necessary repairs. Well, as you can see, it is much cleaner and in better shape than when we moved in. As to the work needed — it will be done when funds allow.'

'You are a thief,' Caleb countered. 'You stole two sewing machines from the workroom. You will give them back or pay for them.'

'Has my cousin's meanness transferred to you in such a short time?'

'Mr Norris is a good businessman, and that does not include allowing anyone to pilfer goods. You either pay me or I will inform the police that you stole from your cousin's business.'

'I will have the money when Lady Galton settles her account.'

'And we all know how difficult it is to squeeze money from the gentry. You will be in prison before that happens.'

Amelia faced him, fear replaced by curiosity. 'What's the matter with you, Caleb? What happened to the kind man who had our best interests at heart?'

'You are living in my house. You belong to me, Amelia Sutton. While you live under my roof you are to remember that, and when it suits me I will call in the favours I have allowed you. Do you understand?'

Amelia stared at him aghast. 'You don't mean it. You surely don't believe what you're saying.'

'Yes, I do. You accepted my terms and now you must abide by them. Do I make myself clear?'

'You're out of your mind, Caleb. I agreed to no such thing.'

'Then you will return the sewing machines and you will pack your things and leave my house.'

Amelia realised with a shock that it was useless to argue with Caleb in this mood. She could never have imagined that he would turn on her in such a way, but his anger was real and the look in his eyes, the determined set of his jaw and his whole demeanour was enough to convince her that he would carry out his threat. If it were just herself she would have told him to go to hell, but there was Mariah to consider and her two innocent children. Amelia drew herself up to her full height.

'I will pay the rent and I'll hire the sewing machines. I can't say fairer than that.'

'You can't afford to pay what I will ask. The rent has gone up since you moved in.' Caleb took a step towards her but at that moment Todd emerged from the house.

'What's going on?' he demanded suspiciously. 'What have you said to upset Emmie?'

Caleb turned on him. 'You didn't waste time in getting your feet under the table, did you? You must have planned to move in the moment my back was turned.'

'Leave Todd out of this,' Amelia said angrily. 'This is between you and me, Caleb.'

'If it concerns you, it concerns me, Emmie.' Todd squared up to Caleb. 'To be honest, I always suspected that you were not the man you pretended to be. What have you said to her?'

Amelia laid a restraining hand on his arm. 'It's all right, Todd. We were just discussing rent for the house. Apparently it's gone up since my agreement with Caleb.'

'That's ridiculous. I thought it was supposed to be cheap because of its semi-derelict condition, not to mention its position here on the marsh.' Todd glared at Caleb, clenching his fists at his sides.

'I've changed my mind. I want a guinea a week.'

Amelia gasped in horror. 'But that's ridiculous, Caleb. I could rent a mansion in Mayfair for that.'

'This old house isn't worth a fraction of that, and you know it. Are you intent on driving Amelia out of her home?' Todd's voice shook with barely suppressed anger. 'What has changed? You were happy enough to enjoy her hospitality when it suited you.'

'And now I am in command of the situation. This had nothing to do with you, Taylor.' Caleb glanced warily at Gus, who had come to join Todd and Amelia. 'And you can keep out of it, too, soldier.'

'Sub-Lieutenant Baker to you, sir.' Gus took a menacing step towards Caleb. 'I heard a little of what was being said. You are a charlatan and a bully.'

'Insult me and the rent goes up again,' Caleb said with a malicious grin. 'This is between me and Amelia. She has to choose. She either accepts my terms or she moves out of my house today.'

'I will pay what you ask,' Amelia said hastily. She could see Mariah and the children standing in the doorway and the thought of telling them they were once again homeless was too much to bear. 'But I need time. When I have delivered the garments to Lady Galton . . .'

Caleb shook his head. 'No. I want the money in advance. You pay me four guineas now or you pack up and leave.'

'That's impossible. I haven't got that much money.'

'Well then, you'd best start packing. I'll wait until I see you on your way.'

'I would help but I can only raise a guinea at the

most,' Todd said worriedly. 'Surely you won't carry out this threat, Marsh. You wouldn't turn out two women and innocent children.'

Gus fisted his hands. 'Let's settle this like men. Leave the ladies out of this.'

'Just a moment.' Dolly pushed past Mariah and stepped outside into the hot sunshine. 'Four guineas a month, I believe you said. Is that correct?'

'Dolly, no!' Gus hurried to her side. 'That is your money.'

She looked up at him with a tender smile. 'Yes, my love, it is. And because it is mine I have the right to do what I think best. I will not see Emmie and Mariah and the children cast out on the street.' Dolly opened her reticule and counted out four gold sovereigns and four shilling pieces. She walked over to Caleb and dropped the coins into his outstretched hand. 'There, sir. I don't know you and I do not wish to make your acquaintance, but I trust you will be gentleman enough to honour your promise that the ladies can stay here. Although shame on you for extorting such a high rent.'

Caleb pocketed the money. 'Thank you, ma'am. I will relieve you of my presence.' He turned to Amelia with a sickly smile. 'But I will return in four weeks' time. I expect to be paid promptly. You may keep the machines until then to prove that I am not such a bad fellow.' He strolled over to where he had tethered his horse and climbed onto the driver's seat of the smart chaise.

'Are you sure you want to do this, Emmie?' Todd said in a low voice. 'I mean, for that amount of money you could move to the West End.'

'I'll have to think it over very carefully, Todd. We're

safe for the moment thanks to Dolly.' She moved away, holding out both hands. 'Dolly. That was such a generous gesture. I will repay you, I promise.'

'I just happened to have that amount in my reticule. I was going to fritter it away on new shoes and a bonnet, but at least it has gone to a good cause. You deserve the chance to prove yourself, Amelia. I will order my new wardrobe from you as well. No doubt I will need more roomy garments quite soon.'

'You will have my very best attention and designs especially for you,' Amelia said earnestly. 'I cannot thank you enough. We are safe for another month at least.'

'I'd have floored him if you'd given me the signal, Todd.' Gus unclenched his fists and flexed his fingers. 'That fellow needs taking down a peg or two.'

'I think I'll pay a call on him in Albemarle Street,' Todd said grimly. 'He won't get away with treating Emmie like this.'

Gus grinned. 'Well, if you need someone to back you up, you can call on me. We'll be in Devonshire for a week or two but I can always return to London if you need me.'

Dolly shook her finger at him. 'It's none of your business, Gus. I think Todd is perfectly capable of handling himself without your support.'

'I will deal with Caleb in my own way,' Amelia said firmly. 'But thank you once again, Dolly. You are a true friend.'

'Remember we are on your side.' Gus took Amelia's hand and raised it to his lips. 'We should leave now, but we will see you again very soon.' He turned to Todd. 'Take good care of her.'

Todd nodded. 'I most certainly will. Goodbye for

now, Gus.'

'I look forward to seeing you on our return to London,' Dolly said as Gus helped her into the chaise. She blew a kiss to Mariah and the children as Gus took the reins and flicked the whip over the horse's head.

Amelia slipped her hand into the crook of Todd's arm as they watched the vehicle drive away. 'You have such nice friends, Todd.'

'They're your friends now, Emmie. I'm so pleased that you get on well with Dolly. I'm still very fond of her, but in a brotherly way.'

Amelia looked up and met his honest gaze with a smile. 'I'm glad, Todd. I can see that she is a special person.'

'I trust that you are sleeping here tonight, Todd.' Mariah marched up to them, her expression uncompromising. 'I wouldn't put it past that fellow to return later. I always thought he was up to no good.'

'Yes, Mariah. Rest assured I will stay tonight, although I have to leave first thing in the morning. I'll try and arrange my duties so that I am here most nights, but it's not always possible.'

'Maybe your pa ought to come and live here, too,' Mariah said thoughtfully. 'He's probably enjoying the attentions of that painted woman, but his first duty is to you, Emmie.'

Amelia laughed. 'I doubt if Pa would see it that way. If he's happy lodging with Mrs Delaney I wouldn't dream of taking him away from a comfortable billet, but I would feel safer if you were here at night, Todd.'

'I've said my say.' Mariah beckoned to Betsy, who was pretending to chase Percy, which he seemed to find hilarious. 'I'll go indoors and start making supper. Farmer Allen left another couple of rabbits this morning, and a few eggs. I think he's making sure of getting his free treatment from you, Todd.'

'Either that, or the gentleman has a fancy for you, Mariah,' Todd said, grinning. 'A widower with five children would think himself blessed to find a comely woman like you living so near.'

Mariah threw up her hands, her cheeks flushed with colour. 'Good Lord, what nonsense you talk. I'm going back to my kitchen. I didn't spend hours cleaning that rusty old range just to have it snatched from beneath me by Caleb Marsh.'

Amelia managed to keep a straight face until Mariah had marched into the house followed by her children.

'You are wicked, Todd,' Amelia said, giggling. 'You made Mariah blush. Shame on you.'

'Well, she is a good-looking woman and an excellent cook. I think Farmer Allen would be a lucky man if she returns his regard, which is blatantly obvious.'

Amelia sighed. 'What a strange turn of events, Todd. We were just beginning to settle down here. I've laid out everything in the long gallery so that I can begin to work on Lady Galton's order, and now Caleb is charging us an exorbitant amount of rent and making threats into the bargain.'

'What threats? What have I missed?'

Amelia met his angry gaze with an attempt at a smile. 'Just nonsense really.'

'Tell me, Emmie. I heard most of what he said, but not all of it.'

'Caleb seems to think that by allowing me to have his old home rent free that I am under an obligation to him, and him alone, if you know what I mean?'

'Are you saying that he made unacceptable advances

to you?' Todd's hazel eyes narrowed and his brows drew together in an ominous frown.

'In a manner of speaking, yes. But I refuted his allegations very firmly, hence his demand for such a high rent.'

'That settles it. You must find somewhere else to live, but if Caleb Marsh pesters you again he'll have me to answer to.'

'I will look for somewhere else to live, of course, but we have a month paid for, thanks to Dolly. I will repay her if it's the last thing I ever do, but in the meantime I am going to start working on my creations. If I can fill Lady Galton's order quickly it might lead to her friends and acquaintances wanting me to design their wardrobes for them. I have to start somewhere, Todd. This is where my hard work really begins.'

* * *

Amelia made a start that evening. With Mariah's assistance she cut out a pattern for the first of Lady's Galton's garments, which was to be an afternoon gown in bronze silk, the colour of autumn leaves, according to Mariah. They worked late into the night, but in the end a mixture of fatigue and the strain of working by candlelight caused them to pack everything away and retire to their respective rooms. However, next morning Amelia was up even earlier than usual and she went straight to the long gallery to begin pinning the pattern onto the fabric, ready to start cutting.

She worked mostly alone as Mariah had household duties to carry out and Percy had found his adventurous spirit, so needed continuous watching or he would wander off into the garden. Fortunately, the old house was surrounded by a brick wall, which was too high for a toddler to climb, but there was unseen danger lurking in the barns and outhouses. Betsy was eager to learn how to sew, but she spent most of her time making sure that her little brother came to no harm.

Ignoring all interruptions, Amelia worked on, cutting, tacking and finally sitting down at one of the sewing machines to begin stitching in earnest.

Todd rode to the hospital every day and managed to swap his night duties so that he was able to sleep at Marsh House. Even so, he was absent for twelve hours at a time, which made Mariah very nervous, although Amelia insisted that she was not afraid of Caleb. During the long summer evenings Todd was happy to work outside in the garden, taming the overgrown lawn and weeding the vegetable patch at the rear of the barn. Then there was the stable to muck out and the horses to groom. Todd joked that he worked harder at home than he did at the hospital, but gradually after weeks of hard work it was possible to see how elegant the gardens must have once been, and how productive the kitchen garden was in its glory days.

Amelia and Mariah finished the silk afternoon dress in record time with the aid of the sewing machines, and the rest of the garments followed one by one. Amelia worked tirelessly, driven on by a niggling worry as to what Caleb might do next. She had no chance of repaying Dolly until Lady Galton's order was delivered and paid for, and then there was another four guineas to find for the rent. She could only hope that Caleb had relented and might be persuaded to cut the sum by half at least, but she had a nagging feeling that he meant business. He would only be satisfied by complete surrender on her part, whether it was giving in to his physical demands, which was unthinkable, or else they would have to leave the premises. Neither option was one she would choose, but she had to be single-minded and make a reputation for herself as a designer and purveyor of fine-quality fashion before she could think of moving away from Marsh House.

Gradually the old house was beginning to charm her in a way she would have thought impossible on first sight. Early in the morning the view over the marsh from her bedroom window was a magical misty vision where the land and sky melted together, and the reeds and sedge were spangled with dew-drops in the pale sunlight. Similarly, last thing in the evening the mist would cloak the land, marooning them within their walled grounds and making Amelia feel as if they were wrapped in a protective shield. It was all her imagination, of course, but nevertheless she could feel Marsh House warming towards her, as if the spirits of the long-dead owners approved of her efforts to keep the old place safe from the destructive forces of man and nature. The creaks and groans of the timbers at the end of the day no longer frightened her, nor did the density of the shadows when she ascended the stairs by candlelight. Perhaps the house itself knew that it was in good hands. She could only hope so, and that made her work even harder. Caleb would not get the better of her, and Mariah's children would be kept safe from anyone who meant them harm.

With the end of August just a couple of days away, Amelia wrapped the grand ball gown, the pride of her collection, in butter muslin before packing it away in the wicker laundry basket she had chosen to transport the clothes to Lady Galton's establishment. The account, noting each item in detail and setting out the cost involved, lay on top of the garments. Todd carried the heavy basket downstairs to the waiting gig.

'I wish I could come with you, Emmie,' he said apologetically. 'But I'm on duty at the hospital. I wish I could find work closer to home.'

Amelia smiled. 'You called this old place 'home'. You wouldn't have done that at first.'

'It grows on you. I don't know why because it's isolated and it's probably very unhealthy living with all the damp humours from the marsh, but it's peaceful here away from the noise of the city, and you and Mariah have made it feel like home. We just need to furnish a few more rooms and get the roof fixed before winter and we'll be set to weather the worst storms.'

'Caleb permitting,' Amelia said dryly. 'I keep expecting to see him riding up the drive to the house with an eviction notice in his hand.'

'He can't do that yet. We've paid the rent and I have half of next month's saved. Unfortunately, my salary isn't large enough for me to cover the whole of it.'

'That seems so unfair on you.' Amelia climbed onto the driver's seat. 'I'll make sure that Lady Galton realises that she must settle her account quickly. Only I'll do it in a more subtle manner. I doubt if she would take kindly to threats of being taken to court for debt.'

Todd laughed. 'No, please don't sink to blackmail.'

'I'll do anything to keep my family safe.' Amelia flicked the whip over Grey's ears. 'Walk on, Grey. We have an important delivery to make.'

* * *

Amelia's request to deliver the order to her ladyship in person were refused politely but firmly. However, she was determined to speak to someone about the urgent need for payment and eventually she was asked to wait in a small parlour off the grand entrance hall, together with the wicker hamper, which she refused to let out of her sight until she had spoken to Lady Galton's maid. She opened it and took out the account, which she clutched nervously in her hand.

Eventually the door opened and a prim-looking middle-aged woman entered the room. Her black bombazine gown was relieved by a white lace collar and cuffs.

'I am Miss Manners, Lady Galton's personal maid. What can I do for you, miss?'

'I've brought the garments Lady Galton ordered.'

'I'll see that they are taken to her room.'

'This is rather delicate, and I don't want you to take it the wrong way, but I really need the account settled quickly. I hoped to speak directly to her ladyship so that she might bring the subject up with Sir Oswald. It seems to take a very long time before payment is made.'

Miss Manners raised a delicate eyebrow. 'That is the way the system works, miss. I can do nothing other than present the account to Sir Oswald's man of business. You will be paid directly.'

Miss Manners was about to leave the room but Amelia pressed the account into her hand.

'Please, Miss Manners, you don't understand. We need the money desperately. If I cannot pay my rent we will be evicted from our home and the sewing machines will be taken away from us. It's imperative that I am paid quickly.'

'Please let me go, Miss Sutton. I will place the account on Sir Oswald's desk but I can do no more than that.' She snatched her arm free and hurried from the parlour, leaving Amelia and the hamper in the middle of the room.

It was not what she had hoped for but Amelia had little option other than to trust Miss Manners to keep her word. Amelia left the mansion in Dover Street and gave her last penny to the boy who had walked Grey and the gig while she was in the house. She had a horrible feeling that Caleb might be waiting for her when she arrived home without the money to pay next month's rent.

18

When Amelia finally arrived home, she was surprised to find Dolly seated at the kitchen table, sipping a cup of tea while Mariah rolled out pastry for the crust of a steak pie.

For an awful moment Amelia thought that Dolly was going to ask for repayment of the loan, but Dolly seemed to have forgotten all about the money. She rose to her feet and gave Amelia a hug.

'It's good to see you again. Mariah has been telling me how hard you've all worked to get out the order for Lady Galton.' Dolly held Amelia at arm's length, her smile fading. 'You look tired. I'm sure you have been working far too hard.'

Amelia smiled. 'I'm just happy to have delivered the garments to her ladyship. Now all I have to do is wait until they decide to pay me. I tried to convince her maid to speak for me, but I doubt if she will.'

Dolly sat down again, taking a deep breath. 'It seems I've come at the right time. We only returned from Devonshire last evening, but I was determined to visit you and put my order in for a new wardrobe. Already my gowns are beginning to feel too tight and it won't be long before they don't fit at all.'

'You've come to the right place,' Mariah said as she laid the pastry over the meat in the pie dish. 'I saw some of Emmie's sketches for your clothes. I think you'll like them.'

'I'm sure I will. Perhaps you could show me,

Emmie.'

Amelia took off her bonnet and laid it on the table. 'Of course. Come upstairs to the long gallery. If you like my ideas I'll take your measurements and we can discuss colours and materials.'

'This is so exciting. When I was younger we had all our gowns made by a woman in Exeter. She was very good, but I feel like a change and I can't keep going backwards and forwards to Devonshire for fittings.'

'I'm sure I can make something suitable,' Amelia said, smiling. 'You can tell me all about Rockwood. You must have grown up with Todd and Gus. What were they like as boys?'

'Gus was constantly in trouble. He's always been a rebel or, as he says, a free thinker, but Todd was the dependable one — the leader of the gang when they were in London, and the good student when he had the opportunity to study medicine. Despite his difficult start in life Todd was always kind and sensitive to other people's feelings. I love him like a brother.'

'That sounds like the Todd I've come to know and appreciate. I don't know what we would do without him now.' Amelia led the way from the kitchen with Dolly close on her heels.

Dolly laughed. 'Do I sense a romance, Emmie?'

'We are friends, that's all. Todd and I both work hard and somehow he manages his studies, too. Neither of us has time for anything else.'

'Hmm,' Dolly said, pulling a face. 'I'm not sure I believe you, but I must say you've both done wonders making this old house into a home.'

'There is so much still to do.' Amelia ascended the stairs with Dolly close behind.

'I think Caleb is robbing you by charging so much

rent for the place.'

'Yes, I agree,' Amelia said over her shoulder. 'And I will repay you when Lady Galton settles her account.'

'That wasn't what I meant. Really, Emmie, it doesn't matter. I just don't like to think of you and Mariah working so hard for so little.'

'Yes, but we have a home and we're safe here.' Amelia came to a halt in the long gallery. 'As I can't pay you in money at the moment, how would it be if I made your whole wardrobe to cover the debt? I am so grateful to you, Dolly.'

'That sounds as if I will benefit more than you,' Dolly said, smiling. 'But I promise I will wear the gowns with pride and I will promote your business by telling all my friends and acquaintances of the wonderful new designer.'

Amelia pulled up a chair for her. 'Do take a seat and we'll go through the sketches I did with you in mind. Also, it will depend upon where you think you and Gus will be based. If you are going somewhere hot, you will need muslins and cottons.' She handed Dolly a portfolio containing her designs and they spent an hour going over each one in detail. Finally, after much discussion Dolly chose her outfits for the next few months, and then they had the pleasurable task of choosing colours and fabrics.

'Gus is coming to pick me up when he finishes his meeting with his superior officer. We should know our posting today, which will mean I can tell you where we are going.'

'Excellent. You must stay for luncheon. I expect the pie will be ready soon. Mariah makes the most wonderful pastry.'

'I'm always hungry these days,' Dolly said with a

rueful smile. 'Pie sounds delightful.'

'I'll just take your measurements and then we're done for today.' Amelia took out her measuring tape and noted down the numbers she required. 'Do you think you might be further advanced than you first thought, Dolly?' Amelia said, frowning. 'I mean, I'm no expert, but it does seem possible.'

Dolly frowned thoughtfully. 'I suppose I could be. From the dates I gave the doctor in Rockwood he thought I'm due in January or even February next year, but I couldn't remember accurately when it was my time of the month. We were travelling so much, I just forgot.'

'Maybe you could talk to Todd about it?'

Dolly shook her head. 'I don't think I could. Just make my gowns a little larger round the middle, and I'll wear capes or shawls to protect my modesty.'

Amelia nodded. 'All right, if you say so, although I'm sure Todd would be very helpful. He is a doctor.'

'And I've known him forever. I believe he had a soft spot for me once upon a time. That's before he met you.'

Amelia felt the blood rush to her cheeks and she turned away on the pretext of tucking her notes inside the portfolio. 'Let's go downstairs and get something to eat. I'm starving, too.'

'That's good, because it doesn't make me look like a glutton.' Dolly buttoned her bodice and wrapped her lacy shawl around her shoulders. 'I wonder if it will be a boy or a girl. I rather fancy a little daughter, but of course Gus wants a son. Maybe it's twins and that explains why I am a little larger than you might expect.'

Amelia laughed. 'Who knows? You'll just have to

wait to find out. Isn't it exciting?'

They were both smiling broadly when they reached the kitchen and were welcomed by the smell of hot steak pie and potatoes roasting in the oven.

Gus had arrived and was swinging Percy round in circles, much to Percy's delight. Betsy watched a little enviously, but she smiled when she saw Dolly and ran towards her, giving her a hug.

'I can look after your baby when it arrives,' Betsy said eagerly. 'I've helped with Percy since the day he was born.'

'That is true.' Mariah opened the oven door and stepped back as the heat blasted into the already hot kitchen. 'Betsy is a very good child minder. She's a proper little mother.'

Gus set Percy on his feet. 'Well, it's a pity that we will be in Bombay, to start with anyway. My posting has come through, Dolly. We're off in a couple of weeks.'

'Then it's muslins and cottons.' Dolly sighed. 'I love you desperately, Gus, but I really would rather stay in England to have our baby. Could I not join you later?'

Gus stared at her in disbelief. 'But you love travelling. You are a perfect army wife.'

'Yes, normally I am, but this is different. I would like our child to be born at home in Rockwood, with Mama there and my aunts to look after me.'

Mariah and Amelia exchanged worried glances.

'I suggest we have our luncheon in the dining room,' Amelia said hastily. 'It's cooler there and we have more room. I'll go and lay the table.'

'That's a good idea.' Mariah took the roast potatoes from the oven and tipped them into a serving dish. 'Take your lady into the dining room, sir. She'll feel better sitting at the big table away from the heat of the kitchen.'

Gus nodded and slipped his arm around Dolly's shoulders. 'Come on, darling girl. We'll talk this over when we get back to the barracks. In the meantime, I can't wait to taste that splendid pie that Mariah is just about to serve.' He winked at Mariah. 'I wish I could take you as our army cook. You could teach them all a thing or two.'

'Get on with you, sir. Take Mrs Baker somewhere cooler before she swoons from the heat. Betsy and I will bring the food.'

Amelia held the door open for them. 'Come on. I haven't had a chance to do much to the dining room. It's a bit like a monks' refectory, but it is not nearly as hot as the kitchen. Betsy, dear, would you be so kind as to fill a pitcher with water and bring some glasses to the table?'

Betsy puffed out her flat chest. 'Yes, Emmie. Of course. You can always rely on me.'

⋆ ⋆ ⋆

'That was absolutely delicious,' Gus said, placing his knife and fork back on his plate. 'The best pie I've ever tasted.'

Dolly wiped her lips on a linen table napkin. 'Thank you, Emmie. I agree with Gus. That was a wonderful luncheon.'

Amelia smiled proudly. 'Mariah is an excellent cook, and she is a brilliant pattern cutter. I would struggle to produce my garments without her skills.'

Dolly frowned. 'Which leads me to the question of whether or not I will need clothes for a hot climate.'

She turned to Gus. 'We have to decide now. Emmie needs to know what to make for me.'

'Are you serious about wanting to remain in England when I'm posted to India?' Gus sat back in his chair, eyeing her warily. 'You always travel with me, sweetheart.'

'I know I do, and I love the life, but I am concerned for the baby. It's a long journey by sea and then we would be travelling on horseback for hours at a time in searing heat. I will join you as soon as I can, but I really want to have my baby at home.'

Amelia rose from the table. She collected the plates and took them to the kitchen. Dolly and Gus needed to be alone to talk things over, but she could see that Dolly had already made up her mind. Maybe she too suspected that her pregnancy was further advanced than was first thought.

'Why the long face?' Mariah demanded as Amelia put the plates on the wooden draining board. 'Didn't they enjoy the pie?'

'They loved it with good reason. You excelled yourself, Mariah.' Amelia sank down at the kitchen table. 'I left them talking over Dolly's decision to remain in England to have her baby. I don't think Gus is very keen on the idea, but it does make sense.'

'Men are never practical when it comes to things like that. I think Dolly will talk him round. She doesn't look like the sort of woman who will give in easily.'

Amelia laughed. 'I think you're right. I'll make a pot of tea and take it in to them.'

'I'd wait until they come out,' Mariah said gloomily. 'There might be fur and feathers flying.'

'I can't believe that.' Amelia filled the kettle and placed it on the hob. 'But you're probably right. I will wait.'

As it happened she did not have to be patient for long. The kettle had barely come to a boil when Dolly waltzed into the kitchen followed by a gloomy Gus.

'It's all agreed,' Dolly said joyfully. 'I am going to remain in London with my uncle Freddie until you have finished my new clothes, Emmie. Then Freddie will take me down to Rockwood where I will stay until the baby is born, and when I am fully recovered I will travel to Bombay to meet Gus.'

'Very sensible,' Mariah said with a nod of approval.

'Yes, I agree,' Amelia added, smiling. 'I'm sure the time will pass very quickly, Gus.'

'Of course it will,' Dolly said quickly, without giving Gus a chance to answer. 'Anyway, you will be so busy with your new posting that you will hardly miss me, darling.'

'I wouldn't say that.' Gus managed a half-hearted smile. 'But whatever is best for you and my son is good as far as I am concerned.'

'There you are, then.' Dolly did a twirl. 'Everyone is happy. I will be staying at Uncle Freddie's mansion in Piccadilly, only he doesn't know that yet. But he will be pleased to see me again, and I am very fond of him. Besides which, Emmie, he moves in high society. If he takes me to social functions wearing your creations, I am certain your business will be established even more quickly.'

'How exciting. I will make sure that your garments are the best that money can buy.'

'I suggest we call in at your uncle's house before we return to the barracks,' Gus said firmly. 'Don't get ahead of yourself, sweetheart. After all, Freddie might be at his country estate. You know he's not fond of town.'

'I'm sure he would come up to London if I sent him a telegram.' Dolly sat down at the table. 'I would love a cup of tea, if you're making one, Mariah. Then we'll leave you all in peace.'

'Your uncle must be very wealthy,' Amelia said curiously.

'He is, but he's not a real uncle. He is a family friend and we all love him dearly.'

Gus grinned. 'I expect Dolly will tell you the full story over a cup of tea. I'll go and harness the horse to the chaise. It's on loan from a friend so we need to get it back to the barracks soon.' He dropped a kiss on top of his wife's flaxen curls. 'I won't be long and then we'd better be off. There's a lot to do.'

Betsy had been quietly listening to the conversation while keeping an eye on Percy, who was playing with a wooden top that Todd had carved for him.

'I'll help with the horse,' Betsy said eagerly. 'I'm good with animals, aren't I, Ma?'

'You are, indeed. Run along then, dear, but don't get in the way.'

'As if I would.' Betsy hurried after Gus as he left the room.

Mariah made the tea and sat down opposite Amelia and Dolly. 'Now tell us all about your uncle who isn't really an uncle, but is very rich. He sounds too good to be true.'

'That's Uncle Freddie,' Dolly said, laughing. 'I haven't seen him for over a year so it will be like old times. I just wish he could find a nice lady to fall in love with. His trouble is that he always chooses the wrong woman.'

Amelia leaned her elbows on the table. 'He sounds fascinating. I do hope you find him at home in

London. It would be lovely if you were so near that we could visit each other, if only for a few weeks until I've completed your order.'

Dolly had just begun explaining how Freddie, the Earl of Dorrington, had become involved with the Carey family, when the sound of raised voices outside carried as far as the kitchen.

Amelia recognised Caleb's voice and he sounded furious. She jumped to her feet and ran from the room, heading for the front entrance with Mariah on her heels and Dolly following more slowly.

Outside, where a white-faced Betsy was holding the horse's reins, there appeared to be a fierce argument between Gus and Caleb, who had dismounted and allowed his horse to wander away, heading for the overgrown parts of the garden to graze.

'What's going on?' Amelia demanded angrily. 'Why are you here, Caleb?'

'Get this brute off me,' Caleb shouted as Gus grabbed him by the collar.

'Who do you think you are?' Gus gave Caleb a shake. 'You come here throwing your weight around when you know you are not welcome.'

Caleb broke free, holding his hand to his throat. 'I'll report you to your superior for attacking me, soldier.'

'Stop this at once.' Amelia placed herself between them. 'Why are you here, Caleb?'

'To collect next month's rent. I'll wager you haven't got a penny piece to your name.'

'But the rent isn't due for another two days,' Amelia said slowly. 'You can't just turn up demanding money whenever you feel like it.'

'If you can't pay up, then I'll take back the sewing machines. They don't belong to you any more than this property does.'

'You heard what Miss Sutton said.' Gus fisted his hands. 'Don't hide behind a woman's skirts, you coward.'

'What's happening?' Dolly pushed past Mariah. 'Haven't you caused enough trouble, sir?'

Caleb shot her an angry glance. 'Mind your own business, woman.'

'Don't speak to my wife in that tone.' Gus took a step towards Caleb, who backed away.

'I have the law on my side,' Caleb said warily. 'There's no need for you to become involved. This is between me and Amelia.'

Amelia nodded fiercely. 'Yes, it is, and I'm telling you to leave, Caleb. This is my property while I'm paying you rent and I don't want you here, upsetting my guests.'

'You know my terms, Amelia.' Caleb lowered his voice. 'I'm tired of play-acting. I've tried being a gentleman but it isn't who I am, and I'm sick of standing by and watching the good doctor fawn over you.'

'Stop it, Caleb,' Amelia cried angrily. 'You're talking nonsense.'

'You'll see what nonsense is if you don't pay attention to me. You accept me as your man and I'll live here and take care of you. Refuse, and I'll seize the machines and evict you from this house.'

'You can't do that,' Amelia said icily. 'I've paid the rent you demanded and the month isn't up yet.'

'But it will be in two days' time. Even if you could find somewhere else to stay I know a certain gentleman who lives in Bow Street, and he would pay me well to learn the whereabouts of his son.'

'That's blackmail, Caleb.' Amelia stood her ground.

'I dislike you intensely and I can't think why you have any interest in me. I wish I'd never accepted your offer of the house. I should have known that it wasn't genuine.'

'At least I've put a roof over your head, which is more than I can say for Todd Taylor. He's using you. He pretends to have feelings for you in order to live here cheaply.'

Gus took a step forward. 'Just say the word, Emmie, and I'll throw this fellow over the garden wall into the marsh and watch him sink into the bog.'

Caleb held up his hand, palm outwards. 'No need. I will abide by the letter of the law. You have two days in which to find the money or to pack your things and move out, Amelia. On the other hand, you know the alternative.'

Amelia eyed him warily. 'Does my cousin know you are doing this?'

'It was his idea.' Caleb snorted with laughter as he strode off towards his grazing horse.

'I wish you'd let me sort the fellow out,' Gus said gloomily. 'He needs a good hiding.'

'Maybe, but it would make trouble for you and for me.' Amelia laid her hand on Gus's arm. 'And that's the last thing Dolly needs just now.'

'I couldn't agree more. I apologise for rushing off so soon, Emmie, but I want to take Dolly to Piccadilly to see if Lord Dorrington is at home.'

'I understand. Please don't worry about me.'

'I don't like leaving you with that fellow Marsh behaving so badly.'

'I can deal with Caleb Marsh. He annoys me but he doesn't scare me.'

Gus grinned. 'You are a spirited woman, Amelia

Sutton. I take my hat off to you.' He swept her a bow, making her laugh.

'Gus and I will stay here tonight if you are anxious,' Dolly said gently. 'What time does Todd return from the hospital?'

'In time for his dinner, as always.' Mariah ruffled Betsy's curls. 'Don't worry, love. That nasty man has gone and if he comes back Ma will hit him with the frying pan and he'll see stars.'

Betsy giggled and hugged her mother. 'He's hateful, Ma. If he's horrid to you I will hit him with the big black saucepan.'

'No one is going to attack anyone,' Amelia said hastily. 'Let's stop this talk of violence and get on with our lives. Caleb Marsh will get his comeuppance one way or another, and it won't involve frying pans or saucepans.'

Gus handed Dolly into the chaise and leaped up to sit on the driver's seat beside her. 'We'll be off then, but we'll be back soon.'

'With good news, I hope,' Dolly added, as Gus encouraged the horse to walk on.

Amelia turned to Mariah with a rueful smile. 'That wasn't how I hoped our pleasant luncheon would end, but Caleb and my cousin won't win. We will beat them, Mariah. When our fashion house is established we can say goodbye to them both.'

Mariah bent down to scoop Percy up in her arms as he had fallen over and hurt his knees. 'That's all very fine, and I agree with you, but how are we going to find the money for next month's rent?'

'I don't know, but I might visit my father at Mrs Delaney's lodging house. Maybe he can help.'

Mariah pulled a face. 'From the little I know of

your pa, I think the only person who might have benefited from his stay will be that painted hussy.' She gave Percy a kiss on his chubby cheek and set him on his feet. 'Betsy, love, take your brother indoors and give him a jam tart. I meant to bring them out to serve with the tea, but I clean forgot, thanks to Caleb Marsh.'

'I don't think Mrs Delaney would thank you for calling her a hussy,' Amelia said, smiling. 'But I think she knows how to get the most from her gentlemen lodgers. Pa was always a soft mark when it comes to feminine wiles, but I'm desperate so I will go and see him and hope for the best.'

* * *

Later that afternoon, having given her father time to return from his duties at the hospital, Amelia arrived at Mrs Delaney's lodging house in Charlotte Street. She tethered Grey to a lamp post and climbed the front steps to knock on the door. It was opened by a very young maid wearing an over-large white apron and mobcap.

'Yes, missis?'

It was not an encouraging start.

'Is Mrs Delaney at home?' Amelia asked, ignoring the fact that the child assumed she was a married woman.

'Yes, missis.'

'I would like to speak to her, unless Dr Sutton is in residence.'

'In residence?' the maid repeated, looking baffled.

'Do you know Dr Sutton?'

'Yes, missis. He give me linctus for me sore throat.'

'Well, has he returned from the hospital?'

'I dunno, missis. I ain't allowed to go to the gents' rooms.'

'Who are you talking to, Daisy?' A voice from the inner hallway was unmistakably that of Ruby Delaney.

'I dunno, missis. She wants the doctor.'

'Tell her she'll have to go to the hospital to see Dr Sutton.'

Amelia had had quite enough of this conversation. She lifted the young maid out of the way and walked into the entrance hall.

'Mrs Delaney, you might remember me. I'm Dr Sutton's daughter, Amelia. I was simply asking if my father had returned from the hospital.'

Mrs Delaney stepped out of a room to the right of the long, narrow hallway. 'How many times have I told you how to deal with visitors, Daisy?'

'I forgets, missis.'

'Well, don't forget again or I'll send you back to the orphanage.' Mrs Delaney clipped the child on the ear as she attempted to sidle past her.

'There was no need for that, ma'am,' Amelia said angrily. 'That child can't be more than eight or nine. She should be in school.'

Mrs Delaney turned to her with a sickly smile on her rouged lips. 'Take no notice, Miss Sutton. Daisy is a charity case and a little simple. I've a good mind to send her back from whence she came and order a substitute.'

'Perhaps a little kindness would go a long way, ma'am. Daisy seems scared out of her wits. I'm sure with good training she would be a benefit to you.'

'Well, you are welcome to try to drum some sense into that thick head. I have tried, so help me. As to your dearest pa, he has not yet come home.'

'Then I will wait for him, if that's all right with you, ma'am.'

'Come into my private parlour. I'd send for tea, but that stupid child will only spill it or scald herself. I really will have to let her go.' Mrs Delaney ushered Amelia into the parlour, which was packed with heavy mahogany furniture and glass-fronted cabinets stuffed with ornaments of every shape and size. The walls were covered with gilt-framed pictures of country scenes and sickly-sweet children with rosy cheeks and spotless white frocks, dancing around idyllic farmyards. The heavy scent of cheap perfume hung in the air and a fire burned in the grate, even though it was still summer.

'It is rather warm in here,' Amelia said faintly. 'Might I wait in Pa's room?'

'No ladies, not even daughters, are allowed in the gentlemen's private rooms. I make that a firm rule.' Mrs Delaney narrowed her eyes, giving Amelia a searching look. 'Might I ask what this visit is about? Not family problems, I trust.'

'I'm sorry, Mrs Delaney, but that really is none of your business.' Amelia could hold back no longer. She had tried to be polite to her father's landlady, but she had gone too far.

'If there's a problem it is possibly my business. I care deeply for your dear pa, Miss Sutton,' Mrs Delaney said unctuously. She wiggled the bare fourth finger on her left hand. 'I don't wish to jump the gun, so to speak, but you might be addressing your future stepmother.'

Amelia stared at her in a mixture of horror and amazement. 'No! Surely not.'

Mrs Delaney's smile froze on her face. 'Why should that surprise you?'

'I — well — you must admit, it's rather sudden, ma'am. My father has known you for such a short time.'

'My dear young woman, love comes when least expected. Be aware that I have your papa's best interests at heart. Now why would you come here in such a state unless you were going to ask him for money? I am right, am I not?'

'It really has nothing to do with you, Mrs Delaney.'

'Oh, but it has. I have to protect my future husband from persons wishing to take advantage of his good nature. I'm asking you politely to leave my property.'

'This is ridiculous,' Amelia protested. 'I am entitled to visit my father if I wish to do so.'

'You want to beg him for money. I know your sort, my dear. I am a woman of the world. Now I'm telling you to leave, or do I have to throw you out? Believe me, I am amazingly strong for such a delicate-looking female.'

Amelia could see that Mrs Delaney meant business and she backed out of the room. 'All right, I'm going but I will tell my father how you've treated me. He won't stand for it, ma'am.'

'Won't he? If you believe that you know nothing about men, Miss Sutton. Your pa will do as I tell him or he will lose all the comforts of home, if you get my meaning.'

'Only too well, ma'am.' Amelia stormed out of the house but came to a halt when she saw young Daisy clinging to the railings, sobbing as if her heart would break.

'What's the matter?' Amelia asked gently.

'Cook beat me because I broke a plate. I hate it here. I'm running away.'

Amelia did not need to stop and think. She lifted the sobbing child onto the driver's seat before untethering Grey. She climbed up to sit beside Daisy.

'Then we'll run away together, shall we?' She flicked the reins. 'Walk on, Grey.'

19

'What on earth are we going to do with that child?' Mariah demanded in a low voice when Betsy had taken Daisy up to her room. The two of them had taken instantly to each other and Percy had managed a smile for her. He had not growled at her once, which Amelia thought must be a record, as Percy was not keen on strangers. Betsy's motherly nature had immediately come to the fore with Daisy. However Mariah was still doubtful.

'She's only little,' Amelia said defensively. 'She's not much younger than Betsy, only she's smaller. Judging by the way Daisy gobbled her tea, I doubt if she has ever had a good meal in the whole of her short life. As to Ruby Delaney, words fail me. That woman allowed the child to be beaten and bullied and now she's got her claws into my poor pa.'

'Perhaps he's happy with things as they are, Emmie. Men are funny creatures when it comes to women. I've no doubt she can manipulate him like a puppeteer.'

'I'm not satisfied. I'll wait until Todd comes home and then I'll find out what duties Pa has and I'll go to the hospital to speak to him.'

'If you do that it will look as if Mrs Delaney is right and you only want your pa when you need money. I'm betting she's the crafty type who will put such ideas into his head anyway.'

Amelia slumped down on the nearest kitchen chair.

‘We have just two days in which to find the rent.’

Mariah stripped off her apron. ‘I’ve allowed you to bear the brunt of all this, Emmie. It’s high time I did my bit.’

‘What could you do to get so much money?’

‘I am owed a few favours. When I was living in Bow Street I helped quite a few of the people that Jasper treated badly. I know for a fact that there are stolen items in his cellar that are worth a lot of money. I’ll say no more, but if you’re happy to see to supper, I’ll take the gig and drive into town.’ Mariah smiled knowingly. ‘Don’t worry about the horse and cart. I’ll leave Grey in safe hands and walk the rest of the way. Leave it to me. By tomorrow evening we should have enough money for next month’s rent.’

‘Don’t do anything that will get you into trouble,’ Amelia said anxiously.

‘Stop worrying. I spent enough years living by my wits to know what’s what. And best not mention where I’m going to Todd. I don’t want him trying to save me from meself. Just tell him I’ve gone to see an old friend.’ Mariah snatched her shawl from the back of a chair and wrapped it around her shoulders. ‘There are sausages on the marble shelf in the larder and plenty of eggs. Farmer Allen brought some round this morning.’

‘He’s getting very keen, Mariah,’ Amelia said, smiling. ‘He’s quite a regular visitor.’

Mariah sniffed and tossed her head. ‘I made some biscuits for his nippers. I feel sorry for the poor motherless little things.’

‘I see.’ Amelia managed to keep a straight face. She had seen Farmer Allen when he was with Mariah and it was obvious that he was quite smitten with her.

'Well, if you're going, you'd best leave now or you'll pass Todd on the way to town and he'll ask awkward questions, but please be careful. Don't take any unnecessary risks.'

'I'll be fine. Don't worry.' Mariah marched out of the kitchen. 'I know what I'm doing,' she called over her shoulder.

Amelia was not so sure, but there was nothing she could do other than to await Mariah's return. She crossed her fingers superstitiously. Even if they managed to scrape together the rent money, they would have to do the same each month just to keep Caleb from evicting them and taking back the sewing machines. It would make her sad to leave Marsh House, but first they must find alternative accommodation, and that would not be easy.

Todd arrived home later than usual, explaining that the clinics had gone on much longer than anticipated. He looked pale and tired, and he did not notice that Mariah was absent until Amelia put the food on the table.

'You cooked this yourself, Emmie?'

'Don't look so surprised. I might not be as good a cook as Mariah, but I can fry sausages and eggs.'

'It's very tasty, but where is Mariah? It's not like her to be out in the evening, unless Farmer Allen has invited her to have supper with him.'

'No, but I expect he will pluck up the courage to do so one day. She's driven into town to see an old friend. I don't know any more and it's none of my business, anyway.'

Todd sat back in his chair. 'You look worried, Emmie. Is it the rent that's bothering you?'

'Yes, of course. I was going to ask Pa if he could

lend me some money, but I discovered that Mrs Delaney has appointed herself as his guardian. She thinks he's going to marry her, but I suspect she will be very disappointed. My pa has had quite a few romantic encounters since Ma died, and none of them ended in marriage.'

'When I get paid I'll gladly give most of it to you. I need some in order to pay the livery stable for taking care of my horse, but you can have the rest.'

'Thank you, Todd. I do appreciate your offer, but I hope it won't be necessary. Mariah might be able to call in a debt from her old friend. That's as much as I know, so we'll just have to wait and see. Anyway, eat your meal before it gets cold.'

Todd picked up his knife and fork. 'Aren't you joining me?'

'I ate with the children earlier. I need to go upstairs to the long gallery before it gets too dark to see. I have the material for one of Dolly's gowns and I need to make a start.'

'This is all wrong,' Todd said, frowning. 'You and Mariah work hard enough as it is. We're keeping this old house in reasonable order for Caleb and he's cheating you with an extortionate rent. I've a good mind to sort him out myself.'

'No, please, Todd. Don't go near him. He'll only cause trouble for you. My cousin is an influential man and you might even lose your position at the hospital if he decides to interfere.'

'I'd rather have my own practice, and I'm due to take my final examination soon. But if it upsets you, I won't do anything, for now.'

'Emmie, I haven't got a nightgown.' Daisy stood in the doorway, tears running down her thin cheeks.

'Who on earth is that?' Todd asked incredulously. 'Not another of your lost souls, Emmie?'

His comical expression drew a reluctant laugh from Amelia. 'This is Daisy and she's come to stay with us for a while. I'll explain everything later, Todd. But now I think it's time for bed, Daisy. Come upstairs with me, dear. I'm sure we can find something for you to wear. Tomorrow we'll buy you some new clothes.'

'You're all heart, Amelia Sutton.' Todd stabbed a sausage with his fork. 'But we'll need to find a mansion to accommodate all of us if you keep taking in waifs and strays.'

Amelia hesitated in the doorway. 'I believe that's what you were as a child, Todd. I can't think that you've forgotten what it was like not to belong anywhere.'

'That's true. I'm sorry, Emmie. Of course you did the right thing. Where would Gus and I have been if Nancy hadn't taken to us?'

'I want to meet Nancy. She sounds like a wonderful person.'

Todd smiled. 'She really is. One day I'll take you to Rockwood and you can get to know my adopted family.'

'That will be wonderful, Todd. But all I'm concerned with at the moment is to settle this little one for the night. Come with me, Daisy, dear.' Amelia led the shy child from the room and took her upstairs. She found her a suitable nightgown and settled her in the truckle bed in Betsy's room. Percy was already asleep in his mother's room, as he had taken to waking in the night, disturbing Betsy, and Mariah had decided to have him in with her. Amelia kissed both girls good night, but she left a candle burning so that they were not plunged into darkness when she left the room.

She would have returned to the kitchen to chat to Todd, but she did not want to get drawn into a discussion about the reasons for Mariah's absence, and she went straight to the long gallery where she lit some candles and set about her work. She pinned, cut and tacked the material for Dolly's next gown and lost track of time as she worked. In fact, she was so absorbed in her task that she did not hear Mariah walk into the room.

'Emmie. It's late. You should be in bed.'

Amelia dropped the piece of material she had been tacking and jumped to her feet. 'Goodness, you gave me such a start.'

'You were concentrating so hard the house could have burned down around you. Come downstairs. I've made some cocoa and I'll tell you about this evening.'

'I told Todd you had gone to meet an old friend. Is he still up?'

Mariah shook her head. 'No. His door is shut and all's quiet. He's probably got his head stuck in one of those boring medical books, so come on, Emmie. Put that away for now, or you'll be making silly mistakes.'

'I think I already did that when I accepted Caleb's offer of this house,' Amelia said with a wry smile. 'I should have known it was too good to be true.'

'Men like him can be very convincing, and I should know.' Mariah sighed as she hurried from the room, leaving Amelia to follow her downstairs.

* * *

The kitchen was warm and the rich smell of hot chocolate welcomed Amelia as she took her seat at the table. Mariah filled a cup and handed it to her.

'Well?' Amelia demanded impatiently. 'What happened in Bow Street this evening?'

'I didn't go anywhere near the old house. I didn't have to anyway because I knew where Jasper's cronies hang out. There's one fellow in particular who bears a massive grudge against him. A few words in his ear and he was only too willing to oblige.'

Amelia sipped the cocoa, which was sweet with sugar and delicious. 'What good will that do us?'

'Grimble is going to swipe the article I mentioned and maybe a few others. I told him exactly where to find them.'

'But do you trust this person? What if he steals the items, sells them and keep the proceeds for himself? What's to stop him from cheating you?'

Mariah laughed. 'I know his mum. She's a woman you would not want to anger. He understands that if I tell her that he has double-crossed me, she will make his life hell.'

'We only have two days . . . in fact it's past midnight so we only have one whole day in which to find the money.'

'We just have to hope it all goes to plan. What other choice do we have?'

'None, I suppose,' Amelia said ruefully. 'But we will have to start looking for somewhere else to live. We can't be beholden to Caleb. I want to put all that behind me.'

Mariah raised her cup in a toast. 'We'll do it, Emmie. We have both suffered in our different ways and that gives us the steel in our souls to make a success of our lives. I won't let you down. Of course, now we have another mouth to feed, too.'

'Yes, that's more or less what Todd said. I suppose I ought to go back to Charlotte Street and tell Mrs Delaney that Daisy is staying with us.'

'I wouldn't, if I were you. She sounds like the sort of woman who would demand compensation for taking away her young servant.'

'Yes, you're right. Anyway, tomorrow — or rather later today — if I have any money in my purse I will take Daisy into town to buy her some clothes. She didn't even have a nightgown.'

'No need for that. I have some garments that are too small for Betsy. She can have those until we are better off. Let's wait and see what Grimble manages to get for us.'

* * *

Amelia was certain she would not be able to sleep that night for worrying, but a combination of hard work, a long day and a cup of soothing cocoa gave her the best night's sleep she had had for a long time. She awakened refreshed and feeling more optimistic than she had the previous day. When she went downstairs she discovered that Mariah was already up, and had the fire going in the range, with a pan of porridge simmering on the hob.

'It's the last day of the month,' Amelia said as she accepted a bowl filled with hot porridge from Mariah. 'How will Grimble contact you?'

'He won't come here, if that's what's worrying you,' Mariah said firmly. 'I'll need to take Grey and the gig into town again this afternoon, if that's all right with you. I'll meet Grimble outside the pub he frequents, not far from Bow Street. If he's been successful he should have the money.'

'And if he isn't?'

Mariah pulled a face. 'The only way would be to do a moonlight flit. It wouldn't be the first time I've had to do that.'

'Me, too. Pa was always getting us into debt because he wouldn't press his patients for money. We had to leave our lodgings quite a few times when I was younger.'

'It will be that, or you will have to persuade Caleb to give us more time.'

'I really don't think that will work. Unless I give in to his ridiculous demands, although I can't believe that he wants me to marry him.'

'It didn't sound like marriage was on his mind, Emmie. I'm sorry to be blunt, but even if it was, I'd tell you not to sell yourself for an old tumbledown house and a pair of second-hand sewing machines.'

'I'd rather live under the railway arches than submit to that man.' Amelia spooned porridge into her mouth, gulping it down and barely taking a breath. 'I've finished. That was good, thank you. I'm going to the long gallery straight away to work on the morning dress for Dolly. I should be able to finish it by this evening, if you could cut out the pattern for the next garment, which is an afternoon gown.'

'Of course. I'll see to the children first and prepare the meals. Don't forget I have an appointment later.'

'You have an appointment?' Todd strolled into the kitchen. 'Are you meeting Farmer Allen in secret, Mariah?'

She tossed a drying towel at him. 'Don't be so

cheeky, Todd. You may be a god at the hospital but here you are just another mouth to feed, as far as I am concerned,' Mariah said with a twinkle in her eyes that belied her words. 'Eat your breakfast before it gets cold.'

'Yes, ma'am.' Todd blew her a kiss and took his place at the table.

Just as Mariah was serving the porridge the kitchen door opened and Farmer Allen stood in the doorway, holding a basket of eggs and a can of milk. His pleasant, suntanned features were creased in a shy smile and he put the can down so that he could doff his cap, a gesture made comical by his shock of sandy hair springing up to create a halo of curls.

'Good morning, ladies. Morning, Doctor.'

Todd's lips twitched but he managed to keep a straight face. 'I hope your family are all well.'

'Yes, sir, thanks to you. I've just come to bring eggs and milk.' A dull flush spread from Farmer Allen's neck to his high cheekbones as he smiled at Mariah, who turned her back on him.

'Do come in, Farmer Allen,' Amelia said hurriedly as she rose to her feet. 'Perhaps you would like a cup of tea?'

He glanced anxiously at Mariah. 'Er, thank you, ma'am. I've got to get back to the farm.'

'Of course,' Amelia said, smiling. 'Maybe another time then.'

Mariah took the basket of eggs from him and began transferring them to a bowl. 'Thanks for the eggs, Jim.'

Amelia and Todd exchanged amused glances. It was quite obvious that Mariah was trying hard not to show any particular interest in her adoring farmer, but it did not quite work.

'I'll empty the can into a pitcher, shall I, Mariah?' Jim eyed her warily as if expecting a rebuff.

'Yes, do that,' Mariah said casually. 'You know where to find it.'

He nodded and opened the larder door.

'You must tell me how much we owe you,' Amelia said firmly as he emptied the milk into two pitchers.

'It's no matter, miss,' Jim said hastily. 'The doctor more than makes up for a little milk and some eggs, and Mariah gives my nippers a few fancies every now and again.'

'Even so, we will pay for your produce. We can't expect you to work for nothing, and your eggs, butter and milk are more than welcome.'

'I have some cheese maturing, miss. I'll bring some next time.' Jim turned to Mariah with a hopeful smile. 'Maybe us could take a walk come Sunday, Mariah? After church, of course.'

'We'll see,' was all Mariah would say, and he backed out of the kitchen, nodding to Amelia and Todd.

'You are hard on him, Mariah,' Amelia said as the door closed. 'The poor man obviously admires you very much.'

Mariah tossed her head. 'It's all words when it comes down to it. All he wants is a good cook-housekeeper and someone to mother his nippers.'

'I don't think that's all he wants, Mariah.' Todd finished his porridge and rose to his feet. 'You could do worse, although I don't know what we would do without you.'

'You'll be late for work if you don't leave now.' Mariah headed for the door leading into the hall. 'Betsy, your brother is crying. Bring him down here, please. You come down, too, Daisy. Breakfast is ready.'

'I'm going right away.' Todd turned to Amelia with a curious look. 'I don't know what you and Mariah are up to, but I hope it's nothing desperate. I get my wages today and they're all yours. But if Caleb bothers you I want to be the first to know. I won't be such a gentleman next time.'

'Thank you, Todd,' Amelia said meekly. She hoped her attempt to look unconcerned was convincing, but Todd seemed to have an uncanny knack of reading her mind. However, he appeared satisfied, or perhaps he was in too much of a hurry to get to the hospital on time, in any event he left the room and Amelia uttered a sigh of relief.

'He knows something is going on,' Mariah said slowly. 'What do we tell him if we get enough money from Grimble to pay the rent?'

'I'll think of something. I'd better get on with making the afternoon gown for Dolly.'

'What about Lady Galton's order? Shouldn't we concentrate on that?'

'Dolly is a friend — she paid the rent for us. Lady Galton will keep us waiting for ages so I know who the most important client is, for now anyway, and I'm going to make Dolly proud.'

* * *

Later that day Mariah went into town, taking Percy with her as he cried miserably when his mother left him. Amelia promised to keep her eye on the girls, which she did by getting them to sort through her button box, arranging the contents in order of size and colour. This kept them quiet for most of the afternoon, leaving Amelia free to work on the garment for Dolly.

It was by chance that she discovered that Daisy was good with her needle. She had been taught to sew by nuns at the orphanage and she was eager to learn, whereas Betsy could not sit still for long enough to concentrate on needlework of any sort. In the end, when the girls had finished with the button box, Amelia gave Daisy some simple tacking to do while Betsy spent her time picking up pins and arranging them neatly on a velvet pincushion. However, she soon grew restive and spent more time gazing out of the window than collecting pins. Amelia was too busy to take much notice until Betsy jumped down from the window and ran towards the staircase.

'Ma is home. She promised to bring us iced buns if she had enough pennies. Come on, Daisy.'

Somewhat reluctantly, Daisy put down her sewing. 'Is that all right, miss? May I go with her?'

Amelia smiled. 'Of course, Daisy. You've done a splendid job. Go with Betsy. I'll be down in a minute or two.' She carefully laid the pieces of material she had been tacking together on the table and followed the girls downstairs. So much depended upon Mariah's success or failure in obtaining enough money for next month's rent. Caleb was sure to call either that evening or next day, and it would be such a relief to send him on his way having thwarted his plan to evict them, or worse.

Mariah was in the kitchen, giving Percy a cup of milk, and the girls were munching sweet buns with happy smiles on their faces.

'Well?' Amelia said in a low voice. 'Did Grimble pay up?'

Mariah nodded. 'Better than I expected, but it

won't take long for Jasper to realise that I must have had something to do with the theft.'

'Why is that?'

'I am the only one who knows what he keeps in the cellar. He's a mean and vicious man but he's not stupid.'

'But he doesn't know where you are. He won't find you here.'

'I hope not, providing Caleb doesn't set him on us.'

'If we pay him in full he has no reason to do such a thing.'

Mariah set Percy down on the floor and reached for her reticule. She took out a leather purse and handed it to Amelia. 'There's the full amount and more. It will help pay towards mine and the children's keep.'

'There's no need of that,' Amelia protested. 'It's your money, Mariah. I wouldn't dream of taking it.' She opened the purse and counted out the rent money. 'There, you keep what you earned. We don't talk about paying for anyone's keep. We're a family now and we look after each other.'

Mariah dashed a tear from her eyes as she put the purse back in her bag. 'It's so long since I had a proper family I can hardly remember what it's like.'

Betsy approached her mother, licking her fingers one at a time. 'Are there any more buns, Ma? That was such a treat.'

'You may have another at teatime but not before,' Mariah said sternly. 'I need you to put Grey back in his stable. Make sure he has plenty of water and straw in the manger. He's worked hard today.'

'I'll help you, Betsy.' Daisy danced on ahead of her. 'I never had nothing to do with horses but I think I like them.'

'I'll show you what to do,' Betsy said grandly. 'Come with me.'

Mariah bent down to catch Percy as he was about to toddle after them. 'No, you don't, young man. You'll get trampled on.'

Percy frowned and growled angrily, but his mother merely laughed and gave him a hug. 'You may have a sugar bun, if you're a good boy.'

Percy gave her an angelic smile and was rewarded with a bun.

'Do you trust this fellow Grimble?' Amelia asked anxiously. 'What will happen if he returns to Jasper's cellar and helps himself to some of the other items stored there?'

'That's between him and Jasper. Nothing to do with me.'

'Maybe not, but I doubt if Jasper will see it that way if Grimble tells him that it was you who gave away his secrets.'

'I'll worry about that if it happens. For now, as you said, we are safe here. I'll put the kettle on. I could do with a cup of tea and then I think I'll take Percy for a walk to the farm. He loves to chase the chickens.'

'And you can chat to Farmer Allen,' Amelia said with a mischievous smile.

'I bought some biscuits for his nippers. He's so good, giving us free eggs and milk. I feel I have to pay him back somehow.'

'Yes, of course,' Amelia said hastily. 'You do that and I'll take my tea upstairs. I'm getting on very well with the afternoon gown. I hope Dolly comes to visit soon as I need to do fittings.'

'Maybe Todd could take a message to the barracks.' Mariah filled the kettle and placed it on the hob. 'I'm sure he would like to spend some time with Gus before he leaves for India.'

'Yes, you're right. I'll suggest it when he comes home from the hospital.'

* * *

Amelia had fully expected Caleb to come to collect the rent that day, but it was her father who arrived an hour later, riding a horse that he said belonged to Ruby's brother, who had paid an unexpected visit to Charlotte Street.

'What is this I hear about you abducting Ruby's young servant, Amelia?' Harold demanded, frowning. 'That was uncalled for.'

'I didn't abduct her, as you put it, Pa,' Amelia said firmly. 'The child was badly treated and she was about to run away. I brought her here, to a place of safety.'

'Ruby is very angry with you, Amelia. She said you were quite rude to her.'

'I am sorry if I made things difficult for you, but I can't warm to the lady, and she was horrid to poor little Daisy. The child is too young to be a servant, anyway.'

'I agree there, but you can't just go round adopting other people's servants, Amelia. It isn't done.'

'I brought her here because it was better than leaving her to the mercy of anyone who found her wandering the streets on her own. If the authorities became involved I dare say she would end up in the workhouse.'

'Possibly so, but can you afford to feed and clothe the child?'

'I can and I will. She has Betsy as a companion

and she will learn to be useful. I discovered that she loves sewing, and I can teach her to be a competent needlewoman. She will always find employment with that skill.'

Harold sighed heavily. 'I see that you have made up your mind to keep her. You are stubborn, just like your poor mother.'

'Did you come all the way here just to chide me, Pa? I am doing my best to earn my own living and I don't ask you for anything.' Amelia did not want to admit that she had gone to Charlotte Street in order to borrow money, which would no doubt give Ruby Delaney a feeling of satisfaction.

'No, and I appreciate that, my dear. The real reason for my visit today is to tell you that I am going to propose marriage to Ruby. I wanted you to be the first to know.'

Amelia was not surprised. Mrs Delaney had told her as much. 'Congratulations, Pa. I am sure she will accept.'

'She's a good woman, despite her quick tongue, Amelia. She owns her house and she works hard. She also understands that I work long hours and am often on night duty.'

'Just as long as you are happy, Pa. That's all that matters. You don't have to worry about me.'

'No, dear. I know you will do well and you have a good friend in Caleb. How many men would give a young woman a large house like this and ask for nothing in return?'

'Yes, I wonder about that, Pa.' Amelia had not seen her father this content for a long time and she had no intention of telling him the truth. It was better that he believed the fiction that Caleb had spread about his generosity.

'Well, my love. I'd better take my leave of you now. As I said, I've borrowed the horse from Ruby's brother, who is a merchant with a thriving business. He thoroughly approves of our match, which is very satisfying. I hope you will come to the wedding.'

'When will it be, Pa?'

Harold smiled coyly. 'I have to ask the lady first, my dear. If Ruby honours me with her hand, I will let you know the date of the nuptials, which will probably be in the New Year. I know ladies like to have time to make arrangements for these things.'

Despite her reservations about his chosen bride, Amelia had not the heart to say anything that would upset her father, and she kissed his whiskery cheek. 'I truly hope you will be happy, Pa.'

Harold picked up his top hat and rammed it on his head. 'Thank you, my love. I'll see you again very soon.'

Amelia saw him to the door but as Harold untethered the horse from a hitching post outside the stables, Amelia turned her head at the sound of hoofbeats and her heart sank when she saw Caleb draw his mount to a halt. The last thing she wanted was for her father to find out exactly what Caleb's intentions were, but thankfully Harold seemed keen to get back to his beloved and had little interest in Caleb Marsh.

'Goodbye, Pa. Ride carefully,' Amelia called out, trying not to sound too relieved.

She forced herself to smile as Caleb dismounted, tossing the reins to Betsy with a curt command to walk the horse. 'You're a day early, Caleb.'

'That must mean you haven't got the money,' Caleb

grinned wolfishly. 'What a pity. You know my terms, and I've come to collect. Get your things, Amelia. You're coming with me.'

20

Amelia thought quickly. 'Wait here, please.' She backed into the house and shut the door. Inwardly she was trembling with anger and disgust at the thought of Caleb claiming her as if she were some sort of chattel, but she was not going to allow him to see that she was upset. She went into the parlour to get the money from her reticule, but she hesitated, taking several deep breaths before facing Caleb again. She walked slowly to the front door and opened it.

'Give me your hand, Caleb.'

He obeyed, eyeing her with a triumphant sneer, which was wiped off his face as she placed the coins into his outstretched palm.

'There is the rent money in full, Caleb.' Amelia slammed the door before he had a chance to say anything. She returned to the parlour and stood by the window, watching him until he mounted his horse and rode off, whipping the poor animal to a gallop. She sighed with relief. At least that had brought them another month's grace, but it was painfully obvious that they needed to find alternative and cheaper accommodation. She knew she must discuss the matter with Mariah, who, despite her deepening relationship with Farmer Allen, still lived in dread that Jasper Cook would find them. However, she need not have worried. Mariah agreed that a move was regrettable but essential. They needed to get away from Caleb as soon as possible, even if it meant returning the sewing machines to the workroom in Nightingale Lane. As to her feelings for Jim Allen, Mariah shrugged and made light of their relationship. Amelia was not sure she believed her, but she said nothing.

That evening Amelia waited until Todd had finished eating the stew that Mariah had created from a chicken — again, a present from Farmer Allen — and vegetables she had purchased on the way home from the farm.

'Shall we take our tea into the parlour, Todd? I would like to talk to you, if you have a moment.'

'I've always got time for you, Emmie,' Todd said, smiling. He turned to Mariah. 'That was a truly excellent meal, thank you. I feel I ought to offer to wash up as you have done all the hard work.'

Mariah beamed with pleasure at the compliment. 'Nonsense, Todd. You've been healing the sick all day. Betsy and Daisy can wash the dishes and I'll keep an eye on Percy. It's nearly his bedtime anyway.'

Amelia led the way to the parlour and sat down, folding her hands in her lap. 'I need to tell you about Caleb, but I don't want you to fly off the handle.'

Todd sank down in the chair opposite her. 'That sounds ominous. I won't promise anything. What has the fellow done now? Just say the words and I'll sort him out.'

'Fortunately for us all, I had the rent money. Mariah provided it — you don't need to know any details but she called in an old debt. Anyway, we're safe here for another month, and after that I hope we can find somewhere else to live. It's a shame because this old house is growing on me.'

Todd clenched and unclenched his fists, but he remained seated, a frown creasing his brow. 'I would still like to settle this man to man, Emmie. You don't know what it does to me to see you bullied and propositioned by that arrogant swine.'

'No, please don't do anything rash. This is his property and the sewing machines don't belong to me. One word from Caleb and I could be facing a charge of theft, but I can't do without them.'

'Could we buy them from your cousin? There must be a way around this without me resorting to fisticuffs or worse with Caleb Marsh. I'm not a violent man, Emmie, but I won't stand by and see you hurt.'

'I know that, Todd.' Amelia reached out to lay her hand on his arm. 'And I appreciate everything you do for us.'

'It's so little. I'm not here when you need me and my hands are tied when it comes to dealing with the person who's making your life miserable.'

'Nonsense, Todd. You've done everything you can and more in order to help us, although there is one thing I was going to ask of you. I need Dolly to come for fittings for her gowns. Could you take a message to her at the barracks? It would help me greatly, and I'm sure you would like to see more of Gus before he leaves for India.'

'I would, of course, and you know I'll do anything to help, but it worries me to think that Caleb just turns up here when he feels like it. I wish I worked nearer. I don't like leaving you, Mariah and the children unprotected.'

Amelia smiled. 'Thank you, Todd, but we are all right, really. Simply having you here at night is a great comfort. I just need Dolly to come for a fitting or two, which will be virtually impossible if she has to return to Devonshire when Gus goes away.'

Todd rose to his feet. 'I'll ride over to Chelsea now that my horse is rested, and I'll have a word with Gus. Leave it to me, Emmie. Don't wait up. I have a key so I can let myself in.'

Amelia jumped up and gave him a hug. 'Thank you, Todd. I don't know what we'd do without you.' She drew away quickly. 'You'd best go now, though. You need to get home before dark in case the mist comes up. It's easy to get lost at night.'

He laid his hands on her shoulders, looking her in the eyes with a tender smile. 'You sound as if you care what happens to me.'

'Of course I do.' Amelia attempted to move away but Todd caught hold of her hands.

'There is one way I could stop Caleb from bothering you for ever.'

She managed a wry smile. 'I don't think murder is a good idea.'

'You know I don't mean that.' Todd raised her left hand to his lips. 'Marry me, Emmie. Marry me and I'll look after you for the rest of my life.'

She snatched her hand free and backed away. 'Don't say things like that just to get me out of trouble. It's really not your problem, but I do appreciate what you're trying to do.'

'You have no idea how I feel. I love you, Emmie.'

The bleak look in his hazel eyes struck a blow to her heart, but she steeled herself to be strong. She knew her plight had touched him deeply, but she was certain that he spoke out of pity and nothing more. 'Please go now. It's not that I don't appreciate your offer — I do — but that isn't the way out of this predicament.'

'I meant what I just said, Emmie.'

'Don't say any more, Todd. I care for you, I really do, but I need to concentrate on getting a business going before I can even think of . . .' She could not go on without hurting him more. She took a deep breath. 'I'm sorry. I need to go to the long gallery. I have a lot of work to do.'

'I'm not letting this go, Emmie,' Todd said reluctantly. 'I know you're upset so I won't say any more tonight. I'll see you in the morning. Don't work when it gets dark. You'll strain your eyes.'

'Very well, Doctor.' Amelia managed a weak smile. Todd's proposal of marriage, even if meant simply to protect her from Caleb, had shaken her more than she cared to admit. She was deeply fond of him, and she could not imagine life without him. However, by putting his feelings for her into words he had changed everything. She needed time to think.

Todd walked to the door. 'I'm serious. I do care about you, Emmie. Believe me.' He left the room and Amelia sank back onto her chair. She could still feel the touch of his hands on her shoulders and the scent of him made her feel suddenly dizzy. She tried to convince herself that her jumbled emotions were just a symptom of relief. Even as the thought came into her head, she knew she was lying to herself.

Mariah opened the door, balancing a tray on one hand. 'I've brought the tea. Where's Todd?'

'He's gone to Chelsea to see Gus. Why don't you sit down and drink his tea? He won't be back until very late.'

'He'd better be careful then. The marsh is dangerous after dark, particularly when the mist comes down and it's getting cold at night.'

'That's what I told him. I won't sleep a wink until I

hear his key in the lock.'

Mariah sat down and sipped the tea she had brought for Todd. 'I have to say this, Emmie. I know you are grateful to Dolly for paying the rent last month, but we should really concentrate on making up Lady Galton's order first.'

Amelia sighed. 'I know, but Dolly is Todd's dear friend and she needs her garments soon.'

'And you are doing it for free. Lady Galton will pay up, eventually.'

'What were you thinking, Mariah? I can tell there's something else on your mind.'

'We need another pair of hands, better still, two experienced seamstresses who are good at using sewing machines.'

'You mean Nellie and Maisie.'

'I do indeed, and I have some money left from the sum that Grimble gave me. I could pay them from that.'

'But they would lose their jobs at the mourning warehouse, Mariah. We can't expect that of them.'

'I know for a fact that they are both in dire need of money and we could pay them over and above the meagre amount of money they get from your cousin.'

'It's certainly worth a try. I'll take Grey and pay a call on them tomorrow morning.'

'Let me go instead. My presence won't excite any curiosity, for one thing. We don't know if all the women who work there are trustworthy. There's one or two who might wish to get on the right side of Caleb by telling tales.'

'I hadn't thought of that, but you're right, as usual.' Amelia eyed Mariah thoughtfully. 'When money starts coming in I will share it with you. We are partners in this business and it's only fair that you should benefit from everything you do.'

'I don't think of money,' Mariah said firmly. 'You have given me and my children a home and that's all that matters, as far as I am concerned.'

'Well, it doesn't suit me. You and I share the work in making the garments and that makes us business partners as well. I won't have any arguments on the subject, Mariah. I've made up my mind,' Amelia smiled.

Mariah had shown her the way to conquer whatever feelings Todd had stirred within her. She had suffered all her life from having a father who vacillated between work and philanthropy, regardless of what difficulties it made for him and his daughter. Caleb had tried to force her to comply with his twisted idea of what was good for her. The future was in her hands and she would not relinquish control to anyone without very good reason. She drank her tea, said good night to Mariah, and went upstairs to her workroom in the long gallery.

* * *

Next morning Todd rushed into the kitchen, his shirt undone at the neck and his tie flying.

'You must have come in very late last night. I didn't hear you.' Amelia stared at him and laughed. 'You obviously had a good time with Gus. You look a wreck. Let me do your tie for you. I often had to help Pa get dressed after he'd been very late on a call.'

Todd pulled a face. 'I'm afraid Gus and I went to a pub near the barracks and drank too much ale. I overslept so I haven't time for breakfast.' He hastily buttoned his shirt. 'I can manage.'

Amelia took the ends of his tie. 'Just tell me what Gus said about Dolly and her friend the Earl of Dorrington.'

'Dolly is staying with Freddie. There's no question about that. She'll come and see you soon, I'm sure.'

Amelia finished tying his tie for him. 'There. Now you look respectable, Doctor. Your patients won't think you've been carousing in the town when you should have been tucked up in bed.'

Todd laughed. 'I have to hurry. I dare say I'll be late but I don't want to make it any worse. I get paid today so I will give you my rent money.'

'Just get yourself to the hospital safely.'

'I'll see you at suppertime. We do need to talk, Emmie.' Todd kissed her lightly on the cheek before hurrying from the kitchen.

'That was a touchingly domestic scene,' Mariah said as she passed him in the doorway. 'You two look almost like an old married couple.'

'Nothing of the sort. He was just thanking me for sorting out his tie. I think he's still a little tipsy after drinking with Gus. He said that Dolly is staying with her uncle in Piccadilly. She'll probably come and see us very soon.'

'I don't doubt it. I'll just see to the children's breakfasts and then I'll take the gig to Nightingale Lane, if that's all right with you, Emmie?'

'Yes, of course. I'll look after the children.'

'I'll take Percy with me. He's getting far too adventurous these days.'

'The girls can look after him. You'll be much quicker if you don't have him with you. I'll keep an eye on all three of them. I can bring some of my work to the front parlour where I can see them if they play outside.'

'All right, thank you. I'll be as quick as I can.'

* * *

Betsy was disappointed that she could not go to Nightingale Lane with her mother. She knew she had been a favourite with the women who worked there. They had spoiled her with slivers of sticky toffee or even a peppermint cream, and had even allowed her to try to work the sewing machines, if they were not too busy. However, she soon forgot her woes when she was put in charge of Daisy and Percy. Her motherly instincts came to the fore and she herded them outside to play in the sunshine. Amelia took her sewing to the parlour as she had promised to keep an eye on them. She sat in the window watching the children and she smiled to herself as she listened to Betsy ordering them about. Daisy took it all in good part and Percy growled at first, but was soon running around shrieking with laughter as the girls chased him. They came to a sudden halt at the sound of horses' hoofs on the gravelled carriage sweep.

Betsy raced into the parlour. 'Two grey horses are pulling the sort of carriage you see outside big houses in town, and the coachman is dressed as fine as anyone I've ever seen. There's another servant sitting beside him. I think the Queen has come to visit us.'

Amelia placed her sewing on a side table and rose to her feet. 'I don't think it's the Queen, but it might be a lord.' Amelia put down her sewing and stood up. She glanced at a fly-spotted mirror on the wall and patted a stray hair in place before following Betsy to the front entrance.

Percy toddled towards the horses but Daisy was closest and she dragged him to safety as the coachman drew the carriage to a halt. The footman leaped nimbly to the ground and went to open the door and put the steps down.

Dolly alighted first, followed by a well-dressed man in his mid-thirties. His pleasant smile enveloped Amelia and she could quite see why he was Dolly's firm favourite.

'Emmie, might I introduce you to my dear friend, Freddie Ashton?'

Amelia dropped a curtsey. 'How do you do, my lord?'

'Freddie, please.' Freddie reached out to take her hand and raised it to his lips. 'Dolly has told me so much about you and your excellent designs that I couldn't wait to meet you.'

Amelia felt the blood rush to her cheeks. 'Dolly is too kind, sir. I am just starting out in business on my own, although I did manage my grandfather's mourning warehouse for a short while.'

'So Dolly told me.'

'Please come inside.' Amelia ushered them into the parlour where the piano had pride of place.

'Do you play, Amelia?' Freddie ran his fingers over the piano keys. 'I had a few lessons as a child but I have no talent for music, unlike Dolly.'

'I play very badly,' Dolly said modestly. 'You said the instrument was here when you moved into the old house, did you not, Emmie?'

'Yes, it was. I don't know who had played it unless Miss Marsh had talents in that direction. I know very little about the house apart from what Caleb told me.'

'I've been hearing about that person.' Freddie exchanged meaningful glances with Dolly. 'It seems you have been having problems with Mr Marsh, and also your cousin, whose reputation has even reached my ears, and I am not at all interested in commerce.'

'Won't you take a seat?' Amelia eyed the shabby furniture with a sigh. 'You'll have to take us as you find us, sir. We have only been here for a few months, but we are not likely to be living here much longer. I can offer you tea.' She broke off, biting her lip. It sounded so pitiful when Lord Dorrington must be used to the finest of everything.

'Nothing for me, thank you,' Freddie said, smiling. 'Dolly has told me a little of your problems, including the exorbitant amount of rent you are paying.'

Dolly sank down on the sofa. 'Do tell Freddie everything, Emmie. He might even be able to offer you some advice.'

'I don't like to impose,' Amelia said shyly. 'It's my problem, sir.'

Dolly patted the space beside her. 'Sit down, Emmie. Tell Freddie about Caleb and his cruel aunt who raised him to become the mean person he is today.'

'Neatly put, Dolly.' Freddie laughed and took a seat opposite them.

Amelia hoped the chair he had chosen was not the one that had a broken leg, but it seemed to be bearing his weight, and she stifled a sigh of relief.

'I know almost nothing about Miss Marsh, apart from what Caleb told me. She was apparently his only living relative, but his miserable childhood made it impossible for him to consider living here himself. He was supposed to be helping me at the start, but now he's resorted to a series of threats and extortionate demands for rent.'

Freddie nodded, leaning forward and fixing Amelia with an intent look. 'Dolly told me much of this, and it sounded a very odd tale to me, so I took the liberty of instructing a private detective to look into the matter.'

'That was kind, sir.' Amelia shifted nervously in her seat. 'Did he discover anything of interest?'

'He did indeed. Mr Marsh is not who he says he is. He did live here as a child, but he was the son of Miss Marsh's cook. According to my source, Caleb Tanner, which is his real name, was spoiled by all the servants and Miss Marsh, who, being childless, doted on him. He was sent away to school and she paid for his education, but the good lady developed an illness that finally took her life. Apparently Caleb rarely visited her and the servants gradually left. When she died her only living relative had no interest in the property. It was left to go to rack and ruin.'

Amelia stared at him in amazement. 'You mean that Caleb doesn't own this property?'

'No, his whole story seems to be a fabrication, apart from the fact that he did spend much of his childhood here.'

'But he showed me his aunt's will,' Amelia said dazedly.

'A forgery, obviously.' Freddie gave her a sympathetic smile. 'I don't suppose you had a chance to examine it closely.'

'He's been using you, Emmie,' Dolly said gently. 'You don't owe him anything.'

Amelia looked from one to the other, momentarily at a loss for words.

'I'm so sorry.' Freddie gave her a sympathetic smile. 'Have you any idea why Tanner might have behaved like this?'

'No. I mean, he's made unwelcome advances, but I can't think why he would want a penniless woman like myself. I could bring little to the relationship other than myself.'

'And your huge talent for designing beautiful garments,' Dolly added. 'Perhaps Caleb sees you as someone who will bring him a fortune as well as beauty.'

'And your cousin must be a wealthy man now that he's inherited Nathaniel Norris's business,' Freddie added. 'Are you his next of kin, Amelia?'

'I don't know. He and his wife are childless, but he might have other close relatives, although I never heard Pa mention any other relations on my mother's side of the family.'

'You could be an heiress,' Freddie added calmly. 'Unless, of course, Mr Norris has decided otherwise. However, it would make sense of Tanner's continuing interest in your affairs.'

Amelia shook her head, frowning. 'This is all so strange. I don't know what to think.'

'One thing is for certain,' Dolly said excitedly. 'You don't owe Caleb anything. He should return the money you paid him.'

'Did your source tell you who does own Marsh House, sir?' Amelia asked eagerly.

'I didn't get a name, but I will find out and let you know. Perhaps you can come to some arrangement with whoever owns the title deeds to the old house.' Freddie glanced round at the peeling wallpaper and chipped paintwork. 'But wouldn't you prefer to live somewhere else? Perhaps nearer to the centre of town?'

'Originally, yes. But I've come to like living on the edge of the marsh, and I have the ideal workroom in the long gallery.'

'Perhaps you could give it some thought,' Dolly said with a smile. 'You've had a shock, Emmie. You need to think things over carefully.'

'Yes, I will indeed.' Amelia turned to Freddie. 'And I am truly grateful to you, sir. I would have been in thrall to Caleb for ever had you not taken the trouble to search his past.'

'I told you that Freddie is a wonderful friend,' Dolly said enthusiastically. 'But aside from all that, I can't wait to try on the gowns you're making for me.'

Amelia jumped to her feet. 'Of course. Come with me, Dolly.' She turned to Freddie with an apologetic smile. 'I'm afraid we'll have to desert you for a while.'

'I'll go outside and make friends with the children. My biggest regret in life is that I have none of my own.'

'But there's plenty of time,' Amelia countered. 'You are still a young man, my lord.'

'Freddie,' he said automatically. 'Thank you, Amelia, but unfortunately I have not yet met a lady who will put up with me.'

Dolly slapped him on the arm. 'Don't be silly, Freddie. Any woman would think herself fortunate to have attracted the attention of someone like you. Come upstairs with us and see the rest of this creepy old house. You can study the paintings in the long gallery while I try on the costumes.'

Freddie rose to his feet, holding out his hand to help Dolly to stand. 'If that's all right with Amelia I would like to see what Marsh House has to offer.'

* * *

The fittings went well. Amelia had been accurate in taking Dolly's measurements in the first place, but it was obvious that her pregnancy was further advanced than Dolly had first thought. Freddie amused himself by studying the portraits in the long gallery, and with Amelia's permission he explored the rest of the house, returning just as Dolly had finished putting on her day clothes.

'This is a fascinating old building,' Freddie said enthusiastically. 'It would be very interesting to discover its true history.'

'Caleb told me it was built by a seafarer in the sixteenth century,' Amelia said as she replaced her pincushion in her workbox. 'I don't know if it was true, but the said sea captain used to store his ill-gotten treasure in the outbuildings.'

Freddie laughed. 'It sounds quite possible. I will definitely do some research into its past, if you agree.'

'I do indeed, and if you could discover who owns it, maybe I could meet that person and we could come to some amicable arrangement as to rent.'

'The private detective is an ex-police officer and completely trustworthy. I'll ask him to continue his investigations.'

'I'm sure we could all do with a cup of tea,' Amelia said cheerfully. 'I'm afraid I can't offer you anything else.'

Dolly gave her a hug. 'Don't be silly, Emmie. We didn't come here to be entertained, and, as a matter of fact, Freddie insisted on sending his butler to Fortnum's before we left Piccadilly. We brought a hamper with us so we can have a picnic luncheon here.'

Amelia headed for the stairs. 'My goodness, I forgot your coachman and the footman. They must be in need of refreshment.'

'They are used to waiting around,' Freddie said casually. 'That's part of their job.'

'Nevertheless, I am sure they would like a cup of tea. Perhaps Mariah has some of her cakes left.' Amelia went on ahead but as she passed the open front door she was surprised to see the coachman, minus his top coat and hat, playing ball with the children while the footman, also without his smart uniform coat, was joining in. Sounds from the kitchen were even more surprising, and as she hurried through to the back of the house Amelia recognised Mariah's voice. As she thrust open the kitchen door she was faced with Nellie and Maisie from the mourning warehouse. On the kitchen table were two more sewing machines.

'Good heavens!' Amelia looked to Mariah for help. 'What's going on?'

21

Mariah puffed out her chest and smiled. 'We have the help we so badly need, Emmie.'

Nellie stepped forward. 'If you want us, that is, miss. Me and Maisie are sick and tired of being the butt of Mr Caleb's spiteful remarks and the way he docks our pay on the slightest excuse.'

'Yes, miss,' Maisie added eagerly. 'We walked out and we took our machines with us. Luckily Mariah was there with the gig, so we brought them here.'

'You stole the sewing machines?' Amelia's voice rose in dismay. 'But Caleb will send the police round to arrest us all for being complicit in theft.'

'Let him try.' Nellie pursed her lips. 'We took them because he refused to pay us. He sacked me and Maisie on the spot because he caught us talking to Mariah. He knows full well that she's your friend and that made him angry. That man's sick in his head, if you ask me.'

'We'll be ready for him if he comes here,' Amelia said stoutly. 'In the meantime, perhaps you'd be kind enough to make tea for everyone, Mariah, the coachman and the footman included.'

'Of course.' Mariah nodded, pointing to the range. 'I put the kettle on the moment we got in. I'll butter some bread and there's some cheese on the marble slab in the larder.'

Freddie held up his hand. 'No need to use your provisions. We came prepared. I'll have the hamper brought into the kitchen. It will feed us all with some to spare.' He strode out of the room before Amelia had the chance to stop him.

'If you'll excuse me, I think I'll go and sit down in the parlour,' Dolly said faintly. 'It's rather hot in here.'

'Yes, what am I thinking of?' Amelia took her by the hand, but she hesitated for a moment in the doorway. 'Of course I will take you on here, Nellie, and you too, Maisie. But I can't pay you much at the moment. Things will get better, though, if we work together.'

'Something is better than nothing,' Nellie said wryly. 'I knew you wouldn't let us down, miss. I think the mourning warehouse will be closed down shortly. Mr Caleb isn't really interested in making it profitable, and we reckon the master will sell it off — if anyone wants it, that is.'

'I would not be surprised,' Amelia said sadly. 'I'll be back in a minute or two. I just want to make Dolly comfortable.' She led the way to the front parlour.

Dolly sank onto the sofa with a sigh of relief. 'You know, I was right refusing to accompany Gus to India, much as I love him. I'll miss him terribly, but if I can't stand the heat from a kitchen range I definitely couldn't have coped with the long sea voyage and the raging heat when we arrived in Bombay.'

'You will be able to rejoin Gus when you are recovered from having the baby, if you still wish to accompany him during his posting there.'

'Yes, of course I do. I love being an army wife, just not at this particular moment. I don't want to risk my life or my baby's life.' Dolly lay back and closed her eyes. 'Where is Freddie with the food? I am starving.'

* * *

The hamper, when it was opened on the dining-room table, was filled with appetising food from Fortnum's, with enough to feed everyone, including Nellie and Maisie. They opted to eat in the kitchen with Mariah, the children and Freddie's coachman and footman, while Dolly, Freddie and Amelia ate more sedately in the dining room.

At the end of the meal, when Dolly was getting ready to leave, she took Amelia aside. 'Freddie is giving a charity ball on Friday evening. I want to wear my new ball gown, but I will need you to make any last-minute adjustments. Could you do that?'

'Yes, of course. I will come whenever you want me.'

'You and Todd are both invited to the ball. Freddie suggested it and I agree.'

Amelia eyed her warily. 'I don't know about that, Dolly. We won't know anyone there.'

'Of course you will. There will be me and Gus — it's his last engagement before he sets sail next week. Freddie will be the host and I dare say Lady Galton will attend with her husband. The rest of the guests will be very wealthy ladies and gentlemen. It will be a good advertisement for your gowns, especially if Lady Galton chooses to wear the one you made for her.'

'But I haven't even started on her gown, Dolly. I wanted to make your garments first. You are the most in need and also you are a friend.'

'That's very sweet, but business is business. You have two extra seamstresses now. You can do it, Emmie, I know you can. Just think of all the rich ladies who will look at my gown and then they'll see Lady Galton in hers and they'll be begging you to design for them.'

Freddie had been sitting at the table, listening to the conversation, and he now rose to his feet. 'Dolly is right, Amelia. It will be a wonderful way to introduce you and your talent to society. After what I've seen today, I will be proud to be your sponsor.'

Amelia looked from one smiling face to the other. 'I can do it, even though it's such short notice. With help from the others I will finish your gown, Dolly, and the one Lady Galton has ordered.'

Dolly kissed her on the cheek. 'Well said. I would help if I could, but I will make sure that Freddie doesn't forget to instruct his detective to find out who actually owns this splendid old ruin. I would love to see it brought back to the fine home it must have been when the old sea captain had it built for himself.'

'And so would I,' Amelia said enthusiastically. 'Thank you both so much. I was beginning to think that nothing was possible. Now I feel so much more positive about everything. I can't wait to tell Todd when he returns from the hospital.'

Dolly's expression softened to a tender smile. 'He's a good man, Emmie. I know he had fond feelings for me when we were younger, but I think he truly loves you. I know him so well, he couldn't hide it from me even if he were to try.'

Amelia looked away. She knew instinctively that Dolly was speaking from her heart, but her own feelings were in a turmoil. She could not afford to allow her emotions to override common sense. She managed a vague smile.

'He is a very special person, Dolly. He will always be my very best friend.'

Freddie sighed deeply. 'I've heard those words before, my dear. They are the hardest to bear. I can tell you that from experience. I hope you don't sacrifice everything in order to achieve success. Believe me, it is not worth the heartache.' He headed towards the doorway. 'Come along, Dolly my dear. Let's get you home so that you can rest before Gus comes to take you out to dinner.'

Amelia followed them to the front door. 'You will try to find out who owns this property, won't you, sir — I mean, Freddie?' she added hastily as he gave her a quizzical glance.

'I most certainly will. It's quite a mystery. I'll enjoy playing detective myself.'

Dolly gave Amelia a fond hug. 'I hope I have your promise to attend the ball on Friday. You will come, won't you?'

'I wouldn't miss it for the world,' Amelia said earnestly. 'I can't thank you enough for everything you're doing for me.' She stood in the doorway, watching until Dolly was comfortably ensconced in the carriage with Freddie seated beside her. They both waved as the vehicle set off and Amelia waited until it was out of sight before returning to the kitchen.

'That was the best meal I've ever had,' Nellie said, beaming. 'Will we get fed like this every day, miss?'

Amelia laughed. 'No, but Mariah might find you something tasty if you're very nice to her.'

'When do we start?' Maisie asked eagerly. 'I can't afford to be out of work, miss.'

'We can begin right away.' Amelia met Mariah's questioning look with a nod. 'The pattern is already cut out for Lady Galton's ball gown. I need it to be pinned and tacked to the material. Which of you has experience in cutting?'

'I'm a qualified cutter, miss,' Nellie said proudly.

'That's excellent. I can do the alterations to Mrs Baker's gowns while you and Maisie work on the gown for Lady Galton. If we work hard we can get it done in time for the ball next Friday. It will show the other guests just what we can achieve.'

'I'll work doubly hard,' Nellie promised, crossing her heart.

'Me, too,' Maisie said earnestly.

'Come with me, then. I'll show you where you will be working.' Amelia turned to Mariah. 'Are you happy with this arrangement?'

'Yes, of course. I'll come up and supervise as soon as I've put the meat on to cook slowly for supper.'

'Rabbit again?' Amelia said with a sigh.

'No, it's not. Jim gave me some scrag end of lamb in return for a couple of loaves of bread. I think that was a fair swap, don't you?'

Amelia nodded. 'What would we do without your farmer friend?'

She smiled as she led the way to the long gallery. It was good to see Mariah looking happy and positive after all the horrors she had suffered in the past. Marsh House had given them all new beginnings and she could only hope that Freddie would discover the identity of the mysterious owner so that perhaps they could rent more cheaply or even buy it from that person when funds allowed. It would be wonderful to be free from Caleb and Cousin Daniel. They were in the past now and the future had never looked brighter.

* * *

For the next few days Nellie and Maisie walked from their homes to Marsh House, starting early in the morning. Under the supervision of either Amelia or Mariah, they worked tirelessly, and every evening, after a good meal, Mariah drove them home in the gig. It seemed only fair as they were putting in many more hours than they would have done working at the mourning warehouse. Fortunately, Caleb had not seen fit to visit them, despite the disappearance of two more sewing machines, or perhaps he had simply not noticed that they had gone.

Amelia waited eagerly for news from Freddie. The future of Marsh House Modes, as she had decided to call her business, hung on discovering the identity of the true owner of the place they now called home.

Working from dawn until dusk every day, Amelia finished the gowns for Dolly, including a beautiful ball gown in pink organza. It was designed to flatter her without placing too much emphasis on her condition, which would have been considered extremely vulgar. In addition to this, Lady Galton's ball gown was even better than Amelia had hoped. The creation in peacock-blue satin, trimmed with sequins, glass beads and waterfalls of Valenciennes lace, was a triumph. It just remained for Lady Galton to have a fitting so that any adjustments could be made. It was two days before the ball and Amelia drove herself to the mansion in Dover Street, hoping that her ladyship would be at home and in the mood to try on a new gown. As luck would have it, Lady Galton agreed to see her and was mildly enthusiastic about the new ball gown.

'If it's convenient for you to try it on I can do any alterations needed,' Amelia suggested tentatively.

Lady Galton glanced at the ormolu timepiece on the mantelshelf. 'I suppose I could. I have no appointments this morning. If you will bring it to my bedchamber I'll send for my maid and I'll try it on.'

Amelia could hardly believe her good fortune as she

followed Lady Galton from the parlour and across the marble-tiled entrance hall to the magnificent sweep of the staircase leading to a galleried landing. Lady Galton's room was just as grand and expensively furnished as the rest of the mansion. The exotic scent of French perfume filled the air and Amelia's feet sank into the deep pile of the carpet as she crossed the floor. She perched on a chair by one of the tall windows while Miss Manners helped Lady Galton to undress and put on the gown. Amelia could have cried with relief. The measurements she had taken and her previous knowledge of Lady Galton's requirements had produced a gown that fitted perfectly. She could see that her ladyship was impressed, even though she was not going to be effusive in her comments.

'It's very nice,' Lady Galton said after twisting and turning to get a better view in the cheval mirror. 'Very nice indeed.'

'The colour suits you perfectly, my lady,' Amelia said cautiously.

'Yes, this shade of blue has always been my favourite colour.' Lady Galton turned to her maid. 'Take care of this gown, Manners. I might consider wearing it to the ball on Friday. I'll see how I feel on the day.'

'I'm glad you approve, my lady.' Amelia rose to her feet and backed towards the doorway, realising that she had been dismissed. 'Good day, ma'am.' She did not expect a response and she left the room quietly, but she did a little dance on the landing, hoping that none of the servants could see. Payment might take a long time to come, however, the mere fact that Lady Galton liked the gown and was thinking of wearing it to Freddie's ball was a triumph in itself. Amelia was tempted to slide down the banisters like an excited child, but the butler and footman were standing by the front entrance. She controlled her emotions with a huge effort and descended the stairs as sedately as if she were Lady Galton herself.

Grey was waiting patiently in the street outside, his reins held by a young crossing sweeper, who grinned delightedly when Amelia over-tipped him. She had Dolly's ball gown wrapped in butter muslin and brown paper beneath the seat, and she flicked the reins, guiding Grey in the direction of Piccadilly. If Dolly's ball gown fitted half as well as the one Lady Galton had just accepted it would be a good day. Amelia was happier than she had been for a very long time.

However, when she finally arrived home, having had a successful last fitting with Dolly, Amelia suddenly realised that she herself had nothing to wear to the ball.

Mariah turned to Nellie and Maisie, who were getting ready to go home. 'We can soon remedy that, can't we, ladies?'

Nellie nodded enthusiastically. 'I saw a bale of beautiful blue silk, the colour of your eyes, miss. It would make a lovely ball gown.'

'I was going to make that into an afternoon gown for Lady Galton,' Amelia said, frowning.

'I think your needs are more important at the moment.' Mariah looked to Nellie and Maisie for acknowledgement and they both nodded enthusiastically.

'Speaking plainly, miss,' Maisie said shyly, 'you need to look even more splendid than the ladies present. They'll all want to know where you got your beautiful gown.'

Amelia laughed. 'I can see that I'm outnumbered,

but I understand what you're saying. The only problem is we have just two days to make me into the belle of the ball. If that's at all possible.'

'You're too modest, Emmie.' Todd strolled into the kitchen, taking off his hat and gloves and tossing them onto a chair. 'You will outshine all the other ladies present.'

'Now I know you're teasing me,' Amelia countered. 'But you will need evening dress. Have you such an outfit?'

Todd grinned. 'I've attended a couple of balls in the country, but never one in London. However, my good friend Gus pointed out the need for me to look smart so I went to Mr Moss's shop in Covent Garden and bought an excellent second-hand evening suit and a dress shirt. I won't let you down, Emmie.'

Close to tears at his thoughtfulness, Amelia flung her arms around him and gave him a hug. 'Thank you, Todd. I can't believe you did that for me.'

Mariah made a move towards the doorway, beckoning to Nellie and Maisie. 'Come along, ladies. I'll drive you home, and tomorrow morning I'll have the pattern cut out for you to begin work on the most beautiful ball gown imaginable for Miss Amelia Sutton, the fashion designer and owner of Marsh House Modes.'

'But I haven't designed one for myself,' Amelia said dazedly.

'Yes, you have,' Mariah argued. 'You did it without knowing, but I can think of a couple of ball gowns that would suit you. One in particular stands out in my mind. I'll leave you to guess which one, Emmie. We're off now, but I'll be back within the hour, if you don't mind looking after the nippers. They've been fed, and Percy is already in bed, but I'll see to the girls when I get home.'

'That's fine by me. I'll keep an eye on them.' Amelia sank down on a chair at the table. 'I'm beginning to wonder who is in charge of this establishment, Todd,' she said, smiling ruefully.

'There's no doubt in my mind,' Todd said stoutly. 'Those women would walk through fire for you. After all, if you hadn't stepped in and helped Mariah in the first place, none of this would have been possible, and the same goes for Nellie and Maisie.'

'It benefited me as much as them. Anyway, it looks as if Mariah has left some stew for us. You must be hungry.'

Todd held up his hand. 'Sit where you are, miss. I'll serve the meal, for a change. We'll eat together while it's nice and quiet.'

'It must be my birthday or something.' Amelia sat back in her seat, closing her eyes, but almost immediately the door burst open, admitting Betsy and Daisy into the room as they squabbled fiercely.

'Woah!' Todd said firmly. 'Calm down, girls. What's the matter?'

'Daisy took my rag doll,' Betsy said crossly. 'It's mine, not hers.'

Amelia jumped to her feet. 'Give it back, Daisy.'

'I want a dolly,' Daisy said sulkily. 'I never had no dolly. I only want to play with her for a while.'

Amelia silenced Todd with a meaningful look. She placed her arm around Betsy's heaving shoulders. 'I know you love Mary-Anne, but you must understand that no one thought to give Daisy a dolly of her own. Perhaps you could lend it to her, just for an hour or so, and then Daisy will give Mary-Anne back to you.'

'Didn't they give you toys in the orphanage?' Betsy demanded crossly. 'She's my doll.'

'Betsy!' Amelia shot her a warning glance. 'What did I just say?'

Betsy thrust the doll into Daisy's arms. 'All right. You can have her to go to bed with tonight but I want her back in the morning.' She took a deep breath. 'Maybe someone will give you a dolly for your birthday, or for Christmas. It's not too far away.'

'Good girl,' Amelia said, smiling. 'I'm sure that someone will give Daisy what she wishes for.'

Betsy sniffed the air as Todd ladled soup into two bowls. 'I'm still hungry. Is there enough for me and Daisy to have some soup, too?'

'I'm sure I can make it stretch if you get two more bowls out of the cupboard, Betsy.' Todd sighed. 'So much for a quiet supper together, Emmie.'

'Another time, Todd. But peace is restored. Let's be thankful for that.'

'After supper might we look at your designs, Emmie?' Betsy handed two bowls to Todd, who filled them with soup. 'Ma said you'd need a gown for the ball on Friday. Can me and Daisy pick out the one we like best?'

Amelia dipped her spoon into the hot soup. 'Yes, of course you may. Perhaps Todd would like to join in, too?' She looked up at him and smiled. 'We are going to be partners at the ball and he has bought himself a very smart outfit.' She reached for a slice of bread and butter.

'Is that your way of asking for my approval of the gown you will wear?' Todd asked quietly.

'Of course it is, silly,' Betsy said without giving Amelia a chance to respond. 'You are going to whirl her round the floor. You want her to look even more beautiful than usual.'

Todd laughed. 'I suppose you're right, Betsy. We'll all take a look and see what everyone thinks.'

By the time the supper things were washed and put away, and the girls were in their nightgowns ready for bed, Amelia brought her portfolio down to the kitchen and set out the designs on the table. After a lot of thought the decision was unanimous, and when Mariah returned from taking the women home, she proved to be in complete agreement.

'This is the one, Emmie. I will take your measurements and cut out a paper pattern tonight before I go to bed.' She turned to the girls with a mock frown. 'You two are up later than usual. Off to bed with you.'

Giggling, the girls ran from the room with Daisy still clutching Mary-Anne.

'I'll go and check the outbuildings before I turn in,' Todd said, rising to his feet. 'You did settle Grey for the night, didn't you, Mariah?'

She scowled at him. 'Of course I did. What do you think I am, Todd Taylor?'

'I was going to do it for you, Mariah. You've had a long, tiring day.' He took a lantern from the scullery and left by the back door.

'That was a bit unnecessary,' Amelia said sharply. 'Todd was trying to help.'

Mariah shrugged. 'Yes, I know. I am tired and you look exhausted. But we need to start on your gown. You have to make a good impression at the ball. After all, that's the reason for accepting the invitation, isn't it?'

'It is, but I wasn't thinking of myself as a model.'

Mariah laughed. 'Who better? We'll make you the

belle of the ball. Come upstairs and I'll take the necessary measurements.'

'Do you really think we can make the dress in less than two days?' Amelia asked anxiously. 'There's even more detail in the design you've all chosen than in the gown I made for Lady Galton.'

'We have all tomorrow and most of Friday. We can do it, Emmie. With a fair wind behind us we'll get it done and you'll make us all proud.'

* * *

Amelia slept badly that night. She was plagued by dreams of herself at the ball wearing an unfinished dress in tattered blue silk. At other times she was wearing just her chemise, but Todd looked incredibly handsome in his evening suit, and she was barefoot. She awakened at dawn and went down to the kitchen to find Mariah and Todd already there.

'You're up early,' Amelia said, yawning.

'I have the last part of my final examination this morning.' Todd drained his teacup and placed it back on its saucer. 'I had an errand to run, but I'm off to the hospital now.'

'Good luck,' Amelia said earnestly. 'But I don't think you'll need it. I'm sure you'll pass with flying colours.'

He brushed her cheek with a kiss. 'I hope I don't prove you wrong.' He snatched up a slice of toast and took a bite of it as he left the room.

'You don't have to worry about him,' Mariah said sternly. 'He's a clever fellow.' She filled a cup with tea and handed it to Amelia. 'We've got a lot to do today.'

'I'm really not sure we can make my gown in time.

It's an intricate pattern and it must be done right or it will do more harm than good.'

'It will be perfect.' Mariah put her head on one side. 'I can hear voices. Help is at hand.' She hurried from the kitchen, leaving Amelia staring after her in surprise. It was unusual for Mariah to get excited at the prospect of seeing Nellie and Maisie, but now it sounded as if there were more voices in the entrance hall than just the three of them. Amelia rose to her feet and went to look. To her astonishment she saw not only Nellie and Maisie, but more of the women from the workroom.

'What's going on?' Amelia demanded incredulously. 'Why are you all here? You'll lose your jobs at the mourning warehouse.'

Nellie stepped forward. 'We haven't got a fairy godmother to magic you a gown for the ball, but I've brought all our best seamstresses and embroiderers. We'll perform our own sort of magic.'

'The workroom is closed from tomorrow anyway,' Maisie added, to a murmur of agreement. 'They've all been sacked so we shut it down a day early.'

'We brought their machines too,' Nellie added. 'If only I could see Caleb Marsh's face when he opens up today and finds everything gone. He's taken to coming early every morning to spy on us. He fines us for being late.'

'Yes, miss,' a small voice from the back of the group piped up. 'We knew we wouldn't get paid so we've come to work for you. Nellie said —'

'Hush, Ivy.' Nellie shook her finger at the young woman. 'I never promised you'd all be taken on. I said it would depend on whether Miss Sutton had orders from the rich folk. But chatting ain't going to get nothing done. I'll show you where you're going to be working.'

'I'd better put the kettle on,' Mariah said, smiling. 'You'll need sustenance before you start.'

'How did all this come about, Mariah?' Amelia asked dazedly. 'I can't promise these women work, even if I get a few orders.'

'We'll worry about that after the ball.' Mariah propelled Amelia back into the kitchen. 'Best cut some slices of bread and butter for them. I doubt if any of them have had breakfast. They'll work better on full stomachs.'

'This is amazing. I really don't know what to say.'

'We are nothing on our own, but together we will put paid to Caleb and his antics. Luckily I made a couple of extra loaves yesterday while you were out. Start slicing, please, while I make the tea.'

Betsy and Daisy danced into the room, Daisy holding Percy by the hand.

'Can we help?' Betsy asked excitedly. 'What are all those ladies doing upstairs, Ma?'

'They are going to help us make Marsh House Modes famous, love. You can help by handing round the bread and tea when they come downstairs for breakfast. You can keep an eye on Percy for me, Daisy, if you will.'

'Yes, Ma. I love Percy. He's like a big dolly.' Daisy gave Percy a hug and he growled at her.

Amelia smiled as she sliced the two loaves and buttered them liberally. 'It's a pity we haven't any jam to put on the bread.'

'There are plenty of blackberries in the hedgerows at this time of year,' Mariah said, pouring boiling water into a fresh pot of tea. 'When we have time, we'll go picking and make them into jam. I remember my mum doing that. We used to walk into the countryside with our wicker baskets and come home with them brimming with berries. We ate as many as we could, too.'

'It sounds wonderful. We'll do that next week when everything goes back to normal,' Amelia said with a sigh.

'Betsy, run upstairs and ask everyone to come down for something to eat and drink,' Mariah said firmly.

'Yes, Ma. I'm going.'

Minutes later everyone was assembled round the kitchen table, drinking tea and munching thick slices of bread and butter. The room was filled with chatter and laughter, but a sudden shout from the entrance hall silenced them all.

Amelia turned to see Caleb standing in the doorway with a savage expression marring his handsome features.

'You're having a party and I wasn't invited.'

22

'You aren't welcome here, Caleb,' Amelia said angrily. 'Please leave.' She faced him defiantly. It was time that she stood up to the man who had been taking advantage of her situation since they first met.

'You must be aware that these women still work for me.' Caleb took a step towards her, his eyes narrowed and his lips drawn into a thin line. 'You've taken them away from their positions in the workroom. Then there's the matter of the stolen sewing machines. What have you got to say to that?'

'Your former employees chose to come here today. You don't deserve them, Caleb Marsh.'

'I'll return with a constable. We'll see how you fare when you're arrested.'

'And I will go to the newspapers in Fleet Street,' Amelia countered boldly. 'I doubt if my cousin would thank you for the adverse publicity.'

Caleb was silent for a moment, his lips working but no sound emanating from his mouth, and Amelia knew she had made her point. She turned to the women with an encouraging smile.

'Do we all think it's time for Mr Marsh to make a hasty exit, ladies?'

The answer was a resounding 'Yes', and the women surged forward, taking Caleb off guard. He backed away holding up both hands.

'None of you will work for the Norris Company again. I will see every one of you in court for threatening behaviour.' Despite his angry words, Caleb left the house, untied his horse and climbed into the saddle. 'You will suffer for this, Amelia Sutton. Don't think you've seen the last of me.'

Amelia had been tempted to tell him she knew that the story he had told her of his past was a pack of lies, but she had decided to keep it for another time. They had Caleb on the run and he proved it by digging his heels savagely into the poor animal's flanks so that it bolted forward, almost unseating him. A rousing cheer from his former workers followed him down the drive, followed by loud clapping.

Mariah called for order. 'Your tea is getting cold, ladies. And we have a lot of work to do today.'

She waited until everyone was settled, munching their bread and butter and drinking tea, before taking Amelia aside. 'He's dangerous. What do you think he will do next?'

Amelia shrugged. 'I really don't know, but we have the advantage over him. We know he is not the real owner of this house. When we find out the identity of that person I will see if I can persuade them to let us keep Marsh House one way or the other.'

'I agree entirely.' Mariah glanced round at the smiling faces as the women chatted amongst themselves. 'In the meantime, we have our workers. If we can't make you the most beautiful ball gown in London, I'll eat my bonnet.'

'That I would love to see,' Amelia said, laughing. Even so, she had a nagging feeling that Caleb was up to mischief and it would not go away. She waited until everyone had finished eating and drinking before leading them upstairs to the long gallery, and the work on her ball gown began in earnest.

After a morning's work with each of the women given tasks for which she was most qualified, they had a brief break for luncheon. When they returned to the long gallery there was a cheerful buzz of chatter as they worked. Satisfied that things were going well, Amelia was able to leave Mariah in charge while she went downstairs for a brief rest. However, she had only just sat in the saggy old armchair in the parlour when she heard the rumble of carriage wheels and the sound of horses' hoofs on the gravel. She jumped to her feet and went to the window. The footman had leaped from the box and was putting down the steps before opening the carriage door. Freddie alighted, but there was no sign of Dolly, which was disappointing. Amelia went to open the front door.

'Is Dolly all right?' Amelia asked anxiously.

Freddie gave her a beaming smile. 'She's absolutely fine. In fact, she went out with Gus today, so I thought I would come and see you. I have had news that will be of interest to you.'

'Please come in.' Amelia ushered him into the parlour and motioned him to take a seat. 'What have you discovered?' she asked eagerly. 'Caleb was here today. Some of the women who worked at the mourning warehouse have come here to help with my ball gown. He had already sacked them all as from tomorrow, but they had with them some of the old sewing machines from the workroom. He threatened to have them arrested.'

'I doubt Mr Norris would sanction that, and I'd be surprised if the old sewing machines have much monetary value. I think Caleb was trying to scare you.'

'He's a bully — that's how he treated all the women, myself included.'

'I'm sorry that they've lost their jobs, but I learned something that will be of interest to you.' Freddie made himself comfortable on the sofa. 'Earlier today I had a visit from the detective I mentioned. What he told me was very enlightening.'

Amelia took a seat opposite Freddie. 'Don't keep me in suspense, Freddie.'

'Apparently this house belonged to the same family for generations. The last in the line was a certain Miss Phoebe Marsh.'

'Was she the cruel aunt that Caleb told me about?'

'No, it was all a lie. Miss Marsh was born here but she married young and left home to become Mrs Sebastian Norris. She married your grandfather's late brother.'

'Surely that's not possible.'

'Do you remember her? She would have been your aunt Phoebe.'

'No, I mean, yes, vaguely. I do remember the name, although I must have been very young when I knew her.'

'Phoebe Norris was childless and she had no living relations. Both she and her husband died of cholera in one of the many epidemics. The house and land seems to have been absorbed into the Norris Company, although it was never official. Caleb must have discovered it while he was working for your cousin, and he found a way to use the knowledge to his advantage.'

'But if it doesn't belong to him or my cousin, who does own Marsh House?'

'The property would automatically belong to Phoebe's husband on their marriage, of course, but he died intestate and your cousin Daniel, being his next of kin, seems to have inherited everything, including the house. Unless, of course, a will can be found.'

Amelia frowned thoughtfully. 'What does this mean as far as I'm concerned?'

'It means that Caleb has no hold over you, but you will need to speak to your cousin about the property.'

'That doesn't bode well. He made it plain that he wants as little to do with me as possible. No doubt Caleb has told him all sorts of lies.'

'I believe that your cousin is married,' Freddie said slowly.

'Yes,' Amelia said thoughtfully. 'His wife's name is Beatrice.'

'Do you think she might help you, Emmie?'

'I only remember her vaguely. She was very elegant and she wore nice perfume, but I don't think she took much notice of me as a child.'

'I've seen her at functions and she is as you describe.'

Amelia eyed him curiously. 'What are you thinking?'

'I believe she is an ambitious woman, very conscious of the family's inherited wealth, and from what I've been told she is keen to rise in society.'

'Have you invited them to your ball, by any chance?'

Freddie grinned. 'I thought it might help.'

'You think that she will want to show off by ordering a gown from me. I doubt if she would even recognise me now, or remember my name.'

'All to the good. She will doubtless be impressed by Dolly's beautiful attire and it seems that you have something equally stunning planned for yourself. I think it might be your chance to make yourself known to her as you are now.'

'And if she likes my designs she might persuade

my cousin to allow us to remain in Marsh House. He might even sell it to me or at least rent it at a reasonable rate.'

'Quite so,' Freddie said, laughing. 'I leave that to you and your ability to persuade your aunt to help.'

'Did you invite them to the ball for that purpose alone?'

'Of course I did. I'll do everything in my power to help you, Emmie. I think of Dolly as part of my family and I'm very fond of Todd, too. I've watched him grow from an unruly boy to a fine young man and an excellent physician. He obviously cares deeply for you.'

Amelia was about to answer when Betsy rushed into the room to announce that Percy had fallen into the horse trough.

'Your servant has fished him out, sir,' Betsy added shyly. 'But Percy is soaked to the skin, Emmie. Shall I tell Ma?'

'It's all right, Betsy.' Amelia leaped to her feet. 'If you find him some clean clothes I'll take care of him.'

'I think that's a signal for me to go.' Freddie rose from his seat. 'Think about what I told you, Emmie, and I'll see you at the ball tomorrow.'

She laid her hand on his arm as he was about to leave the room. 'I can't thank you enough. You've given me hope, but the rest is up to me.'

Amelia followed Betsy out of the parlour and found Daisy clutching Percy's hand. He was very wet and his hair was covered in green slime, but it did not seem to worry him.

'Take him into the kitchen, please, Daisy. I'll wash him and dry him before we put him into clean clothes.'

'Should I tell Mariah?' Daisy asked anxiously. 'It

weren't my fault, honestly.'

'We won't bother his mother,' Amelia said firmly. 'No harm has been done. Percy will be fine and a dip in cold water might make him less bold next time.'

Of course, Mariah found out what had happened. She came downstairs to start preparing supper and found the clothes that Percy had worn earlier that day washed and hanging on the line in the stable yard. She was alarmed at first, but then she saw the funny side of things and laughed, to the obvious relief of both Betsy and Daisy. She gave them a lecture, but it was a short one. Amelia left them in the kitchen and went upstairs to the long gallery to supervise the next stage of making her gown.

With so many expert hands working hard, progress was fast and the gown was ready for its first fitting at the end of the day. Amelia tried it on and stood very still while Nellie and Maisie did the necessary alterations to make it a perfect fit. Even in its unfinished state Amelia could see that the gown was going to be eye-catching. She thanked everyone for their efforts and congratulated them on their work, sending them home tired, but smiling happily.

Amelia watched them as they made their way to the lane at the end of the drive.

'If we were to take them on properly I think it would be vital to arrange some sort of transport for them, Mariah. It's too far for them to walk after a hard day, especially when the weather turns nasty. It's getting dark earlier and earlier.'

Mariah nodded. 'I agree. Let's hope all goes well tomorrow at the ball. A few wealthy customers will see us through the harsh weather, providing we can stay on here.'

'There might be a way. Come into the kitchen and I'll tell you what Freddie's private detective discovered about the real owner of Marsh House . . .'

* * *

It took all next day for those who were most expert in adding the trimmings to the gown to work their magic, but the result was spectacular. Amelia was close to tears when Nellie handed her the completed garment.

'You must try it on now,' Nellie said firmly. 'The girls want to see the result of their labours.'

This remark was greeted by a round of applause, which Amelia could not ignore. With the help of both Nellie and Maisie she tried on the shimmering ice-blue gown, to gasps of admiration and cries of delight from those who had worked so hard to achieve a minor miracle. The fading sunlight set the bugle beads dancing and glittering as if on fire, and the silk caressed Amelia's body, sending shivers down her spine.

'It's beautiful,' Mariah said. 'I'm close to tears meself.'

'I can't thank you all enough.' Amelia caught sight of herself in the tall cheval mirror and her hands flew to cover her mouth. The gown was so perfect that it moulded her slender figure, curving in the right places and minimising her small waist to a mere handspan. 'It's wonderful,' she added breathlessly.

'If that don't get us orders from the toffs, nothing will.' Nellie sniffed and smiled. 'Well done, everyone. Ain't that better than making them blooming black crepe gowns for funerals? I feel as though I could put on a pair of dancing slippers and trip the light fantastic meself.'

'I'd give a week's wages to see that,' Ivy piped up from the back of the room, and everyone laughed.

'If this doesn't prove our worth, nothing will.' Amelia smiled and clapped her hands. 'Thank you all again. I hope this ball gown is the first of many that we will make together.'

'We love you, miss,' Ivy said boldly. 'But we all got to eat. I don't want to sound grasping and greedy, but we do need to get paid.'

'And you will, I promise. The moment I get the money from Lady Galton I will make sure you all get what you've earned, with a bonus for what you've accomplished in two short days.'

'Ta, miss. I knows you won't let us down.' Ivy clapped her hands and everyone joined in.

'Todd will be here soon,' Mariah said urgently. 'We need to put your hair up and you must change your shoes. You can't wear high button boots beneath a ball gown.'

'I haven't got any dancing slippers,' Amelia said aghast. 'It's something I hadn't considered. In fact, I've only got these boots.'

A ripple of consternation ran through the room. 'You can't wear black boots, miss,' Ivy said sadly.

'My gown covers my feet — almost.' Even as she said it, Amelia knew it was not true. The scuffed toes of her boots showed with each movement.

'Take 'em off, miss,' Maisie said urgently. 'Give 'em to me. I think I can do something with 'em.'

'What are you thinking of?' Mariah demanded.

Amelia sank down on a chair and began to unbutton her boots with Maisie's help. 'What can you do, Maisie?'

'Mariah, have you got some blue powder for whitening washing and some starch in the kitchen cupboard?' Maisie asked eagerly.

'Yes, of course. I'm proud of my washday whites.'

'Then give me the boots and show me where you keep those things, and leave the rest to me.'

'Are you sure you know what you're doing?' Mariah demanded suspiciously.

'Of course. I wouldn't say so if I didn't think it might work.'

'It's worth a try,' Amelia said firmly. 'I have no choice other than to wear these boots. Do what you can, Maisie, and thank you.'

Maisie tucked the boots under her arm. 'Leave it to me.'

Amelia went to her room and sat at the dressing table with a cracked and fly-spotted mirror while Mariah coiffed her hair, piling it in loops of curls on top of her head. She finished it with white rosebuds that Betsy had picked in what remained of the rose garden.

'Todd is all dressed up,' Betsy said enthusiastically. 'He looks so handsome and he's waiting for you, Emmie.'

Amelia glanced at her reflection in the mirror. 'My hair looks wonderful, Mariah. Thank you. I just hope it's not too windy. Travelling in the gig is not the best way to arrive looking immaculate, especially so late in the year.'

Betsy giggled. 'There's a surprise for you, Emmie. I ain't supposed to tell, but there's that lordship's carriage outside, waiting for you. You'll arrive just like a proper lady.'

'Except for my boots,' Amelia said with a wry smile.

'Maybe I should go in my stockinged feet, Mariah.'

'I done what I could, miss.' Maisie hurried into the room, holding out the boots, which were now coated in starch mixed with the blue powder they used to rinse the sheets in on washdays. Oddly enough, although slightly patchy, the result was reasonably effective. 'They'll be fine, but don't rub the leather or the starch will brush off.' Maisie went down on her hands and knees to help Amelia put on the finished boots.

'They look all right,' Mariah said grimly. 'At least they match in with the colour of your gown. We've just got to hope and pray it doesn't rain.'

Maisie fastened the boots using a button hook. 'There, they don't look bad, if I says so meself.'

Amelia rose to her feet. 'Thank you again. Thank you, all. This wouldn't have been possible without you.'

Mariah patted her gently on the shoulder. 'You look really beautiful, Emmie. Really, lovely. I'm so proud of you. I can't wait to see the look on Todd's face when you walk down those stairs.'

* * *

Todd gazed up at Amelia as she glided down the stairs, one hand trailing the banister rail, the other holding her skirt so that she would not trip.

'Emmie, you look beautiful. You'll be the best dressed woman at the ball.' His tender smile widened into a grin. 'But the boots are quite amazing. Are you starting a new fashion?'

She reached the foot of the stairs and allowed her skirt to cover the offending footwear. 'Don't laugh, Todd. It's not funny.'

‘Haven’t you got another pair of shoes?’

‘No. These are all I have.’

Todd’s smile faded. ‘If only I’d known. I’d have made sure you had a proper pair of dancing slippers. I’m ashamed of myself for being so thoughtless.’

‘You weren’t to know, and to be honest I simply didn’t think about my feet. Besides which, no one will notice. The blue powder and starch mixture is almost the same colour as my gown.’

Todd shook his head. ‘We’ll have to hope it doesn’t rain.’

‘Mariah just said that,’ Amelia said, laughing. ‘I am so excited about this evening, Todd. I don’t care about my shoes. I just hope that everything goes to plan and Lady Galton wears her gown, as well as Dolly. This ball means so much to me.’

‘I know it does.’ Todd slipped his arm around her shoulders and gave her a gentle hug. ‘Come along then. Freddie has sent his carriage for us. He’s a splendid fellow, for a lord.’

Amelia took her cape from its peg in the hall and Todd wrapped it around her shoulders. He hesitated for a moment, looking at her with an inscrutable expression in his hazel eyes, and then he smiled.

‘You deserve recognition for your talent, Emmie. If the rich women at the ball don’t fall over themselves in their efforts to get your attention I’ll have to stand in the middle of the dance floor and proclaim you the queen of couture.’

‘Such a fancy word for a country doctor,’ Amelia teased.

‘You mean a soon-to-be-specialist in paediatrics, Miss Sutton. I really think I did well in the examination. It was a matter of luck but I knew the answers to all the questions.'

'It wasn't luck, Todd. It was all those hours you spent studying that made it seem easy. I'm so proud of you.'

'That means more to me than accolades from the medical profession.' Todd swept her off her feet and carried her out to the waiting carriage, setting her down on the padded leather squabs. He climbed in after her and took her hand in his. 'This is your night, Amelia Sutton. I know it will be a triumph.'

* * *

Amelia was suddenly nervous as she entered the mansion in Piccadilly on Todd's arm. He gave her an encouraging smile as they waited outside the ballroom to be announced.

'You seem quite at home here,' Amelia said in a whisper as she glanced round at the palatial setting. The vast entrance hall was lit by two gasoliers and gas wall lights, as was the ballroom, but in addition, the crystal chandeliers were casting romantic candlelight on the dance floor and surrounding tables. The air was filled with the scent of hot wax, expensive hair pomade and French perfume. To Amelia it was like stepping into another world, a fairy tale with handsome princes in evening dress squiring beautiful princesses wearing ball gowns and dazzling jewels.

'I've been here once or twice,' Todd said casually. 'Gus and I more or less grew up in Rockwood Castle. Dolly's family are wonderful people. Heaven knows where we boys would have been without their support and generosity.'

They reached the top of the stairs and Todd gave

their names to the master of ceremonies, who announced them in loud, clear tones. Freddie was there to greet them, performing the duty on his own. Amelia felt instantly sorry for him. It seemed so wrong for a man such as Freddie Ashton to be receiving guests without the support of a loving wife.

'I hope you enjoy your evening,' Freddie said, smiling. 'And I hope that you make many influential friends, Amelia, my dear.'

Amelia bobbed a curtsey. She did not know if it was considered the correct etiquette, but it felt natural. 'Thank you, sir.'

Todd led her through the crowd to the edge of the dance floor, from where they could get a better view of the assembled guests.

Amelia clutched his arm. 'I see Dolly and Gus, and I do believe that's Lady Galton. She is wearing the ball gown I designed and made for her. Todd, I think this evening is going to go well for us.'

'You are the one who deserves all the credit, Emmie.'

She smiled up at him. 'I couldn't have done any of it without your help. You chose to stay with us at Marsh House.'

'I'm sure I have the best of the bargain. Mariah is a wonderful cook,' he added laughing.

Amelia nudged him in the ribs. 'And you have my company in the evening. That must count as something.'

'That too,' Todd said casually, but a teasing smile curved his lips.

Amelia was suddenly serious. 'As it is, we are on borrowed time. I need to seek out my cousin Daniel's wife, Beatrice, and introduce myself. I doubt if she would recognise me after all these years.'

'Do you recognise her?'

'No, not really, but I see Daniel over there by the potted palm tree. I think the lady with him must be his wife.'

'Perhaps you can catch her on her own at some point,' Todd said in a low voice. 'I suggest we join Gus and Dolly. I know there is a serious point to all this, but we might as well enjoy ourselves.'

'I agree entirely. I am so nervous that I doubt if I could think of anything to say to Lady Galton. Perhaps I should go and thank her for wearing the gown I designed for her.'

Todd shook his head. 'I don't think that would be the way to go about it. Be subtle, Emmie. You are dealing with people who look down on tradesmen and merchants, even though their families might have made their fortunes that way in the past.'

'I'll have to be guided by you and Dolly. I don't want to spoil my chances of making good connections because of ignorance.'

'Not ignorance. You just aren't acquainted with the ways of the world, and that's not a bad thing.' Todd raised his hand to acknowledge Gus as they made their way through the throng to the table where Dolly had taken a seat.

'I thought you were leaving today, Gus.' Todd pulled up a chair for Amelia and she sat down beside Dolly.

'I'm leaving at midnight,' Gus said cheerfully. 'I will be like Cinderella fleeing the ball before the clock has struck twelve.'

'Don't joke about it, Gus.' Dolly sniffed and blotted a tear away with a lace hanky. 'I wish I'd agreed to go with you now.'

He leaned over and kissed her cheek. 'You made

the right decision, my darling. You and our son, or daughter, are the most important people in my life. I want you to be safe and healthy and then you can join me abroad.'

'I suppose so,' Dolly said reluctantly. 'I cry easily these days. I don't know why.'

'I've seen ladies in your conditions weeping like fountains over nothing,' Amelia said gently. 'We'll always be here for you, and you look really lovely in your new gown. It makes me feel very proud to think it's my design.'

Dolly's eyes brightened. 'I've already had ladies asking me who made such a flattering creation. Of course, I gave them your name.' She glanced over Amelia's shoulder. 'I can see women staring at both of us now. I think they've noticed your exquisite ball gown, too. You have surpassed yourself, Emmie. It's really beautiful.'

'Thank you for your support. I'm truly grateful.' Amelia leaned forward, lowering her voice. 'I need to speak to Cousin Beatrice. It's a long story, but Freddie discovered that the Norris family own Marsh House. I'll explain everything later.'

'I know your cousin by sight,' Dolly said slowly. 'The lady with him is his wife.'

'There's little chance of Daniel helping me in any way, but Beatrice might be more amenable, especially if she realises that I have a connection to Freddie. I think she is a social climber.'

'Well, now might be your best chance, Emmie. It looks as if Mr Norris has gone to fetch her a glass of wine or fruit cup. If you're quick you might catch her on her own.'

Amelia rose to her feet. 'You're right. Wish me luck.'

She made her way quickly between the tables, apologising to a gentleman she almost bumped into in her hurry.

Beatrice Norris was seated beside a potted palm. Her fingers drummed nervously on the sparkling white tablecloth and she kept glancing over her shoulder, as if aware of being watched, although the only person heading towards her was Amelia.

'Excuse me, Mrs Norris?' Amelia said shyly.

Beatrice turned her head to stare at Amelia, her lips closed tightly and her eyes narrowed. 'Do I know you?'

'Amelia Sutton, ma'am. We haven't met since I was a child.'

'Amelia? Harold's daughter?'

'Yes, ma'am.'

'You've grown up.' Beatrice eyed Amelia's gown with a hint of jealousy twisting her thin lips. 'You look very — prosperous.'

'I designed and made this gown with the assistance of my seamstresses.'

'Are you trying to sell me something? If so, you may leave now. I've been told that you importuned my husband.'

'I do have a business, but that's not what I wanted to speak about.'

'I don't want my husband to see us together. Say what you have to say and be quick about it.'

'I wanted to ask you about Marsh House. I believe your husband inherited it from his aunt, the former Phoebe Marsh.'

'I know nothing about such things.'

Amelia took a deep breath. 'Did you know that Caleb Marsh claimed to own the house? He's been charging me an exorbitant rent to live there.'

'No, I didn't know, but I have nothing to do with business matters.'

'But you should, ma'am. The house was left to your husband. I have grounds to believe that is true. Caleb has been stealing from you.'

'What is this? What has she been saying to you, Beatrice?'

Amelia leaped to her feet at the sound of her cousin's voice, but in doing so she knocked his arm and a cup of fruit punch spilled onto her boots as she tried to move her skirt out of the way. She stood very still, staring at the mixture of alcohol trickling through the blue-coloured starch to reveal the black toes of her footwear. A sliver of peach slid to the floor.

Daniel Norris threw back his head and guffawed with laughter. 'Just look at the little fraud. All dressed up in an attempt to make herself known to my lady wife, and she can't even afford to buy a decent pair of dancing slippers. Get back to the slums where you belong, Amelia Sutton. You are just like your feckless papa. You shame us by your brazen behaviour.'

23

'No, cousin. If I am like my papa then I am proud to be so. He is a better man than you, by far. As it is, you have a criminal in your employ who has been extorting money from me for the rent of Marsh House, which I believe belongs to you.'

'What nonsense is this? Anyway, whatever it is, this is not the time or place to discuss such matters. Go away and don't come near me or my wife again.'

Amelia stiffened her shoulders. 'No, sir. I will not leave this table until you hear me out.'

'People are staring, Daniel,' Beatrice said angrily.

Amelia was ready to argue it out, regardless of the stir she realised she was creating, but Todd was suddenly at her elbow and Freddie was making his way towards them.

'Leave them, Emmie,' Todd said in a low voice. 'They are not worth bothering about.'

Freddie extended his right hand to Daniel with a friendly smile. 'Mr Norris, I believe. My man of business tells me that you are looking for an investor.'

'Your lordship, I'm honoured that you recall such a trivial piece of information.' Daniel bowed over Freddie's hand as if addressing royalty and Beatrice fanned herself vigorously.

'Mrs Norris, how kind of you to grace us with your presence this evening.' Freddie raised her hand to his lips, causing her to blush rosily.

'I — er — thank you, my lord.'

'I hope you both enjoy your evening,' Freddie said graciously. He proffered his hand to Amelia. 'As the host, I must lead the dancing. Would you honour me by being my partner, Miss Sutton?'

She was so surprised that she merely nodded and allowed him to lead her into the middle of the dance floor as the orchestra struck up a grand march.

'I don't know how to dance,' Amelia said in a whisper.

Freddie smiled at her. 'I'll lead, don't worry. Just look beautiful and enjoy yourself. All eyes are upon you and your wonderful gown.'

'But my boots, Freddie. Everyone will laugh at me.'

'You might start a fashion, my dear. Hold your head up high and hold my hand. We will show them all how it's done.'

Amelia had little option other than to do as Freddie requested. He gave her fingers an encouraging squeeze and they processed around the ballroom with couples falling in behind them. After the first agonising moments Amelia forgot about her unsightly boots and began to enjoy herself. When the grand march ended Todd claimed her for a waltz and although she barely knew the steps he held her firmly and she was able to follow as if they had danced together all their lives.

'When did you learn to dance?' Amelia asked as he whirled her around the floor.

'Nancy made sure that we boys had a rounded education, and that included social skills,' Todd said casually as he steered her expertly through the dancers.

Amelia abandoned any attempt at conversation and gave herself up to the pleasure of being held in Todd's arms, but after the waltz ended it was Gus who took her round the floor in a lively polka. If people were staring at her boots it did not seem to matter. The fact was that she was loving every minute and she felt she could dance all night, which was what actually happened. Of course, Todd was her main partner, but other gentlemen were introduced to her and none of them seemed to have noticed anything untoward about her footwear.

During the break for supper in an adjoining room Amelia was approached by several women, the younger ones enquiring shyly about her gown, while the older ladies demanded to know which French couturier had suddenly arrived in London.

It was sad to say goodbye to Gus at midnight, and Dolly retired to bed soon after, having made a brave attempt at staying until the end of the ball, but eventually exhaustion won and she said good night. Amelia knew that Todd was working next day and they should have left for home, but he swore that he was enjoying himself far too much to leave before the end of the ball and she was easily persuaded.

It was the early hours that they finally said good night to Freddie. Amelia thanked him profusely for his kindness in helping her to recover from her embarrassment and also for teaching her not to be afraid to step out on the dance floor, despite her lack of knowledge. He kissed her on both cheeks and congratulated her on her success in catching the eye of some of the wealthiest women in London with her wonderful designs. It was a compliment to her skill in making them into infinitely wearable and beautiful gowns. He insisted on sending them home in his carriage and neither Todd nor Amelia chose to argue. Hailing a cab at this time in the early hours and demanding to travel out of town would be as bad as asking a cabby to take them south of the river.

Amelia leaned against Todd during the carriage drive, and she fell into a deep sleep so that when the carriage eventually came to a halt outside Marsh House she could hardly believe that they were already at home. Todd helped Amelia to alight and he unlocked the front door, but she stumbled tiredly as she stepped over the threshold and he lifted her off her feet, carrying her as if she weighed next to nothing.

'Put me down, Todd. I can walk upstairs.'

It was dark in the hall with just a little moonlight filtering through the windows but she could see his lips curved into a smile. 'You are worn out, and rightly so. You need to get some sleep, Emmie.'

'And you have to go to the hospital in an hour or so.'

He took the stairs easily, even with her in his arms. He opened her bedroom door and sat her on the bed while he unbuttoned her boots and laid them on the floor. She fell back onto the pillows, too tired to think of anything but sleep. With astonishing tenderness Todd helped her out of her ball gown and slipped her nightgown over her head. It all seemed like a dream and she did not want it to end, but he leaned over the bed and brushed her hair back from her face with the tips of his fingers. They were so close that she could feel his warm breath on her cheek and she was tempted to slide her arms around his neck, holding on to him as if she would never let him go, but she was too exhausted to move.

He kissed her gently on the lips. 'Sleep well, my love.'

* * *

It seemed that she had only just lain down in her bed when suddenly there was a blaze of early morning sunshine as someone drew back the curtains. The scent of a steaming cup of tea and childish voices demanding to hear about the ball made it impossible to go back to sleep.

Betsy slumped down on one side of the bed with Daisy perching on the edge.

'Wake up, sleepy head,' Betsy said cheerfully. 'We've brought you a cup of tea. It's mid-morning and Ma is doing all the work on her own. She said to tell you that the sewing ladies are here in the long gallery, waiting for you to tell them what to do.'

Amelia snapped into a sitting position. 'Heavens! Is it that late? Has Todd gone to the hospital? He'll be in trouble if he's still in bed.'

'Ma said he must have changed his clothes and gone straight to work. His bed hasn't been slept in.'

The memory of his tender words and the touch of his lips on hers made Amelia suddenly nervous. She glanced at the pillow at the side of her, but there was no indentation of another person's head. Perhaps she had dreamed that he carried her upstairs and helped her into bed before kissing her so tenderly. She reached for her cup of tea and swallowed a mouthful regardless of the fact that it was still piping hot.

'He left early,' Daisy added casually. 'I woke up and heard hoof beats, so it must have been Todd going to the hospital. I love Todd — he's so kind.'

'Me, too.' Betsy nodded emphatically. 'I want to marry Todd when I grow up, unless you do, Emmie. I think he loves you really.'

Amelia shook her head. 'Why don't you two go downstairs and I'll get dressed and come down, too.'

'But we want to hear all about the ball, please.' Betsy made a moue, fluttering her eyelashes, which made Amelia laugh.

'I will tell you everything, when I come downstairs. I promise.'

'You must come down quickly. There's a parcel arrived for you by special messenger. I think someone has sent you a present.'

Mystified, Amelia frowned. 'I can't think what that would be. I'll be down directly. Now, both of you, leave me in peace to find my everyday clothes.'

Daisy picked up the discarded boots. 'This didn't work too well, did it, Emmie? Shall I take these downstairs and wash off the mess?'

'Please do, but don't make them too wet. They're my only pair of shoes.'

Betsy made for the doorway. 'Ma says that you'll soon be rich when all the ladies order their gowns from you. Then you can have as many pairs of shoes and boots as you like.'

'Yes, that will be wonderful.' Amelia put her cup down and swung her legs over the side of the bed. 'Now, go. Or do I have to chase you both downstairs?'

Betsy and Daisy raced from the room with shrieks of laughter.

Amelia filled the basin on the washstand from a pitcher, and had a quick wash in refreshingly cool water. She dressed, put up her hair and went downstairs in her stockinged feet, hoping that Daisy had cleaned the sticky starch from her boots.

Mariah, as usual, was in the kitchen chopping vegetables, with Percy chasing a chicken round the room.

Amelia came to a sudden halt. 'Where did that chicken come from?'

'Can't you guess?' Betsy asked cheekily. 'Jim loves Mum. He gives her eggs, butter and cheese, and now he's given her three hens. That one is called Hettie the hen.'

Amelia sighed. 'We'll have a cow and a goat soon.'

'It's not a bad idea,' Mariah said, smiling. 'We need a lot of milk, especially with the girls working here. They love their cups of tea at break time.'

'But hens? Don't they need a special henhouse or coop? What if a fox gets them?'

'There is a henhouse behind the stables. I'll wager you've walked past it a dozen times.'

'Do you mean that shed with half its roof missing?'

'Yes, I mean that shed, but Jim has mended the roof and now it's a safe place to lock the feathered ladies at night.'

'We've already had three eggs,' Daisy said excitedly. 'Me and Percy collected them this morning while you was asleep.'

'And there's your parcel.' Betsy picked up a package wrapped in brown paper and thrust it into Amelia's hands. She unwrapped it, trying not to appear too excited, although it was unusual to receive presents. Pa had often forgotten her birthday and she had become used to expecting very little.

'Do you know what this is, Mariah?'

'Don't look at me. I have no idea. A messenger brought it this morning.'

'While I was asleep, I suppose. I doubt if I'll ever be allowed to forget that.'

'I have to get up early,' Betsy said primly. 'We all do.'

'Hush, Betsy. Don't be impertinent,' Mariah scolded. 'Do hurry up, Emmie. I'm dying to know what it is.'

Amelia tore off the wrapping and gasped in amazement as a pair of beautiful white satin dancing slippers fell out, landing on the kitchen table.

'Quick, pick them up,' Mariah said urgently. 'It's unlucky to put new shoes on the table.'

'There's a note with them.' Amelia unfolded the piece of paper. 'Oh, my goodness. The dancing slippers are from Todd. He rode into town this morning without so much as a wink of sleep. He found a dolly shop open and bought these. They're second-hand, but they're perfect.'

Mariah sniffed. 'Hmm. Maybe he should have bought you a new pair of boots. When are you going to wear dancing slippers again?'

'I don't know,' Amelia said with a sigh. 'But it was a lovely thought. If you'll sit down for a moment, Mariah, I'll tell you what happened at the ball last night.'

'I hope you're going to tell me that we've got a list of new clients.'

'More than likely. It was a great success and everyone admired the ball gowns.'

'All the more reason to go upstairs and tell Nellie and the girls what they are supposed to be doing. I can't do everything round here.'

Amelia stared at her in dismay. 'Why are you so cross? Did you want to go to the ball, too?'

'No, of course not. What would someone like me be doing at a ball with all those toffs?'

'Believe me, Mariah, you are worth ten times my cousin Beatrice, for instance. I went to speak to her about Caleb and I told her what he did with Marsh House, which belongs to her husband. I hoped she might use her influence on him to allow me to rent Marsh House, but she brushed me off like an irritating insect. It was because of her that Cousin Daniel spilled wine over my boots and made them all streaky and ugly. Then Freddie asked me to open the ball with him at the head of the grand march, and I had no idea what to do. Anyway, he led me onto the floor and everyone could see my black boots streaked with starch and blue dye. Every step I took showed them off more. It was so embarrassing—' Amelia broke off, staring at Mariah and the children. 'Why are you laughing?'

Mariah wiped her streaming eyes on her apron. 'Because it's so funny. I would have given anything to have been there and seen the faces of the other guests when they watched a pretty lady in a wonderful gown, dancing like a clodhopper.'

Amelia looked from one to the other and she began to giggle. 'It was rather funny. But I have to say that Freddie was wonderful. You'd think he was dancing with a real lady.'

'You are a lady, Emmie,' Betsy said earnestly. 'If I'd been there and anyone laughed at you I would have given them what for!'

Amelia smiled and patted Betsy on the cheek. 'I know you would, darling. You are a good girl, but we just ignore people who are unkind to us, even if we feel like hitting back. They just make themselves look mean and spiteful.'

'Yes, Emmie is right,' Mariah said firmly. 'Now get back to scrubbing those potatoes, please, Betsy. And you, Daisy, take Percy into the piano parlour and give him his bricks to play with. Don't let him out into the yard, for goodness' sake. I don't want him falling into the horse trough again.'

'When you girls have finished your chores I can find nice things for you to do in the long gallery,' Amelia suggested, smiling. 'I need my button box sorting out again, and the bead trays have become muddled. As to the ribbon drawer, that is a nightmare. It needs a small pair of hands to tidy it up for me.'

'I'd do it,' Betsy cried eagerly.

'Me, too,' Daisy added.

'I'll go upstairs now, Mariah.' Amelia glanced anxiously at her friend. She was sad to think that Mariah, who had always worked tirelessly to keep everyone safe and well, had felt left out. 'But please come up as soon as you can. I need your help to make paper patterns for the rest of Lady Galton's order.'

'I will. I don't suppose you could manage without me.'

'No,' Amelia said firmly. 'I most certainly could not. We are a team and it doesn't work if one of us is not there.' She left the kitchen quickly without giving Mariah a chance to elaborate on her grudge. Hopefully she would be feeling less put upon now, but her brief outburst had made Amelia stop and think. She had taken her friend for granted and perhaps she had not thought enough about Mariah's feelings while she had put so much into making the gowns for the ball.

Amelia held the slippers close to her breast as she mounted the stairs. She could not believe that Todd had done something so out of character and so romantic. It was truly touching. He had kissed her good night. It had not been a dream. She could still feel the softness of his lips on hers, and the scent of him would stay with her for ever. Suddenly everything was crystal clear, as if she had just stepped out of the marsh mists into the sunlight on the other side of the River Lea.

She took the dancing slippers to her room and tucked them away in a drawer with a lavender bag. Maybe one day she and Todd could dance together again. But now she must put all that aside and get on with the business in hand. She checked her appearance in the dressing-table mirror before leaving her room once again and heading for the stairs to the long gallery. Now the real work must begin. There were two more day gowns to make for Dolly as well as two lace-trimmed blouses and a fine merino skirt and jacket for Lady Galton.

There was a round of applause when she walked into the long gallery, which took her by surprise.

Nellie stepped forward. 'We heard all about it from young Betsy. She couldn't wait to rush upstairs and tell us how you danced with a real lord. Did you impress the rich ladies? Do they want us to make them new gowns?'

'Hold on a moment, Nellie. One question at a time. Yes, the ball was delightful, although my boots suffered a mishap when someone spilled wine over them, but that's not important. I think the gowns made their mark, but we'll just have to wait and see if we get orders from the ladies who were present.'

'We all need to know, miss.' Ivy spoke up from the back of the room. 'We've got to eat and feed our families, miss. We can't afford to work for nothing, even if we do get fed nice meals.'

'Of course,' Amelia said hastily. 'I will pay you all at the end of the day. Tomorrow is Sunday, so you will naturally be at home. There is enough work here to keep you all busy for at least another full week. I wish I could promise you permanent work, but it does depend upon getting enough orders.'

Nellie frowned at Ivy. 'We understand that, miss. We'll all do our best.'

'I know you will,' Amelia said earnestly. 'I've seen how hard you worked at the mourning warehouse. We'll make a success of Marsh House Modes and we'll all benefit from our efforts.'

A murmur of assent met her remark and Amelia set about delegating tasks to each of the six women. She knew that Nellie and Maisie could work alone but, however willing, the others needed supervision. Each had her own special talents and Amelia was determined to encourage them to develop even more. Jane Jones and her sister, Polly, were particularly good working on the sewing machines. They could turn out perfect seams quickly and neatly, while Sally Miggins was an expert when it came to shirring and making fine, even pleats. Ivy was infinitely patient when it came to sewing on trimmings of every sort, while Nellie and Maisie excelled in every way and could be trusted to oversee the others for short periods of time. From her experience in Nightingale Lane, Amelia knew that the chit-chat amongst the women helped them to work, but occasionally arguments flared up and it needed someone with a cool head to keep the peace. Mariah would stand no nonsense and the others seemed to respect and defer to her. Amelia was certain they were on the brink of achieving success in the world of fashion — all it needed was one good order followed by others at regular intervals. It seemed a lot to ask, but Amelia had been impressed by the number of well-dressed ladies at the ball, and she suspected that they all vied with each other when it came to fashion.

That evening Amelia and Todd sat together in the piano parlour after supper and Amelia shared her thoughts with him. As always, Todd listened sympathetically to her ideas.

'You've made a good start,' he said calmly. 'I think you will hear from some of the ladies who were present last evening. They were certainly eyeing your gown enviously.'

'The trouble is money, as always. I had to pay the women before they went home this afternoon. I couldn't give them as much as they deserved, but I gave them every penny I had.'

Todd took a leather pouch from his pocket and tipped the coins onto the table beside his chair. 'There's my rent money and a bit more. It's all I have but it's yours to use as necessary.'

'You can't get by on nothing, Todd. And you bought me those lovely dancing slippers. I could have cried when I saw them.'

He laughed. 'Tears of happiness, I hope. I know it wasn't a practical gift, but there will be other occasions when you need to dress smartly.'

'I know, and I appreciate the thought, but money is tight.'

'All the more reason to treat you to something that makes you smile. You've had a hard enough time of things, Emmie. One day I will buy you a brand-new pair of dancing slippers and you will wear your best ball gown and be the height of fashion.'

She eyed him thoughtfully. 'Maybe that's the answer, Todd. We need to hold a fashion show in a smart venue and invite people of wealth and standing.

That does not include the Norrises.'

'I agree. That sounds a wonderful idea, but first you need to make the garments.'

'Of course, and I need the money to purchase materials. I've almost used the fabric bales I bought in the first place, and then I have to pay the women a fair wage. They are walking a long way each morning to get here and the return journey at night. It will be especially hard in the depths of winter. I don't know if I can expect them to keep it up.'

Todd put his coffee cup down on the table. 'I stopped to talk to Jim Allen on the way home tonight.'

Amelia put her head on one side, smiling. 'Did you ask him what his intentions are towards Mariah?'

Todd laughed. 'I think they are quite obvious, and I have to say, most sincere. He's a decent chap. He told me that the local doctor is retiring from his practice after forty years of caring for the locals. I have a chance to purchase the goodwill and buy the practice. I think I could do well looking after the people on the marshes and in the villages nearby.'

'You left Rockwood because you wanted to work in a London hospital, and you want to specialise in treating children. You said you've done well in your examinations.'

'Yes, Emmie, but I need to have the funds to set up a practice of my own if I wish to become a consultant. I can live here and save money as and when I can. That way I could drive into town each morning and pick up your workers and take them home in the evening.'

'You mean you'd have a surgery here, in this house?'

'Would that be so terrible?'

'No. It would be a good thing, but aren't you

forgetting something? We don't own Marsh House. Telling my cousin's wife that Marsh House belongs to her husband might have been a mistake.'

'Why do you say that?'

'Judging by Daniel's attitude, I have a horrible feeling he will evict us from the property when he checks and discovers that he does own this place. Even if he sacks Caleb, I can imagine it might be his last job to throw us all out onto the marsh. I love your ideas, Todd, but I feel as though we are sinking into the morass and I have to fight my way out.'

24

Despite Amelia's fears they heard nothing for weeks and the silent world of the Hackney Marshes remained a tranquil haven from the bustle of the city. The autumn weather turned cold and in the early mornings the marsh was iced with hoar frost. If Daniel Norris was going to throw them all out of the house, he did not seem as eager to make it happen quickly. Amelia was relieved to be able to get on with her work but she was not complacent. She suspected that her cousin was too busy to bother much about a tumbledown property, and Beatrice was too occupied with clawing her way up the social ladder to give it a second thought. Perhaps the knowledge that Freddie Ashton was a personal friend might have had something to do with the unexpected reprieve. Amelia neither knew nor cared; she spent her days working hard on her designs as well as supervising the women who had started on Lady Galton's spring wardrobe, her winter garments having been delivered to Dover Street.

Freddie proved to be a stalwart friend. He brought Dolly for fittings until all her gowns were finished, and he insisted on paying for them, saying they were a belated wedding gift for Dolly and Gus. Amelia was in no position to refuse and she used the money for the women's wages and to purchase more fabric for her creations. One of Dolly's acquaintances, Lady Shelmerdine, ordered two ball gowns, several skirts and blouses and a fur-trimmed mantle. Dolly was thrilled to pass the order on and she accompanied Lady Shelmerdine on her first visit of many to Marsh House. Then there were enquiries from other wealthy ladies who had attended the ball. It was all very gratifying.

Todd had purchased the goodwill from the retiring village doctor with a loan from Freddie, which Todd agreed to repay with interest. It seemed to give Freddie a purpose in life, helping them to establish themselves. He was obviously fascinated by the history of the house and the almost forgotten area of East London. While Dolly was being fitted for her new wardrobe, Freddie would don his overcoat, hat and boots and take long walks, exploring the marshes with Jim Allen's eldest son as his guide. When Dolly came for her final fitting she announced that her mother had insisted that she return home to Devonshire for the remaining months of her pregnancy.

'It does make sense, I suppose,' Dolly said reluctantly as she nibbled a hot biscuit fresh from the oven. 'Freddie has to return to his country estate and I don't want to stay in London without him. I suppose I'm a country girl at heart, and I miss Gus terribly. Perhaps being at home in Rockwood with all my family might take my mind off being parted from him.'

'I'm sorry you're going,' Amelia said sincerely. 'But it would be best to travel now, before the really bad weather sets in. Farmer Allen thinks it might snow soon and then the roads will become impassable.'

'You have a good order from Florence Shelmerdine. That will keep you all busy for weeks. I believe her friend Sophie Challoner is very interested in your costumes. I met her at a soirée last week and she said she will be contacting you.'

'That's really good news.'

Dolly sighed. 'I envy you being so busy. I am not the sort of person who enjoys sitting about doing nothing all day. I once tried to make my way on the stage, but then I married Gus and became an army wife. You are lucky to have so much to do and so many people around you.'

'It does get rather hectic at times. Since Todd began running a surgery from the house there is always something going on. I have never been so busy. My father even comes here to help out on his days off. I think he misses being a family doctor, even though he is very successful at the hospital.'

'He'll be sorry if he marries that woman,' Mariah said darkly. She rinsed her hands in the sink and dried them on a cloth. 'She'll make his life a misery if he doesn't do exactly as she says.'

Amelia sighed. 'We don't know that, Mariah. She might be totally different with Pa than she is on the odd occasion she visits us.'

'I know her sort,' Mariah said, pursing her lips. 'Do have another biscuit, Dolly. You are eating for two now.'

'Thank you, Mariah. They are delicious as usual, but I really must not eat too much or my lovely gowns will need to be let out again.'

'You will return before Christmas, won't you, Dolly?' Amelia said eagerly. 'I'm having my fashion show in the long gallery just before Christmas.'

'That seems rather close to the festive season. Wouldn't it be better to have it earlier?'

'I thought of that, but I need to make more garments than I have at the moment, and I'm hoping to get orders for gowns for the next London season.'

'I hadn't thought of that. I will definitely come to your fashion show. I wouldn't miss it for the world. That is, unless my child decides to arrive early.'

'You aren't due until January or February, is that right?'

'Yes, so the doctor says, although Mama thinks he's wrong. Anyway, I am coming up to town in December to buy Christmas presents, and I wouldn't miss your debut into the fashion world for anything.'

Mariah tut-tutted, shaking her head. 'You shouldn't keep jumping on and off trains in your condition.'

'I am young and strong and I refuse to stay at home and be coddled. I'll be in town for your show, Emmie. Anyway, Freddie has promised to travel with me and we get the best of treatment from everyone. It's not simply because he tips well — everyone does their best to please Freddie because he is such a dear. I wish I could find him a suitable wife, but I'm afraid there is no one quite good enough for Freddie Ashton. At least, not since Nancy married Uncle Tommy.'

'He is a wonderfully kind and generous man,' Amelia said earnestly. 'And he's been so good to us. We all love Freddie.'

'I know. I keep looking for someone for him, but he never exhibits any interest in the pretty young women he meets.'

'Matchmaking never turns out well,' Mariah said firmly. 'You should take care of yourself, Dolly, and your baby. He or she is the most important person in your life now, except for Gus, of course.'

'You are always right, Mariah,' Dolly said, smiling angelically. 'Maybe we could match you up with Lord Dorrington.'

'No, that's not a good idea, Dolly.' Amelia wagged her finger at her friend. 'Mariah won't admit it, but I know she is spoken for, and we rely on Farmer Allen to supply hay for our horses and feed for the chickens. I believe he is going to present us with a couple of goats, too. We mustn't upset Jim.'

Mariah rolled her eyes expressively. 'You young ladies have too much imagination and too little to do.'

'I think that is my cue to leave you in peace.' Dolly rose to her feet. 'I think that's the carriage arriving anyway, so I'd better leave now or it will be dark before we cross the river. I don't like the marshes at the best of times. I always fear the carriage is going to get stuck in a bog.'

'I'll see you out.' Amelia stood up and followed Dolly from the kitchen. She helped her on with her fur-lined mantle. 'You'll be glad of this. It's very cold for November. I think we're going to have a hard winter.'

'I expect even the sinister marshes will look pretty when covered with snow.' Dolly stepped outside, pausing only to blow a kiss to Amelia before she climbed into the carriage.

Amelia closed the door and was about to walk past the parlour where Todd held his surgery when the door opened and Todd stepped out into the hallway.

'Have you finished for the evening?' Amelia asked eagerly. 'It would be so nice to have supper together for a change.'

He smiled, shaking his head. 'I need hot water to bathe a nasty gash that one of Jim's workers suffered. And carbolic soap to clean the area.'

'You'll have to ask Mariah. She will know where it's kept.'

'You look tired, Emmie. I think you're working too hard.'

'Nonsense. It's the poor light in the hall. I'm perfectly fine, Todd.' Amelia was about to walk past him but he caught her by the hand.

'I know how hard you're working. You need to take things more slowly or you'll be one of my patients.'

'I'm not the one who is on call night and day, Todd Taylor. You need to take a dose of your own medicine.' Amelia stood on tiptoe to plant a swift kiss on his cheek. She backed away instantly, suddenly aware of the nearness of him and remembering the multitude of confusing emotions she had experienced on the night of the ball. 'It's almost time for the girls to be taken home, Todd,' she added in an attempt to break the sudden tension between them. 'It will be dark soon and it's really cold.'

'I've got several people waiting to see me,' Todd said, frowning. 'It will be at least an hour before I can drive them home.'

'I'll do it then,' Amelia said briskly. 'The fresh air will do me good.'

'Let the women wait for a while. Give them some supper or something.'

'They have families to get home to, Todd. I'll be all right. I know how to harness Grey to the wagonette we bought from Jim Allen.'

'It's too much for you to handle on your own.'

'No, it isn't. I can do it and you must look after your patients. Maybe one of them will pay you with money instead of free shoe mending or a bale of hay.'

Todd laughed. 'I don't like it, but you must take care. If it's foggy you must wait and let me take them home later.'

Amelia merely smiled and nodded as she headed for the staircase. She had driven the wagonette on a couple of occasions and had no qualms about driving through town at night. There were two good carriage lamps to light the way, and Grey could do with the exercise. She hurried upstairs to tell the seamstresses to get ready to leave for home.

It was pitch dark by the time they crossed the River Lea, and the choking fog, thick with smoke from homes and factory chimneys, had followed them from the marsh. But it was too late to turn back and the women were eager to get home to their husbands and children. Sure-footed Grey plodded on, dragging his heavy load of women muffled up to the eyes in scarves and thick boat cloaks. Despite the fog they reached Whitechapel safely and Amelia dropped the women off as near to their homes as possible before turning Grey in the direction of home.

Ivy was the last as she lived close to Nightingale Lane and, having seen Ivy safely home, Amelia could not resist the temptation to drive past the mourning warehouse. She was eager to find out if her cousin or Caleb had rented the house and workroom to another tenant, but as she drew closer she saw the door open and a familiar figure stepped out onto the pavement. She had no alternative but to drive past. However, Caleb had spotted her in the light of the streetlamps and there was no escape. He stepped into the road, causing Grey to rear in the shafts. Caleb caught hold of the reins and drew the startled animal to a halt.

'Have you come to spy on us, Amelia?'

'Certainly not. I'm on my way home.' She clutched the driving whip in her right hand, holding the taut reins in her left hand. 'Let go of my horse, Caleb.'

To her surprise he obeyed, but before she had a chance to tell Grey to walk on, Caleb had leaped up to sit beside her on the driver's seat.

'What do you think you're doing, Caleb Marsh? I know that is not your real name. Does my cousin know that you are a thief and a liar?'

'Because of you I've lost my job. Mr Norris accused me of attempting to cheat him out of his rightful property. He terminated my employment and refused to give me a reference. After all the years I've given to the company and now I've been thrown out. That's why I was here. I still have the keys to the house. I've nowhere else to go, thanks to you.'

'You've finally got what you deserve,' Amelia said angrily. 'Get off my vehicle or I shall scream for help.'

'A scream in this part of London is unlikely to raise an eyebrow.' Caleb snatched the reins from her and ordered Grey to walk on.

'What do you think you're doing, Caleb?'

'You should know by now that I do what I wish, and I intend to teach you a lesson you will not forget in a hurry.' He snatched the whip and cracked it over Grey's head. The frightened animal broke into a canter.

Amelia was shaking, but with anger more than fear. She put two fingers in her mouth and emitted a piercing whistle, which brought Grey to a sudden halt. It was a trick she had learned from Todd, and Grey never failed to respond. The wagonette shuddered to a halt and, catching Caleb by surprise, Amelia gave him a hefty shove and he toppled off the high seat onto the cobblestones below, landing with a sickly thud and a howl of pain. Or was it rage? Amelia did not stop to find out. She grabbed the reins and urged the frightened horse to a trot and then a canter. She did not try to slow him down until they were at a safe distance and she did not look back to see if Caleb was injured. She had known in her heart that he would take his spite out on her in some way, although she had thought it would be a battle of words. She had not been afraid of him — until now.

The drive home was slow and the fog was so thick that when they crossed the river Amelia had to rely on Grey's instinct to keep them on the right track. It would take very little to topple the large wagon into the ditch at the side of the road or, even worse, for Grey to take a wrong turn and flounder in the treacherous mud of the marshes. It was a relief when she recognised the white picket fence that surrounded Jim Allen's farmhouse, and she knew at last that she was getting close to home.

She had never been so glad to see the rusty iron gates of Marsh House. Although the fog had lifted, the temperature had plummeted. Grey pricked up his ears and quickened his pace. Amelia smiled grimly as she drove past the stark bare branches of the dead tree that was supposed to have been Caleb's refuge during his childhood. Perhaps part of that had been true, but knowing him as she did now, she suspected that he had hidden there because of some misdemeanour he had committed and was avoiding his just deserts. She had put him out of her mind until this evening, but now she realised that he was still a real danger to all of them.

She was about to drive round to the stables when Todd emerged from the house holding a lantern. He greeted her with a worried frown. 'I was just about to saddle up my horse and go out looking for you. Are you all right, Emmie?'

'Yes, it was not very nice driving in such thick fog but Grey brought me safely home.'

Todd helped her down to the ground. 'You're shaking.' He slipped his arm around her shoulders. 'You're white as a sheet. What happened?'

'Nothing really. I'm just cold and hungry.'

'That's not the whole truth, is it? I know you so well. Something has occurred to scare you, and it wasn't just the fog.'

Amelia could see that he was not going to let the matter drop and she sighed. 'Caleb stopped me outside the mourning warehouse. It was my own fault for driving past it after I dropped Ivy off, but I just wanted to see if there was a new tenant.'

'He stopped you?'

'He jumped out and caught hold of Grey's reins. Before I could do anything about it he'd climbed up to sit beside me. He was furious because he'd lost his job, for which he blamed me.'

Todd took her in his arms and held her close to him, ignoring the flakes of snow that had started to swirl around them. 'I knew I shouldn't have allowed you to drive into town. Are you hurt, Emmie?'

'No, it all happened so quickly. He whipped poor Grey into a canter but I remembered how to call him to a halt and I whistled. Grey stopped so suddenly that it almost unseated Caleb and I shoved him as hard as I could. He fell to the ground but I drove off and I didn't look back. I might have killed him, Todd.'

'Damnation!' Todd hugged her so close that she could feel his heartbeats. 'If I could lay hands on him now I would finish what you began. I'm going to have it out with Caleb tomorrow. That man isn't going to frighten the woman I love and get away with it. No one treats you that way, Emmie.'

'I'm all right, Todd. I wouldn't have mentioned it if you hadn't insisted.' He was obviously so angry and distressed that Amelia chose not to press the point. She made an effort to sound calm. 'I need to take Grey to the stable. Then I'm going to get something to eat. I hope Mariah has saved my supper for me.'

'I'll see to Grey, you go indoors and get warm. Tomorrow I'm going into town to sort Caleb out once and for all.'

'No. Don't do that, Todd. Caleb has been found out. He's lost his job and he's powerless to hurt me now. He might even have ended up in hospital. Either way, I don't think he'll bother us again.' Amelia walked into the house without giving him the chance to respond. She peeled off her gloves and her damp cape before going to the kitchen.

'Well, you took your time!' Mariah said crossly. 'We've all eaten and I've finished clearing up. What kept you?'

Amelia took a deep breath. 'I've just had all that from Todd. I don't want to go through it again. I'm cold, tired and very hungry. Did you put something aside for me?'

Mariah's expression softened. 'Of course I did. Sit down and I'll serve it up. You can tell me about it later. You've certainly upset Todd. He's been pacing the floor like a caged tiger. I think he was about to set off looking for you.'

'It was very foggy,' Amelia said mildly. 'It took a very long time to get anywhere, but now the fog has lifted and it's started to snow. Don't worry, I won't attempt to cross the marshes at night again.'

Mariah sniffed as she ladled stew into a bowl. 'I should think not.' She placed it in front of Amelia as she took her place at the table. 'There's bread and butter and I made an apple pie, if there's any left after the children have been digging into it.'

'Thank you, Mariah,' Amelia said meekly. 'This is just what I need.'

* * *

Amelia lay in bed that night, unable to get to sleep even though she was exhausted. Caleb was unimportant now that she knew he was not the owner of Marsh House. Although that left her with an even bigger obstacle. The house had come to Cousin Daniel and he had made it plain that he wanted nothing to do with Amelia or her father. She doubted if he would lower the rent, even if he agreed to let them stay on. If Caleb had proved to be a bad landlord, Cousin Daniel was likely to evict them without warning. She closed her eyes, hoping that the morning would bring a solution to the problem.

Awakened by the sound of children's voices and laughter, Amelia leaped out of bed. Daylight streamed through the window when she drew back the curtains and the world outside glistened white with a dusting of snow. She dressed hurriedly, brushed her hair and tied it back in a knot at the nape of her neck. She could hear the sound of sewing machines clattering away in the long gallery and the cheerful exchange of chatter from the women as they worked. Amelia hurried downstairs to the kitchen.

'Why didn't you wake me, Mariah?' Amelia sat down at the table. She reached for the Brown Betty teapot. 'I have so much to do.'

Mariah treated her to a reproving look. 'Todd told me what happened to you yesterday. Why didn't you say anything at supper?'

'Because I knew you would look at me as you are now. I know I shouldn't have driven the women into town, but it was sheer mischance that put me in harm's way.'

'Caleb isn't the forgiving sort. You realise that, don't you?'

'Yes, of course I do. He's lost everything because of me.'

'He's lost everything because of his own folly and dishonesty. But that makes him even more dangerous. I'll send word to Grimble. He knows people who will put an end to Caleb's antics for good.'

Amelia smiled. 'I don't think violence is ever the answer, but thank you for wanting to help.'

'It's my future I'm thinking of as well, Emmie, and that of my kids. We'll be homeless if we lose Marsh House.'

'It won't come to that, even if I have to beg my cousin on bended knees to let me rent it from him.' Amelia poured herself a cup of tea and sipped it thoughtfully. 'Where's Todd? Is he seeing patients this morning?'

'I almost forgot. He's taken one of the farm labourers to hospital. The poor fellow was gored by the bull in the ten-acre field. Very nasty.'

Amelia rose to her feet. 'I need to go to the hospital, anyway. I want to find out if Caleb was admitted last evening, and I need to have a word with Todd. He was furious with Caleb when I told him what happened. I don't want him to do anything rash.'

'He loves you, Emmie. Knowing Todd, I don't think he'll let Caleb get away with trying to harm you.'

'That's what I'm afraid of. I'll be as quick as I can.'

'Go carefully. It's really icy out there and it's going to snow again, judging by the heavy clouds. The children have been out throwing snowballs at each other since first light.'

'Todd will have taken the pony and trap, but I can ride his horse. That animal knows the way to the hospital blindfold.'

* * *

Mariah was right about the weather. Snow began to fall in earnest just before Amelia reached the hospital. She left Todd's horse at the livery stable and walked the rest of the way, slipping and sliding on the icy pavements.

The clerk at the reception desk was not in the best of moods, but after a little persuasion he leafed through the attendance ledger and found an entry pertaining to a street accident the previous evening. The casualty had suffered contusions and a broken leg.

'Was he admitted to a ward?' Amelia asked anxiously.

'Are you a relative, miss?'

Amelia knew better than to deny it. She nodded. 'I'm his sister.'

The clerk frowned. 'He was treated for his injuries, but he was taken away by the police. Arrested, it says here.'

'Oh! I see.' Amelia stared at the perfect copperplate

writing. It was legible, even seen upside down, and sure enough it said that Caleb had left in the custody of the police. She turned to leave but hesitated. 'Did Dr Taylor bring a patient in this morning?'

The clerk rolled his eyes. 'This is confidential, miss. I'm not supposed to give out information.'

'Dr Taylor is my intended,' Amelia said firmly. 'I need to speak to him urgently.'

'Is there anyone in the hospital who isn't related to you in some way, miss?'

Amelia glanced over his shoulder and waved. 'There's my pa. Sorry to have bothered you.' She hurried through the crowd of waiting patients to catch her father before he disappeared into one of the cubicles.

'Pa, have you got a minute?'

'Amelia. What are you doing here?'

'Caleb has been arrested, Pa. Were you on duty last evening?'

Harold ushered her into an empty cubicle and closed the curtain. 'I was here when he was brought in. I sent a message to Daniel, thinking that Marsh was still in his employ.'

'Did Cousin Daniel have Caleb arrested?'

'Daniel came here in person. He was not in the best of moods. Apparently he had sacked Marsh for renting the property to you and keeping the money for himself, but he also found all sorts of discrepancies in the books. Marsh had been cheating your grandfather for years without being discovered and he thought he could still get away with it. However, he reckoned without Daniel, who had him arrested. He won't be swindling anyone for a very long time.'

Amelia sighed with relief. 'Thank goodness for that.

Caleb tried to abduct me last evening, Pa. It was I who caused his accident. He leaped onto the driver's seat and snatched the reins from me. I pushed him and he fell to the ground, but I didn't stop. Will the police want to question me? Will I be in trouble?'

Harold laughed. 'You'll probably get a medal, my love. Self-defence is not a crime, and you helped to bring a criminal to justice.' He gave her a hug. 'Well done, my dear.'

A nurse parted the curtains. 'Are you ready for your next patient, Doctor?'

'Yes, of course. My daughter is just leaving.' He stepped outside and Amelia followed. 'I was planning to visit you, anyway. Ruby told me that she had been quite rude to you when you last met. She was very ashamed of herself and hopes you forgive her.'

'She was rather abrupt. Are you really going to marry her?'

'She's a good woman at heart, despite her rather quick temper. We plan to get married in the New Year, and I hope we have your blessing.'

'If she makes you happy, Pa, that's all that matters. Perhaps I didn't give her a fair chance.'

'Thank you, that means a lot to me.' Harold kissed her on the forehead. 'All right, Sister. I'm coming.' He gave Amelia an apologetic smile before hurrying off in the wake of the nurse.

It was with mixed feelings that Amelia left the hospital. She was deeply relieved to think that Caleb would be tried and sentenced, which could mean years in prison. She was happy for her father, if a little doubtful about his choice of bride, but she would give Mrs Delaney a chance to prove herself. If Pa thought she was the right woman for him, who was she to argue?

He did so much for others, he deserved to have someone who could give him love and show him tenderness. Amelia was not entirely convinced that Ruby Delaney was that person, but she could always hope.

She realised with something of a shock that the snow was settling fast, making the short walk to the livery stable quite hazardous. Thankfully, Todd's horse was a sure-footed animal and, although it took twice as long as usual, they finally made it to Marsh House. Amelia rode into the stable yard to find Freddie's carriage outside the front door. She was greeted by a hail of snowballs, as the coachman and footman had taken on Betsy and Daisy with a little hindrance from Percy, who kept falling over and having to be set back on his small feet.

The coachman held up his hand. 'Stop now, mind the lady.'

The footman hurried forward to hold the horse while Amelia dismounted. 'You're soaked, miss. Allow me to take care of your horse while you go indoors and get dry.'

'That's very kind of you . . . ? I don't know your name.'

'It's James, miss. I've been with his lordship for many a year.'

'Well, thank you, James.' Amelia smiled and nodded. 'Betsy and Daisy, don't stay out too long. Maybe you should take Percy indoors before he catches cold.'

'Don't worry, Emmie. We'll take care of him,' Betsy said, grinning.

'He'll only growl at us if we try to get him away from the snow,' Daisy added hastily.

Amelia nodded. Percy was a sweet child, unless he

was crossed, and then he turned into a little growly bear.

She hurried into the house.

Freddie was seated at the kitchen table, sipping coffee with Mariah.

'You're soaking,' Mariah said crossly. 'You'd best get changed or you'll catch your death of cold.'

Amelia peeled off her wet mantle and draped it over a chair close to the range. 'It's snowing harder than ever.' She turned to Freddie, smiling. 'It's lovely to see you, sir — I mean, Freddie. Is everything all right? You haven't come about Dolly, have you?'

Freddie shook his head. 'No, Amelia. I came to see you. Dolly is well, as far as I know, and I will be travelling down to Devonshire next week to bring her up to London. It's later than she planned but she is still determined to do her Christmas shopping in London. Once Dolly has made up her mind there's very little chance of gainsaying her.'

Amelia pulled up a chair and sat down. 'Is there something I should know?'

'You are so impatient.' Mariah filled a cup with coffee and placed it on the table in front of Amelia. 'Drink that while it's hot. It will warm you up.'

'I hope I didn't overstep the mark, Amelia,' Freddie said cautiously. 'But after the ball at my Piccadilly house Dolly told me what passed between you and the Norrises and I was concerned about your well-being.'

'They know the truth now, and Caleb has been arrested, although I don't think it will change my cousin Daniel's attitude to me.'

'Daniel Norris is not a nice man and he behaved very badly at the ball.' Freddie smiled ruefully. 'I can still see your ruined boots as we did the grand march. I really admired the way you carried yourself, despite the difficult circumstances.'

'Do tell her, sir,' Mariah said impatiently. 'Tell Emmie what your detective discovered.'

'I should have waited to tell you first, Amelia, but Mariah has a way of interrogating a fellow.'

'I know what you mean.' Amelia laughed. She clasped her coffee cup in both hands, allowing the warmth to bring her chilled fingers back to life. 'What did your detective find out?'

25

Freddie sat back in his chair, smiling triumphantly. 'On my instructions the detective looked into the background to Marsh House. He applied for a copy of the last owner's will, which was interesting reading.'

'I thought it said that Phoebe Norris's husband left everything to Daniel.'

Freddie shook his head. 'Not so. The house and grounds were left to you, Amelia.'

'No! That's impossible.' Amelia stared at him in astonishment. 'I'd never heard of Marsh House until Caleb brought me here.'

'Apparently, your father was Miss Marsh's physician when she was taken ill with cholera while staying at a house in Clerkenwell. Miss Marsh was the sister of Miss Phoebe Marsh, who married into the Norris family. Your father was a young man, newly qualified, but he pulled Miss Marsh back from the brink of death, and she believed that part of her recovery was due to Dr Sutton's four-year-old daughter, who visited with her father and kept her amused during her convalescence. Miss Marsh was childless and she never forgot you, Emmie. She must have known that her sister, Phoebe, married well and had a home of her own, or perhaps she had no particular fondness for Daniel, who should have been next in line. Whatever the reason, Mildred Marsh left her beloved home to the little girl who made her laugh.'

'I don't believe it. There must be some mistake,'

Amelia said dazedly. 'I don't remember visiting an old lady, Freddie. She must have been thinking of some other child. It can't have been me.'

'It's there in beautiful copperplate writing. I have a copy of the will at home, but I wanted to tell you first.'

'But why didn't my father know about this?' Amelia looked from one to the other. 'I saw him this morning. Surely he would have remembered the old lady who used to live here.'

'Not necessarily,' Freddie said firmly. 'I doubt if he ever visited her at Marsh House. As I said, she was staying at a friend's house in Clerkenwell when she was taken ill. Your father was not her regular physician. She could have left the house to him, but she obviously saw something in you that she wanted to nurture, even after her death.'

'Could my cousin contest the will, Freddie?'

'Neither he nor his wife seem to have taken much interest in the actual details. Your cousin doesn't appear to have been bothered about the estate until you brought up the subject. He didn't even ask Miss Marsh's lawyers for the deeds. I suggest we make an appointment for you to see them as soon as possible.'

'I still can't believe it, Freddie. I'm sure when we see the lawyers we'll discover that there has been a mistake somewhere. This sort of thing just doesn't happen to me.'

* * *

Amelia left the solicitor's office with the official copy of Miss Marsh's will and the deeds of Marsh House. The solicitor had offered to keep them in a strong box, but Amelia was not about to let them out of her sight. Perhaps she would purchase a safe, when funds allowed, but it was still hard to believe her good fortune.

Freddie and Dolly walked on ahead of her, although Dolly was moving a little slower these days. Amelia was concerned for her friend, thinking that perhaps the lure of Christmas shopping in London was too great for a woman expecting her confinement in a matter of weeks. Dolly, on the other hand, insisted that she was perfectly fit and could continue to do normal things until the last minute.

Amid the excitement of discovering that she was indeed an heiress, Amelia had been very busy with her designs for the fashion show just days before Christmas. The women in the sewing room had worked incredibly hard to make the gowns ordered by Lady Galton, which had been delivered and accepted. Now her ladyship's payment of the bill was uppermost in Amelia's mind, although she knew the money would come eventually.

Lady Shelmerdine had been delighted with her gowns and had ordered a complete spring wardrobe for her debutante daughter, Grace. This, Dolly said, was a great coup and would establish Amelia's name without a doubt. Other matrons would be clamouring for their daughters to be outfitted by Marsh House Modes.

The old house reverberated with the clatter of sewing machines turning out garments at a surprising rate. Nellie was even talking about hiring more help to cope with the influx of orders and, of course, they could do with a couple more sewing machines — new ones this time. Amelia could only agree.

Almost immediately after the show it would be

Christmas. Until now, there had been little reason to celebrate the festive season. In the past her father had been busy patching up the heads of drunken brawlers or setting broken bones from falls on icy pavements, leaving Amelia to sit by the fire to celebrate the festive season on her own. This year it was entirely different.

Despite the cold snowy weather, Marsh House was filled with warmth and laughter. The scent of boiling plum puddings, baking cakes and spicy mince pies wafted from room to room. When the children were not playing outside, building snowmen or hurling snowballs at each other, they sat by the fire in the piano parlour and made paper chains. Their excitement was building as they counted the days until Christmas. Amelia loved to see them so happy, but she had other things on her mind. The workroom hummed with activity and the clatter of the sewing machines accompanied the cheery chatter of the women as they worked.

Two days before the fashion show, Todd braved the snow and arrived home with a huge pine tree on the back of the wagonette, together with boxes of glass baubles, hanks of tinsel and strings of beads. Betsy and Daisy fell upon them, draping themselves in garlands of tinsel and dancing round the tree, which Todd secured in half an oak barrel filled with damp soil. Mariah brought cups of hot cocoa for them all to sip while they decorated the branches, and the scent of hot chocolate and pine needles filled the piano parlour. Betsy, being the tallest of the children, was given the honour of securing the paper star at the very top of the tree. She had to stand on a wooden ladder, held by Todd, as the point of the star touched the ceiling. Having charmed everyone into the Christmas spirit,

Todd took the girls in the wagonette and returned a couple of hours later with a load of holly and ivy, which they used to decorate the entrance hall.

The fashion show was due to take place in the long gallery, and on that day the machines were all stored out of sight. Every chair in the house was brought upstairs and set out in lines so that the prospective customers could get a good view of the garments. Amelia had persuaded Nellie and her girls to model the clothes themselves and Dolly offered to help them change their garments while Mariah opted to do their hair. Betsy and Daisy were given the task of showing the guests to their seats and Todd was put in charge of Percy, who did not take kindly to strangers.

They had a dress rehearsal the day before the actual show, but the weather was Amelia's main worry. There was a definite threat of more snow to come, and the sky seemed to be leaning heavily on the marsh. There was nothing they could do but hope that the worst of it held off until the guests had enjoyed the show and, hopefully, ordered some of the gowns. After that it was up to them to make their way back into town. Mariah was gloomy about the attendance, even though they had invited everyone to arrive in the early afternoon. Would the fashionable ladies want to travel so far into the East End to view the fashions from a virtually unknown designer? Amelia tried to be optimistic. After all, rich ladies might think it was exciting to go out of their way if only to relieve the boredom of their pampered lives. There was only one way to find out.

The dress rehearsal went well enough, although Nellie's girls spent most of their time tripping over their long skirts and giggling. Surprisingly, it was Betsy and Daisy who took things most seriously and

Betsy even scolded Maisie for not paying attention to Amelia's instructions. Amelia gave Betsy a quick hug.

'You are so good at this that I'm putting you in charge of sending the models out one by one. Wait until each is on her way back to the dressing area behind the screens, and then send out the next one.'

Betsy puffed out her chest. 'I will, Emmie. They won't play up when I'm in charge.'

'You are your mother's daughter,' Amelia said seriously. 'I think I'll train you to be my assistant.'

Betsy ran off to tell her mother, leaving Daisy looking crestfallen. Amelia felt sorry for the child and she gave her a hug, too.

'And you have the very important job of showing the ladies to their seats, Daisy. Do you think you could do that?'

'I should say I can,' Daisy said importantly. 'Leave it to me, and I'll do my very best.'

'I'm sure you will.' Amelia smiled and went to find Todd, who had just seen his last patient that morning. She found him in the kitchen filling the kettle at the sink.

'It's gone really well so far,' Amelia said eagerly. 'I just hope we get a good audience tomorrow and some orders, too. We're doing quite well but we need work to keep us going through the winter.'

'I'm sure your wealthy lord will help out.'

Amelia stared at him in surprise. 'What did you say?'

Todd turned to her, clutching the kettle tightly in one hand. 'Lord Dorrington is a frequent visitor. I think he has his eye on you, Emmie.'

'What gives you that idea, Todd? He's an aristocrat and I'm a doctor's daughter. What would a man like him see in someone like me?'

'That's just it, Emmie. He's a man and you are a beautiful and talented young woman. He's let his chances pass him by and now I believe he's set his sights on you.'

'Todd! I don't know how you came to such a wild conclusion, but it's ridiculous.' Amelia turned her head as Mariah burst into the kitchen.

'Lord Freddie is here again,' Mariah said breathlessly. 'He's brought Miss Dolly and I've done nothing for luncheon. What will they think?' She clapped her hands to her bosom as she gasped for breath. 'I ran all the way from the long gallery. I'm not as young as I used to be.'

'There, what did I say? Why would a man like Dorrington want to attend a fashion show?' Todd marched out of the kitchen without waiting for an answer.

'What's the matter with him?' Mariah demanded. 'Why are you two quarrelling?'

'We weren't. It's just that Todd has got some silly idea about Freddie being interested in me. I never heard anything so far-fetched in my life.'

Mariah sniffed and tossed her head. 'Well, you are the only one who can't see it. That man might be a rich lord but he's still a man, and it's obvious that he fancies you.'

'Nonsense,' Amelia said, but without much conviction. It was true that Freddie had been paying her a lot of attention, and she would never have discovered that she had inherited the house had he not hired a private detective. She had always put his kindness down to his affection for Dolly, but now she was not so sure.

The door opened and Dolly breezed into the kitchen. Her cheeks were rosy and her eyes bright with excitement.

'This is such a thrill, Emmie. I can't believe that in an hour or so the guests will be arriving for your first fashion show.'

'I'm beginning to doubt if it will happen at all,' Amelia said slowly. 'If the distance from here to the West End isn't enough, I think the threat of snow will put everyone off.'

Freddie followed Dolly into the kitchen. 'Don't worry about small details, Emmie,' he said smiling. 'People will flock to Marsh House, if only out of curiosity, but that will change when they've seen your show.'

'It's just nerves,' Mariah said hurriedly. 'Now if you will kindly leave my kitchen I will make luncheon. We're all behind this morning.'

'Of course. We'll be in the piano parlour when you're ready.' Amelia ushered Freddie and Dolly out of the room. She shot a wary glance at Freddie as he walked at her side. It was madness to suggest that someone of his senior years and standing would be interested in her, a poor woman struggling to make a living. She led the way to the parlour where a huge log fire burned merrily in the grate. 'Make yourself comfortable, Dolly.' Amelia gave her a searching look. 'Are you sure you should have come today? You look a little flushed.'

'I wouldn't miss this for all the tea in China,' Dolly said, smiling.

'I just hope that the snow doesn't put people off.' Amelia sighed. 'We've worked so hard to get everything ready.'

'Both Dolly and I have been extolling your virtues and undoubted talent at every opportunity.' Freddie gave her an encouraging smile. 'Be brave, Emmie. I know you'll take the fashionable world by storm.'

'Of course you will,' Dolly added eagerly. 'Take me, for instance. I look elegant even if I am the size of a hippopotamus.'

'You look wonderful, Dolly. I do appreciate your support, but should you really be doing so much travelling?' Amelia said anxiously. 'Maybe your mama was right and you ought to be at home with her in Devonshire.'

'Darling, I am an army wife.' Dolly pulled a face. 'Had I returned to India with Gus I would doubtless be riding a horse over unspeakably rough terrain and sleeping on a charpoy. Following the gun is not for the faint-hearted. My son will be born in comparative luxury and we will both have the best of care.'

'I suppose you're right.' Amelia met Freddie's sympathetic smile, but there was also a deeper expression in his blue eyes that brought a blush to her cheeks and she turned away.

Fortunately, at that moment Mariah burst into the room to tell them that luncheon was ready. 'I've heated up the soup and made some ham sandwiches,' she said firmly. 'It's not very grand, my lord, but we have been very busy these last few days.'

'I'm sure it will be delightful, Mariah.' Freddie proffered his hand to Dolly and helped her to her feet. 'I suggest we eat in the kitchen to save you the trouble of taking everything to the dining room. We have a fashion show to put on, remember?'

* * *

Amelia's worries proved ill-founded. Soon after one o'clock carriages began to arrive, spilling out their elegant passengers. They entered the house chattering and looking around as if they had come to view a spectacle. Amelia greeted everyone at the door and Daisy led them upstairs to the long gallery. It had been Freddie's idea to serve the ladies with glasses of ratafia wine together with tiny almond-flavoured biscuits, and the pitch of excitement grew as they sipped, ate and waited for the first of the models to process along the polished wooden boards of the long gallery. Fires burned at both ends of the room, sending out heat and the scent of applewood, together with the aroma of a pine tree that Todd had set up late that morning aided by Betsy and Daisy. Snow had piled upon on the outside sills of the mullioned windows, adding to the charm of the scene. Amelia felt her heart swell with pride. None of this would have been possible without the help of her surrogate family. She owed it to them to make a success of the show.

Amelia did the commentary, describing the garments as they were modelled to a very enthusiastic response. Perhaps it was the wine, or maybe the ambience that affected the normally staid wives and daughters of wealthy men, but the atmosphere was exhilarating. At the end of the show Mariah and Betsy brought trays of tea and cake to the long gallery. Freddie, in an aside to Amelia, said wryly that perhaps more wine would encourage sales, but she did not have a chance to reply as a tall, grey-haired matron summoned her with an imperious nod of her head. Amelia seized a notebook and pencil. She was ready to take orders and was agreeably surprised to find that most of the gowns had found eager buyers.

When the last guest had departed Amelia made a note of the interest shown, planning to follow up the requests for private consultations. However, it was already dark and she was concerned for her workers, who needed to get home. Freddie offered the use of his carriage and they were all delighted to accept, although Ivy was a bit anxious as to what the neighbours would say if she arrived home in such a smart vehicle. It had stopped snowing, although there had been a significant fall during the afternoon and it had settled. With the night temperature dropping fast, the going would soon become dangerous. Amelia said a final goodbye, thanking her faithful workers yet again as she closed the front door.

Amelia went to join Freddie and Dolly in the piano parlour. Todd had gone out on a call earlier but they had not had a chance to clear the air between them. This bothered her more than she cared to admit, although, of course, he was being unreasonable. There was no hint of anything romantic between herself and Freddie. The idea was ridiculous. Dolly was sitting by the fire, sipping a cup of tea. She looked up and smiled as Amelia walked into the room.

'It's been so enjoyable, Emmie. Did you get many firm orders?'

'Yes, I did. I need to check with Mariah, who also took some down. There were a lot of enquiries, which I will follow up, too. I think we have enough interest and firm requests to keep us going throughout the winter.'

Freddie took Amelia's hand in his and raised it to his lips. 'Well done, Emmie. I am so proud of you.'

'We all are.' Todd strode into the room, taking off his hat and overcoat and tossing them carelessly onto the piano stool. 'Emmie is an amazing woman and she's going to head a fashion house to rival Worth.'

Amelia stifled a sigh of relief. Todd had obviously had time to think about what he had said and realised that he had jumped to the wrong conclusion.

She smiled up at him. 'I don't know about that, but I'm agreeably surprised that we did so well, and that people travelled all the way to Hackney Marshes to view our work.'

Freddie glanced anxiously at Dolly, who had gone alarmingly pale and was holding her side. 'Are you all right, Dolly?'

She raised her right hand, shaking her head. 'Just a bit of a pain. I've had them on and off all afternoon, but that was a bad one.'

'I think you'd better come into my surgery, and I'll take a look at you. That's if you don't mind, Dolly?' Todd said gently. 'You could be in labour.'

'No, it's too early,' Dolly protested. 'I have a month or two to go.'

Amelia moved swiftly to her side. 'I'll come in with you, if that helps.'

Mariah was about to enter the room, but she took in the scene with a single glance. 'Let me go with her, Emmie. I've had two babies and I've helped many others into the world.'

'Don't worry, she'll be fine.' Todd raised Dolly to her feet and helped her from the room, followed by Mariah.

'What shall I do?' Freddie asked urgently.

Amelia sank down on the sofa. 'We can't do anything, Freddie. We just have to do as Todd says. He's a very good doctor.'

Freddie sat down beside her, taking her hand in

his. 'Emmie, I know this is probably not a good time, but I never manage to catch you on your own.'

She withdrew her hand. 'I don't know what you're going to say, but can't it wait?'

'I need to tell you that I've formed a deep attachment to you, my dear. I know I'm a lot older than you but my feelings are totally sincere.'

'Freddie, if this is what I think it is, please don't. I have the highest regard for you, but I love Todd. I think I fell in love with him from the start. I have deep affection for you —' She broke off as he rose abruptly to his feet.

'I'm sorry, Amelia. I just hoped that perhaps you might find it in your heart to care for me. I could take you away from all this. You would be safe and secure for as long as you live.'

'I'm deeply honoured and flattered, and I hate to hurt your feelings, but none of that matters to me. I'm used to living on the edge of society and I don't even mind being poor, but I couldn't marry a man I didn't love with all my heart. I am so sorry.'

He nodded sadly. 'It seems I am doomed to fall in love with the wrong woman, but I don't want your sympathy. I think I knew what your answer would be. I just had to take a chance.'

'Dolly is more important at this moment, Freddie. We both love her.'

He smiled reluctantly. 'You're right, of course. I did try to persuade her to return home as soon as she'd done her shopping, but you know Dolly — she has a will of her own.'

They lapsed into silence until at last Mariah marched into the room. 'There's no doubt about it. The baby is on its way. I'm going to make up a bed for her. She won't be going anywhere this side of Christmas, your lordship. Maybe you should go home.'

Amelia jumped to her feet and went to the window. 'It's snowing again. Your coachman hasn't returned yet, Freddie. I think you might have to stay here anyway.'

Freddie nodded. 'I won't leave until I know that Dolly is all right, and her child, too.'

'It's going to take a good few hours,' Mariah said, frowning. 'It could even take all night before the baby is born.'

'Then I must definitely stay,' Freddie said firmly. 'If that's all right with you, Emmie?'

'Of course it is. We have plenty of rooms. We can put your coachman and the footman up when they return although, looking at the way the snow is coming down, they might not make it back tonight.'

'I'm going to make up a bed for Dolly,' Mariah said firmly. 'I'll put out clean linen for you, too, my lord.'

Freddie held up his hand. 'Please don't go to any trouble on my account. I can sleep anywhere.'

'I'll make sure the children have their supper and get to bed on time,' Amelia said calmly. 'Don't worry about Percy. We can handle him between us.'

'With all the excitement today they should all be worn out,' Mariah said with a wry smile. She hurried from the parlour, closing the door behind her.

Amelia was left facing Freddie. She could see that he was concerned and anxious. 'Don't worry, Freddie. Dolly will be fine. Todd is an excellent physician and I dare say he's lost count of the babies he's delivered.'

'You really do love him, don't you?'

She smiled ruefully. 'Yes, I do. It's taken me a long

time to realise it.'

'I hope he's worthy of you, Emmie.'

'You'll find someone special one day, Freddie. I hope we can always be friends.'

Freddie clutched her hand and raised it to his cheek. 'Always.'

'I must go and find the children or they'll be outside playing in the snow instead of going to their beds.'

There were tears in her eyes as Amelia left the room. She hated hurting anyone, especially Freddie, who had been so kind to her, but she had to tell him the truth. It had taken her long enough to acknowledge her feelings for Todd, but now, at last, they were out in the open. She went to look for the children.

26

Dolly's daughter was born in the early hours of the next morning. Amelia had fallen asleep on the sofa and Freddie had dozed off in a chair by the fire when Mariah burst into the room to give them the good news.

'Mother and baby are fine,' she said with a tired smile. 'Considering it's her first child, Dolly did extremely well. She's sitting up drinking a cup of tea with the baby snuggled in the crook of her arm.'

Amelia rose somewhat shakily to her feet. She yawned. 'That's wonderful. Can I go and see her?'

'You go, but, Freddie, I suggest you wait until daylight. Dolly is very tired and needs to rest.'

Freddie subsided back onto his chair. 'Of course. After all, I'm not a relative.'

Amelia frowned. 'Maybe you're not related by blood, but Dolly thinks of you as part of her family. We'll both go just to congratulate Dolly and admire the baby, and then we'll let her rest.'

'Suit yourself. I'm just the midwife here.' Mariah stalked out of the room.

'Don't worry about Mariah,' Amelia said in response to Freddie's startled look. 'She's exhausted. Come with me. We'll be very quiet and we won't tire Dolly.'

'Of course.' Freddie went to hold the door open for her. 'You are a remarkable woman, Emmie. Todd is a very lucky man.' He stepped back as Todd appeared in the doorway.

'What do you mean by that?' Todd eyed him warily.

'I hope your feelings for Emmie are as sincere as the love she has for you.'

'What do you know about how Emmie feels, Lord Dorrington?'

Freddie smiled tiredly. 'Talk to her and maybe you'll understand. And thank you for taking care of Dolly. She means as much to me as if she were my own flesh and blood. I'll go in and see her now, but I promise I won't stay more than a minute or two.' Freddie headed towards the staircase.

'What was he talking about?' Todd asked wearily.

Amelia could see the lines of exhaustion on his pale face and she moved swiftly to his side. 'There's only one man in the world for me, and it's not Freddie.'

Todd took her in his arms, holding her close. 'Do you really mean that, Emmie?'

She answered by pulling his head down so that their lips met in a timeless kiss. She could feel his heart beating to the same rhythm as her own, and her body moulded to his. He was the first to pull away.

'Do you really love me, Emmie?'

She was torn between tears and laughter as she stroked his cheek. 'Yes, of course I love you, Todd. I'll always love you, no matter what. I don't care if I never design another gown just so long as we're together.'

He smiled and covered her face with soft kisses. 'I love you, too. I fell in love with you the first time we met, but I didn't think you would look twice at a humble doctor.'

Amelia stood on tiptoe to kiss him again. 'You're forgetting that I am a doctor's daughter. I know the advantages and the disadvantages, but I don't care. I love you for who you are, Todd. I really do.'

'I'm sorry I acted like a jealous fool over Freddie.'

'That's all forgotten, Todd.' Amelia drew away. 'We've got the rest of our lives together, but now I really want to see the baby.'

'We'll go up together.' Todd slipped his arm around her waist and they made their way through the entrance hall, lit by moonlight on the settled snow, and up the stairs to the room Mariah had hastily prepared for Dolly.

Freddie was seated in a chair at her bedside but he rose to his feet with a guilty smile. 'I'll go and find Mariah. I've just realised that I'm starving. She always rises to the occasion when anyone is hungry.'

Amelia laughed. 'You're right, Freddie. Mariah loves to feed people. It's the way to her heart if you enjoy her cooking.'

Amelia leaned over to get a better view of the baby, who was fast asleep in her mother's arms. 'She's beautiful, Dolly. What are you going to call her?'

Dark shadows underlined Dolly's eyes but she smiled proudly. 'She was born during a snowstorm so I'm going to call her Blanche. She'll be Blanche Rosalind Amelia Baker.'

Amelia leaned over to kiss Dolly on the cheek. 'Thank you. That's such an honour.'

Freddie was about to leave the room when Mariah entered. 'What's all this?' she demanded. 'Dolly needs to get some sleep.' She bustled forward and took Blanche from her mother's arms, laying her in a drawer taken from the clothes press and padded out with a blanket. 'I've made a jug of cocoa and a plate of sandwiches. I suggest you all go down to the kitchen.'

Amelia exchanged amused glances with Dolly. 'Yes,

Mariah. We're going, but I'll be back later, Dolly. I want to enjoy having you and your baby here for as long as possible.'

'I'll send a telegram to your parents when my coachman gets here, the snow permitting,' Freddie said as Mariah shooed him out of the door.

'Gus will be so happy and so proud of you,' Amelia added as she left the room. 'Are you coming, Todd?'

'In a moment. I just want to make sure that Dolly is comfortable.'

Dolly smiled broadly. 'You've done it, haven't you, Todd? You've told her how you feel and Emmie's admitted that she's been in love with you all along.'

Amelia blew her a kiss in answer and hurried from the room.

* * *

There had been a slight thaw, allowing Freddie's coachman to get through later that morning, and Freddie had returned home with a list of Dolly's things that she wanted brought to Marsh House. The children were delighted to greet baby Blanche, although Percy was not keen at first and he growled at her, but then relented and brought her a cake that he had taken from the larder. Betsy tried to explain that babies could not eat cake and only drank milk, but Percy was not impressed and he toddled off to find something more interesting. Daisy cried because she wanted a dolly and not a baby. Amelia gave her a hug and told her to wait and see what Father Christmas had brought for her, and there was not long to wait now.

In addition to getting ready for the fashion parade

Mariah had spent hours preparing a feast for Christmas dinner. Amelia said they should go to the nearest butcher's shop and purchase a turkey, but Mariah said she had a capon she had been fattening up for the purpose. Jim Allen brought them a huge ham, smoked over the range in the farmhouse kitchen. Amelia thought secretly that the taciturn farmer might actually propose to Mariah on Christmas Day, but Mariah kept her feelings private and refused to be drawn on the subject.

Ignoring Mariah's advice to rest, Dolly was up and about after spending only a day in bed. She was besotted with her baby and delighted to show her off, especially when Freddie arrived, bringing with him the baby's layette, carefully collected by Dolly during her pregnancy. He had with him a valise filled with Dolly's clothes, packed, he said, by his housekeeper who did not trust a mere man to know what a lady needed, even if he was a peer of the realm. He also brought a large hamper from Fortnum's packed with delicious cooked meats, pies, pickles and relishes. To the delight of the children there were chocolate bars and fancy biscuits as well as peppermint creams and toffees. The biggest treat of all was a large turkey, plucked and ready to be stuffed and cooked in the range oven. Even Mariah was impressed and the capon had a lucky escape. However, not to be outdone, Mariah made a huge plum pudding, which she boiled in the copper outside in the newly renovated wash house. Freddie hinted that there was another surprise waiting for both Amelia and Dolly.

On Christmas morning the old house echoed with the sound of happy laughter and the bubbling excitement of the children. Even Percy forgot to growl when he saw the presents wrapped in brown paper and coloured ribbon piled up beneath the Christmas tree. Amelia prayed that there would be no emergencies for Todd to attend and they all breakfasted together in the dining room. Percy actually behaved himself, although he cast suspicious glances at baby Blanche, who had become the centre of attention.

Amelia ate her porridge laced with sugar and cream, silently comparing it with the same time last year when such luxury had been just a dream. How long ago that seemed, and how much better life was now. She had to pinch herself surreptitiously to make sure she was not dreaming.

She glanced round at the rosy faces of the children and she exchanged smiles with Todd. There was no need to tell him how she was feeling. The warmth in his gaze filled her with happiness and hope for the future. He raised his coffee cup to her in a silent toast and she responded in kind.

'When do we open our presents?' Betsy asked eagerly.

Mariah gave her a reproachful look. 'Finish your breakfast, miss. You'll wait until you're told you may get down from the table.'

Betsy and Daisy exchanged mischievous grins, but they did not argue.

* * *

It was impossible to keep the children away from the excitement of the gifts waiting beneath the tree in the piano parlour. Daisy was given the honour of handing them round. There was a wooden horse pulling a cart with wheels that actually went round for Percy, a pair of new boots and a tartan dress with a white lace collar for Betsy, together with a copy of *Alice's Adventures in Wonderland*. There was also a new dress for Daisy as well as a beautiful doll with golden hair and blue eyes. Then there was the general opening of presents for the adults with no one left out, even Freddie, although Amelia had thought long and hard of what to give someone who had everything. She had solved the problem by drawing a group sketch of them all, including Freddie, in pen and ink. The frame had come from the attic and had cleaned up nicely. Amelia was very proud of her effort and Freddie was clearly delighted. Mariah had made small cakes for everyone, iced with their name, and Todd had enlisted Betsy's help in purchasing silk scarves for Mariah and Dolly. He had not as yet given Amelia her gift and she wondered if he had forgotten her as she handed him the small shagreen-covered box containing a gold tiepin she had purchased from old Scoggins. She tried not to feel piqued when everyone else had received their presents, but it was a day to be happy and she refused to be miserable. No doubt Todd had an answer; she would just have to wait.

When the excitement of the presents had died down, Dolly went to the piano and played carols while Betsy rocked baby Blanche in her arms. The sound of an approaching carriage made the children rush to the window. Looking over their heads, Amelia saw a hackney carriage draw up outside and two people stepped out onto the snowy cobblestones.

'I didn't know that Pa was coming today.' Amelia turned to Todd who was standing behind her. 'Did you have anything to do with this, Todd?'

He smiled. 'I need to ask his permission to marry

his only daughter.'

'Haven't you forgotten something?' Amelia asked with a mock frown.

'I thought after the other night it went without saying. However, I want to do this properly.' Ignoring the fact that Mariah had ushered Harold and Ruby into the room, Todd went down on one knee. From his inside breast pocket he produced a small box, which when opened revealed a sparkling diamond ring.

'My darling Emmie, will you do me the honour of becoming my wife?'

Amelia looked up and saw her father was beaming and nodding his approval. Ruby stood behind him and she too was smiling.

'Yes, Todd,' Amelia said softly. 'Of course I will marry you.'

He slipped the ring onto her finger. 'One day I will buy you a much larger diamond.'

'No, this is perfect, Todd.' She raised him to his feet and slid her arms around his neck. 'I thought you'd forgotten me.'

He kissed her, to the delight of the children, who whooped and danced around them.

'I could never forget you,' Todd said, holding her close. 'You are always in my heart, my darling Emmie.'

'You will look after my daughter, Todd,' Harold said with a mock frown. 'Otherwise you will have me to deal with.'

Todd shook his hand. 'I will do everything in my power to make her happy, sir.'

'I know we got off on the wrong foot,' Ruby said in a low voice, 'but I wish you every happiness, Amelia.'

'Thank you, Ruby. We'll start again, shall we?' Amelia gave her a hug. 'All I want is for my pa to have a good life.'

'It may surprise you, my dear, but that's what I want, too.' Ruby eyed Freddie with an arch smile. 'And you must be Lord Dorrington. I've heard so much about you, sir.'

Freddie bowed over Ruby's hand. 'It's a pleasure to meet you, ma'am. And you, too, Dr Sutton.'

'Thank you, my lord.' Harold beamed at Freddie and they shook hands.

'Congratulations to you both.' Dolly wrapped her arms around Amelia and Todd. 'I know you two are going to be very happy. I just wish Gus could be here.'

'I notified his commanding officer in London of the happy event,' Freddie said hastily. 'The good news will catch up with Gus soon. I couldn't magic your husband back from India but I have done the next best thing.' He glanced out of the window where a second cab had drawn up. Dolly uttered a gasp of delight as a good-looking gentleman emerged first and proffered his hand to an attractive woman wearing a smart blue velvet travelling costume with a matching fur-trimmed mantle.

'It's Mama and Papa. They've come all the way from Devonshire.'

Freddie smiled. 'I knew they'd want to see you and little Blanche as soon as possible.'

Amelia stood close to Todd, watching the tearful reunion as Rosalind and Alex Blanchard greeted their daughter.

With her new granddaughter in her arms, Rosalind Blanchard turned to Amelia. 'I've heard so much about you, my dear. You've been a wonderful friend to Dolly.'

Alex Blanchard shook hands with Todd. 'Thank

you for taking care of my girls, Todd. I'm proud to know you.'

'And Nancy sends her love,' Rosalind added, smiling. 'You must bring Amelia down to Rockwood very soon, Todd. Everyone wants to see you and meet your betrothed.'

'How did you know?' Amelia asked breathlessly. 'Todd has only just proposed.'

'The diamond ring gives the game away,' Alex said, laughing. 'Congratulations to you both.' He slapped Todd on the back. 'You've done so well, Todd, but we all miss you.'

Amelia turned to Mariah with a smile. 'We just need Farmer Allen to join us now and we'll be a big family.'

Mariah's rosy cheeks deepened into a blush. 'As a matter of fact I invited him and his children to join us for Christmas dinner, since Freddie has been so kind as to bring enough food to feed an army. The turkey has been in the oven since before breakfast.'

Amelia leaned against Todd with a contented sigh. 'This is all so wonderful. I can hardly believe it's happening.'

He looked up at the mistletoe someone had craftily hung from a beam. 'Happy Christmas, my darling Emmie. This is just the beginning. I will do my utmost to give you everything you want and deserve.'

He drew her closer and kissed her, until she drew away to catch her breath. She glanced at Blanche, who was now safely back in her mother's arms and she smiled.

'I know exactly what I want, Todd, but first I would love to have a white wedding with all my family present. Happy Christmas, everyone.'

Other titles published by Ulverscroft:

DOLLY'S DREAM

Dilly Court

1874. Dolly Blanchard dreams of a bigger life. She wants to make a mark on the world, not simply wait for a husband to come along. So when an impoverished actress offers her a lifeline, Dolly flees to London, determined to make it on the stage and prove to her family — and herself — that she can strike out alone.

But the dark city streets are full of danger. With her dreams fading to dust, Dolly soon finds herself in peril. And with the family's future at Rockwood Castle under threat, and secrets tumbling out of the shadows, she faces a difficult choice. Will her heart call her home? Or will her dreams lead her astray?

SNOW BRIDE

Dilly Court

Nancy seems to have found her happily ever after. She is surrounded by family and engaged to marry the man of her dreams. But when her fiancé's father insists they wait a year to prove that their love is true, the young couple's feelings are put to the test.

The path of true love never runs smooth, but as the snow begins to fall, Nancy will need to trust her heart for her Christmas wishes to come true.

SUNDAY'S CHILD

Dilly Court

Left on the steps of an orphanage when she was just days old, Nancy Sunday was brought up in hardship — until the kindly Rosalind Carey took her in. Now eighteen years old, Nancy is an adopted member of the Carey family. But she can't help wondering who her parents really were.

When Nancy is sent away to finishing school, she finds herself in the midst of London society. There she meets Freddie Ashton — kind and warm-hearted, he might just be the man of Nancy's dreams. But she knows his wealthy parents would never let him marry a penniless foundling.

And she has also caught the eye of another man — the charming and dangerous Gervase North, who has reasons of his own for discovering Nancy's parentage . . .